ILLYRIA
BOOK ONE

BETRAYAL
OF ANGELS

Armin Shimerman

D1555848

Jumpmaster Press
Birmingham, AL

Copyright Notice

Library Cataloging Data

Names: Shimerman, Armin (Armin Shimerman) 1949-

Title: Betrayal of Angels / Armin Shimerman

5.5 in. × 8.5 in. (13.97 cm × 21.59 cm)

Description: Jumpmaster Press™ digital eBook edition | Jumpmaster Press™ Trade paperback edition | Alabama: Jumpmaster Press™, 2020. P.O Box 1774 Alabaster, AL 35007 info@jumpmasterpress.com

Summary: The Queen's conjurer, Doctor John Dee is an Elizabethan mathematician, cryptographer, and mystic commissioned by Her Majesty's spymaster, Sir Francis Walsingham, to suss out a noble Count who governs an island in the English Channel. Dee's mission? Uncover treason, reveal terrorists, and unveil threats to The Crown.

ISBN-13: 978-1-949184-33-4 (eBook) | 978-1-949184-31-0 (paperback) | 978-1-949184-32-7 (hardcover)

1. Queen Elizabeth I 2. John Dee 3. William Shakespeare 4. Alternate History of 12th Nite 5. Sir Francis Walsingham 6. Espionage

Printed in the United States of America

For more information on Armin Shimerman
twitter.com/ShimermanArmin

ILLYRIA
BOOK ONE

BETRAYAL OF ANGELS

Armin Shimerman

Acknowledgements

David S. Rodes for my education;
Michael Scott for initial inspiration;
Mary Lambert for further inspiration;
Ghia Truesdale, Kate Zentall, Kathryn Ann Swink, and
Diana Lenney for editorial guidance;
and Henry Condell and John Heminge

...well, just because

For Kitty Swink

A muse of fire that brightens my life and inspires me
with powers to lend these subject light

P

"Fut."

"What sayest thou, thou naughty knave?"

"I said, 'Fut.'"

There is menacing reserve in his voice. "Be that some untoward profanity?!"

"No, sir. A mild Midland's oath for, 'i'faith' or 'e'en so'."

Having foresworn much travel in his life—too dangerous—he has no way of knowing what country idioms are beyond London's walls, hence the youth's employer lifts an eyebrow and harrumphs. Reaching across the tavern table and over stoups of beer, he snatches the foul papers piled between them on the table. Though the *oeuvre* has just been read to him, the theater owner scans the pages perfunctorily for a second time. Perturbed by the risk this play presents to purse and reputation alike, the cheek of James Burbage twitches dangerously.

"I should fling you back into the streets for your disobedience. Have a care. You are my apprentice, my drudge, my menial, my non-entity who shovels horse's dung from afore my theatre. Damn me for looking favorably on thee. And..." His clenched hand waves the sheets perturbedly. "...*this* is how you repay me?"

"Master Burbage, I'm also your poet who, penning lines that will live eternally, will render you celebrated—I am your newest playwright."

"You are too bold. Your ambition overweens too much."

"Perhaps. But do not think I flatter when I say, 'fame and *your* name will be interchangeable'. Men will praise the name of Burbage everlasting for giving me a chance, and *that* shall stand proof against the scythes of Death and Time, my good master."

"Boy, do not loose your purple language on me. I've heard it all before and by your betters. You are no Kidd, nor Kit Marlowe." As though he were a lawyer at a trial, he holds up the ink-blotted papers he has just rifled. "I tell thee these words of thine will make the Royal Censor blush and prohibit our further performance."

"The Censor? Edward Tilney?!" The boy frowns. His high forehead furrows. "How say you by that? Instance? Instance?"

"Conceive. As of this year, have we the Crown's patronage, or have we lost it?"

Your loss, not mine, thinks the menial. "We are still beloved."

"Strive not to confound my argument, rogue. Which company is Her Majesty's favorite?"

"The Queen's Men."

"Aye boy. There you are in the right. The Queen this past March was mightily deceived by Master Secretary Walsingham who, saving his Grace's pardon, stole the best of my players for the Royal Revels. God be praised,

I still have Kempe. But I digress. Master Tilney alone may license a play..."

Putting on his best face, the lad interrupts. "He will revere mine and swear it has no equal."

Burbage raps the wooden table with the rolled up manuscript so forcefully that the tankards totter and nearly spill. "Who bade thee speak? Know your place." His balding head rears back. He glares. "What false angel bade me employ an upstart wretch and entrust him with the writing of a play?"

"Your lack of funds, master Burbage, which have thrust the more established poets from trusting your credit."

"Why you impertinent toadeater, you meaningless nog, how dare you answer me thus?!"

Foregoing his sweet transitory moment in the sun, the youth presses his palms together.

"Good sir, I meant no disrespect but thought you had posed the question *to* me, and I was required to answer. You are the finest *connoisseur* in London theater." He lowers his gaze and stares at the ground. "It is an honor to stand in your shadow. I assure you, good sir, I never meant any disrespect."

Burbage's eyes narrow, knowing he is being played for a fool. Yet the boy is talented, and the difficulty is that the rascal *is* at present the only playwright who will work for him. Swallowing the insolence, James Burbage clears his throat.

"Sirrah, there is much in here that will not stand." He grimaces as if the paper smelled of rancid piss. His cheek twitches again. "If Tilney perceives aught that offends in this, we will lose all. You will have squandered your opportunity, and, me, my money in this play of yours, this *Prince Amleth.*"

"To what, good sir, do you refer?"

"I mean this half-arse attempt at Seneca and his plots of revenge—with a *ghost* no less."

The hapless poet regards the theater impresario as if his employer seeks to desecrate a religious shrine. "Nay, master Burbage, the language is lofty, the arguments sententious, and the plot exquisite. It shall surpass."

"Again in the right," Burbage feigns concession; the lad brightens. "It shall surpass. It shall pass gas and be weighed as a fart, being lowly in language, sentimental in feeling, and having a plot that is excrement. If you do not improve on this before the week is done, I swear I will sue you for breach of contract and abjure you from ever scribbling in London again and so farewell your dreams of being a poet—"

"—And your fame, noble sir, will be unborn, an unseen meteor, a nomination that loses the hope of prosperity."

Burbage shakes his head at being interrupted and at the flattery, but inwardly admits that the boy is not without spirit. "You reechy varlet, were you born impertinent? Or have the whores and the Godless players corrupted you?"

"I meant no harm. I ask only that you show me what needs correcting."

"Then listen. What name have you christened the King's counselor?"

"*Corambis.*"

"A character as like the Lord Treasurer, Lord

Burleigh..." brays Burbage, thrusting two index fingers in the boy's face, "...as these my two fingers?"

"I wanted to inject political tragicomedy, social commentary if you will, to give the lordlings satiric understanding and the groundlings comic sport."

"'Comic sport' call you it? I am not a scholar, but my Latin is enough to tell me that *corambis* means *cabbage*. Do you call the Lord Treasurer, The Honorable Burghley of Her Majesty's Privy Council, a *cabbage*?"

"No, master. The nearest translation is *reheated cabbage*, good sir."

"Do not mock me, boy, or by Heaven, I shall have thy thumbs broken. Consider scratching out words with such a disability. Speak thus again, and thou were best look to't."

The fledgling dramatist is chastened.

"The Lord of the Revels, Master Tilney," Burbage inflects sharply, "will not allow such a slander to shame the Queen's chief counselor. So, re-christen the good man and forego your sportiveness and your social significance. And, *this*, above all, temper your anger against the character of the King. Give him a speech or two to justify his acts. We cannot show Royalty to be utterly contemptible or we shall all be hanged."

"I cry you mercy if I have offended. I will mend what needs mending. My ignorance will learn from your tutelage, and I will repay you for whatever villainy I have done with current repentance and future magnificence."

"Do so. Or *this*..." Burbage chucks it across the table at the boy, "...shall be your last, Will Shakespar!" The pages flutter about the eviscerated wretch.

1

Having spent the better part of an hour keeping pace as amanuensis, the old scholar, Dr. John Dee, looks up from his frantic note-taking. Before him, Edward Kelley emerges from a trance.

At dawn, the two necromancers had convened. A half-hour of fervent cleansing prayer prepared them for the séance well before the more sluggish members of Dee's household had commenced their morning toilets.

The sun streams through the east-facing windows, yet the room darkens as the gleam of the polished Abyssinian showstone flickers quixotically and fades, stolid upon its ceremonial plinth. Not daring to profane the divine ritual by realigning the black slab back into the sunlight that lingers on the far wall of his library, in order to coax the Delphic angel to return, John Dee's only option is to reanimate the channel of conversation with the Divine through contrite prayer.

Spiritualist Dee invokes Anael, the angel of Principality, who—for nigh on a full hour—has educated him of God's divine plans, conducted through the medium Edward Kelley.

"Heavenly Anael, be my speed and plead the following at the Holy Throne for me..." He lowers his head and voice in reverence, "O God of Angels. God of principalities, God of Reason, God of we the seekers of thy truth: O Lord, be my help, that this my work be allowed to progress a moment or two more in thy instruction to thy Glory, O God. Show me but one more instance that the world shall be reformed, religious peace shall reign throughout Europe, and your servant, Our Royal Queen, will lead humanity and as the Imperial Governor of all Christian kings, Princes and States. O Lord, remain in master Kelley's mind that I may learn of all thy works." The shadows in the room persist, and the philosopher must accept the inevitable end of another session with the Divine.

The scryer, Edward Kelley, rubs his eyes, yet John Dee probes for more.

"Edward, rememberst aught else?"

Still dazed by both the light from the polished stone and the images to which Anael has made him privy, Edward Kelley shakes his head *no.*

"What did Anael share last, Edmund?"

"'What is on high dwells below; what is below dwells above'," Kelley replies vaguely.

Visions of the morning's séance waft away like the diffused shadows in the room; Kelley nods weakly. "What do you make of it, Doctor Dee?"

"It further confirms the invisible golden chain of influences that stretches from Our Father to his ministering angels and their celestial orbs to the sublunary world that we abide in."

"Aye, that chain of perfection has been iterated many times," says Kelley quietly, knowing his employer is now too busy to be aware of aught but the old man's chronicle in his worn notebook describing today's revelations.

At forty-seven, the ancient is still devoted to discovering the hidden truth in Nature to better come into harmony with Heaven. Having no organs for voice, angels with God's permission, Dee believes, convey guidance through trance-like communications. These are initiated in the pristine sunlight of early day and coalesce through focused light reflected upon a polished surface. Angelic inspiration, Dee further believes, is the cause of all inspiration in man or what the vulgar blithely call an *epiphany.*

John Dee's backdrop during that last week of September of 1583 is set somewhere in the middle of that exuberant period known as the Elizabethan era. Therein Europeans are conceiving fantastical theories and shattering the superstitious shackles of the Middle Ages whilst discovering hidden truths of the complicated existence in which they are enmeshed. Navigators are finding new lands. Astronomers reshape the celestial map. Optics, lens, and perspective are redefining art and how the mind perceives. To Doctor John Dee, the natural philosopher, everything is open for consideration and investigation, especially in this propitious year so close to the coming imperial conjunction of Saturn and Jupiter. In Whitehall, the home of Her Majesty's government, spidery men of power focus on freeing themselves from the Continent and do so through extraordinary political skill and tactical prudence. The invasion of the Spanish Armada is a long five years away, but the groundwork for its assault is already being assembled in Paris and Madrid and Rome. Its viciousness and self-righteousness, forged out of the fires of religious controversy, is inflamed further by new ways of canonical thinking.

England, at present a Protestant country, is at peace with the world, yet at civil war with herself. A tremendous sense of religious conflict hovers over all of the country. Its drama is grander and more pernicious than any historical shadow-plays enacted in theatres or on makeshift scaffolds. Her Royal Highness Queen Elizabeth has constantly been the inspiration for theatrical intrigues—machinations by her mother to make her birth legitimate, conspiracies inspired by her half-sister to murder her, aspirations to place her on the throne, courtly cabals to keep her from that throne, and administrative in-fights to get her married. But now, late in her reign, there are designs to eliminate her. The culprits are reverend Englishmen and women loyal to their Catholic roots who cannot bear the infidel Protestant Queen any longer and would willingly martyr Her, rather than be ruled by Her. Some have tried. None has succeeded. Nervous government Privy Councillors keep a constant vigil for malcontents who would lead dissidents into hellish sedition. The leaders of Whitehall, the Queen's foremost advisors, have put Mary Queen of Scots, Elizabeth's estranged cousin, the great royal hope of Catholics abroad and at home, under house arrest for *safekeeping* at Chartley. But, in every smoky tavern of the English realm, whisperings abound around the likelihood of Mary's reign and of the possibility of uncrowning the aging, childless Elizabeth.

❧   ❧

Following the Thames River southwest of London, in the village of Mortlake, stands the home of Dr. John Dee. The Doctor's *Interna Bibliotheca*, his private study, is nestled in the rear of a two-story split-timber house that watches over a small bend in the country's main thoroughfare. In this room, politics is forbidden, not that the infamous scholar is immune from governmental policy and succession which have affected his life and career more than most. But this is his sacred workspace, his sanctuary, dedicated solely to the acquisition and distillation of the arcane. While monks and their studies have been outlawed in the realm for a generation, Dr. John Dee's monastic cell is off-limits to all except the privileged, like Edward Kelley, who has just left their morning séance with the Angel Anael.

Dee's private investigations that have made him notorious cannot be compromised by political distractions. Books and pamphlets and the paraphernalia of erudition proliferate. It is here that he deciphers the language of the angels for his *Enochian Dictionary*. In his secret and sacred chamber, the philosopher ponders the aggregate riddles of alchemy, astrology, literature, cryptography, mathematics, and geometry. Though nigh two score and a half in years, Dee, like his times, is a student of the Renaissance, that other era that found keys to true wisdom through the studying of ancient scholars. In those postlapsarian times, man walked nearer to God and better intuited the Deity's omniscience: the golden source of intelligence from which the present corrupted modes of wisdom are, Dee posits, only baser metals.

In the sanctity of his *Interna Bibliotheca*, lead glass windows overlooking the busy river are never opened, and the room has the gritty taste of burned ash from a smallish stone hearth set in the middle of the northern wall. No magician's lair was ever as private or as unknowable. Though even in this dim room, English law expressly forbids investigations into the invisible world through reasoning, intuition, magic, as well as mystical experiments. Yet, the magus believes he is an agent of Heaven. As another John baptized the Christ, so this John believes he will help bring in a new millennium of peace and ecumenicalism.

Presently, a woefully lost tree toad, no larger than a carpenter's thumb, makes its way indoors and across the parquet pattern of the floor. Entering through an unplugged crevice in the Tudor paneling or through a momentarily-opened door, the intruder's brilliant green coloring—camouflage in the nearby marsh—contrasts all too sharply here in the dull tones of the library's well-worn floor timbers and whitewashed walls.

The meandering toad takes its time, leaps over the pocked planks spattered with drops of ink, and heads for the sooty throw rug that depicts the labors of Hercules. The frayed carpet betrays the Doctor's mental labors during ruminative hours of pacing. It is badly singed—not from hellfire, though Dee's detractors would swear otherwise—but from wayward embers spat from the fire. And it is there the intrepid amphibian rests for the nonce to gather its bearings.

Tarrying for a breath, it hops again with unwitting vigor. Circumnavigating the swells in the furrowed woolen rug, it pays no attention to the whitecaps of forgotten candle wax embedded in the Olympians' story woven into the rug. For a moment, the toad is masked from the mathematician's sight by scattered pamphlets and scrolls cluttered at the legs of the pine reading-table. Unhappy with the darkness, soon it leaps out again into the light only to skitter away faster than Dee's young students from their books. Finding itself in a corner of the room, it vainly thumps against a rampart of esoteric volumes standing at odd angles on the floor. They are too fat, too weighty to be pushed aside. If the little beastie had the gift of analysis, it might be intrigued by their tattered condition. These hefty tomes once bound in sumptuous vermillion velvets and brilliant tawny leathers are now faded to rose and butter. Some are charred at the edges and appear to have just barely been rescued from the flames of intolerance. During the Tudor Reformation, Anglican worshipers had disapproved of such books that for centuries had been collected or hand-copied by monastic antiquarians. Considered a threat to the true faith of Protestantism, such-like beautifully illuminated volumes with their meticulous calligraphy had been hauled away by the cartful to be blackened by bonfires. Zealots' axes had hacked mercilessly at forests of knowledge. The reformed Church taught that geometrical designs appearing in these texts signified that the content was satanic—not fit for proper Christian minds. Since

Henry's VIII's dissolution of the Catholic friaries and cathedrals, those text pages had more often been used for wiping one's backside than for improving minds.

In resistance, John Dee has become England's primary book collector, spending most of his pitiful inheritance and earnings on their rescue. He has saved whatever he can, though he prefers Natural Philosophy. The other collection of books in his house, the *externa bibliotheca,* holds the larger part of his archives, currently the largest library in England. Attacked for his actions, Dee maintains that he is a practicing Anglican dedicated to a life of intellectual curiosity. To him, books (and the knowledge and art they contain) are civilization's salvation. If by the grace of the blessed Trinity, he can unlock their secrets, the knowledge made manifest through him will be humanity's salvation allowing the void between man's understanding and nature to be filled.

A *machina horaria* strikes three, its tin warrior bowing mechanically with each tinkling of the silver bell. With its tolling come shrill caws from the cupboard where a raven in an osier cage presently gives warning of an invader. The bird, all in black like Dee himself, might be taken as his familiar and indeed is a cherished—albeit captive—guest in this room. The bird is a gift from former student, Henry Percy, Ninth Earl of Northumberland, and one of the highest peers of the Court of Elizabeth.

Troubled by the screeching raven, the amphibian flexes its hind legs and leaps for the bright parallelograms on the floor cast by the sun. This light, patterned into Euclidean forms, neither interests nor intimidates the little toad. It is warmth that attracts it. There it basks taking no notice of the velvet slipper that suddenly intercedes. The hovering shoe shifts position, and the intrepid toad, more disgruntled than startled, blithely leaps upon it. Discomfited suddenly the creature effectuates its mightiest leap, and at the apex of its trajectory, a hand with ink-stained nails plucks it from the air. Rendered motionless by its incomprehensible loss of liberty, the captive's short life is thusly changed.

Cupping both hands together, John Dee is careful not to crush his newly ironed wrist ruffs or snuff out the life of the intruder. With the loss of light, the little prisoner's panic becomes palpable—continual thumps betray attempts to break loose. Freedom from dark imprisonment is an instinct instilled in all God's creatures. Alas, the vanquisher has no sympathy for the vanquished. After all, it is of lesser rank on Nature's chain of being, and the philosopher never considers freeing it. *Fortune smiles upon me,* thinks Dee, *I need but desiccate the specimen and remove the crapandina.* By removing the toadstone from the cranium, Dee can cure the swelling of an envenomed bite of rat, spider, or wasp. Nature's antithetical temperament is not lost on the scholar; this soulless inhabitant of the marsh is both a loathsome thing and a precious source for healing. *But for now, the little villein has invaded my inner sanctum, interrupted my meditations, and must be dispensed with.*

Retrieving a glass jar below his draw-top table, deftly he imprisons it. Peeping cheerfully in roomy confinement the toad is willing to accept its fate. The marsh-dweller quieted, Dee returns to his reading of Bruno's Oxford lecture on divinity. In April of that year, Giordano Bruno, a defrocked Italian monk now an advocate of ecumenism and currently a protected guest of the French Ambassador, Michel Castelnau, posited an astounding theorem. Bruno set forth that GOD is an actual sphere of which the center is everywhere and the circumference nowhere. God's presence being infinite, there must exist an endless image of his divine presence throughout a limitless cosmos; there must be countless worlds inhabited by infinite beings, which in turn reflect God's majesty. If this is so, then in this unbounded universe, it is unreasonable to think of Earth as the center of God's creation. Originally, Dee believed Bruno had advocated an heretical Copernicus-like heliocentric solar system ruled by mathematics. But, after several readings, on this very day it is patently clear that Bruno scorns numbers and calls such proof artless pedantry. A cosmology where man is not at the center is an overpowering idea quite at odds with all Christian theology, it is no wonder Bruno has been demonized throughout Europe. At his desk, Dee finds the conclusions, though fanciful, plausible, though he opines the monk's disdain for mathematics to be a childish discredit to his argument. And yet the Mortlake scholar wholeheartedly supports Bruno's principle that all religious intolerance is shamefully partisan, and that newer holy dogmas of radical Christianity often tear down the good works of inspired men who have come before.

"We are taught certain doctrines and disciplines in our homelands," writes the Italian, *"where we also are taught bigotry for the tenets of opposing views. Just as the roots of zeal for our own deployment are planted in us by the natural force of breeding, so in others an enthusiasm for their own different customs is equally instilled."*

John Dee's left foot has grown uncomfortably colder. Not without concern, he has noticed his advancing age renders his feet to need more wool to warm them. Looking about for his misplaced slipper, he spots it on top of the side table and absent-mindedly reaches for it. In so doing, a pewter saltcellar tumbles to the floor, losing a quarter of a teaspoon or more of its cubic granules. *Spilled salt is a wicked omen*, he warns himself. *Best take precautions.* Bad luck exists in this world. Better to follow superstition than risk misfortune. He pinches the spill several times with index and thumb and tosses it over his left shoulder. Remembering the arcane proverb, he allows a sour smile to spread across his lips—*it is wisdom to make the best of a bad thing.*

Dee returns his thoughts to Bruno. *"The outcome is a sense of comforting pleasure at the oppression and slaughter of the detractors of our faith. From this grows the fervent thanks that the Deity has shown 'the righteous' the true path to Heaven and salvation."* Licking the few grains of salt from his fingertips, he turns the page. *"But there is a way out of this intolerance,"* says Bruno, *"A way out of the thorny self-inflicting thicket that we build around ourselves. It is a persuasive argument that can weaken not only your enemies' convictions, but remodel your own. Success at this will lead men out of the abyss of blindness into the clear and tranquil light of those stars in all their variety that are scattered over the dusky blue mantle of Heaven. Such men will lift up their voices for the unaccustomed gladness in their hearts."*

He glances at the toad dappled in sunlight with its bulbous head resting on its folded forearms, seemingly on its way to amphibian slumber. *Almost human*, he thinks. Another artifact catches his attention. Disappointed, the scholar peers at the black slab of Abyssinian stone standing impotent on its pedestal.

If only the light had not faded earlier and Aneal had, like the archangel Michael, confirmed an Annunciation of the new era of ecumenical understanding led by Elizabeth Regina. Is not the truth of it foretold in the upcoming fiery conjunction of Saturn and Jupiter? Bruno and I are but worshipful men like the Baptist preparing the way. But the cynical world, will it heed what is in the night sky for all to see? Heed or not, Europe—nay all humanity—would in time know the truth of it. Though baffled, Dee's studies have taught him nothing if not acceptance. The sweet nearness of *Pax Britannica* outweighs the morning's frustration. *All things come soon enough if we can have the patience to stay for them.* Temporary setback is acknowledged and accepted.

Sucking on his inner cheek, Dee becomes aware of the salty taste in his mouth and craves more. Stepping to the buffet, he stabs at a sliver of Stilton: a morsel left over from last night's late studies. Jane, his wife, had made sure the savory delight was brought before one more check on their little son, Arthur, and turning in herself. Momentarily breathing in its tanginess, recalling Jane's kindness, Dee finds the cheese runny from sitting fireside and savors the curdled richness. How he loves cheese and wonders, if deprived, could he live without it? *Certainly, there must have been a time ere men knew the process to make it. God be praised, we live in blessed times.* He then wipes his lips with the back of his liver-spotted hand. *Port would be good right now,* he considers, *but it muddles the mind.*

It is of note that a neatly-trimmed, pointed beard—designed to replicate a triangle—surrounds the scholar's thin mouth. The English *D* is the letter *Delta* in Greek, and its symbol is the triangle. It is a ridiculous affectation, but it also has its purposes. It makes John Dee's long face even longer and gives it a sinister appearance. His fearful persona as a Doctor of the Occult Arts has been a role that, at times, has served him well. By the light of this autumnal morning, the old man's countenance has the alien pallor of a drowned man at the bottom of the sea. His probing black eyes, deep-set in their sockets, look as though they can pierce men's thoughts. It is sweet satisfaction that his unsettling countenance can prompt men to give way. He treats himself to another serving of blue cheese and continues reading. There is a particular passage that he can't help but read twice, "...*the sun, the universal light, is reflected in its shadow, the moon, which is the world of universal nature, Diana, in which the enthusiast hunts for the vestiges of the divine, for the reflections of the sun's divine light in nature, and by doing so the hunter becomes converted into what he hunts after. He becomes divine.*" It is a pleasing conceit that touches his pride and self-importance, as pleasant as the salty taste of runny cheese in his mouth. Nodding in satisfaction, he reads on, finding less pleasant matter, "*Therefore now that we have been in the dregs of the sciences, which have brought forth the dregs of opinions, which are the cause of the dregs of customs and of works, we may certainly expect to return to a better condition.*"

Dee shoves the book away from him. The central premise that science is bad is a conclusion that is wholly irrational and unsubstantiated. Not to mention, it does precisely what Bruno had accused others of doing—tearing down good works. It is often thus with Dee, spending time weighing an unwieldy argument or statistical conundrum that cannot easily be confirmed. There is great satisfaction in struggling with mysteries until their complexity is mastered. This he might define as the highest state of the human reason, the quest for an answer. Too often lofty sentences and fantastical figures, though difficult, are not as profound as they seem. So the philosopher reminds his students, "Though the line is sonorous, the sentiment may not be sound." As he rubs his woolly chin to puzzle out how Bruno can be so right about some issues and utterly wrong on others, he finds crumbs in his beard. It has a nasty habit of collecting the refuse of meals: bread crumbs, porridge, and pudding. Like a nursing baby or a consciousness lost in second childhood, it often demands attention.

He glances again at Bruno's text but has not the frame of mind to focus longer. Moreover, with the unsettling numbness in his feet in the last two years, he finds it harder to distinguish the smaller print so prevalent in current publishing. Infirmity brings a world of woes. But perhaps it's not the smallness of the print, but that he is always restive. Whatever the pretext, the scholar decides to give his beard a proper brushing and searches for a boxwood comb he had recently bought from an East Indies sailor, inbound from the remote Bermudas. With no particular patron in mind, he had purchased the comb with a thought of giving it as a gift. It did not matter; a unique gift could always be counted on to be a Trojan horse to a future benefactor's Ilium. The question remains, where has he put it?

The room is surveyed. It is not on any of the library shelves. Yet, he knows he most definitely had seen it on one when dinner was brought. Did he put it in a safe place, now totally fled from memory? It is not lost on him that lately newer memories are the sooner forgotten. Knowing it cannot be anywhere but in front of him, he is determined to find it. Careful to topple neither the saltcellar nor anything else, he lifts the trencher on which he had cut his meat that still lies un-cleared on the parson table. He seeks high and low, in drawers, through books, under his sable-lined cloak thrown over some books. Magically, the beard comb has disappeared. Perhaps a group of cherubim is playing blind man's buff with him, and, like Proteus, one of the deities has taken on the image of something other than that which now mysteriously blocks the comb from his vision? He lifts the two or three mummified animals scattered on the floor. Nothing there. The toad watches through his glass. Is the Doctor's futile search any less senseless than its own had been?

In frustration, Dee gets down on his knees to peer beneath the standing celestial globes—a present from his fellow student, Gerard Mercado. According to Bruno, there must be an infinite amount of such orbs in the sky above them. A throbbing constriction around his lower legs where his skin-tight nether stockings, fastened by garters, pinch him painfully. *Blast, French hose*, he thinks, *Fashion is an enforced livery wearing out more clothes than a year's work.* One must either refrain from the ink stains of work or give up all finery. Then, beneath the curio cabinet across the room he discovers the comb; or rather he sees the boxwood case wherein it resides. Fallen from the cabinet where Dee put it when Mr. Marley jostled it with a serving tray the day before. He congratulates himself as he crawls toward it, *The plotline of our lives is constructed of mingled instances—tragic and comic.* For Dee, on hands and knees smarting from his exertions and his tight stockings, this is not an auspicious moment to start an adventure.

Nevertheless, one starts. For at that moment, Ludavico, a resident scholar from Padua who has come to Dee to further his studies in engineering, shambles into the library.

"One Faunt, newly come from London, is asking for you, master," the boy, Ludavico announces.

Unperturbed at finding his learned mentor like a crab scrambling on the floor, Ludavico yawns, readjusts his scholar's skullcap and then, turning his back on his teacher, picks his way through the bookshelves for a needed text. Small for his age, the lad stands on tiptoe to peer at the titles on the spines. This is only his second visit to the inner sanctum, and there are so many wondrous books in the room to peer at.

Uncomfortable that his ward finds him in this awkward position, the master of the house scolds, "Have I not told you to forebear entering my study when the double doors are closed?"

"The outer one was open, *Signore*."

"Oh." The old philosopher belatedly recalls having forgotten to fasten the second door as Marley left. It is becoming a mistake he often makes, forgetfulness being another symptom of advancing age. "I know no Faunt," replies the flustered Doctor as he stands. "Might it be Phanto? Phanto from Saltzburg?"

"*Forsa*." The boy can't be sure. "He is *un uomo*, skeleton," replies the Italian as he moves the ladder to search. Spotting what he needs halfway up the bookcase, he asks, "*Signore*, can I *burrow* your Geometry book for my lessons?"

Permission granted, but only after a grammatical lesson is given. "In English, we use 'may I' to make a request." A dutiful nod is given. Dee retrieves the book, a newly-printed adaptation of Dee's *Euclidean Geometry*.

It is handed over, and the lad fingers the pages carefully, searching for a forgotten hypothesis or a spiritual inspiration, studying mathematics after all is one and the same.

"The *bruto* yanked me as I stepped outside, demanding *fortemente* to *see-a* you. *Signore* Faunt has a Machiavellian *humour*. He wants kindness," and then under his breathe, "and liberality." The young scholar's thoughts then drift to some arcane reality where only numbers and symbols exist.

"From London?" questions the Doctor. His heartbeat quickens. "Was he of the Court?"

Still transfixed by what he is reading, Ludavico murmurs, "*Si, Si... Forsa*, he is of the *Court-a...* He *was-a* from London.*" Looking up from the text and in a louder voice the student continues, "*Signore*, explain to me *encora* what is the spiritual meaning of the monad. I know it is the marriage of the sun and the moon, but how effects it sublunary? Is it a mystery, *Maestro*?"

"Not now. *Via* to this Faunt. Show him in. Wait. Is he alone?" A sudden concern overtakes the scholar, "Speak, boy!"

At Dee's urgency, Ludovico shakes off his schoolboy haze and remembers his obedience, "*Si*. He *come* alone. I see him come from the High Road. Right against the church. Enter your field at the great gate. No others."

Dee's first thought takes root. "Mayhap, it is a courier from Her Majesty. Go at once and bring him to me. Tell Mr. Marley to make sure the liquor cabinet is supplied. Oh, and tell him to serve a salver of cheese." *Salver* is too difficult for the young foreigner to understand. Dee explains, "a board, a board of cheese. Waste not a moment. Usher him to me. We will hear this Phanto, this Faunt, *adesso*."

Ludovico scurries out the door, mindful of his master's fearful authority, his student gown swinging about his ankles like a clapper in a clarion bell.

"Have a care, boy, in the future," scolds Dee. "Be quick about London guests."

"I will do all, *Signore*," rings the reply as it reverberates from around the corner.

Dee walks to the footstool where Ludovico has unwittingly abandoned *Euclid*. He looks at the forgotten book and thinks of the trembling expression on the student's face and laughs. *He's a good boy and, though he is from Sienna, knows his manners, yet such an untidy mind.* Dee tells himself he must spend more time with the boy who, after all, wants nothing more than to understand the world he lives in. But for now, the schoolmaster lifts the oversize text and hugs it in his arms. He had once presented Her Majesty with just such a copy of his work of Euclidean Geometry. She had seemed pleased. Did She deceive him? *She is certainly good at that. Were Her blood not Royal, She would have made a convincing player.*

His unspoken hope remains that Her Majesty might be sending word to grant him the Chair of Philosophy that he so covets at Cambridge University. Dee had spoken to Sir John Cheke about it last spring, and the Court scholar had then promised to put in a good word on Dee's behalf at his next Royal interview. Has the hoped for cynosure come at last? Elizabeth is, he knows, much taken with the good Sir John, but Her favorites, like Her *humours*, are as changeable as weather in

March. Had not Her long-time royal favorite, Leicester, fallen? He reminds himself it was not Her wont to bestow such suits speedily—*blast Her!* He lifts a finger to his lips in forbearance. As Ludovico has reminded him, authority must be respected. With a sigh, he scolds himself for putting the cart of his ambitions before the horse of proof. There is no proof for any of his speculations. Man being a reasonable creature, there can be nothing more worthy than the employment of one's thoughts, but alas, one could too easily overthink a thing and worry it to death. His predilection isn't helped by the queasy state of his wretched finances. The flow of students is presently no more than a trickle, and his current books aren't as popular. His investment in the Moscovey trading company is a shambles. So much for being the premier scholar of the realm. He needs employment soon, especially now with another child on the way. Even at the advanced age of forty-seven, he has never learned to patiently abide things in their due course. *Patience. Patience is what I need.*

For decades, Elizabeth has promised him personal advancement. Even as long ago as their first meeting in remote Woodstock where Her reigning half-sister, Mary, had imprisoned Her. The mewed up Elizabeth had been fascinated with Dee's astrological powers to peer into the future and make predictions. He had tutored Her for an hour on the mathematics of it. She had politely laughed and clapped Her hands when he showed Her how Her dominant planet in conjunction with the hour of Her birth affirmed that Her fortunes were auspicious and that She would lead a long and eventful life. And, She had roared boisterously when he had shown Her Queen Mary's inauspicious charts. Later, Her ladies would tell him that they had been very startled by the unfamiliar sound of Her Ladyship's joy. King Henry's bastard child, Elizabeth, they would confide, was too solemn for her youth and spoke too often of the peril of her position. "Sick with melancholia," in hushed tones they would share that "Her Ladyship will prove a hard wife." But Dee's prognostication soon had proved the more accurate.

He reminds himself that now decades later, unlike many of the Queen's privileged courtiers, including those solemn Ladies, he has been blessed to hear that deep, commanding Royal laugh for these many years. *Basso* at times. Where others had vanished, he lives to listen to Her mature *basso* playfully execute wounding flouts and jests of biting wit. He must bide his time. "She will reward you one day, that's certain. But *when*?" chides his inner voice in a pique. He sighs in resignation and, before the arrival of his courtly guest, reaches up to return the *Euclid* to its proper location. The velveteen book slips comfortably back into its niche. Neither his charts nor his scrying has ever given him an answer to that question. Nor for that matter has *She*.

Knowing that, in moments, the Londoner will be presented to him, the aging scholar studies his personage in the long glass. He adjusts his stiff ecru ruff so that his graying beard will fall handsomely over it. His fingers comb it into a carefully shaped isosceles triangle. The entire learned world knows that there are occult secrets locked up in the inner nature of triangles as there are in the other Euclidean figures. In his youth, the world eagerly waited upon him to set those secrets free. But as yet, the geometric forms stubbornly refused to relinquish their complex meanings. While he had mastered much of the known occult mathematical allusions, he had contributed little to the storehouse of what is already known. He prays daily that, in time, a vision might be granted him. One last look in the mirror confirms his hairline recedes above his Patrician forehead and deep wrinkles fan his eyes. Time is not on his side.

2

Despite the early hour, refreshment is served to Nicholas Faunt. Hospitality and plentiful drink are the hallmarks of a good house and a man of means. At table, Faunt sloshes in his mouth the raspberry wine that tingles his palate. Forcing his cheeks inward, he funnels the liquor down his throat. This is so much better than the tavern swill he is used to—watery dregs of ale that force one to nose through a cloud of froth and foam to sip but a lady's thimbleful of beer in an entire flagon. *This* justifies the two-hour journey from London on a nag with thick wind and a chink in the chine.

Burrowing in, young Faunt bleats, "Ill luck and abandoned hopes are my boon companions of late."

"Why is that, young sir?

"My current political career at Whitehall is unsatisfactorily stalled. Despite my scholastic promise at Oxford, I am chained to a clerk's desk with naught to do but the drudgery of note-taking. Certes, from my chair at Whitehall, I have been given a lovely view of Tyburn brook, but what of that? The dismal sight of the marshlands will not buy me a new wardrobe." He swishes the Grenache watching its slow-moving wine legs streak down the side of his glass. "At best, my recent trip took me abroad to the splendors of Paris to seek out enemies of the Crown and gain further advancement. But to what avail? The mission was brief and a failure."

After his second glass, Nicholas Faunt shares, "I had planned to arrive at Mortlake by breakfast and savor some of your goodwife's eggs and salted bacon, but the cold and the damp and my fool of a horse forced me from that hope somewhere just past Putney. Now it is past nine, and the return journey still lies ahead."

A water taxi would have been easier, but then there was the ferryman's expense. His half shilling from the Secretary's *per diem* is certainly not adequate compensation for his aching joints, the chafing in the fleshy part of his upper legs, and the cramp in the arches of his feet. Glass three inspires a catalogue of Faunt's medical woes. And Dee learns that tomorrow his guest must to the surgeon for some salves, dear as they might be.

Faunt shares, "My groaning back and sore arse are momentarily tolerable."

"Master Faunt, may I pour you another?" The doctor moves to the sideboard near the door and lifts the decanter of wine. Across the table, the self-satisfied face perched above the filthy ruff nods in succession, each time more emphatic than the last. As Dee moves to replenish his cup again, he regrets his original offering of a rich vintage. *It is too good for this lout. 'Tis but midmorning and the pintpot drinks as if it were Twelfth Night. Yet still not a word of his mission.* From the sideboard, Dee uncorks a lesser vintage—*Bait.*

Eager for the next round, the menial brays, "Sir, Mortlake's wine is surpassed only by mine host's liberality. I will not say you nay. Here be my glass," adds the smiling, rooster-chested young man. He is clad in worn peasecod doublet with bishop sleeves padded in the forearm and, in the old style, tapered at the wrist. He extends his arm. "Will you not join me?"

Reaching across the pine-planked table, Dr. Dee tips the bottle toward his visitor and slowly pours but a dram into the Venetian goblet. "My boy, I dare not touch a drop till my day's labors are done. And I satisfy your mission..." As he pours, he watches the boney, blond-haired youth rapaciously turn his attention to the elegant design of grapes etched in the glass. The hand holding the glass is no longer steady. This grinning jackal, best used as a footboy, the old scholar observes, is obviously a scrivener; his finger tips are indelibly stained. As Dee withdraws the bottle, the sot realizes no further libation is forthcoming and wobbles the goblet to his nose clownishly inhaling its bouquet. The perfect host adds, "And invariably, I find Spanish wine upsets my stomach and gives me the headache." Indifferently, Dee's glances out the window that looks out on the garden where the grass is damp and russet autumn foliage sways in the wind.

"Good Doctor Dee, I have come on government business from London." He snorts self-importantly, "I am nobody's boy. I, clerk for Sir William Cecil, Lord Burghley, the Chief Secretary of The Privy Council of England, am to serve this writ of summons..." His fingers fumble inside his doublet and manage to produce the document, his voice is almost as wobbly as his fingers, "...for one Dr. John Dee to come with all haste to Whitehall." The writ served, it is duly examined. "You must come today. There can be no objection."

"With no choice, I shall obey." Obedience, thinks Dee, is every Englishman's duty. We owe it to God, to the Queen, and to all who are bound to the Commonwealth.

Propped up with one elbow on the table, Faunt returns to supporting his drunken face on his hand. His pose speaks volumes: there is no danger for Dee yet. He recalls the discomfiting process of such a petition two years prior; none of Dee's captors then had been so casual, so slack, so breezily disrespectful—and rightfully so, for as it turned out, he had been exonerated by proving his "crimes" were "on Her Majesty's behalf."

No, there is no danger, Dee reassures himself, no enforced lockup in the occultist's immediate future. Elizabeth's punctilious secretary would not have sent a young scamp of a clerk to do the roughhouse work of a constable. But Sir William Cecil, Lord Burghley, Dee realizes, is not one who might dispense a university chairmanship to Dee. *Still, nothing to worry poor wife,* Jane, Dee reflects. But neither, alas, will there be a remedy for his pressing financial circumstances. That will not please Jane. But praise God, Providence must be trusted.

Despite his insistence on leaving presently, Faunt hungrily eyes the *divers* bottles in Dee's liquor cabinet, licking his lips in anticipation. His host considers the situation: What to make of this official invitation to London? And what of the morning urgency? Might there be some pressing profitable employment? Royal employment? In the hope that generous amounts of alcohol will fully unbridle the clerk's tongue, Dee grudgingly brims Faunt's glass and uncorks yet another bottle to breathe. "Certes, young sir, you have ridden far for Lord Burghley. I am eager to understand what His Lordship requires of me. There is not an Englishman alive who does more reverence the man than I, and we all thank heaven for Sir William's longevity. Surely it cannot be but some mean task, sith I am at best an inkhorn who dabbles in signs and mathematics."

"An inkhorn who possesses the honorific of doctor," snorts Faunt, passing his palm over his lips. "At Oxford, only you rare minds were made doctors." Disdainfully, pulling at his pencil-shaped beard, the belligerent clerk asks, "Did you not lecture divinity at Louvain and thereafter in Paris? And are you not an inward of Her Highness the Queen? Her astrologer, Her doctor, and cartographer?" As Dee nods in the affirmative, so does Faunt. "Master Secretary gave me certain details."

Taking in the inebriated messenger's ingratiating smile of smug conviviality, Dee thinks ruefully, *And, are not these achievements decades gone, and am I not a forgotten old man?* Yet, he returns the swaggerer's smile.

"You'll forgive me for saying this. You have not been seen at Court in years. Though I'll grant Queen Bess seems to favor you—probably for nostalgia's sake."

The blond scarecrow lifts the goblet to his lips and studies his host for a moment. Dee is sure Faunt is about to say more but has stifled whatever it is and drowns the idea with another long swallow. The doctor obligingly waits upon his pleasure, watching the rogue's prominent

Adam's apple slide obscenely as the wine gutters down his gullet. In silence, Dee stares, wanting to smash it flat as one would a fly on a window.

Bad news for Nicholas, notes Dee—wine stains the clerk's leather doublet. Faunt mops the spill with a ratty kerchief brought up from some nether region and loudly sucks the spilled liquor from the cloth. Dee traces the blood-red path of the wine from the corners of Faunt's mouth to his chin and thence to the seam sewn down the center of his leather doublet where it will doubtless settle in a hempen shirt beneath. The dripping Spanish Malaga leaves an indelible dark purple vein on the young man's garment, joining others of its kind. Yet what can Dee do about this lout? The rogue serves Lord Burghley. The corners of John Dee's mouth turn upward in a welcoming grin even as his tongue—unseen—pushes hard against his teeth. Blithely, Faunt inhales deeply and belches with gusto.

His patience strained, the Queen's old retainer focuses in. "Young man, I believe Her Majesty hath conceived a goodly opinion of my studies mathematical and geographical in times past. I have done *divers* calculations on Her behalf that have ever pleased Her. I praise God for Her. Have you journeyed here at Her behest as well?" With that, Dee, seats himself opposite his guest at the narrow table, leans forward, and whispers conspiratorially, so that nosey students cannot overhear, "Is there a service at *Her* bidding that the secretary requires of me?"

"If there be," replies the inebriate, "I know not." He shrugs, laughs heartily, and leans back in his chair. "I have come here solely for William Cecil, Lord Burghley. He is much taken with your last treatise on naval defense and would hear *more*." *Or at least that is what I was instructed to say*; Faunt snickers to himself. In his drunkenness, he now betrays more than he should. "He has only given me to understand that it is to that matter and the greater concern of the Realm's protection that he sends for you."

"The *Realm's* protection?"

At that, Nicholas Faunt's nail-bitten hands flutter the question away. The cockerel turns away in his chair, but Dr. Dee catches a flicker of unease in his tipsy guest. Pushing against the table, his chair arching back, the clerk remains mute and fixes his glassy eyes on the ceiling. Clearly, this summons has nothing to do with a possible lay rectorship at university. Though who better to lead a university than he? *What could the Lord Treasurer be after?*

As the cry of an English bullfinch warbles from without, the courier, eager for any distraction, looks for its red breast out the window. Leaning back to admire the bird's plumage, Nicholas' unwashed mane of hair falls back to reveal his ruddy face. His dusty blond head suddenly catches the sunlight and for an instant, Faunt's profile is purified of the ravages of the English weather and excess drink. He is now not so much a self-important barnyard cockerel as a perfect Giotto painting, the archangel Michael haloed in gold announcing the good news to the blessed Virgin. But the image is as brief as an epiphany, and once the songbird has moved on, Burghley's lackey folds his arms around his chest and returns the chair and himself to a proper sitting position.

"I keep a linnet bird caged at home," Burghley's messenger says expansively. "God knows when he'll get fed."

Every man, it seems, believes in his own importance and is ready to think he is such to others without once having the wits to know his affairs have no more weight with others than theirs have with him.

Faunt stretches and yawns broadly. It is a wonder that he does not break his jaw. Instead, the messenger selects a crabapple from a bowl of fruit. Tossing it high in the air, he watches it descend.

"What Her Majesty desires or does not desire is out of my sphere," he announces, emphatically holding up the apple to make his point. Pleased with his rhetorical pun, Faunt takes a healthy bite. His weak mouth sucks at the crab's tartness. The question of the protection of the Realm is forgotten or purposefully ignored.

Disgusted, irritable, but not deterred, Faunt's host presses on in a courtly manner.

"Truly, Her Majesty's designs are known only to a select circle. Though surely Lord Burghley is an influential quadrant of that right perfect circle. Excluding Leicester, Her recent favorite, Her Master Secretary knows more of Her mind than any man alive—and has been privy to Her noble thoughts for as long as they have been Royal. He has ever been there at Her side, and pray God that he always shall be."

Etiquette requires that Burghley's man reciprocate the prayer on behalf of his master's welfare, but instead, taking another bite, Faunt finishes off apple and core, spitting the seeds toward the nearby fireplace. This gross indecency, this churlish disregard for his master's wellbeing, or Dee's home, has crossed a line. A man without respect or loyalty is as faithless as a masterless dog, and the doctor has come to the end of his patience.

"Have a care, boy! I'll not have you treat my home as waste ground. Has intimacy with the best of the English Realm taught you no manners? Were you born in a pigpen?"

This sudden upbraiding from the ancient jars Nicholas, he stammers, "Why, sir... I, sir..."

Merciless, the Queen's wizard will have none of it. "Nay, make me no hollow apologies. Take not Mortlake's hospitality as a license for your upstart forwardness. And do not scant your obedience to your betters. Rather, on your knees, scoundrel, and police after yourself."

Faunt hoots faintly, undaunted, "And if I do not? Will you call your schoolboys and steward and chastise me? Surely you are aware how that would appear slight courtesy to the Master Secretary, mistreating his envoy for adding three apple pips to an already-filthy floor." The liquor has rallied the boy's bravado. Unsteadily, the youth rises from his chair to his full height and thrusts his pigeon-boned chest at his accuser.

Boldness invariably born of constraint often intimidates and overwhelms those who are either shallow in judgment or weak in courage. Stone-faced, Dee takes his measure. And so, calmly and steadily, Dee replies, "Whelp, you abuse Your Lordship's patronage, and I must not show offense to him. I will call neither student nor Marley, my steward—they would but bloody your saucy mouth. No, I will chastise you myself in a manner that will bring no offense to Lord Burghley." Nicholas merely sniggers. But now the voice is all steel and threat. With only nostrils flaring, Dee continues, "You fear not my reverence and assume I have but little strength. Perhaps with others of my age that would be true. But alas for you, you have forgotten in whose house you are. I am, as I know you have heard, a necromancer of dire degree. I converse with Heaven and have command over the lightning to rive the oak. Think twice before you awaken my ire, for I have the power to afflict. I will wrack your bones with aches and make you moan with the ague for an eternity of time beyond your reckoning. No mark will show, and no man can ever prove I beset you. I say again, get you to the floor and gather up your refuse."

The color in the upstart's face wanes, and his jaw slackens. The London courier is a man of the world, educated at Corpus Christi College. Magic is a charlatan's trick. But lively invention is something to which the young are most susceptible, rooted as it is in less life experience, with drink only heightening susceptibility and weakening one's strength of mind. Every man has heard of Dee's reputation. It is said even the Queen Herself acknowledges his powers. Most counselors merely raise a prudent eyebrow at Her gullibility, but one or two of the wisest secretly suggest that John Dee's investigations of the unseen world have uncovered the darkest secrets of hidden powers. The young clerk cannot be certain whether Dee's threat is a practiced performance or a genuine harbinger of powerful witchcraft. Uncertainties multiply when the old man lays hold of a gnarled oak bough leaning by the fireplace, and raises it easily aloft with both hands. Not daring to breathe, Faunt stares at a living portrait of the biblical Moses who could transform staffs into snakes and part seas with an uplifted hand.

It takes but a moment in time—an eternity to Faunt—for his imagination to get the better of him. Obedient hands slip from his hips, and he bends to the floor to retrieve one of the pips sitting on the flint tile of the hearth. Cupping it in his hand, he examines it as if it were a ruby; he does not wish to threaten Dee by looking up at him but steadfastly keeps eyes on the floor, searching for the other seeds. His tousled locks hang down around his face like a curtain rung down on a play. At this angle, a scab in his hairline becomes noticeable, a purplish target waiting for a blow from above. Faunt fears being struck, but not by Dee's staff. He's been clubbed and whipped before; the familiar can be borne. The fear is of the possibility of everlasting torment. Could the older man truly make that threat real? The Bible talks of witches; could he deny them?

There is great anguish in not knowing what may befall us that astonishes the mind and enfeebles the extremities. Although a part of this upstart's brain reasons that this is all a ruse, an older, more superstitious part of it cannot be certain. His heart palpitates under his tight-fitting doublet. He feels the coarse cloth of his breeches cut deeply into his crotch. Though he tries, he cannot will himself to look up at the magus. He is fully aware of how abject a figure he presents, but there seems to be an iron halter on his head and shoulders that keeps him bowed. He silently curses his own weakness but has not the fortitude to protest. Dee watches in stony satisfaction at the boy's disquiet—yet having no doubts that this moment will be re-imagined later. The villain at the alehouse will stand before his cronies, swearing that it was a spell the satanic Dee had visited on him via his damned wine. *Well,* thinks Dee, *it is your lie to tell. My angels know the truth.*

In a very long minute, Faunt finds all his effluent seeds and does not put them in the fire but holds them fast in his hand and then swallows them. Only after swallowing hard does he look up to see the satisfied doctor lower his staff and return it hearthside. Not a word is spoken. The ingrate's bended knee is statement enough. Order has been restored—order, the underlining spine of Elizabethan life, the calcified skeleton whereby society hangs: order, bred from infancy into every member of the Commonwealth. Every tinker has his limitations, every nobleman has his responsibilities, and even the Queen has her parameters. The laws of England rigorously insist on preserving decorum, and the English constabulary slavishly enforce those laws. No one is immune; all know their place.

Boot steps approach the door. There is a respectful knock. Whoever it is waits patiently for an answer.

Sensing that the inimical presence is staring at him, Faunt whispers, "Your worship, I meant no disrespect."

"And what of Lord Burghley?"

"His Lordship has and will ever be in my prayers."

There is a silence as the two regard each other. "Mr. Faunt, I suggest that you stand, unless you wish Johannes Marley, my steward, to find you like a papist pilgrim bussing my floors with your palms and knees."

Faunt rises up and weakly repeats, "I meant no disrespect."

But Dee is no longer interested in Faunt or his apologies. His mind is beginning to prepare for his trip to London. "Come in, Johannes. I am in want of your help."

Marley pushes open the wooden door and tips his head a bit toward his master in obeisance. He is a squat, middle-aged man dressed in a brown gown as befits his office. There hangs around his thick throat a necklace with a key that is polished daily until it gleams with the sun's radiance. He has the straight-backed importance of an ex-military man who prides himself on foreseeing unforeseeable difficulties. On quick inspection, he deems there is no danger present in the room, only a whey-faced puppy who looks as if he has seen the devil.

"How may I be of service, doctor?"

"First, I will need my horse saddled for a journey to the city. I expect I shall stay overnight. Moreover, since autumn's nip is in the night air, fetch my heavy cloak."

"You will require a warm hat, sir."

"Aye, but I like not to bring attention on the road. The woolen cap will do."

"Sir, that laborer's cap befits not your station. Let me fetch you your beaver that Sir Walter brought back from the New World."

"Fine. Fine. The beaver," says Marley's master with a flintiness that discourages any further discussion. "If I remember rightly, it yet rests in the trunk by the kitchen. As for my station, pack me my dancing rapier given me by the Duke of Northumberland. That will become me finely."

"Anything else, sir?"

"Yes, clear away this food. Young Faunt is finished."

Nicholas Faunt looks up, startled at the mention of his name.

"Unless, of course, master Faunt would like another apple." Dee looks over at him briefly and then returns his attention to Marley. "This young man seems particularly interested in the apple pips of our region."

3

The Dees have but one horse, and so the mare sniffs in curiosity at Faunt's unfamiliar roan that whinnies by her side.

"Mr. Marley, I leave the charge of the household in your good hands," says the master of the house adjusting his saddle straps there in his barnyard.

"Gramercy, sir. I shall endeavor to keep all well and mindful in your absence." Out of many years of habit, George Marley inadvertently touches the key at his neck, his badge of office, acknowledging his duty.

Mounted, Faunt clutches the reins tightly, dreading the ride to London with the dark-*humoured* sorcerer. The nipping country air with its smell of the river have gone far to sober him. He envisions the deadly silence of the return trip knowing it will be harder to bear than that morning's discomfort. Worse, what if this accursed witch practices his black arts on him while they ride alone in the woods? His dread is evident. As the wise William Cecil has often said, "Truth can be found even in forbidden communications with spirits." Foreknowledge is a political asset and a counselor against national calamity. Turning in his saddle, the callow youth looks toward London where his future safety surely lies.

London means not being alone with this menace. London is a stiff drink with fellow-minded lads like himself, but that is at least two hours off. Much can befall-between then and the present.

Surreptitiously ignoring Faunt, Marley holds firm the bit-collar for his master's horse. "Doctor, be there anything that I may retrieve for you in the house?" Though he looks dutifully to his employer, all the butler's thoughts are concentrated on the insipid rake twisting uncomfortably on the adjacent horse. This Faunt is too silent, too nervous, too mealy-mouthed. Marley is known to dislike couriers from London who invariably bring bad news—the fall of the Dudleys, the departure of Pickering, and most especially the *pursuivants* of two years ago who had come to arrest his employer for devil worship.

"I cannot harbor a guess of what that might be," states Dee as he approaches Marley, "But, perdition, I shall have forgotten something that is certain." With that, one hand on Marley's shoulder, Dee steps into his butler's cupped hands and vaults into his saddle, taking the reins from his man and looking down into George's broad face, "Mr. Marley, you are the governor of my household now. See to provisions while I be from the house. Of necessity, my absence may extend two or even three days. Look to the students whom I leave in your care. Let them not revel overly much in their master's absence." There is no steel in his voice, only concern. "Remind them of their studies. Each must translate either from the Latin or Greek a page a day of the manuscript they study. Master Herbert is behind in his tuition and must be urged to seek funds from his father. The old reprobate, Black Will, shall not fob me off again."

John Herbert, Earl of Pembroke, *Black Will*, had once promised John Dee an excellent salaried position in his household as his astrological advisor, but had conveniently forgotten. Taking in his son had been scant reward for what Dee had once thought was a certain path to financial security. Worse luck, the position had been given to John Prestall, an unscrupulous cunning man who had none of Dee's learning. "Remember to lock up all when the family retires and see that you quench the fires and the lanterns. Most especially, have a care that no one set foot in the *interna bibliotheca*." Any discovery of his private magical literature, the waxen tablets that he uses for scrying, his journal of angelic conversations, or his copy of *de occulta philosophia* would mean the end of his reputation—possibly his life— in addition to squelching whatever chance he had of securing a new sinecure from Elizabeth. Too many unschooled minds already thought him a conjurer of devils and whispered the Lord's Prayer whenever he passed. A mindless mob had burned his library once, and without a Court patron, he had been powerless to obtain reparations.

"That I will, sir, as I always have," George Marley reassures his master.

"Aye, that you have." Dee looks out across his field to the road to London. A bitter country wind blows. "Odd's my life, I was to procure hay. You must look to that as well."

"Farmer Blakely as usual?"

"Nay, not him. He is a pettifogging knave. We shall not do commerce with him again."

"Understood. I will endeavor elsewhere."

Dee nods. Feeling keenly the seasonal chill in the air, he takes a reading of the cloud-swept sky. Venus is entering the house of Capricorn. "Like as not, we shall have rain, Mr. Faunt."

Surprised at being addressed, Faunt stirs uneasily in his stirrups and faintly answers, "Very like, Doctor," then looks away. He scolds himself to show some mettle. "My horse has it in the nose too." Like a groveling ostler who knows only to keep his eyes averted and lips sealed, Nicholas ducks his head and pats his mount's mane. But then one last peep, "The sooner started, the sooner there, sir." It is not lost on either of the men how pitiful this sounds.

With his calloused hand shielding his eyes from looking directly into the sun, Marley remonstrates, "Your riding gloves, sir?" His hand moves to his mouth to cover it from the billowing dust and bits of hay the breeze blows about, "You bought them purposefully for your next visit to London. They become you well. Shall I fetch them? They but rest in the foyer."

"You are a godsend, Mr. Marley. Yes, on your way now, yes, they will indeed become me well." It is best to look prosperous. "Don't forget, bring me the beaver hat." For the Puritans serving in the English government, like Burleigh, poverty bodes misfortune and shows a loss of God's Grace.

Marley jogs back to the house. Reflexively, Dee

reaches down and searches the pocket of his riding cloak for his diary. It is an unsettling fear that he might leave it behind; it is his constant companion and counselor. The discipline of daily entries makes him pay closer attention to the innumerable details of his life. What use being a student of the Heavens if one does not study oneself? Meaningful instances present themselves often. The eye sees not itself but by reflection through one's own actions.

Thankfully, the diary rests deep within his pocket. On the blank page opposite its frontispiece is the signature of Henri II of Navarre who had offered him two-hundred crowns to be the King's Mathematical Instructor. That was back in the halcyon days when Dee had been the doyen of the intelligentsia packing university lecture halls with his lectures on Geometry. As a royal gift to him, a Parisian bookseller had been commissioned to bind a bespoke diary of vellum pages in precious red leather. Though it teems with observations, there is yet room for more. It is filled with dates and impressions and observations that seek to understand the natural world as completely as Jesu would allow. Oh, that his life's work would survive him and be read by thousands. The thought is a consolation to his once hopeful ambitions. *Was it a misstep rejecting Navarre's offer?* Then there had been so many assurances by the powerful that he was destined for great things. Alas, his potential never translated to success, and, consequently, he is now pressed to make ends meet. He fingers the familiar wrinkles in his journal's spine, willfully banishing the image of himself as a French *philosophe.* As an Englishman and a Welsh descendant of King Arthur, his duty is to the Tudors in London and not to powers abroad. The familiar feel of the leather is as comforting as laying his hand on Jane's thigh. He can be parted from neither. Both are essential.

Marley reappears with the gloves and hat—the trifling preparations of their journey complete. Doctor Dee stares toward London. What is to become of him there? Ill Fortune or promotion? He had dreamt of falling the other night. *What did that bode?* He scrutinizes the sulky sot beside him, too frightened to match his gaze. No help there. Only Time can bring Truth to light.

"Many thanks, Mr. Marley." Dee slips his hands into the fleecy gauntlets, ready to embark on whatever Fortune has in store. "Westward ho, Mr. Faunt!"

They ride in silence. Wary, the government's lackey is scrupulous to keep Dee ahead of him. They pass shoulder-high hedges and flourishing apple trees just inside the boundary of Dee's property. Lavender, orange, and tawny yellow leaves peek out among green boughs. In two weeks, Mortlake shall become an exquisite tapestry of color.

The unruly roots of his small orchard tilt Dee's stonewalls at an obscene angle, yet not enough to hinder travelers on the road. The community council requires that landowners' walls be maintained and that an estate's vegetation and debris along the public highways be kept groomed. Many landowners grouse that it is cheaper to pay the Council fines than to hire the gardeners to hew the brambles and briars. Though the

Dees scrimp on expenses, ever dreaming of Royal patronage, John and Jane agree that civic obligation must be obeyed. To that end, Mr. Walter Hooper has been hired who, of late, is barber in Cheswick. He maintains the hedges and knots in good order at a salary of five shillings per annum plus some food and drink. For that, all is to be pruned twice the year.

The journey's way doglegs to the left past the new church with its limestone walls, flat-arched windows, and square tower as prim and proper as the vicar who preaches there. The road widens; deep gullies in an uneven highway hinder their horses, making the ride difficult. For the first half hour, nothing is said. In time, farmhouses and yards disappear, replaced by misshapen scrub pines slanting in every direction, blocking what little there is of the late morning sun yet providing some degree of buffer from the increasing ferocity of the wind. Frantically waving tree branches threaten to topple the riders from their mounts. The wind blows at their backs whistling eerily. Tree roots, raspberry bramble, and wild antique white roses grip the landscape with their talons. Thrashing tendrils latch on to anything and everything. More than once, a thorn lashes out at a face. None of this is to Faunt's liking.

"*Pam'pinus*, the Latin for briar."

The Oxford graduate lacks the gumption to grumble more than, "I know"; at pains to keep his teeth from chattering, the nipping chill allows him to say nothing more.

"The French call them *pampre*. They don't seem so pampered now."

There is a lift at the corner of Dee's eyes, and Faunt wagers secretly that beneath the old man's muffler a smirk betrays Dee's pleasure at his own pun. *Enjoy your drollery while you can,* thinks the writ server.

Crossing a meadow of grazing sheep, Dee notices rivulets of runoff rainwater sluicing downhill through the grass and St. John's wort, forming ponds along the flatter spaces of the hillside. The riders slow their pace, careful to keep the watery sheep dung from splashing on their clothes. The northern chill invades their clothes and stiffens their joints. Faunt rubs his chafed cheek. The older man is aware the younger has no muffler. Either, he is chronically ill-prepared or a fool. *Doubtless, both are true.* Only a third of their way through the ride now, and most of it has been in grim seclusion; both men long for its end.

Just before they exit the pasture, under a copse of trees, Faunt reins in his horse and reaches into his saddlebag to withdraw a stained clay pipe filled with tobacco. Bad luck for him, he finds no matches. No matter. With its stem firmly clenched in his mouth, he sets his aggrieved jaw against the chill, giving him some sense of control. There is comfort in the briar's familiar redolence and bite. The phantasm of its former warmth seemingly alleviates the cold. By the smugness of his curled lips, it is clear the youth heartily congratulates himself for having brought it.

Citing an old adage, Dee reminds with brittle contempt, "Tobacco taken without measure *stealeth* a man's wit." While visiting Mortlake, Raleigh had forced him once into a smoke that had almost immediately made him uncomfortably lightheaded. Dee approves of nothing that dilutes reason. *Where the fascination?* Like all adages, truth is revealed in proverbial wisdom.

"It is an old wives tale," is all the taciturn replies.

A quarter of an hour passes silently until they come across a family of wandering beggars. *Moonmen*, they are called. There are eight of them dressed in the unwholesome rags of castoff clothes. Six are children—four girls and two boys, none of whom are past fourteen years of age. The smallest is a lumpish babe wrapped in a coarse hempen blanket; the woman protects it from the weather, hugging it to her chest. But truth be told, the entire tribe huddles together to shield themselves from the wind. Some have nothing but remnants of footwear—toeless slippers and slashed boots. The youngest two have nothing at all, and their feet are as brown as hooves and have bunions of mud caked on them. On seeing their betters hastening forth on horseback, they make no move to relinquish the road. At first, Faunt refuses to cede the way, but Dee signals to hold up and let them pass.

"Alms, kind sirs," pleads the oldest and, no doubt, the father of the family. As he comes closer to Faunt, he extends his arms showing him his inflamed sores, saying once again, "Alms, alms, for Jesu's sake." Faunt's mount whinnies and sidles. "My family is destitute," the moonman whines. His oldest boy, who is also the scrawniest, removes his cap and cups an empty hand in the universal gesture of begging, whimpering all the while like one who has just this day lost his favorite dog. The troop is almost comical in their practiced routine.

Faunt kicks at the grasping hands with his boot. He has a moral aversion to the poor, a revulsion of the stinking masses—society has taught him a religious respect for those with property. Conversely, those *without* are contemptible. "Fie, thou foul smelling lousy knave. Naught comes of naught. Your mort and thee have spawned godless rogues and vagabonds. Get thee from our sight. We are at Her Majesty's business."

Scurrying up to Faunt's horse, the beggar woman raises her head and stares at her husband's attacker. "Have a care about you, young sir," she hisses, "I will set the evil eye on you. Have a care."

Looking at the two urchins at his ankle, the Doctor sniffs, "More like you will infect us with some disease." Maneuvering his horse nearer the beggar woman, "Madam, we have nothing for you, except to demand that you and your kinchins continue on your way and leave us to ours."

Resolving that no coin will be cadged from these two, the husband and wife gesture for their children to leave off, and so they do, but not without low mocking bows from some and catcalls and insulting gestures from the others. From their gesticulations, despite the wind, a palpable stench emanates from them. Dee lifts his muffler a little higher to his nose. Without hurry, the vagabonds pick their way past, meandering like lazy mountain goats and reeking much the same.

"These knaves would rather hazard death than do a day's work," *tskes* the civil servant, clenching the pipe even tighter in his mouth. Few in government could separate the cause of the recent spate of England's homelessness from the clergy's insistence that it was a sign of God's rejection. *In its everlasting wisdom, Heaven ordains poverty and wealth,*" said the pulpit.

"They fear nothing, no not the stocks nor a whipping."

"Do they not? One day, I must enquire. But I do think you are in the right."

As Doctor Dee proceeds on his way, his till-now-sullen companion draws closer to press the opportunity for a chance at conversation. "Doctor Dee, does not your constable, perform his office, and lock up this vagrancy? Is your village not oft waylaid by these moonmen? They are lousy and belike carry the plague. They besiege us in London. Bridewell is overrun." Bridewell, a former Royal residence at Ludgate Hill near Fleet Street, had been converted into a place to train the poor for work. But it quickly devolved to little more than a stinking prison.

Dee looks back, slightly surprised at the man's newfound loquaciousness. "Aye Will Hunt does what he can," Dee points back in the direction of Mortlake. "But they are many and more than Will can cope withal. What few he claps in irons must abide in his small jail until the tardy magistrate comes round to set them to trial. We here in the country are overrun by rogues that you in the city escort to London's walls and push out upon us."

"But is it not the law to do so?"

"Aye. That it is, a city law, and a bad one. Would not the Commonwealth be better served to set these beggars to work? And not confine them in the corruption of Bridewell. Let them for hire rather repair the city's ditches that are the reservoir of the city's privies and the engendering of much pestilence. The doing of it or the fear of this manner of work will fright them into good husbandry."

"It is a just and reasonable answer to our country's dilemma," Nicholas says, removing the pipe from his mouth as they plod forth leaving the urchins behind to ready themselves to accost the next passersby. "But London is overwhelmed daily by a flood of humanity. It's not just the poor but also all the foreign-born strangers. They buy up houses with jobs that they have stolen from trueborn Englishmen. They threaten our way of life by snapping up custom and place. They keep to themselves and constitute a commonwealth within our own. Particularly egregious are the foreign merchants and handicraftsmen who take their profits from us and export our currency back to their unholy lands."

"Work is the remedy. Judgment is only found through industry. It physics the mind. Her Grace must convince her prosperous classes to employ more and at a decent wage. More, the walling off of the Common's lands by the wealthy for their particular sheep and cattle has engendered naught but misery amongst those who once tilled the land. There must be a fairer sharing of our nation's wealth."

"If something is not done soon and that betimes, then belike the honest strivers by which I mean the apprentices and journeymen will in time sore beset the brute Belgians and the faint-hearted Flemings. And drive them back across our Channel and from the betrayal of our Kingdom." *The clerk has found his voice,* observes the philosopher, *speaking for reform, a tendency often found in the young.*

"What say you, Master Faunt, do you as a functionary of the government now speak for revolution by the lower classes?"

"I care not for the idle nor the worthless who through their own faults deserve sharp justice." A glow of rectitude comes into his face. "But for those unfortunates whom we call the true poor and deserve our charitable help and sustenance. They deserve better than we have provided."

"And how might that be accomplished? Would you have us be Anabaptists?"

"Nay, I am no Hutterite who dies for goodness and never sees the world. I only speak of charity.

"Our nation containeth a great store of poor people who of necessity must be relieved by wealthier citizens. Else they starve and come to utter desolation. The Word doth bind us to make daily provision for them."

"Would you raise our taxes? Which in fact often is the very cause for many of these unfortunates being thrust into their wretchedness?"

"Nay, the nation can ill afford that. But something must be done for those who *cannot* find gainful employment." Putting both reins into one hand, he begins to gesticulate with the free one. "As you say, working wretches are being daily evicted from their pelting farms and are forced to bear necessity's hard cruelties."

"But I put it to you again, how would you remedy the situation?"

The dialogue so long in coming continues with much passion for the rest of the journey. The two college men eagerly pursue the lively thesis and antithesis of the remedy for national poverty. The weather's rawness is forgotten as friendly arguments ensue. Though the wind rattles, the two make every effort to speak above it. Hypothesis, instances, and convictions are shuffled back and forth and the day's gray sickly sun mounts to its apex. They enter London by way of the Thames crossing over the London Bridge, joining the unruly throng, and slowly pushing their way through traffic. The enormous crowd is confined to a structure only twenty-six feet wide. Carriers of vegetables, riders, livestock, carts, and peddlers with their wares—all jostle for entrance. It is a half-hour before Dee and Faunt manage to pass the northern gatehouse of the bridge. The urban woes of overpopulation are immediately apparent: jutting tenements overhang dark narrow streets wherein the bedlam of animals, clanking carts, and carriages compete with fulsome cooking smells, street peddlers, and store-front merchants loudly hawking their wares, travelers hoping to either get home or find lodging before nightfall—the entire city shouts to make itself heard. Worse are the smells of the reeking mid-street gutters with their open drains polluted with stinking refuse. Everything and everyone is painted over with the thin black soot of the city's smoke and its acrid smell. Nearby pitchmen shout and wave to get their attention, but Faunt, now in the lead, spurs his bay to get past, leaving Dr. Dee to follow as best he can.

4

The residences in this part of London teeter almost touching each other across narrow Leadenhall Market Street. Fostered by the aging London docks, there is an algae-green seediness to the neighborhood. Nicholas Faunt draws up to one of the three houses before them, followed by Dee. A rickety lad of fourteen addresses them; the boy is a victim of one of London's seasons of the plague and looks up at them with a palsied eye, the right side of his face paralyzed.

"S'Death, Mister Nich'las, the master is past patience expectin' you. Indeed, 'a has cursed your delay well these two hours. 'alf the day is spent." Only his good eye squints at Faunt. "What 'as kept you?" The young ostler has the guttural accent common to the North Country.

"I am here, by the grace of God, and that is all that matters," the Privy Council's clerk protests. In a peremptory voice as much for Dee as to put this boy in his place, Faunt demands, "Where is your employer?"

"Within. In his sitting room. He studies paper *thingies*," advises the ostler, who communes easier with horses than humans. Like the weather of his Yorkshire Dales, he is cold and cloudy.

"Patrick, see that Dr. Dee is well taken care of. Show

him at once to the hallway study." Then, with neither a *by-your-leave* nor a backward look, Nicholas Faunt dismounts and hustles himself through the open door of the gray three-story house, never to be seen by his riding companion again.

"Patrick is it? Boy," asks Dee as he thinks to dismount and then doesn't. The ground here is muddy. "who is the master of this place?" He hands his reins to the menial who reeks of his profession.

"Why sir, this be Thomas Phelippe's 'ouse," is the curt reply. Left unspoken is the tail end of Patrick's sentence, *any fool knows that.*

"And who be he, sirrah?"

"'ee, sir, why, 'ee sir is boon companion and confident to Mr. Secretary Francis Walsingham," wheezes the boy as he cozies up to the horse. His frozen face traps his words in his nose like lost prisoners, attempting escape through the unready way of his misshapen mouth. "'Ee be the Secretary's secretary," says Patrick sniggering over his rudimentary pun. No matter the class, all Londoners—even young ostlers— seem to have a smug superiority over visiting country bumpkins. "Master Thomas is the Secretary's *aide-de-camp.*" The French *aide-de-camp* in the boy's mouth sounds like an anapest galumphing out of a frozen field. *Secretary's secretary* is more a repressed sneeze.

This Patrick treats me as an old nothing, thinks Dee, *and yet doesn't care to hide the fact that like a pack of hounds before the hunt they have been expecting my and Faunt's arrival since early day. It's evident that he honors my horse over me.* Another thought dawns. Is this testiness an act distracting from sharing information about his master? *Perhaps he will not be so guarded about his master's master.* "What of Secretary Walsingham? What of him?"

"'Ee be 'ere already. I 'ave but fed and brushed his mare this past two hours. Came early 'ee did." He strokes Dee's charger. Smelling hay on the boy, the horse is eager to make friends.

Taken by surprise, the doctor sits straight in his saddle. So the old fox *is* here. *That knave, Faunt, said it was Burleigh I was to meet. What meaning is in this our coming here? Not so fast.* Is Walsingham's presence here chance or purpose? *With Walsingham, it's always wheels within wheels,* reasons the doctor. Walsingham's enemies have always said that Sir Francis is incapable of telling a truth. He runs an army of spies for the Crown, dishonorable men pretending to be other than they seem. Intelligencers—Walsingham's men of the spy trade—are notorious for deception and betrayal. They are disaffected troublemakers who prosper by betraying confidential conversations, infiltrating households, and rifling through private diaries. Dee feels for his own. *Scum who lie in their throats and, in comparison, make hell's ministers seem angelic. Portsmouth curs have more honour.*

Yet, he is reminded of the peril in which all of Europe stands. First, the Queen and Her Commonwealth must be protected from the *Papal Bull of 1570* that suggests a call for Her death. In the coming year, papists would show their lethal capabilities with the assassination of Prince William of Orange, the Protestant martyr of the

Low Countries. But did England need the gruesome spectacles of beheadings and disemboweling that are daily staged to horrify the populace into a cowed acceptance of Protestant rule. Poor imprisoned Catholics are brought down daily by Walsingham's disingenuous agents—these intelligencers—who secure their freedom by repeating to their jailers the testimony of fellow prisoners. Men, and women too, are tortured for nothing more than a word mindlessly blurted in anger, that later is shamelessly repeated against them by Sir Francis' *eyes and ears*. And for what? Even the staid scholars of Oxford whisper in their dormitories that there is very little difference in the way of religious tolerance between Elizabeth and Her Roman Catholic predecessor, bloody Mary Tudor. Their father, King Henry, rather enjoyed the pageantry of the Popery he destroyed.

Catching the boy's wary look, Dee offers, "You must guard your every word in this household. Must you not?"

Patrick lowers his voice, saying, "Oy, sir. They say 'ee 'as ears everywhere." Looking at the still-open door, Patrick stints at continuing this particular line of thought. As Dee's mount chomps her lips for food and water after the hard journey, the palsied ostler strokes the horse's sweaty flank. Careful not to be caught with his opinions showing, Patrick moves to the horse's mouth and focuses on feeding her oats from his pocket. "Oy. Sir," is all he says out loud. There is a quick stab at the door with a grimy finger. "Nich'las bade me bring you inside." Frustration at being in something over his depth, slurred words tumble out, "S'blood, it is not my office to see to the guests nor to blather with'em, neither. That be Walter's job." Another look at the door. "I'll call for 'im." With that, the ostler brings his free hand to the good side of his mouth and halloos, "By Gist, Walter, 'ave a care. 'ere be the guest to Master Phelippes."

There comes an answering yell. "Anon, I will come anon." The annoyance in Walter's voice is unmistakable.

Despite the mud, Dee dismounts. *Though expected, I'm definitely not welcome here*, thinks Dee.

Before the doctor can reprimand the ostler for ill treatment, he is met by Walter, Phelippes' gentleman usher. Breathless from excess of household duties within, he rushes toward Dee, pulling wisps of hair from his sweaty cheek. He stands just over five feet and is a little past his prime being in his late thirties. Wide as he is tall, he is a jiggly fat man whose body continually ebbs and flows like tides in a lake. He wipes his hands on a tattered apron that grudgingly surrounds his waist.

Walter pants with inquiries, "May I enquire of your worship's desires? Have we kept you long? Has the Doctor dined?" Though his wheeze addresses Dee, Walter casts his attention on the ostler's turned back and large ears. Presumably Patrick always makes a bad first impression, and Walter is eager to offer apologies.

"Gor, this 'eres the fellow traveler of Faunt's," says Patrick, waving his hand disingenuously in the direction of the stranger. Then shouts, "Opinionated, 'e'is!"

Dee straightens and growls, "Me sirrah? Why I have said not a word this last two minutes."

Patrick never looks back. "Don't need to. I know them looks." With that, the lad *harrumphs* and turns the corner of the building, guiding the mare to the barn. Dee is not unaware of the muffled epithet muttered in his direction as Patrick shambles off.

With great decorum, Dee focuses on blubbery Walter. "I am Dr. John Dee, of Mortlake, from whence Faunt and I have traveled this dank day. Faunt spoke of a hallway study. By your leave, may I rest inside?" Walter's eager nod sets his entire body rippling, "...and await my courier who it appears has deserted me for something or someone in the house."

"Of course, of course, Your Reverence." Walter smiles and hustles backward. "Master Phelippes would have it no other way." He nearly trips over the threshold of the doorway. But as he stumbles, his hand catches the brass latch handle of the door and he steadies himself. Never missing a beat, yet never quite catching his breath, Walter reiterates, "Welcome, welcome to you, Doctor. Let me show you to a fire." Entering the house and passing through a narrow vestibule, they reach a study, with a well-stocked library. "Doctor Dee, your worship, can take some comfort here," urges the courteous usher. "You shall not want for drink. You have my word. It will be brought anon." He opens the door and yells, "Tom!"

"A tankard of mulled wine if you have it?" replies John Dee, thinking, *as they all like to shout in this household, ALL must be deaf.*

"You shall have it, my dear sir. You shall have it," he reassures, but some worry seems to accompany the statement. Walter adjusts a wooden stool so that it is closer to the fire. "Rest you here, sir? Certes, you must be fatigued from your travels."

"Aye, that I am, Walter. Your fire relieves the chill." With that, Dee rubs his chafed hands before the open grate. There he remains to allow the numbness in his palms to thaw into nettlesome pricks. Stiff fingers unbutton his traveling cloak, and the man sets himself on the offered stool. As if nothing would please him better, Walter claps his hands together in a gesture of personal satisfaction, happy indeed to see a stranger made comfortable. The man has an innate affability that radiates like a woman's kindness. His face is framed by steel grey hair trimmed like a hedge just above his eyes, but on the sides of his head, tresses hang to his shoulders. After time spent with the enigmatic Faunt, Dee lets himself relax in the warmth of this gentleman's good cheer and hospitality. Seeing his guest's muddy boots, round Walter offers Dee the opportunity of removing them, either for the Doctor's comfort or to keep the house clean. Finding a stool, the tired traveler raises his right booted foot in the direction of the gentleman usher. *Here is a man,* Dee thinks, *with whom it would be a pleasure to sup.* Stretching his stockinged legs out in front of him toward the fire, he declares, "Tis good to rest. T'was a long, tedious jarring. Your Mr. Faunt was a cold companion at the start. He is hard to warm to."

"Oh, Faunt is not one of *our* household," shares the fat man but says no more. Old Tom, the yeoman of the Chamber, enters. It would appear Tom has never been quick about his business. "Tom, bring mulled wine at once." Tom turns to go. But Walter has had a history with him and is put out. "My dear fellow, have you seen to the arras? Have you broomed it?" On the wall hangs the Flemish tapestry, a pastoral scene populated with trees, a forester in Kendal green, and hounds standing guard, a white fence pens in a recumbent white unicorn. Walter slaps it with the flat of his hand and a cloud of dust appears while he *tsks* reproach. "Tom, 'tis shameless. You have been again derelict in your duties." The waving tapestry undulates, much like Walter's midsection, and the unicorn seems to retreat from its captivity.

Looking at the muffin-man as if he were as inconsequential as a pin, the terse yeoman flatly replies, "Don't make a Star Chamber matter of it. I will attend to it."

"We will speak of this anon, Tom. Now fetch some wood from the back and replenish this fire. Mr. Phelippes would not like a guest to catch his death for lack of kindling. A lemon bough or two will give the chamber some sweet fragrance."

Tom leaves as stolidly as he had entered.

With two fingers to his brow, Walter peeks around the doorway down the hallway to check on a forgotten commandment, or perhaps to keep an eye on Tom, reprimand him for some other forgotten household responsibility. Whatever the reason, Walter returns presently giving his full attention to his guest.

"From here, Mortlake is a *not-altogether-worrisome* ride. But for pity's sake," at that Walter pads his oversized bum, "why not hire a ferryman? 'Tis speedier and easier on the frame. 'Tis the common practice, is it not?" London born, the chatty Walter has never left the security of the city's walls. Not waiting for an answer, "I tell you truly, I like not horses nor being bounced about like M'Lady's pearls. The Thames runs less vigorous at Mortlake, does it not?"

"Aye, it doth," Dee answers quickly, not unhappy to hold up his end of the conversation. "Though, truth be told, I am loathe to travel by boat. My feet," Dee confides, raising one of his elegant boots in the air, "must be ever planted on *terra firma*. I am uncomfortable on boats of any size. I'd fain die a dry death."

"Aye, verily," having never seen the sea, the merry usher agrees. "I'd forgo a thousand furlongs of sea for an acre of barren ground." At that, the affable Londoner slaps his forehead and declares, "About my brains, what a lackabout, I am." The round man turns with unimagined dexterity to the door. "Here you sit tired and hungry and I prattle of nothing but seas and such. S'death, what keeps Tom? Ever the tortoise!" Annoyed, he bustles to the door. "I will personally see about your refreshment." With that, he gives a small courteous bow with more bending at the neck than at his oversized midriff, and the stout barrel rolls out of the room, the library noticeably larger in his absence.

Soon the fire does its work, and the traveler removes his heavy outer clothes. Needing a spot to lay his fine beaver hat, he glances about then lays it on a reading table at the back wall near the main door. Behind it, a bookcase frames a small window. A frosty late September sun scantily lightens the room. Eschewing the broadsides and parchment that lay scattered about, Dee gives his attention to the bound volumes on the shelves.

A kindred academic spirit, opines Dee happily regarding his host's collection of books that appear to be mostly unbound manuscripts. Bound books are an expensive luxury. As he peruses Thomas Phelippes' collection, he ponders the pronunciation of his host's surname. *Is it Phillips? Or Fee-leaps?* That is how the inhospitable ostler had pronounced it.

Many of the writings are journals of governmental procedures. Amongst them is a bound tome—a battered copy of *The Common Prayer Book*. The presence of this required volume of the Church of England in such a public room openly declares to all where Mister Phelippes stands as to the bitter religious controversy that divides England and Europe. The black book's pages are well-thumbed, and the book's binding is separating, leaving no doubt that the owner of the house is a devout Anglican. *The man studies his scripture.* Of course, being the Secretary's secretary, it could be no other way. Practicing Catholics were legally forbidden from filling governmental positions in Elizabeth's England unless they acceded to the *Oath of Supremacy*—which few did.

Carefully, Dee replaces the text on the shelf. Hunting further, he discovers small collections of poetry, map books, accounting records, and some works from the ancients. All seem to be categorized—a good sign of a disciplined mind. But as he scans the volumes, he finds some texts out of alphabetical order. The mis-cataloging of books is Dee's *bete noir*. Like many of his countrymen, he abhors disorder. At home, he knows the exact location of every item in his library as well as the precise reason why he has placed them where he has. Purposefully, he sets about repositioning the books more rationally. His obsessiveness is interrupted by the slow, purposeful sound of heavily-weighted feet along a seemingly endless hallway. A glum Tom enters laden with extra wood.

"Walter doth apologize to your worship about the want of grog. It was needful that he attends elsewhere. I shall return with a faggot in a trice." He shakes his head at the memory of that recent conversation. "Jesu, lemon boughs no less." It is evident to Dee that Tom hasn't done any task "in a trice" for quite some years now. The philosopher watches the man shuffle his way out. Dee can't help but think Old Tom is as thick and as dour as a headstone in a graveyard. At the doorway, the slab turns with the sobriety of an undertaker, "I hope these," he indicates the new logs on the fire, "shall please."

This brings a smile to the tired guest, and he chortles, "Tom, it doth please me well."

Satisfied, Tom shuffles out of the room on his way to fetch lemon boughs to fragrance room. His weary footsteps are the tread of an ox inexorably yoked to a mill wheel. *Once again, I am left alone to cool my heels*, thinks Dee, *All this is sheer impertinence. And still no wine!* His restive eye darts around the room, returning to the books. Perhaps it is the crimson color of the leather or the fact that the book lays on its side resting on top of the others, but Dee is drawn to a large tome in easy reach. Looking at the title, he startles, and, wrestling the weighty volume into his lap, opens the clasp that binds it shut.

"Miraculous," he murmurs. It is a rare copy of della Porta's *de furtvis literarum notis*. Della Porta, a renowned linguist, had compiled a masterly treatise on the mathematical use of ciphers as secret codes. *Della Porta makes much of substituting one word for another or one number for a letter*, Dee recalls. *It scrutinizes the architecture of language and makes suggestions on how to build new ones.* It is a rarity; Dee knows of only two or three other copies in all of Europe besides his own sequestered within his *bibliotheca interna*. *This learning should be treasured, not left carelessly dangling in some out of the way public antechamber*, chides Dee, *Such negligence insults the book's goodly estimation—mere impertinence.* As Dee reverently turns the leaves of the large book, he savors the enlightened theories on *gematria*, so valuable to his studies. Eschewing comfort, food, or drink, the doctor grows enthralled reviewing the knowledge of cryptology that is before him.

And so, he never hears the door open.

"John. Welcome to London, old friend." Dee looks up in surprise. "I see you are enjoying what is only claptrap to most. It was just brought to us from Flanders. I had the servant leave it where you would find it."

Despite the closed door, the imposing figure in his early fifties has manifested itself like a ghost. Quite a *coup de theatre*—as it is intended to be. There is a self-assurance in the older man that speaks of responsibility and success. With it is a grimness that has always set John Dee's teeth on edge. Behind his hooded eyes power resides. Dressed in black, here is death's executor topped with a modest black skullcap like John's own. The poor antiquarian tips his head both in recognition and respect.

"Good evening, Sir Francis."

"It is good to see you again, John."

"And you, Your Excellency." Though the two men have history, Francis Walsingham does not attempt to do away with formality. Never has. It is his due as the Foreign Secretary of England. "Will His Lordship vouchsafe why I was waylaid into coming here?"

"For matters of State, friend Dee." An enigmatic half-smile or rather a rounding of one at the corners of the Secretary's mouth, "I have always found you to be an honorable man who loves his country and her Queen."

"Your Lordship knows—"

Interrupting, "S'truth, man, I know nothing. I have learned not to trust any man where religion is concerned. You are no exception, Dee." Sir Francis let's the accusation hover in silence like the smell of intolerance. "Were you not chaplain to the hated Bishop of London, popish Edmund Bonner who served Our Queen's half-sister Mary? As merciless an interrogator and as wicked an inquisitor who slaughtered countless godly Protestant martyrs as Heaven ever put on this earth!"

For the love of Christ, thinks Dee, am I never to be forgiven for past mistakes? He suddenly remembers he is without shoes. Sir Francis Walsingham deigns to give the old man time to struggle into his boots. An exercise that is rather awkward for both men, though it gives John time to stew. Elizabeth's regime uses Bishop Bonner as a byword for the Devil. Yes, the Marian cleric burned men and women who had the bad luck or bad timing to be un-Catholic during the papist Queen Mary's short reign. But it was another time—though not so different than now—when Englishmen followed obediently their Queen and her chosen religion. Elizabeth's people, Protestants all, had shown mercy to many of Her half-sister's ministers, but Bonner and his minions were the exceptions. Bonner had been a monster. *Curse the day that I fell in with him.*

The task completed, the man on trial stands but is not allowed to speak. "Though I have never heard you talk of it, it is not unknown to me that you swore vows as a priest."

Where is this going? Dee wonders.

"Else, you could not have served as his *chaplain*."

The last words are more an accusation than a question. A discomfort touches John Dee and his throat contracts pushing saliva down to meet bile on its way up. It is witless to deny history. And just as foolish to expect any kindness from Sir Francis in matters of state. *Doubtless,* considers Dee, *Walsingham has access to all the files in Whitehall, even those decades old. Better to watch and evaluate.* "I am not proud of what I have done," comes Dee's humble reply. "I saw my vows as the sole path to preferment under the former Queen. For measure," he adds, "I was never a true believer in Rome." That is a cowardly defense. When Dee was ordained as a priest, he had sealed his vows to the Mother Church by receiving the sacred host. He believed in its sanctity then, but now he is not so sure. Only God knows the truth of whether that wafer is Christ's body, yet, warring Englishmen of good faith go to their deaths for the belief that they know the answer. Dee tacks, "As I do love Her Highness, that employment was a fault to heaven which *ever* sorely grieves my penitent heart, and I seek your forgiveness."

"Do you equivocate with me, sir? Which Highness do you swear by?"

"By all that is holy, the current one," fumes the ex-chaplain. Walsingham, enigmatic as ever only hoods his eyes in acceptance. "Your Lordship, were it in my power to alter my past, I would surely have done otherwise."

"John, had you such necromantic powers to alter the past as your enemies proclaim, for friendship's sake, I would you could." Sir Francis peers at Dee over his stiffly starched ruff weighing some consideration. But that choice is postponed when the door opens. Walsingham turns his head to a new man, but does not attempt to stop him from entering. Instead, the Queen's high Secretary approaches and holds the door open so that the bearer may easier deliver a tray of comestibles.

"Welcome to my poor abode, Doctor," the newcomer says blithely. The tray is set beside Dee's fine hat. An ink-stained hand extends. "I am Thomas Phelippes. Though we have met before, I see you do not remember me. Understandable. We were introduced in Paris. I served there as an aide to the English Ambassador. Moreover, at university, I had the good fortune to attend your lectures on geometry. You amazed us with revelations of divine knowledge hidden in geometric forms."

Unsure of what is happening or this man's purpose, Dee responds warily, "You are very kind, sir. I am delighted to be reacquainted with you." Not sure why this man is here, Dee wades deeper, "Though I must confess you are unfamiliar to me."

Dee looks to Walsingham for how to behave, but the dark-eyed minister gives but one clue, just a succinct, "Thomas is my private secretary."

Pointing at the tray, the balding Thomas Phelippes offers, "These delicacies shall do much to relieve your weariness. You have had inclement weather all day, have you not?"

The question goes unanswered; rather Dee eyes the sweetmeats on the tray. There are three cakes with spiced wine drizzled over the top. Beside them, a glass of Madeira. As was his wont, he had fasted in preparation for his early morning angelic séance, nor has he eaten much this day. Yet, he shows his manners, "Sir Francis, will you partake?" and then turning to Phelippes, "And you, sir?"

With a stony countenance, Walsingham shakes his head and sniffs, "I have not tasted wine these seven months. I am a martyr to my stomach."

Either the day's enforced fast, or his need for courage pushes Dee to forego further courtesies, and he gulps the proffered wine. Its warmth fills his throat. Staring at the fluid still left in the glass, it strikes him that this drink could be his last. "I compliment you on your cellar, sir. And your generosity."

But though his words go to his gracious host, Dee's attention is on the imposing older man with whom acquaintance is borne of a mutual love of arcane knowledge. Sir Francis Walsingham's estate, Barn Elms, lies but five miles east of Mortlake. Each often made the short trip to borrow books or talk about the possibility of sailing the Northwest Passage or the chances for an English Empire. There had even been two or three times when Master Secretary had asked—ordered really—his neighbor astronomer to cast an astrological chart for him as to the success of a particular Elizabethan enterprise. It had surprised John that the powerful Chief Foreign Secretary had accepted being his son, Arthur's godfather. Could it have been the result of their camaraderie hunting game? Had John caught Francis on a good day? Obviously, today is not as favorable, perhaps an ill-fated one.

"*Steganographia*," pipes Thomas Phelippes, pointing at the book now on the stool. "You praised it in your lecture."

"*Stegan—?*" Sir Francis stammers.

"...*o-graphia*, Your Lordship. It means—"

"I know my Latin! It means *hidden meaning*."

"The same." Back to the Doctor. "You spoke eloquently of Abbot Johannes Trithemius' text, *Steganographia*, and his thesis concerning ciphers and secret messages. You schooled us on how easy it is for ciphers to replace letters in secretive messages and thereby forbid any outside reader from knowing what passes between the two correspondents. Using a mathematical formula of the correspondent's own design, private intelligence is made impregnable from any unschooled eyes. You inspired in me a desire to study it the more."

"Yes, but you are missing the more profound philosophical importance of the Abbot's work. Trithemius would have us decipher symbols in Nature to unlock the language of the unseen world. With such a key, we could parley with the angels themselves, and learn the mysteries of the Heavens, learn G—" He is about to say "God's" but that word is forbidden in Puritan households. "...that the Divine wishes for us. For surely the end of days is coming."

Waving away the Doctor's criticism, "I always understood your larger purpose," answers Phelippes. Turning to the Foreign Secretary for approval, he continues, "I simply employed your cryptography for more practical purposes. Such that His Lordship finds useful for political communication and statecraft."

Though he has heard it before, Sir Francis mutters in derision, "end of days," and looks away to avoid offending his neighbor with a withering look of mockery. Dee's fortunes and ambitions have been thwarted many times by powerful men who deemed him a fool for his quest after the arcane, some say *forbidden*, knowledge. Research in natural philosophy, symbolic geometry, Middle Eastern mathematics, *Kabala*, and metaphysics inspired in him unsociable ideas, including an apocalyptic new world sprung from man's understanding of the night's sky and the *Book of Nature*. What Dee saw as God's truth, others saw as heresy or, worse, witchcraft. His supporters called him a "white magician" but the superstitious citizenry of London often spat when he passed. *Am I being charged with this?* Dee stares at his adversary.

Walsingham frowns sternly, brooking no argument. "Master Dee, I have no doubt you believe in the Deity—"

"Aye, the Lord of hosts sits in his throne and rules all." Then Dee insists, despite the frown, "...and I believe in angels, heaven's ministers and servants."

"Aye, for the Bible advertises such."

Here is safe ground. Despite all religious controversies, all Christian sects and dogma agree on angels. Controversy only lay in the belief if they still visited mankind. Proceeding respectfully but firmly, Dee continues, "Then surely a man's mind can hope to plumb the truths of natural philosophy that which we two have oft spoke, and I seek to know." The Secretary's practiced frown deepens. "Because through the divine gift of Reason, the human mind can always course after Truth, concealed as it may be. Anon, like a burrowing fox, it can and must be flushed out."

"Must it?" A well-timed pause lingers between the men. "Perhaps."

Another judicious pause blooms and withers. The puritanical Secretary cannot fault the argument only the seeming impiety. Sir Francis' somber tone breaks the silence, "John, I attribute no heresy in your belief in ministering angels, nor in your belief that there is a path to find them. But verily, it is the sin of pride to actively look for Heaven's revelation before the Divine has chosen to reveal it to us. We must obey not only the Almighty's law but also his timetable." His Lordship touches the corner of his mouth with his thumb and wipes away imaginary crumbs. Always calculating, always cautious, he reaches back to the open door behind him and closes it firmly. "If the Deity had looked favorably on you, he wouldn't have burdened your life and career with such a catalog of setbacks. When you published your book on celestial resonances... what is its title again?"

Phelippes replies for Dee, "propaedeumata aphoristica," then adds quietly, "It explained the alchemical measurement of occult rays and celestial influences."

"There is no sacrilege *there*, Sir Francis," Dee defends himself. "Her Royal Majesty told me privately She thought it had much merit."

"My point exactly, our Prince has praised it in private and yet refrains from publicly rewarding your efforts." Dee looks away. The lost revenue had been a blow. "*Why?* One might ask."

"De Lannoy and his damned foolishness of swearing he could turn lead to gold."

"Yes, you did have the misfortune, or we might say the *bad timing* to publish just as Her Majesty's government realized it had squandered a fortune in propping up the Dutchman's laboratory and his alchemical attempts," Walsingham concludes.

"He's still in the Tower." This from Phelippes.

"Her Highness believes in the power of alchemy and my search for the philosopher's stone."

"But, Dee, perhaps, Heaven is telling you your timing is off."

"Ideas are divinely given, as is the time they are given."

"Are they? Were you divinely inspired when the three wax images of Her Highness, Sir William, and myself were found and purportedly left under a dunghill to conjure murder against us?"

"I employed goodly magic against the conjuring. Secretary Wilson will avouch for me. He saw all."

"So you said—"

"And still say!"

"But was it divinely inspired?" posits Walsingham. Phelippes can't help but snigger. "You and Leicester swore it was all part of a Catholic conspiracy. Catholic magic. It turns out you were very wrong."

"Love-conjuring, was it not?" Phelippes clarifies playfully.

"Aye, Thomas, to induce a woman named Elizabeth to fall in love with a jilted suitor. Bad timing again. In fact, every time your star seems to ascend, it always seems to immediately fall. Therefore, my reason tells me your investigations, and you yourself are not part of Heaven's timetable."

John Dee listens in silence. He is determined not to argue. His best efforts to educate with his eschatological revelations always seem to be thwarted. The lost labors have cost him position, favor, and solvency. At those times of deep despair, he has considered and agreed with Sir Francis' conclusion.

Feeling a catch at his neck, the Privy Council pokes at the inside of his starched ruff with two jeweled fingers. "I believe both you men have a mutual acquaintance in my nephew, Thomas." Walsingham's dark set eyes find Dee's baleful countenance. "Was he not a familiar of yours in Paris, Dee?"

The shift in the conversation is unsettling for the put-upon man on trial, as is being addressed so rudely. His studies and their merits are no longer on the table. Unable to defend himself further, Dee answers dutifully, "Aye, that he was, he like Mr. Phelippes attended my lectures at the French University. I owe my life to that noble young man. During the eve of St. Bartholomew 1572, a fatal date for any English traveler in Paris, I made my escape from the massacres the de Guise family rained down on our fellow countrymen and all Protestants on that night of slaughter." The name de Guise stiffens each of their spines. "Your nephew took me into your household when you were Ambassador, and we abided with fearful incomprehension the outcome of that hellish night. I have never forgotten his or your generosity or kindness on St. Bartholomew's Eve."

Most mindfully the Secretary intones, "That butchery will never be cleansed from England's memory."

Phelippes again changes the subject and hints at something deeper. "Secretary Walsingham, whose constant duty is to protect all Englishmen, is a man who knows the value of loyal citizens. He has long made use of men who serve our country in diverse ways. It is evident England cannot afford to lose such a worthy man as yourself."

"My thanks, sir," John Dee responds politely but

warily. He finds himself caught in a defensive rigidity, still reasoning out the necessity for Francis closing the door or the need for Phelippes' presence and what use Walsingham means to make of him. "I say again. I am in absolute ignorance of why I am here? This entire scenario beggars my understanding."

With a liver-spotted hand, Sir Francis sits with his back to the fire, motioning Dee to take the opposite seat. One of the Secretary's bejeweled fingers bids Phelippes sit behind the Doctor. "First, my sincere apologies. But as I said, we are here on matters of the state." Dee sets his jaw in preparation. He is no lawyer, but he must not allow himself to be put out of his depth. "Second, Lord Burghley, whom I know to be a perpetual friend of yours, has no knowledge of your arrival in the City. That was a scheme of mine to lure you from your studies and seduce you to come to London. Let us move on to the need for the lie. It was necessary that I might press you into service of Your Queen, your country. Pray, John, slake your discontent. Learn why your government is in need of you."

As he has had occasion to do in the past, Dee studies the analytical intensity of the Secretary's dark eyes. Walsingham, waiting for the expected answer, gets it. "I love my country as I do my Queen."

A flicker of a smile plays about Sir Francis' mouth. "Good sir, Her Majesty's government is well aware of your loyalty." Dee cannot discern whether the smile is friendly or one that mocks him. "Well, to the matter, you are not the first priest I have interviewed." Again the enigmatic smile and the domineering black eyes. "You are aware of the last *Papal Bull* from the iniquity of Rome?"

"The *Regnans in Excelsis*?"

Walsingham nods. "Master Dee, you will explain its significance to me. My secretary will take a disposition as to your answers."

What's this? What's this? Sir Francis knows the import of the *Bull* better than any in England. And why the amanuensis? Sense seems to have left the room. But now is not the time to cavil. "Pope Pius published a Church decree to be read to all English citizenry that Our Good Queen Elizabeth is a heretic." Here Dee stops. *Can there be treason in repeating the Bull's contents?* "Sir Francis, I in no way sanction this edict of the Church of Rome."

"Mr. Phelippes, you will take note of Master Dee's assertion." Turning again to his neighbor, "Now, John, do you know the *Bull's* contents?"

"Sir Francis, do you mean to entrap me in some lawyerly game of words?"

"As a man of honor and these many years as a friend, I shall not double deal with you. But, I must needs have some sureties ere I make plain my intentions." He pauses and looks directly at Dee. "And so I am obliged to have certain answers."

John Dee must take him at his word, yet he inwardly scoffs at his calling himself a *man of honor*. Dee sighs deeply with the futility of what he has been asked to do. "It proclaimed Her Majesty a heretic and an excommunicate. It absolved Her subjects from having any allegiance or loyalty to Her Highness or Her government. This was published a lifetime ago."

"And yet many still credit it."

"But, I do not." Dee is vehement.

"Despite the fact that, when you were made a priest, you took solemn vows always to obey the Church of Rome and its Bishop Bonner?"

The point is not missed. Dee is left without a rejoinder, only contrition. *Vows sworn on the body of our Lord no less*, reproves the ex-cleric. Can anyone trust a man who has foresworn his word? Dee turns deliberately to the secretary. "Take this down verbatim, 'on perdition of my soul, I have never once countenanced the *Papal Bull of 1570*, and I forever renounce any and all of my former oaths to the Catholic Church.'" *Though I burn in hell for it.* Having made such an oath and not meant it as flat blasphemy, regretfully, he acknowledges to himself the allegiances he has sworn to and foresworn after living through an age of religious upheaval wherein questions of religion define criteria for political choice. His past religious associations are an embarrassment that he must live with, though better men than he have laid down their lives for the same commitments. Unresolved doubts on some matters still exist in him. Angelic conversations had never given satisfactory answers. Standing before a religious zealot like Sir Francis, it is best to keep doubts to oneself and steer clear of ecclesiastical scruples. Not happy, Dee hides any show of self-reproach or indignation.

"Thank you, John. It was necessary for me, and a witness to hear. Though I knew it could not be other." Fire dances behind the hearth-grate flicking out short-lived spasms of light and heat. Fire, the godliest of the four elements, is a double natured force being both a source of comfortable security as well as a destructive, deadly menace. Even as it burns snugly in the hearth, one can always sense its danger. In the presence of fires, even the most benign flames, one often prefers to draw back. And, coughing, the Secretary does so. "John, trade places with me. The smoke takes prisoner of my breath and chokes my lungs with—" Another cough, this time accompanied by a wince.

Walsingham and Dee exchange chairs. Still stationary, Walsingham's man informs, "His Lordship has suffered several bouts of colic lately." Walsingham ignores the mention of his infirmity as he does the gripe in his stomach. There is more pressing business to deal with.

"Tell me, Doctor, are your monuments flourishing?"

The choice of the word *monuments* is not lost on Dee. *Even in discomfort, the fox plays the game, and he reminds me that he has all the chips*, thinks the disconsolate doctor. *Monuments* was the term a nearly thirty-year-old Dee, then friend to Edmund Bonner, had used in his request to Elizabeth's predecessor, Her nemesis, and half-sister, Mary, to beseech the Crown to save the written works of ancient writers. In days long past, Henry VIII had ordered destroyed all the popish churches with their centuries-old collections of Catholic and pagan manuscripts as the Protestant populace had ransacked the vestries and scriptoria for anything worth the taking. Dee had begged Queen Mary to allow him to retrieve lost volumes, create a sanctuary, and establish a

Royal Library that would be a national resource to settle the doubts and fine points of academic research. He had argued that having such *monuments*, English power could be much advanced. With a national library, England could outdistance Europe in material success and military preparedness. But the plan had had no Court backing, and Dee had been left to collect books on his own, costing him his life's savings.

"Aye, I have had to transform a large room in my small house for the maintenance of my collection. 'Monuments' as you term them are challenging to find and dear to purchase." Dee turns to Phelippes, the fellow book collector. "Perforce, I have managed to get some on loan. His Lordship and others have, on occasion, made me such loans. My school-boys copy them o'er, and then I return them to their owners." He turns back to Walsingham. "You have not called me here because of my failure to return three or four manuscripts to Barn Elms? Have you? If so, my work on them is not yet complete, but you shall have them anon." Dee studies his questioner endeavoring to discover what lies behind this part of the interrogation. Walsingham's masked thoughts give no clue. "My Royal request was years ago. I was but twenty some-odd-years." He is not ignorant of Elizabeth's government being always on the lookout for Marian threats—and by that, Catholic threats. Such associations often meant death.

Short of breath, Walsingham, with some effort at a more benign smile, dismisses the scholar's obvious fears. "No, on the contrary, you know I agree with you on your work of hoarding knowledge as a potential

English weapon. My works are yours until all your scrivening be done. The wisdom of the ancients can bring a modern nation out of darkness. It may also bring other nations to their knees."

Dee braces for the next attack, but none comes. Instead, the Secretary places his hand above atrophied lungs, and makes a concerted effort to breathe.

From behind him, a kinder tone murmurs, "Your writings have always intrigued me, Doctor Dee." Phelippes continues, "One must understand the celestial reverberations that are invisibly present in the sublunary world. I have often shared with His Lordship your ideas that letters are not merely the building blocks of words, but also have an intrinsic numerical value. Certain numbers are more holy, more divine. Yet each has value."

From Walsingham, a nod and, "Her Majesty agrees."

Really? The poor scholar ever in need of Royal favor must know more. "Her Royal Highness?" Dee asks without a hint of exuberance for his inquisitors to leverage.

"Aye." Another meaningful pause. "Does that intrigue you?"

"How could it be otherwise? I have longingly desired Her Majesty's approval for my suit of the *National Library* project."

"I will share with you that Her Royal Highness is near to granting your petition. She deems your request a great advancement for the Realm. Naught is settled on at present, but I counsel you to keep a watchful eye. Your long neglected petition may soon be granted."

Fortune has turned her wheel. Tension giving way to curiosity, Dee gives thanks even as he suspects there will be a bribe. Nevertheless, a bribe can be rejected.

Before another prologue to some weighty pronouncement, Francis Walsingham, Secretary of State to England coughs. Clearing his throat and leaning forward, he avers, "Doctor, your country has need of you." Dee, with the solemnity of the moment and trepidation in his mind, leans his head toward the humbled man before him. "No doubt you are not unfamiliar with the constant threats that daily beset Our Majesty from traitors who deny Her very right to rule. I labor continually to squash the papist schemes that threaten Her and this country of ours." His Lordship never takes his eyes from his friend, nor waits for a response. "Many have had their fortunes risen with my employment. Her Majesty looks favorably on those who have in the past made mistakes but have redeemed themselves in my employ." Walsingham reaches for and pinches his prominent nose, his fingers lingering on its bridge as if to focus his thoughts. Hooded eyes flicker— a thought alters their conversation. "Is it not Jew *Kabala* that teaches you to seek out Heaven's design?"

Astonished by the comment, Dee's mouth flinches as if an unseen wire pulls it. He speaks unwittingly, "How sir, do you know that I study the *Kabala*?"

Mr. Secretary glances at his associate. "Did not this man abandon both his wife and scholastic employment to journey covertly to Bohemia endeavoring to master these wicked arts?" Phelippes nods.

This is magic indeed, thinks Dee, *No one in England*

can have known of my private meetings with the Rebbe of Prague. Unsure of the repercussions of acknowledging Jewish study to a Puritan zealot, and fearful of what may be read into his testimony, the doctor remains mute, imposing on his face an impenetrable mask. He reaches for his unfinished wine.

Sitting imperiously, Sir Frances begins a patronizing grin, but a catarrh gets the best of him, and he reaches into his sleeve, withdrawing a scarf of silk to catch the phlegm. "Dear friend, do not be amazed at my intelligence. I am well advised of all the foreign activities of our Realm's more prominent citizens. You were abroad for a long time, and your government had to know why."

"Master Secretary should have a care about nosing about in my privy business." Undeniably heated, Dee replaces his glass upon the table with emphasized force.

Dee's neighbor takes no umbrage, dismissing Dee's anger as he would a clucking aunt. An unseemly chortle follows that fills the small wood-paneled room as a large circle fills a square. The spasm in his gut is seemingly forgotten. "Master Dee, the same has been said of your unlawful pursuit of the hermetical arts. Many would say you should have a care prying into the Lord's business." He draws himself straight in his chair. "Doubtless, the hunt for Truth by a scholar such as yourself can far outstrip government's petty ordinances—even England's. You left without passport." Walsingham's dark eyes seem to sparkle; his tongue lolls lazily in his mouth.

Dee has lost patience with Sir Francis' circumlocution.

His use of the rack has taught him to torture by infinitesimally minute degrees. Though various emotions war within, composure trumps all as any admission of his covert past might cost his freedom, or worse, inflict danger-upon his family. The Dee family is no stranger to political consequences. He and his father had both suffered in the Tower for willful words. His inquisitor continues in some pain. Why exasperate him? Dee casts his eyes down, acknowledging his clandestine affairs.

"Thomas, are you getting all this down?" Walsingham looks back to Dee, changing the dialogue again. "We shall discourse more on the rooting out of Truth before the day is done. Grace has raised men and imbued them with reason partly to give praise to Heaven's glory, and partly that man might finally comprehend the Truth of his nobleness and worth. We are all sacred in His endeavors."

Then why do you slaughter so many innocent souls? "Aye, I couldn't agree more." But inwardly, the natural philosopher does not agree. He would love to cite what is so obvious. Churchmen of Europe continually argue over transmutation and the primacy of Rome. Still, if they could lay aside their pride, their particular ceremonies, and their inability to agree, they then might be capable of reading from the *librum naturae*. With all its secrets of Knowledge and Nature thus visible and available to our Reason, might not our faults be amended and would not heaven and earth glory in the reformation. *Would that such a paradise existed now, alas, the world must wait another five years for that pre-ordained perfection.* He dares not share what the angels have revealed to him. Just five years' time, according to the angel Anael, this age of ecumenical understanding shall come to be. And he, John Dee, would be a Moses leading Europe to a miraculously new existence, free from contentiousness. All remains hidden behind lips and teeth. These men of intrigue have no inkling of the *timetable* his angel has assured him will happen.

Contentedly, Sir Francis continues, "'Tis a consummation devoutly to be wished."

With that, the silk scarf appears again, and three trumpeted attempts are made to clear his nose. He saws the nose rag three times across his face and then slips the kerchief back up his sleeve, tugging at his woolen doublet's sleeve three times to straighten the line. This repetition of three does not go unnoticed by Dee. His studies have shown that three always has significance. One had only to think of the Holy Trinity or St. Peter's three rejections of the Son of God. But what omen for good or evil does this iteration of three presage? Dee makes a mental note to chronicle the event later in his diary if ever the Secretary gets to his point and allows the scholar to get home.

Adjusting his beard over his ruff, Sir Francis lectures, "But afore all else, we must make certain that reactionary forces do not rein us back into the ignorant times of popish heresy. We must be vigilant. We must be ever fearful of any insidious threat to the new Church and to Our Gracious Majesty who is its chief defender. You are aware of the constant recusant plots that daily threaten Her and by extension our entire weal? The Catholic gentry are a peril to all our estates and country." There is neither sarcasm nor deviousness in his voice, only sincere concern. Walsingham's secretary does not record any of the last statement.

Dee now believes his loyalty is not in question. Perhaps there is no visit to the Tower in his stars after all. He had charted this month's horoscope and had not seen anything inimical. Perhaps His Lordship is seeking something else. Perhaps their old comradeship has saved him.

Walsingham pushes himself out of his chair and stands over his guest. His ring finger uncharacteristically twiddles his thumb, standing like a wife gone to market, deciding whether to spend on a pricey cut of meat. "John, for every give, there is a take. I have the power in me to free you from all financial burdens. You could buy your books, take your scientific trips abroad, even buy your good woman, Jane, some finery that she deserves and has done without. All this, I am willing to confer on you, but you must do your part." Closer to the fire's fumes, Francis coughs into the back of his hand. Having no stomach for being used as a wicked instrument for this consumptive man's deceit, the impoverished antiquarian girds his loins with trepidation for the bribe he knows must come. To lose one's honor is to lose one's self. "As I say, Her Majesty has need of your especial services.

"What services?" *Come on, come on you old pettifogger, and come to the point.*

"Those that you and you alone can perform. Her

Grace would have you journey abroad and do her business. Identify recusants who threaten her reign and her life."

"You'd have me be a base intelligencer?" he snaps.

Undeterred by Dee's anger, practiced as he is in dealing with stubborn recruits, Walsingham shrugs, "Aye, that is the manner of it. Both Thomas and I believe you have all the specifications to do this exceeding well."

"A spy! S'death, I like it not. It stinks of Judas. I am a man of science, a natural philosopher, a loving husband, and a child of God." Regret springs immediately from uttering that last word, that un-allowed word in Puritan households, *God*. Frustrated, Dee hates that the spymaster has gotten calmer.

"There you have hit on it. The Crown must gather information on a Catholic Count whose island dukedom, Illyria, stands betwixt England and Her enemies. Her Grace must have information on where his loyalty lies—either with Her or the See of Rome. We have it that Phillip of Spain is mustering a navy to invade our English shores. This fish-eater, Orsino of the English Channel, espouses love for Britain, but like many of his kind, he may be duplicitous and eager to abet Her Majesty's enemies. The Catholic threat has o'er-shadowed our peace since the Norfolk and Babington plots. These Papists—they are the Anti-Christ—these vermin plot assassination continually. If you love Your Queen, you will do all to prevent this abomination."

Dee now rises to his full height. They look eye to eye. There is an inflammation in Dee's left eye. A small blood vessel has broken. "I will not add one jot to the national shame of one Englishman betraying another. You do hunt Catholic worshippers as wolfhounds do harts and partridge. And, much like game, after their capture, with too much relish, you publicly disembowel and dismember them, and, like butchers, then hang the severed parts for display."

Walsingham overrides Dee. "Not with relish but as a warning to others."

Two men intent on their beliefs stand judging each other, armored with warring moral points of view. This close to Sir Francis, Dee detects the floral aroma of civet covering up the foul traces of phlegm and discharge. The man's courtly manners like the cat-piss perfume on his hands and clothes disguise the hatred they disguise. Sir Francis likes not the pedant's disregard of Crown and Country. The scene is a microcosm of England's bitter civil divide.

Mr. Secretary speaks first. "I understand your reluctance. The work appears odious to you, but it is necessary. Her Majesty has commanded me that She will only accept the legitimacy of reports on Orsino, a man of high gentry and family, from one whom She personally trusts. Orsino is a Count and a handsome one. You are whom She has chosen." With that, Sir Francis restrains another cough, and Thomas helps him back to his seat. Walsingham's infirmity does nothing to mitigate Dee's disdain. Sir Francis, aware of this, takes a different tack. "We hunt Catholics, as you put it, to ferret out traitors to the throne. Which I am certain you are not. You are born and bred of this Realm and owe an allegiance to your Prince. That is your duty as an

Englishman. My duty is to root out evil. You are a Catholic priest—"

"I *was* a Catholic priest," Dee snarls, his tone defensive, cold, stripped of obedience. Undeterred, he releases a breath—the image of authority.

"So you say, yet we have naught but your testimony to the contrary. We know you to be in possession of heretical, necromantic books that violate the *Act of Witchcraft* laws, you are considered a pariah by many of the nobles, and you are in debt to your creditors. For any of these, I could arrest you as a malefactor." He sees Dee's rectitude melting with the growing appreciation of the checkmate that Dee is in. "I am commanded by my Queen to enlist your services. Would you deny Her and me when what I offer in return is fair and goodly wages? Her Majesty has a long memory. Take it from me; She does not easily forgive. For a man of your discerning, how can you say me nay?"

"How will my absence be explained?"

"You have but to advertise that you have gone on one of your intellectual expeditions."

Phelippes adds, "It is why we were so secretive with you. So that neither your wife nor your household would know of this meeting."

"Must I not tell Jane the true reason for my leaving?" The next thought is unbearable. His eyes glow with pleading intensity. "No! A way must be found for her to journey with me, she and the child. They are everything to me."

"Your safety and hers are best kept by her not knowing. Catholic spies secret themselves everywhere. A woman's loneliness or her fears will oft turn to reckless gossip. If Orsino is guilty and learns of your true mission, you are a dead man. Worse you lose yourself... and them."

John Dee is barely hearing. He takes short breaths and feels that he must sit down but dares not show weakness to this Satan in a white ruff. "What shall I tell this Orsino? He will want an explanation and an introduction."

"You shall be given letters as to your appointment as first Postmaster to Illyria."

Dee has lived in poverty too long and, without friends at Court, he cannot hope to defend his name nor continue his studies. Most have already deserted him. "Is that all?" *All*, he ponders. *All* is his family. *How will I live without them?*

"No, you shall judge the best occasion to reveal to the Illyrian Count that you were a priest."

"Why?"

"To creep into confidence and thereby be advised of his conspiracy."

"Must I pretend to win his confidence?"

"It is essential."

"More damnable betrayal."

"Betrayal to a traitor. Loyalty to Your Queen."

"I have no choice," winces John Dee.

"You have only yourself to blame for that."

Blocked at every turn, Dee twists away in anger.

Phelippes pours Dee another Madeira. "Welcome to Her Majesty's service."

5

There is a rapping at the entry: No louder than the hammering a silversmith would make fashioning a goblet. Phelippes eyes his master. After considering, Sir Francis nods and grants, "You have my leave."

The door opens slowly. It is old Tom, "I have brought the lemon boughs Walter bade me fetch for the room." Walsingham frowns but does not forbid the man's entrance. Risking censure, the elderly retainer reaches down carefully and pulls a scrap of paper from his boot, sheepishly offering it to Mr. Secretary, "For Your Lordship. From Mr. Faunt."

Walsingham, raising his kerchief to his mouth, reads the message. Nothing is spoken, and the menial does his work. As the flames erupt, Walsingham grimaces at the smoke. "Thank you, sirrah, you may go now."

Tom backs out of the room. Somewhat concerned, Sir Francis coughs painfully, but then addresses both men, "I must return to my lodgings on Seething Lane. My nephew, Thomas Walsingham, has a matter of importance." Phelippes hands his scrivener notes from the meeting to Sir Frances. The Privy Council tucks them in his sleeve. "John, my secretary Thomas Phelippes will instruct you in all that needs to be known. He is ignorant of very little, I commend you to him." Bringing the kerchief closer to his face, Walsingham flinches. "I could not have remained here much longer. The air is too close in this room. I take my leave of you both. Good day."

The commoners rise, bowing in courtesy to His Lordship. Dee, standing behind the Secretary's secretary, is aware of the back of Phelippes' neck. Whereas Walsingham is tanned, his secretary's neck is as white as albumin. *His duties must keep him continually imprisoned inside.* The old philosopher pictures the retainer's days of long hours researching, scrivening, sending, and receiving messages—a dog's life. He seems somewhat cognizant of cryptology. *When has he time to study?*

"Mr. Secretary does not stop his work when he is out of sorts," Thomas mutters almost in awe.

"So it seems."

"We must follow by example." As no one has touched the sweetmeats on the tray, Thomas slips one of the cakes into his mouth. After nibbling crumbs from his fingers, he says, "For your especial safety, none but Mr. Secretary will keep accounts of your employment for fear word should get back to the suspect—the Count—or worse, to your political enemies." Dee catches sight of della Porta's work. Both he and it are now properties in the theatre of false witness. Almost as if it is biblical, Phelippes intones, "We must all wear a mask." Dee could not help but remember old Bishop Donner saying something very like that. Perhaps, politicians have their own translations of the Bible.

"I will begin my investigation unbiased. Orsino is

neither friend nor foe, but noble far above my station."
Dee pulls at his collar. The heat in the room is indeed
close. And less than an hour ago he thought it too cold.
He feels misused. He cannot forgive himself for not
having put up more resistance to Walsingham boxing
him in. "As to my employment, I demand remuneration
of a hundred crowns plus expenses in advance for travel
and lodging."

"Knowledge is never too dear. Her Majesty's
government is honored to provide pains and charges."

Dee is not finished. "I should like to be awarded the
deanery of Gloucester when it becomes vacant. The
revenue from its lands would cover the costs of my
investigations into Natural Philosophy and add to
defraying the costs of my considerable library." There is
confidence in his voice. His brown eyes pierce. His
countenance is uncompromising.

For a time, nothing is said. Dee wonders if Phelippes
will haggle. "Good sir, I have no power to make such a
promise. That is a matter for both the Queen of England,
the Convocation of the Bishops, and the Archbishop of
that region."

"Your master has much sway with Her Majesty, has
he not?"

"Aye."

"I trust Sir Francis can work his magic there. But
know you and tell your Lordship that I have not
completely acceded to this villainy."

"We have your recorded acceptance from your recent
interview that you *have* acceded."

"Depending on my remuneration," cavils the new

recruit. Thomas politely shrugs at the point. The tiger is caught. The cage is secure. "But, I will think on it."

"You will *think* on it?" Phelippes purses his lips, changing the subject. "You have England's thanks. Our beleaguered island is like a hapless good woman who is set upon and mistreated by popish miscreants and knows not why she is savaged and bruised."

Dee's voice rises. "Nay, master Phelippes, lecture me not on Catholic thuggery. I have just passed a half-hour being schooled in it by your better." Again, Phelippes shrugs. The matter is of no consequence to him. "But you surely know there is wrong on both sides."

"That is why Sir Francis has need of *you* especially. Knowledge is preferable to understanding," says Phelippes, as if he were preaching at a Sunday sermon.

"What mean you?"

Thomas Phelippes has heard the maxim repeated so many times by Mr. Secretary that it is now as familiar as his own name. "Why sir, no other meaning than understanding is that which is written and reported while knowledge is the putting of that understanding in its proper context. But knowing a thing is *only* valuable if it is true and verifiable. It must be substantiated by a trusted witness." Much like an actor, the man has a practiced sincerity of tone, "The Crown must be sure of the reportage from your mission. Its honesty must come from one the government can have no doubts about."

"Tell me of this, Orsino."

Like other intelligence officers, Thomas Phelippes is energized by the offer. The urge to confide hidden knowledge swells inside his breast, and the only relief for it is to let it out as an anecdote, a history, a perception, even a half-lie. The festering secrets of intelligence work continually seek freedom and, like political prisoners, always threaten to escape their cramped confinement. "Count Orsino is a sober-blooded man of his mid-thirties with a pretty young French thing for a wife. His family has long maintained the island he commands for the English Crown. By fervent letters and other communications, he has professed himself a loyal subject to Elizabeth Regina, but he was born Catholic. His father, the Count senior, never reproached the King's for putting away his Catholic first wife, but never visited Henry's Court again after the divorce. And he was invited. Many times." Now the damning secrets against the Count break their levee and pour themselves out. In the intelligence trade, all are deemed guilty. "Moreover, we have it from goodly sources that popish contraband—pamphlets and artifacts—are routinely smuggled into England through the island's ports. After arriving there from Europe, the heretical materials find their way to popish printing presses that, within days, distribute their treasonable falsehoods to England's disenfranchised, fanning sedition and intrigue. The inflow of this filth into our country must be put to a stop. Mr. Secretary cannot believe that Count Orsino is not so ignorant of his populace as to be unaware of the business. Either he turns a blind eye or lends a helping hand. Neither is good. He cannot be innocent."

"And if he is?"

Again the equivocal shrug, "Then you must find that out." Dee sulks. Craving more Madeira, he reaches for the ewer, but Thomas overrides him. "Moreover, the Spanish who are ever eager to put a Catholic ruler on our throne are even now in earnest preparations to have their Naval Armada attack our shores."

"That is unthinkable," objects John Dee shifting in his chair, anxious to have his drink.

"Perhaps from where you sit. But under our watchful stewardship, we have the vantage of access to people and testimony in the households of our enemies." Thomas Phelippes never hesitates but leans further forward. Secrets flow from him like a man on the rack. "Their hope is to fright the English citizenry and give secret infiltrators a chance to raise an uprising in our land of peace. To that end, the Church in Rome has long been organizing itinerant priests from Louvain and Rome who preach sedition to godless wickedness. We believe Romish priests disguised as seamen are smuggled onto the Count's island on their journey to England. As you know, our harbor watchers in Portsmouth and Gravesend are less careful of inbound cargoes, especially if they are aboard 'English' vessels, rather than foreign ones. You are not ignorant of what I speak. Your father, Roland, was a watcher in Gravesend. Was he not?" More secret intelligence spills out. "This Orsino was educated at Oxford and is a close companion to Lord Strange."

Dee holds a hand up with his palm in Thomas' face in the universal sign to stop talking. His desire for drink overrides, and he pours one for himself. "I am well acquainted with the good Lord Strange, Ferdinando Stanley, who is a close cousin to the Queen. His Lordship made my acquaintance as he was in need of architectural drawings for his public houses here in London." Dee savors the Madeira and allows it to dampen his qualms. "I was invited several times to gatherings at Stanley's home in Lancashire. On those weekends, men of the Arts and Sciences shared *divers* discoveries." Taking another sip of wine, "There is no want of good cheer and good conversation at the Stanley's." Dee smiles at the memory. He had a particular fondness for Stanley's Lady Alice, a witty member of the fairer sex who could hold her own in any man's company. "His Lordship has the art of making every man feel comfortable in his noble presence. Lord Strange is an honorable man."

"Is he?"

"I doubt it nothing." But, Stanley's advocate cannot help but admit to himself that he might conspire against the Queen. As he drains his drink, he considers that Lord Strange, though not born into Catholicism, is adamant about still allowing the practice of the old religion. Hearing Mass is now forbidden in England. His Lordship seconds the National Catholics who argue for moderation in enforcing the new strictures recently being imposed against Catholicism. In the North, few are not still Mass goers. It is no secret—even in the parish of Mortlake—that Elizabeth turns a blind eye to Her cousin's inconveniently sluggish obedience as She did to so many others of the northern estates where the old religion holds sway. Even though Walsingham, Cecil, and other Privy Councillors have often advised Her Royal Highness to take a more aggressive stance against Northern recalcitrance. Open debate, they argue, leads to secret convocations that, in turn, lead to treasonous actions. During such council meetings, it is said that the Queen just closes Her eyes and shakes Her head balefully, muttering, "Lest you forget, Lord Strange is my cousin."

"You seem lost in thought, Doctor," Thomas Phelippes reels him back into the future mission, "We keep a watchful eye on his visitors and intercept his communications when we can."

Dee blanches. Whitehall has spies everywhere. It is a daunting and horrible realization. Now they are placing *him* in Count Orsino's home. "Was not the Queen's cousin born into the Anglican faith," Dee counters.

"Aye. But he is surrounded by Catholics. Strong advocates of Roman popery. There is Langton, Heskeths, Houghton, and that mother hen to seminary priests, his brother, Sir Edward Stanley." Before Dee can speak further for his friend, Phelippes adds, "Though our practices may not be your liking, Ferdinando—"

"You refer to the Lord Strange. He deserves your respect—"

"The Lord Strange, the future Fifth Earl of Derby, is very probably an enemy to the State." Suddenly, Thomas Phelippes is reticent, either in respect for His Lordship's reputation or the remembrance that his listener is still *thinking on it*. Lord Strange's father's great uncle was Henry VII and his mother was the daughter of Eleanor Brandon, Elizabeth Tudor's first cousin. Phelippes sees no reason to mention to his guest that Lord Strange's name is continually present in captured communications from Spain, where hopes run high that he shall be the new Catholic King when Elizabeth is removed and he is converted. Britain's checkered history is rife with such noblemen who risk all for the chance of sitting on the English throne. The last few drops of Thomas' covert statecraft dribble out, "We will ask you to learn more of that—if you can."

"You seek for me to betray a friend. By my faith, I cannot do that."

Both men eye each other and think a bit more. Dee cannot help but be reminded of *Ecclesiastes*: *"He that toucheth pitch shall be defiled therewith; and he that hath fellowship with a proud man shall be like unto him."* He looks at Phelippes, lost in his own reverie, and notices that the man's hands have crept further inside the waist of his pantaloons. The philosopher can only guess at what the man is searching.

Then Thomas says, "But to return to the main—" The clerk speaks with a stronger tone of voice than before.

Dee interrupts, "Sir Francis mentioned my being an official of the mail—"

"It is an ornamental posting, and you have naught to do. None will think this odd since you will give out that you have accepted the post as a pension from our generous Queen. It may be of interest to you, but I am told that Count Orsino, like yourself, has a large collection of ancient texts. Indeed, Orsino's library may be nearly as extensive as your own. He is an antiquary like you. Does that not whet your appetite to go? You may find much intellectual satisfaction in this secret theatre of falsehood, as you have labeled it." Dee purposefully makes no show of pleasure. Thomas clears his throat and reiterates, "But to return to the main...

Count Orsino's most trusted confidante and chamberlain is Lord Griffin, as wise a politician as can be found in the Channel Islands. He is a master at administration. Lord Griffin is said to have the common touch with the gentry. The people love him as their benefactor."

Setting down his Madeira, Dee distractedly leaves through the open pages of *de furtvis literarum*. "But how shall my reports be brought safe to London. Must I scurry across the Channel when something urgent is to be reported to Mr. Secretary?"

Phelippes dismisses the *naïveté* of that scenario with the snigger of a man grown bold in his profession. "No, in your absence, you might miss much. Mail boats arrive there regularly. You shall have an Ambassador's pouch, and we will see to it that your messages will be conveyed only to us." Lifting the nearby volume, *Steganographia*, "For your further protection, you will employ your knowledge of secret messaging to encode your communiqués, fashioning your intelligence to seem like cargo invoices. Thus, the number of Spanish ships shall become bottles of Madeira... Would you care for more? You seem to like it." The Doctor, embarrassed, makes a show of refusing the offer. Thomas continues, "...and discovered recreants shall be ships, times of meetings, in turn, vessels' arrival dates. An easy thing, I believe, for you to do. Urgent packets should be marked with the gallows mark; Mr. Secretary will be instructed to read those first."

"I like not that word gallows. What danger lies in this?"

"Why, good sir, there is danger in crossing Piccadilly Circus. You will be England's official Postmaster, and moreover, you are a man well known for your learning. That will keep you from harm. Many of our other agents have far weaker protection."

Dee laughs, derisively. "Master Phelippes, I am not so much a youngster as not to know that many believe me to be a necromancer. It would be an easy matter to eliminate me on some trumped-up charge of devil worship."

Dee moves to the window and thinks twice about this Royal mission and its consequences, never forgetting his loss of Jane, and his five-year-old son, Arthur. *How can I leave them for so many months? And what of the child on the way?* Yet, his analytical mind weighs the alternative. *But of the good that might be bred? How can I leave them penniless? For that they shall be if I lose all friends at Court. They must not be reduced to a pauper's existence—like the miserable indigents on the road this very morning.*

"Master Dee, listen to me," says Thomas rudely. The philosopher is taken aback by this unfamiliar lack of courtesy, "You cannot shrink from this now. I have told you too much. And have you forgotten what charges of lewdness will be brought against you by The Privy Council of England if you perform this not? Calculating, conjuring, and witchcraft! By the ancient laws of our Kingdom, your actions deserve death. Have you forgotten your house being sealed and your books and papers seized as evidence? Have you forgotten your time in the Tower with your torturer, John Bourne?"

With disbelief and astonishment, John sputters, "Marry, that was thirty years ago."

Phelippes cannot but correct the mathematician on his arithmetic, "Nay, sir, it was twenty-seven. And think you how many more valuable papers and *ancient monuments* are now in your keeping since the Queen took pity on you. If you fall from Her favor, you stand in jeopardy of losing all." Phelippes changes to a more conciliatory tone, "Should you balk at the government's request, Mr. Secretary has instructed me to make you summon up remembrance of that dark time long ago when you were indicted. More, he desires me to instruct you that presently in these times of civil and religious unrest, the Queen and Her government would not stand by what you yourself term 'a devil worshipper.' You stand presently on a precipice."

6

The mind of Dr. John Dee is shattered beyond any salve of remedy. There is no solace, none, from his current circle of hell. He fears he shall go mad. What reprieve? What's to be done? *Calm. Calm yourself. All will be well.* Years ago, he had watched Bishop Bonner and his other chaplain, Nicholas Harpsfield, masters of this art, force men of great families and will into untenable positions. Nor had he been spared. *Yet he had survived.* Sir Francis Walsingham, Elizabeth's chief Machiavelli, is the current era's master of this game. Men without conscience of this sort were formidable enemies. *What's to be done?* Repeats the fearful inner voice. *There is no way but one- perseverance,* answers another more pragmatic one.

"I know you are not pleased, reverend sir. If I may offer this consolation, Mr. Secretary would also have you know that should you agree to the Crown's request, you will have his word that you shall never have to dirty your hands with this work again. Whilst Elizabeth is Queen, and he has the power, you shall evermore be free from persecution. He will swear to it."

"In writing?"

"Even so."

Dee finds himself staring at the geometrical patterns in the wainscoted walls. Looking for some semblance of comfort, the man from Mortlake lays his fingers in the troughs of the wall's joints and traces their upward path. The feeling of their undeviating straightness reassures, steadying his mind and allowing him to quiet his thoughts. "Master Thomas, I have been given a grievous decision to make. No devil could pinch me more." His index finger now moves downward along the groove. "Though hateful, I have but one viable choice." He inhales and lets his decision slowly crawl out "Tell His Lordship... I will leave for my new posting... after I have settled my affairs at home." Having said that, he feels sick to his stomach. "But now, I quit this loathsome room and its stink of evil... or I shall go mad." He walks with purpose to the door. "Unless there is aught else you would burden me with?"

Shaking his head no, Phileppes' last words are, "You must be there as soon as preparations and excuses can be made."

Wearily, Dee nods then putting on his hat, departs from the room without so much as a cordial goodbye.

After exiting Phelippes' main entry, wanting only to escape this house of villainy, John Dee must wait fifteen minutes of insufferable delay for his horse. Galloping down Leadenhall Market Street, he eventually ends up nowhere, finding himself at the bank of the Thames and the moorings of London Bridge. Filled with uncertainties, he is unsure of where to go. Scanning the area bustling with human traffic, he stares at the city's great harbor area before him—the *pool of London*—

filled to overcapacity with flat barges, small barks, and great galleons canopying the river with a quilt of sails. Searching for calm, his first thoughts are to ask aid of Sir William Cecil, his university friend, protector, and Sir Francis' superior in the government. But, on review that is pointless. Surely, Cecil, because of his premier position, would have to have been told of his mission, and, must have given consent.

Moreover, a commoner—even a fellow graduate from Cambridge—doesn't just storm into the London residence of the Lord Treasurer of Her Majesty's Most Honourable Privy Council. His porters and halberdiers would mistake him for an assassin. *What about Dudley?* No, his son, Phillip, is newly married to Frances Walsingham, his persecutor's daughter. No help there. Lord Strange is an obvious choice, but he is wintering in Ludlow. Harry Percy, ex-student and reliable friend, lives too far away in Northumberland. Not even his raven could fly there from Mortlake in a few days. Whom can he turn to? There is no one. He must resign himself that in London his studies in alchemy and natural magic have marked him for a political leper. His compromised history of allegiances and the slander of his enemies have proven to be an exceptionally sharp ax to his good name. A price is exacted for one's choices in life, and now the consequences have come home to roost. *I am not the first who, with best meaning, have incurred the worst. The consumptive fox, Sir Francis, has tricked me into the henhouse, cozened me, and left me with no way out.* In fury, he rages, *Must I sully my honor and forego my essential studies to help them when I have so much to do? In five years' time, when the new age, the age of harmony and prosperity arrives, my erudition and guidance will be needed. I must prepare. Why must I suffer under these fardels? Oh Lord, why have you beset me so?*

The early evening dusk darkens toward night, yet it is only five of the clock. The daylight, like his fortunes, is on the wane. Twilight river winds breeze in from the south and cool his frustration. From behind the overhanging clouds, the moon cohabitates the evening sky with the sun. Soon, an entourage of familiar stars appears; he envies their freedom. *Fie. Fie.* He rebukes the sinking nausea in his gut. His astrological charts—not to mention heavenly angels—have promised him great tidings. As one of the elect, he must expect to be tested. *This is but a beneficial tribulation imposed by Heaven to better prepare me for the glorious apocalypse to come. It is proof I am part of divine History. As the strawberry grows beneath the nettles, always I have been an outcast while growing toward God's perfection. Always have I prospered.* He repeats the mantra to quiet the wild whirligig images of his despair. *The strawberry grows beneath the nettles.* The Pool with its thousands of ships is suddenly an image of assurance. Despite the filth that is thrown at the river, Father Thames tells him, it endures. *And so shall I.*

More concerns trickle up. *Any one of these vessels in the pool could be carrying contraband or arms to England's enemies, even here in the heart of London. Ignorant of their passengers, hundreds of watermen are ferrying foreigners ashore tonight. How many are villains? How do Walsingham and Burghley and their watchers do it? How do they protect England from invasion and rebellion when access is so freely given?*

Perhaps there is a way. Tomorrow, with all discretion and tact, he will appeal the decision to his old friend, Sir William. Cecil, will no doubt say *no*, but it is worth the doing. *Doubts are oft traitors that betray the good that we might achieve.*

No reasonable answers can come tonight—more time must untangle this. He turns his horse toward home, but the hour is late, the road too dangerous at night, and he needs to stay in London if he is to see Sir William in the morning. It has been an arduous day. No one in Mortlake is expecting him. He aches for Jane, yet already regrets the lies he will have to tell her.

Settled, Dee wheels around toward Cheapside and his accustomed inn, the *Ville Royale*. There he finds accommodations, but no peace of mind in a pitifully small room. Claustrophobia only presses his dilemma in on him. To escape, he wanders aimlessly north, passing drunkards in the gloom pissing in the streets and mongrels licking it up. Oafs with cheesy breath bluster oaths at him and swaggerers strut by preening. Eventually following the crowd with their torches against the dark, he finds himself at the Theatre and that night's performance.

The acting troupe owes its existence to Lord Leicester, a longtime patron of his. But tonight's script is claptrap. A third rate piece of prattle that knows none of the rules of the unities of time, nor of common sense. The main character is a tiresome speechmaker in need of revenge against a murderous uncle. There is none of the choreographed swashbuckling of Kyd, nor the wit of Greene, and it wants the heroic language of Marlowe. *A wasted hay penny*, thinks Dee as the play's mediocrity revives his gloom. The predictable last scene cannot come soon enough. He pushes his way out of the stalls into the street, past the torches, past the doxies of the evening, and the gallants hoping to make their acquaintance, only to hear his name hallooed over the cries of the jostling crowd.

"Doctor Dee!" Thomas Harriot, a hatchet-faced former student of Dee, now employed by Walter Raleigh, shoves his way through the crowd. "How do you, John?"

"Well," the brooding scholar replies crisply. His own foolishly curt manner only maddens him the more.

"For old time's sake, pray, join me for food and drink. My treat." Dee, in no mood for company, tries to beg off. "I will not let you say me *nay*. I will not allow you in your dark *humour* to skulk away to your bed."

Grumbling, Dee concedes, "I will walk with you awhile, for friendship's sake."

Having no light but the full moon, they pick their way over to Cheapside. The narrow streets of the city are perilous at night, both for the danger of pickpockets and the human refuse from upper windows, raining down on the cobblestones. At night, it is best to have company and walk nearest the walls of the buildings. Thomas Harriot is eager to talk about his recent work with two natives of the Americas captured by Raleigh. This surprisingly brings Dee out of his funk.

"The 'redmen' are visibly awed when first seeing many of Europe's scientific instruments. These are to them beyond strange. And so far exceed their capacity to comprehend their use or creation that they think our machines are the works of gods rather than men."

This leads them to discuss their mutual belief in harnessing hidden principles of physics to perfect the limitations of nature and, by extension, all of humanity. Dee is insistent, "The time will come, and trust me soon enough, when the discovery of the current secrets of Natural Philosophy will so inform European minds that you and I will seem today as ignorant of the Laws of Nature as your redmen are ignorant of our clocks and telescopes."

At the front door of the *Mermaid Tavern*, Raleigh's man once again pleads, "Come, let us break bread and share a stoup."

With the crisp night air and Thomas' good company, Dee realizes that he is indeed hungry. Not willing to face his tiny cage again with its wasp nest of poisonous choices, Dee agrees. Happily, Thomas Harriot swears, "*The Mermaid* is as well victualed a house as any in London, and frequented by the best wits in London." He promises it to be a remedy for all that ails.

"Stewed beef for me."

"By Gis, a good choice," says the boy waiter perfunctorily, having this night more tables to attend than usual. "It will arrive in a giant bowl, and tonight there is a goodly amount of suet on the bones," he reports. Flicking some breadcrumbs from the table, he makes to move off, nervously eyeing others who shout at him for service. But before fully turning his back on them, Harriot restrains the server.

"Do you know whom you serve?" Thomas Harriot extolls, "England's greatest scholar is here tonight and has had not a morsel today. Have a care. We'll not be made to wait long. See to it. And put no lime in the ales. Hear me. We'll not be fobbed off."

On the move and never turning his back, the menial responds, "Aye, sir. Anon, sir," but, now, instead of moving to the next table, he makes his way to the secret domain of the kitchen.

The Mermaid has a crowd of about fifty men and if Dee peers into the darker corners, maybe three or four women. All sit on an assortment of stools in and around plank tables. Torches flicker though there is a good-sized hearth that keeps the autumnal night chill at bay. The incessant din is at first off-putting. Many of the customers have been at their cups all day. There are frequent explosions of roaring oaths, swearings, and curses. But soon, Dee finds the swaggering festivities and ensuing conviviality are lifting his spirits, diverting him from the painful realities of his distasteful future. The stone floor is covered with rushes that look as if they have been recently scattered. From the smell of it, Dee knows wormwood has been added as well to keep the fleas out. Gallants are displaying their newest clothes, lawyers recounting their triumphs at unwinnable suits, and players and scribblers out-jesting and out-anecdoting each other. Through it all, a handful of drawers keep the gaiety bubbling with tankards of beer and salvers of roasted meats and more beer.

Harriot and Dee share news of mutual friends, gossip from the Court, and the war in the Lowlands. Dee has many questions. The world is abuzz with Walter Raleigh's expeditions to Virginia. All of Europe is wondering whether Spain will allow Elizabeth some territories in the Americas.

"Philip, the Great Castile, has threatened Her Majesty with war if Raleigh and his half brother, Adrian Gilbert, continue to send English ships to the new Indies. So says a gunner's mate from Valencia. He recounts, vast swaths of Spanish forests are hewn down every day for planks and masts to build a score or more of tall ships in Madrid. He says *armourers* in that country do naught but fashion cannons. According to the *Treaty of Tordesillas*," Raleigh's man adds, "England has no right to *that* part of the world. For you know Pope Alexander VI bequeathed it to Spain."

"Not so, Master Harriot, it is manifest to me and others of a like mind that Our Royal Highness has real and legitimate claims to *novus orbus*, which the vulgar call America. In the last century, the sea voyages of John Cabot and the Welshman, Madoc, have secured vast territories for us. Her Highness has even elder claims. There is Mercator's assertion that King Arthur with four thousand men laid claim thereto, giving England a *Title Royal* stretching from Barbados northerly."

"If this be true, will the Privy Council have the mettle

to uphold the claim?" Harriot fumes. "Or are we to be berated as a nation of farmers and sheep? For Raleigh swears great treasure is there in commodity and gold that would prosper the economy and the Commonwealth. Her Royal Highness is but a woman after all, passive and accommodating. Will She fight for Her rights in the New Lands?" He pauses for dramatic effect, then slams his empty tankard on the table. "By all that is holy, I know She will. She is made of sterner stuff."

"Aye, that's the tune. Elizabeth Regina has as great a heart in fighting for what is Hers as any swarthy Spaniard or wine-puking Frenchman. The Christmas star that streamed so bright eleven years ago emboldened Her Highness to seek what is Hers to take."

Suddenly a comparatively loud commotion from a group in the alcove at the window drowns out their conversation. A young reveler with a Midland's accent and a high forehead has pushed himself away from the table and tumbled awkwardly into a waiter, overturning a tray of beers. The falling drinks splash foam and ale on expensive doublets and hose causing a great row of anger.

The reveler, a young boy no more than sixteen, impervious to the crowd's curses jumps to the top of the table, shouting, "'I am Amleth! Give me revenge!'" The last word is more sung than spoken and with it comes a clenched hand raised in defiance. If he expects applause, he gets none. Instead, spattered customers go for him, but he draws a hacked dagger expertly holding them off.

"Will, put that prop away! You'll be imprisoned if you

are seen having it," says one of his companions. But the boy continues to menace until his detractors grudgingly return to their seats. From his position of power atop the table, the young tosspot glowers down at the helpless server who is now on his knees mopping up the spill. "Have at you, you *minimus.*" Then drunkenly, he declaims at the beer on the floor, "Take away this bull's pizzle and bring me some sack. Know you not who I am?" Wrestling the dagger from him, the young man's friends seek to quiet him, to no avail. He rants about the magnificence of his characters, his plot, and his conceits. Annoyance fills the tavern, bellowing him down.

An older man in his forties who must be the proprietor flies out of the kitchen, concerned. "Sirs, Sirs, I beg of you! Shall we not have peace and decorum? We'll have no mayhem here! For charity's sake! Peace and decorum!"

A young spade-bearded man of eighteen, a compatriot to the reveler, tries to coax the drunken teenager down from the table. "A word in your ear, you must calm the tempest of tonight's cold reception in your mind and listen to reason." The king of the mountain waves the advice off with exaggerated swivel of the head that nearly topples him from the table. But his friend will not be deterred, "Will, it is but a play, you will write others."

Staggered by the suggestion, the young playwright whines, "Others?" Twisting his sideburns into elflocks, he bleats, "There will be no others. James Burbage, that whoremasterly poet-baiter, said he would chance me but the one chance as poet. Did you not hear the catcalls from the galleries, or were they drowned out for you by the brays of the groundlings? My future is naught. I am lost. I am undone!"

"Then, if the theatre is not your destiny, you must return to *poésie* where you have shown great talent. Follow your talents. Leave off these theatrics. If you continue playing the fool, you'll have Kempe here in a fit of professional jealousy."

The befuddled whiner shows no sign of being placated but instead bemoans his fate the more. "But, Kit, I labored for a month. I poured my heart into it. I sacrificed my marriage for it. My Anne, my new-old wife with the shrewish tongue and the colossal bum, has left me and returned home to live as far from me as our meager expenses will allow." Scrambling down to his knees on the tabletop, he implores, and as he does so, his regional burr thickens, "I pray thee, Kit, tell me my play pleased *you*. A word from *you*, and I shall be able to face the world's harsh tongue." Will grabs his friend's shoulders, perhaps in as much to keep his balance as to look into his eyes, the windows to his soul.

Harriot, never one to bridle his impatience, shouts, "Your play pleased none of us. It was as nightmarish a presentation as one could wish to behold. If the gate had been free, it would not have been worth the price of admission. As it is now, it isn't worth a fart."

From another corner of the room sails, "Nay, a fart would have been loftier."

Many in the room echo Thomas' feelings with the other more blistering reviews. Will, the failed playwright *cum* reveler, slashes his knife at Dee's table where the first of his critics sits. His friends make to stop Will from lurching from the tabletop, but happily, his's diet of small beer sends him into slight vertigo, buckling his knees. He crashes clumsily backwards into the arms and laps of his friends. Some of the fallen poet's more effeminate associates lick his face and buss his drunken ruddy cheeks. They tickle his ears and grab his buttocks. The proprietor does his best to have the boy removed, but his theatrical entourage, well-known regulars at *The Mermaid*, will not have it so.

Thomas Harriot turns back to his old mentor. "This same sodden-headed boy may have skill in his dagger, but none in his quill. In his case, his sword is mightier than his pen. Keep us from barren entertainments like the execrable *Prince Amleth*." Thomas looks over his shoulder to where the theatre crowd congregates, and lifts his fist, intoning, "For *Amleth*! Revenge!" Both men laugh. So do two nearby playgoers. In the play, the old Danish ghost demanded repeatedly of his son, "*Amleth! Revenge!*" Senecan tragedies with ghosts and murders are all the rage on stage, but London audiences insist on elevated language.

A dog from the kitchen wanders out and slips between the tables, begging at each. Carelessly, Dee strokes his mangy back. The cur rubs his flanks against Dee's stockinged leg in an act of utter love. Dee scratches the dog behind an ear and feeds him bits of bread. *A dog's affection medicines a troubled mind.*

Dee looks up just as Thomas Harriot exclaims over Dee's shoulder, "You sir, are not welcome here."

Doctor Dee turns to see the young playwright no

longer swaggering, instead, he wrings a dirty workman's blue hat in his hands as he approaches Dee.

Harriot shouts to the crowd, "God help us! He has come to beg us for money."

"I do not desire your welcome. I do desire to apologize, reverent sir," the young man pleads, but not to Harriot. Still tipsy, the teenager does his best to make a grand flourish, performing a large arc with the blue hat starting above his head, Will then scrapes the rush-laden floor. At last upright, hat behind his back, his eyes are puffy with drink, yet mirthful. Grim-visaged Harriot, not partial to effeminate boys, *harrumphs* his displeasure.

Dee, however, acknowledges the gesture and awaits what reverence this boy means to offer. "Let him have his say."

In a theatrical posture, the player obliges with a voice reminiscent of a Roman orator, "Gracious Sir, by your leave, I ask your pardons for my churlish actions. I had no idea just now that I was addressing the Duke of Leicester's architect. One who is able to construct divinity on the ashes of a cockpit. Pardon worthy, Sir, pardon."

"What's this? What's this?" snaps Dee's companion. "What drivel is this? Away you rogue. You are drunk, boy. Have a care not to upchuck over us."

"Indeed, I am not well. Tonight, I have shipwrecked my future on the shoals of my own inadequacy. But though I own drunkenness, I am not so besotted as to forget my manners and not give credit where credit is due."

Dee allows a small smile of thanks for the Baroque compliment. He has grown accustomed to his fame, but not his infamy. At least, the rogue hasn't spat at him. Turning to his former student, "What the boy alludes to and perhaps unknown to you, Harriot, is that I was employed by His Lordship Robert Dudley, Earl of Leicester, to furnish for his players a harmonic plan for a theatre and tyring-house. The result is the Theatre."

"Why harmonic?" queries Harriot.

"Because all the angles and proportions are posited on the numerical quintessence of seventy-two. It is the number of the names of God in the Hebrew. Architecture must have a celestial resonance, an affinity with the sacred."

The Warwickshire boy sheepishly shrugs. "Your meaning?" The two seated scholars regard him as no more than one of the unwashed unlearned. A group that in the current times had grown in number, and, with what Dee's studies indicated, was a sign of the deterioration of their dying era. "I know nothing of Architecture, nor Hebrew, nor seventy-two. But there is a divinity in the acoustics of our theatre. And you have put it there. Not a seat but has excellent hearing." Will flatters them with a toothsome smile.

"You have made your introductions, now get you gone. It is time for your exit."

But the playwright has other plans, though poorly conceived. Rather than flee the scene, he draws up a nearby chair and without a *by-your-leave* joins the table. Thomas and his anger rise, stalled only by Dee's mitigating hand on his friend's arm. They share a look and then Thomas collapses back onto his stool with a disapproving grunt, his brawny arms entwined waiting for a provocation. Undaunted, the boy looks gaunt; it is obvious he has not eaten a decent meal in some time. Nevertheless, he is pranked out in a silken brown doublet comically puffed out to have a *peascod-bellied* look. The buttons down the center are carefully set and made of bone. It seems very expensive. Master Shakespar emulates the fashion of the times when men would rather starve themselves than be seen in other than *haute couture*.

"What's your name?" asks Dee.

"Will Shakespar."

"Is that your real name or a *nom de plume*?"

"What do you think?"

"Still, Will Stage-poor would be a more appropriate one, or by the look of you *Rake-spar*." Thomas sniffs, either at the playwright, or *The Mermaid's* foul air.

"I think you are exceedingly bold and peremptory," replies Dee, happy to lord it over someone today. "I am John Dee, Doctor of Natural Philosophy, and this be Thomas Harriot, newly employed by Sir Walter Raleigh—a man of formidable fame, courage, and position."

"The Lord or his lackey?"

"Both," replies Dee, smiling at his friend.

"*Enchanté*," Shakespar offers his hand, but Harriot, with a thunderous disgust, pointedly refuses it. It could not have been more rudely rejected had the lad shat in his palm before offering it. Dee disdains to shake, as well. Not to be put off by the rebuff, the intruder grips the table with both hands, keeping his bleary focus on Dee. "You were both at the play? *Prince Amleth*?"

"Aye, *Prince of Denmark*," Dee teases weakly.

"I must know your evaluations. Did you not find it thrilling?" The look on the boy's face momentarily reminds Dee of the begging dog beneath the table.

At that moment, while laden with several platters perched precariously on his other arm, the drawer delivers the stew. Sliding the serving onto the table and wary to avoid wobbly Shakespar, the waiter sloshes some of the briny contents over the side of its pewter bowl. Making no excuse for his clumsiness, the waiter is instantly gone even as he shouts, "I'll fetch the ales anon."

"Aye, you do that," shouts the less-than-pleased Thomas, more than eager now for his drink or a fight.

Just as loudly, John Dee adds, indicating the emaciated Shakespar, "Bring this man some veal and ale. Bring it apace when you return with our ales."

"You liked the play then?" asks Will hungrily. "It appealed to your more refined taste."

"Master Shakespar, I ordered you a meal sith it seems that you have refrained from eating for quite the while. I ordered you the ale so that you might better withstand the criticism we are about to heap on you."

The garrulous playwright ventures nothing more than a pale, "Oh."

And, there they sit for the next quarter of an hour raking the evening's tragic fiasco over the coals. Dee makes suggestions on how Amleth might be less a trickster. Thomas Harriot, begrudgingly now a part of the discussion, suggests sullenly that perhaps, like himself, the Prince might be a student of Philosophy. The neophyte's feelings are obviously hurt by the critique. Grateful that the ale has come and with it the veal dinner, humbly, he makes no objection to the evisceration of his first work. As the food sobers him, John and Thomas trash the dialogue of *Amleth* for not providing insights into inner secrets of man and his works.

"Look you," says Harriot, pointing back at the actors' table, "your friend Kit Marlowe, he knows how to write. Borrow his books and learn about allusion, majesty, and poetry. Learn what great minds have said about honor, sacrifice, nobility. Your *Prince of Denmark* bores us with its inane blood and guts." Knowing his place and that these are men of Letters, Will, uncharacteristically, holds his tongue.

As long as Will is quiet, Thomas can abide his presence. "Spurious rhetorical reasoning," insists Thomas.

"Reasoning. Your characters must reason," Dee says repeatedly.

To this Shakespar does speak. "Unlike yourselves, I am in want of university learning and am unacquainted with proper logic. My father, who was bailiff of our town, stumbled financially just when I should have attended." He glances back to the table where his friends sit. "But I have more poetry and heart than any of those Oxford twits. Even Kit Marlowe. Certainly more than Chettle."

"Well then, what was the point of the ghost?"

"It is a Senecan device."

"Then write like Seneca!" shouts Harriot.

The player enacting the part had gotten lots of laughs that evening. Which, of course, was not Senecan at all. Will had envisioned a magnificent guardian angel inciting his son to terrible action but, instead, had written a blustery *miles gloriosus*.

Dee peers sharply at the boy. "Ghosts, like angels, are superlative beings not drunken soldiers with booming voices."

At that, both Harriot and Dee set off on a long involved discussion on the nature of angels and how, if correctly summoned, illuminate God's will. Dr. Dee is articulate on the subject.

"Cherubim communicate in a language not so much of words, but of mathematical constants."

"Perhaps in musical tones and harmonies," ventures Thomas.

Young Shakespar, finishing his third tankard, is visibly out of his depth. The two bookmen take notice.

"Master Shakeshaft—"

"—Shakespar!"

"Shakespar. You need to study more, travel more, and acquaint your pen with the rich lessons the *Book of Nature* suggests to us." It is a speech the schoolmaster Dee has made many times to his students. "Your writing will never succeed without proper study. Without it, you are doomed to failure."

"Go to Virginia." Blithely, the winking Thomas adds, "Learn from the savages. Or read Montaigne!"

Downcast, the boy shakes his head bitterly. A *failure* is what Will's father had called him when the lad had declared his intention to become a playwright, "That profession will bring you nothing but failure. Failure and venereal disease." And tonight the reception to his play rekindles fears that his father spoke truth. *If life has not prepared me to fulfill my ambitions as a poet, and if I cannot be great, what is the point?* Sullenly sliding his chair back and holding tightly to the back of it, Will Shakespar rises from the table thanking his host for his generosity and time.

Then he squeaks, "*Prince Amleth* will stand the test of time." It is a weak protestation rendered to save a bruised ego. Will had hoped to mine complements at the table of his betters. Instead, a witch's caldron of disappointment prevails. Again, the lad bows to Dee, his flourish less self-assured.

Dee watches the despondent youth limp back to his friends. Though they greet him with caresses and applause, the boy responds to his mates half-heartedly, his earlier panache having evaporated like beer froth. This gloomy demeanor bores his playmates; soon, they abandon him to his melancholy humour. The table takes up singing a ballad, John, Come Kiss Me Now and they make eyes at the prettier sailors wagging in from the docks.

Dee feels for the lad. Were it not for a few years difference, the fate of Dee's own father had been as the boy's. *The sad player and I suffered the same tragedy— one's youthful ambitions ripped away by a parent's failure to do right by you.*

Following his old teacher's gaze, the ex-pupil quips, "Shakespar looks like he has feasted on toad."

"What mean you?"

"Why sir," Thomas grins, eager for the opportunity to teach his teacher, "You yourself instructed me that the toad is a vile creature and if eaten leaves the eater with a venomous breathe. See where his companions have deserted him, and he sulks there as green as a sick girl. Looks he not like he has eaten a toad?"

John Dee nods weakly in approbation. "Methinks we'll have no more plays from master Will Shakespar."

7

The meeting with Sir William Cecil, Lord Burghley, dressed in his sober black velvet, is frustratingly brief. John Dee receives compassion but no reprieve from his old patron. The Lord High Treasurer lays it out plain.

"The Royal Commission is yours to accept or not, John." As he speaks, Burghley's grizzled beard, like a fidgety bird in a cage, twitches manically over his stiff white ruff. "The consequences would be swift and devastating should you decline. And you need no astrological guidance to assure you of your future should that be your will. My advice to you is to embrace your fortune and thank Her Highness for the employment."

At their conclusion, Dee stands by the door when in passing the Lord Treasurer inquires, "How fares our Jane? We miss her at Court." The question is rhetorical, as Lord Burghley does not wait for an answer. "And how goes your perfecting of your magical elixir, *pantaura*? I have again been attacked by the pleurisy, Doctor." Burghley demonstrates by having to sit. "With all speed distill that alchemical remedy, and the Queen will appoint you Royal Doctor on the next day following."

Dee acknowledges with nothing more than a curt

bow as he leaves. Having worked for years on the calculation for the panacea for all diseases, the *pantaura*, Dee's success at distillation is still far off. *My race against time is nearly at an end. Now, Burghley and his ilk enforce me to delay my research and run off on some fool's errand that any wretch might do?* Despairing of finishing any of his work, he ruminates, what right had these authorities to trample on his life? *It is insupportable.*

As the hobbled man rides away, he reflects on his life from a great altitude. Dee is the Secretary's and the Queen's chosen man for this mission, and the Secretary will not—*cannot*—have another. To foreswear Walsingham's assignment is, in Burghley's words, "foreswearing Her Royal Highness," and that is "patent treason."

But what of his Jane, his beautiful auburn-haired Jane, and the sweetness she has brought to his otherwise drab academic existence. His former wife, Katherine, had been a millstone. How utterly bereft of joy she had been. In comparison, Jane is radiant sunshine. How could he leave her love or his pretty Arthur, the son who has so late graced his life? *And is not a son a more perfect and more meaningful legacy than any academic work I have ever penned? And one on the way!* Risk his loved ones' wellbeing? Unthinkable. Sacrifice beyond all reason! Have his beloved England threaten to frown on *them*? This mission of Walsingham's, this Judas intelligencing—or call it what it is, *spying*—what is it but as vile an occupation as ever this miserable world had for a man who prided himself on maintaining his honor? There was no remedy in fleeing for Scotland or Europe, leaving behind books, his few benefactors at Court, his chances for promotion, and to discredit his life's work. Walsingham had spies everywhere. Good Sir Francis would not rest until one of his assassins had found and slaughtered Dee and his family in their sleep. Who would mourn a deserter, worse a traitor? Or worst of all, to be delivered back to England and the executioner where the sentence for blasphemous witchcraft might be death by fire or, worse still, disemboweling.

Many, like John Prestall, his rival alchemist, always jealous of Dee's close proximity to the Queen, had already tried several times to discredit him. Only his friendships with the Secretaries and Her Majesty keep Prestall's libels at bay. *No*, he tells himself, *any attempt to escape Walsingham's control is foolhardy. Bereft of favor, none will recognize me. What alternative then remains when family, life, and honor is in the hazard?*

The more he twists the problem in his mind, the more the Gordian knot infuriates him. *My mind is like a blind horse at a mill.* He curses his stars. He curses the bald toady, Thomas Phelippes, who pretends sympathy. He curses Nicholas Faunt, who brazenly deceives. He curses his father, who left him without sufficient livelihood or protection. Still, mostly he curses Walsingham. The irony does not escape him that if he is indeed the magus that the populace dreams him, the power to smite his tormentors with vengeful spells should be in his reach. *How sweet that would be*, he thinks.

Arriving home to Mortlake, Dee tries to escape his suffocation by returning immediately to his lectures. Gathering his charges, Dee and his wards begin reviews of his theorems on the measurements of the parallax of a star. The calculations are challenging, but Dee will brook no mistakes from his class. Bristling at their questions and ridiculing their ignorance, Dee is more brusque than usual.

"Ignorance is the mother of presumption and error," he commands, "I am disappointed and marvel at the want of study in every one of you muddy mindless louts—to my great grief."

When the students whisper that something horrible must have happened in London, he upbraids them for their nattering and scolds them to rather concentrate on their work. Suddenly, he stops mid-sentence, and, without excuse, leaves them for his *interna bibliotheca*.

For the next several hours, Dee locks himself away. The more literary of his scholars alludes to Achilles shutting himself up in his tent. A young astronomer then studies their teacher's personal astrological charts and attributes his foul *humour* to the charge of Saturn, it being in ascendancy. In wonder, Jane, like all the household forbidden to enter Dee's private study, keeps an eye on the closed door. *Will my Johannes unburden himself to me when door opens?* She despairs, knowing her husband is a proud man who grows more sullen as he broods. Hopeful, she remembers with joy his warm embrace after his recent return, calling her "my sweeting" and "my mouse". He had been so very affectionate—yet distant. His words of love gladden—a brief sun shower—and, now, all the house is chilled with the master's inclemency.

When the lead key finally turns, and John Dee emerges, he is silent and pale as a corpse. Fearing for his health, Jane immediately brings him *aqua vitae* purchased from an itinerant barber. She will not budge until he has drunk every drop, and he gratefully downs it as a sailor weathering a bitter storm. Color slowly returns to his cheeks.

"For this relief, dear heart, much thanks," he says quietly to his doting wife.

"Are you not well, my husband?"

"Well in my body, but not in my mind. There is great sorrow there."

Concerned, Jane opens her arms wide, hoping to hug him into happiness. But he makes no effort to embrace her. Playing with the glass between his slender fingers, he cannot find a way to look her in the eye. He is tetchy and unapproachable, and the goodwife, knowing her Johannes is a good man with many responsibilities, knows not to meddle. She wraps a woolen blanket around him as he sits on a high backed chair. Standing behind, Jane reaches to cradle him in her arms.

"Some griefs are medicinable. You have but to abide the time."

"School me, sweet Jane. Is there remedy for separation?"

"What means my husband?"

"I must leave thee, Jane. I must to Poland within a two month's time."

A tiny involuntary gasp escapes Jane's lips, her milky white complexion blanching further. She listens, trembling as he informs slowly, "I have decided to accept Count Laski's kind invitation to study and lecture in Krakow."

She makes a face of incomprehension. "And this is why Burghley sent for you?"

"Aye," he lies. "He had heard of the invitation and requires me to report on the doings of the Hapsburg Court."

Suddenly hopeful, she hugs him a little tighter. "And cannot Arthur and I journey with you?"

"Nay, beloved, I would for the world you could. But you must not. Winter is a-coming, and the sojourn will not be an easy one. I dare not risk yours and our future child's health. You must remain in the comfort and safety of our home with friends about you, for your well-being and the safety of the birth."

"May I ask why you must needs go now? Can you not tarry till spring, after the birth?"

Jane feels her husband's back stiffen, and the loving grip he has on her hand loosens immeasurably. These are the tiniest of movements that only a wife can notice.

"I am bid by my betters. It *must* be ere the old year is out." His eyes, the silent revealers of thoughts, are shuttered. "Ask me no more."

"Then, dear John, let us not waste time and breath talking." And she draws him toward the bedchamber.

A crushing weight it is to deceive; it is a sin of infidelity. The family share a cold, nearly wordless evening. Despite his abjectness at having no choice, his calculating mind broods, revisiting his scheme. An absence from home excused with a trip to Poland will not be questioned. Count Laski has been suggesting one to him since their first meeting in May at Greenwich. Jane knows that, as does the household, and so do his neighbors. Thus, a sudden lecture trip abroad for scholarly reasons would not be questioned by any, and would surely be further rumored 'mongst the populace by his neighbor Sir Francis Walsingham. After putting off at Illyria, he shall make excuses to Laski afterward about arriving late—stormy seas, impassable roads, or sickness—no one will be the wiser. If he dies in the undertaking, his friends will assume he has perished *en route* to Poland. If word arrives from Orsino and his Court about treacherous activities, there will be confusion and talk. But, at least, this proffered, plausible lie will provide his family a shred of decency for them to cling to. If he succeeds, he will continue on to Laski, none ever knowing his true purpose on the island of Illyria. As to the infamy of what he is about to do, stanching heretics in the Channel Isles, Heaven will not judge him too harshly. What sin you do to save your Monarch is accounted small. Sins of compulsion are pardonable. Though a considerable risk to his family's good name remains, his initial discontent eases as the

Gordian knot loosens. He must put his trust in the Almighty as all men must do who serve God and country and are buffeted by the caprices of Fortune.

Later that night at prayer on his knees alone in his study, he swears by all that is holy that he will make amends for his actions to his matchless, peerless Jane. "I have been false to her who is the dearest to me in the world," he confesses in his prayers, "To abandon her in her condition and perhaps not be here for her comfort is an act too wicked to bear. Jesu, have mercy. Let her not hate me."

Dee spends the next month at Mortlake as best he can with the schooling of the boys. Those who can continue will do their research in his massive library under the supervision of Jane or Mr. Marley. Three young scholars, two brothers from Suffolk, and a boy from Flanders are recent charges in the Dee household; all are instructed to go home with permission to study further at Mortlake when the master returns. At least the cost of their feeding can be saved. On the day before they depart, All Hallow's eve, an unseasonably warm afternoon, Jane puts together a holiday outing and treats the boys to mulled wine and honey cakes.

To an open field that overlooks the river, they hike up the palisade to fly a kite. A gentle breeze sets it aloft, and there it hangs in the bright blue sky floating tentatively beneath banks of clouds. Soon, a blustery wind catches it, and its tail begins gyrating like an eel trapped in the shallows. Struggling for control of it, the boys watch in gamesome pleasure as the novelty leaps ever higher in the sky, or sometimes, with a will of its own, dips down to hover over the meadow, inciting shouts of joy from the schoolboys. Jane joins in as they revel in the whirligig pitching wantonly in the buffeting wind.

The blustery gusts often override and distort the cheering, and, Dee, at times, is deaf to the intermittent shouts of excitement. Mostly he stands by the rug laid on the ground, rapt in this day's pleasures: the dappled red and white hawthorn bushes bending over the Thames with its endless comforting splash and gurgle, the scudding clouds, and the echo of faraway neighbors at work. Most of all, he fixes wistfully on Jane with her auburn hair pulled neatly from her forehead and gathered in a French weave. Unable to afford a proper hair-tyre Jane has improvised an excellence of woven yellow and rust-colored leaves into the snood that holds it. *Mine own autumnal nymph*, Dee muses. A few windblown strands of hair escape confinements and, like the kite, dance in the breeze. He daydreams about how suggestively long and luxuriant her tresses are at night when she releases her magnificent hair from matronly bondage. He can close his eyes and smell its smoky fragrance. It is a perfect afternoon, and the memory of this day, of his beloved's beaming face, is a gift that Dee will revisit often in the exiled months to come.

Shadows stretch out as students and family amble back toward the bluff for home. There, moving quickly up the steep path to meet them is Marley. Wincing as he climbs, his arthritis is plainly hurting him. Nevertheless, on arrival, he insists on removing from his mistress' arm the empty wicker basket that she carries. Dee has the rug, and two boys share the kite. It is clear from Marley's breathless hurry that he has brought news.

"Good Doctor, there is one come from London," Marley pants his utterances, "more boy than man who waits in the great room upon Your Honor. He claims he comes to be tutored by you."

"S'death, Did you not tell him, I go abroad these next weeks, within the next full moon," grumbles Dee and then allows his wife to nuzzle close, feigning to help him with the rug. She smells of Earth and woman. "This young man has lost a journey, and you have acquired naught but pains in coming here, Mr. Marley."

"For the lad, Sir, he has been *told*. Yet, he says that is *no-nevermind*. He must needs commence his studies forthwith. He is a garrulous boy who can sling a word or two and will not be denied. Aye, will you, nil you, he says, but he *WILL* study." And there, the usually taciturn Marley ekes out a smile to his mistress. "Verily, his name is Will Hall."

"His name well becomes him, he will have his will with us," Jane laughs.

Dee wonders if it is some colleague of Faunt who has come to spur him on his way. "Well, this Will Hall will have to limp back to the city," grouses Dee.

"Husband, be kind. It is a long journey from London, and we must be gracious to our guests." Picking up Marley's trope, she prettily says, "Will you or nil you, you will entertain this Will."

The students clap at the lady's cleverness. She has hoped to tease a smile out of her distant husband. She and the boys have tried all day to alleviate his melancholic *humour*.

But Dee is not of a mind to smile or squander time with anyone but Jane. This day is too perfect with its flax-blue sky to tarnish it with unlooked-for intrusions. Dee's reputation for being a magus, unfortunately, brings many scoundrels to Mortlake. Wastrels often apply for his tutelage, but after a week or a month at most, their avowed fascination with Mathematics or Astronomy fades with the waning moon. They only seek to be inducted into the secrets of white magic or alchemy, wanting to transform base metals into gold. No, a true scholar must have an innate yellow *humour* and be content to while away the hours immersed in study forgoing even sleep, food, comfort, time, and, most of all, oneself. The joy of hard study is the acquisition of knowledge. Of course, former students, Thomas Digges, renowned astrologer and the Ninth Earl of Northumberland, the distinguished scientist, both men of great liveliness and mathematical acumen, are the exceptions. Each of them having early on made a deep commitment to learning each was spurred to burn the midnight oil, persevering where others grow vanquished. Their wit and witticisms made long classes so much more agreeable for Dee. Always having the academician's love of sobriety, Mortlake's tutor would forgive them for their aberrations. In return for being the teacher of these accomplished men and others, Dee's reputation had increased. Yet, with that increase, a flood of knaves would find his doorstep.

Marley suggests that cook can put all away, but the

master of the house will have none of that, wanting only to delay the inevitable. He clutches Jane a little tighter, knowing she shall soon enough be lost to him, and, with her gone, so too shall be his contentment. When they reach the house, Marley and the boys make their way to the Great Room, while Dee follows Jane to the kitchen. There, he helps Jane return the picnic *equipage* to cupboards and shelves, and the flatware to its chest. Persuading Jane to share the last of the cakes, Dee will not leave her side until she has eaten every crumb.

Once more with a full heart, he whispers ardently, "My mouse." Kissing her warmly on her pale cheek it ripens with happiness. Finally, with a sinking sense of obligation, he goes to meet the would-be student from London and endure the usual blandishments and everlasting small talk.

"Master William." Marley indicates that the youth should stand. "This be John Dee, doctor of Philosophy and Medicine."

The young man of sixteen makes a courtly bow to his esteemed host. Then ducks his head almost to his knees in obeisance to the lady of the house. His taffeta hat, sitting like a forted castle on his high forehead, has a belfry of feathers that waft in the air as he breaks a leg. Having served Elizabeth as an attendant for years, Jane knowingly claps her appreciation for his panache. Will Hall accepts her approbation with aplomb. To the irascible Dee, his attitude is too cavalier, too fantastical. Its outlandishness roars with outrageous self-esteem as does the boy's leather-quilted doublet that hangs just to his privy member. The young guest showers them with a burst of flowery language praising Dee's renowned intellect and Jane's beauty.

Dee perfunctorily acknowledges, "Sir, my pleasure to make your acquaintance."

"But, surely Doctor, you must remember that we have met?"

Taken unawares, Dee squints at the stranger and realizes his mistake. The feathers on the hat and the rosettes on his shoes proclaim him an actor. In fact, Dee recognizes the wardrobe from the play in London. The costume is that of the character Osric, a landowner.

"Husband?" Jane quizzes.

"It is not Hall at all, but *Shakespit*, is it not?" Dee says with nettled distaste. Why has this theatrical come to maim a perfect day? "This, dear wife, is the ham-fisted scribbler of *Amleth, Dunce of Denmark*."

Smiling graciously at the lady who is quite charmed by the lad, Will Hall deliberately ignores Dee's snide remark. "My father's name is an unfortunate one. *Hall, Shakespar...*" With that, Will gyrates his hips to punctuate the meaning of *Shakespar*. "...or, *Shakespit*, they are but names, and names are but words. What's in a name, but airy nothings, a breath? Words are as interchangeable as grains of sand. Hall has a more grave and impressive import. I like the direct monosyllabic-*ness* of it. I have adopted it as one would take on a new wardrobe of clothes and, thus, newly garbed, I, and my new name stand before you."

Dee takes offense, "Without language, our lives have no meaning. A name is to be defended. To abandon one's name is to betray one's honor," immediately upbraiding himself for having squandered as much time as he has on this popinjay. *Get to the point.* "Young Master Shakespar or Hall, whatever you call yourself, be brief. What dalliance has brought you to my home, and what would you of me? I would fain be about my business."

The boy has expected the question and has conned a speech ready for the answer.

"Sir, when I set about my life's journey, I looked upon study with an ambitious suitor's eye, forgoing my childhood romance with books for a more ambitious marriage with money. But, now, my failure that you and all the world have seen makes me rue my choice. Now, I harken back to my former love and feel the thronging soft and delicate desires of learning. Not a moment has slipped by since last we met, but your wise words on scholarship have haunted me. And I quote, 'For, though the commons care for naught but blood and swordplay, yet the gentles crave allusion and reason.' I am quit of the *theatre* for now as I am quit of my father's name—until that time, when I can write with style and wit." A look of practiced sadness appears in his face. "I am neither moneyed nor scholarly enough for Oxford or Cambridge, but I am young enough to serve you," with a gesture to Jane, "and your comely wife." Will extends both hands above his head. "Here in the comfort of your home. I ask only to seek the mastery, or should I say mystery of my craft."

"Master Hall, I am not wealthy, and, when employed, I am handsomely paid for my tutelage. There are no free lessons here!" He makes to end the meeting.

"No good sir, you mistake my meaning. I request not your especial presence but crave your leave for three months' time to communicate with your magnificent library, of which all the world knows contains a goodly sum of the world's learning. I shall be as loving with your books as a heifer with her calf, as gentle as any mewing cat. In trade whereof, I will do all as you desire, perhaps as messenger, scrivener, or *Johannes factorum.*"

"I have no need of any such."

But with that, Jane, ever the accommodator, retrieves her husband, tugging at his sleeve, and aside murmurs, "The boy but desires a chance. You will be gone dear husband for an equal span of days, and the library will stand unused. Oft have you faulted young poets for their lack of education. Here is one after your liking. And the boy is so charming."

"Aye, his request is witless, mad. An unschooled scribbler expects to suck up learning by merely tasting as much of the nectar of the ink and the leaves of parchment as a bee might." John Dee croaks a dry, joyless laugh. Abruptly swinging back to Shakespar, he barks, "How do you expect to hold a clear understanding of what you read in a mere three months. Your Marlowe studied for years at Cambridge."

The cocky lad smiles mischievously. "Kit Marlowe has not my ability at retention. In that commodity, I am exceedingly blessed."

"What mean you?" asks Jane.

"Madame and kind Sir, Heaven has seen fit to empower me with an ability far beyond the common capacity. Since my early days, I have been ware that upon reading a quotation or passage, it sticks in my remembrance as a fly in a web. And if I but shut mine eyes, every jot and tittle of that memory stands before me."

"Surely, the exact details vanish within the smallest part of an hour?"

"No *Madame*, I have but to be prompted by correlative smell, a sound, a texture, and the writing is again there no matter the hiatus. Transfixed on the back of my eyelids or in my mind's eye as if just seen."

"Husband, what make you of that? Is this not miraculous?" Jane's short time with her wizard husband has acquainted her with sights and strange vessels and scientific instruments that regularly astonish her. But this tale of a perfect memory is as marvelous as any of her husband's collected wonders. Before her marriage, Jane would have suspected satanic causes for Shakespar's abnormality. John has taught her to forgo these childish thoughts and instead recognize aberrant talents as gifts from a benevolent Heaven.

Moreover, the boy's wit is quick and very amusing. Even at Court, she had rarely heard better. She turns to Dee for his recognition of God's glory. Instead, her husband is again lost in his own thoughts. He looks at the boy in his outlandish finery, thinks on his exaggerated histrionic manner, and seems to resolve on a course of action.

"When was the day and hour of your birth? Your

birthplace?"

"I am of Stratford-upon-Avon, Warwickshire. God blessed me to be born on the feast day of St. George, England's patron saint."

"You are proud of that, it seems."

"Aye. That I am. It is a singular comfort to myself and were I given to superstition, a sign from above that I shall slay dragons."

"And the hour?

"Of that particular, I live in ignorance."

Less than pleased with the boy's lack of this essential astrological detail, Dee reprimands him. "Sirrah, you are mightily careless of your beginnings."

Shakespar, at the least, is nonplussed, not knowing why so unimportant a fact should elicit such rebuke.

Mistress Jane instructs him, "My husband's meaning..." She gives a wifely look to Dee. "...is that without the exact hour, he wants the means to create your astrological chart. Without letters of recommendation, how otherwise might he know your character?"

"Men are men," he laughs. "I defy augury. There is no special providence in the fall of an eagle. Men are not shaped by their stars but by their command of the moment."

"You misquote, boy. The proper biblical reference is *the fall of a sparrow. Matthew 10:29.*" Dee smiles haughtily. "Your repudiation of the unseen world only further manifests your want of education." The boy does not protest, but nods resolving never to make that mistake again. "And your religion? Are you of the new religion? Or the old?"

"I am loyal to My Queen!" There is defensive steel in his voice.

"Are you now? A goodly quality in an Englishman," he says dryly, "and as politic a statement as one could make. One that you might rehearse and remember should you perform someday on the hangman's stage. But, this is not, *videlicet*, the answer to my question. Be of a good cheer, young sir, I am no Sir William Lucy, who persecutes law-abiding Catholics. Nor am I a follower of bloody Bishop Donner, who, you may be too young to remember, was a most diligent pursuer of Protestant martyrs under Our Former Majesty. It is of *no-nevermind* to me nor pertinent to my consideration of your request to study in my home what dogma you follow."

Jane *tsks* her husband. She will not have papists in her household. Though the truth is she has had, but has never known it.

"Then why enquire of the matter?"

"That is insolence." A look from Jane softens him. "I have my privy reasons."

The boy seems to weigh his options. "Then, I will impart to you that I was born in the Roman faith, which I no longer practice. My current religion is the worship of nature—a hedonist *I*!" Though Will expects another *tsk* from the lady of the house, he gets none. *Praise heaven, he is not a papist*, is her only thought, accompanied by a demure smile. After all, her husband, a natural philosopher, is devoted to the same following. Not needing to excuse himself, Will takes the wind out of his own youthful sails, leaving him with a sobriety that he has not shown before. "It is loathsome to me that the aforesaid Thomas Lucy indicts my Uncle John for so small a thing as failing to attend Protestant church services, which, for mine uncle, is a great matter of conscience. This is a crime that hurts not a soul in the Warwickshire parish, except perhaps his own."

"My husband is no friend to Lucy, as that vicious and unforgiving Member of Parliament is a disciple of Puritan John Foxe who has libeled my husband in that lying book of his."

"He that chronicled—

"—It is not an honest chronicle."

"*The Book of Martyrs?* In it, did he not name those who, under the rule of Bloody Mary, savaged the Catholics of England?" questions the young man. The book is nearly sacrosanct these days. The lad's supple back straightens. "What offense do you find there?"

"None in Foxe," replies a protective Jane Dee. "Though he limns my worthy husband as accomplice to an inquisitor."

"Which I was," reminds her husband.

"Aye, husband. *Was.*" She turns her attention back on the boy. "It was in another regime when advancement for my husband meant serving powerful masters he did not accord with. But, he has ever been a true advocate of Elizabeth and her religion—even when she was but King Henry's bastard daughter. God forgive me. All the world knows in what peril my John stood when he did favors for Princess Elizabeth and what punishment he suffered at his arrest by the *quondam*

Queen, her sister."

The boy is not one of those who knows or cares, and he shrugs. It is all ancient history to him.

Dee puts a period on the matter. "Relentless hounds, Prestall, Murphyn, and Lucy will not let the matter rest. They rake up the ashes of my past and blow on the coals of suspicion and thin accusation to set them ablaze again. I am belied, and many know not the truth of it."

"Then Doctor Dee, I pray you be kind to me whose family suffers even now at Lucy's hands." With that, Shakespar retells the history of how that Warwickshire Member of Parliament continually persecutes his mother's family, the Ardens. His uncle, who had occasionally criticized the national *Prayer Book*, had been severely fined for each of his pronouncements and then, in the local courts, denied standing by the MP. John Dee responds in kind by repeating Lucy's slander accusing the necromancer of practicing black magic. "The English can be astonishingly indifferent to the fate of others until they are personally threatened," observes Jane.

The three swap stories until Jane leaves to organize refreshments. During her absence, the philosopher and the young poet discuss the principles of poetry, initiating a dialogue that endures throughout their *connaissance*. Dee is a man of ethics, a doctor of natural philosophy and religion, a scholar, a man who rubs elbows with Queens and Emperors. As a writer, Shakespar, the rebellious son of a provincial shopkeeper, has no desire to be dutiful to antiquated forms or long-dead philologists. This day, youth and maturity clash as they always have, neither side giving any ground.

Dee posits, "There should be no trace of country comedy in serious literature."

Shakespar hoots, "Without it, the sentiment is as dry as straw."

"Poetry of late," says Dee, "is filled with naught but romantic proclamations of love. I fault Ovid for that." The doctor frowns at the thought of the elegiac frippery of *ars amatoria*. "I find these warbled love-notes sung by poetasters insincere if not downright unbelievable. Where are the stanzas that strain to find the truth about existence? Where is the felicity of expression one finds in Horace? The logic of Cicero?" demands Dee.

At that, Shakespar does an about-face and agrees with the learned scholar, "That is why I have come to read your books that I might pierce the veil of my ignorance and teach the world a thing or two with conceits composed with wit and grace."

Dee can't help but bray with laughter at the inflated aspirations of the bombastic glover's boy. More than once, Dee calls him an untrained peacock, yet all the while acclimating to the lad's company.

At the end of two hours, Arthur, who has been screaming tetchily in want of sleep and his mother's presence, emerges bawling from his room. Dee, the soon-to-be-absent father, feels he must attend to his son and quickly shakes hands with his new acquaintance telling the player he may use his library as long as he is careful of the books, but Shakespar is strictly forbidden access to his secret library, the *interna bibliotheca*. Shakespar gratefully makes his goodbyes, and Dee happily plays with his son's fingers as Arthur nestles in his mother's lap. Once the Dees are alone, Jane wonders what John thinks of their visitor.

"He is a poltroon to come marching in here flying false colors and calling himself Master *Hall*. But, it is evident that he has a good mind." He chews on that for a while. "It is his mind, dear wife, that intrigues me."

"You mean his power of memory."

"Aye that. Much might be made of that. He has a strong desire for distinction. A slayer of dragons, indeed," says the bemused academic, rolling his eyes.

"You favor him?"

Not daring to reveal his innermost thoughts, he answers her ambiguously, "He might prove the perfect secretary. One has but to pen some notes, have the boy read them, and then confidently destroy them, being in no danger of losing one's records."

"Why would you desire that?"

The old man's eyes look inward and, eventually he responds, "Fewer weighty journals to lug about in Europe." She gives him a stern look for such an absurdity.

"And his Catholicism? I'll have no heretical beads nor papist crucifixes in my home."

"You may well be assured of that."

Jane takes another tack. "Could not Lucy and the others see some collusion there? Should we fear that?"

"Collusion? No. He is but a boy. A boy from Stratford, with no name or family to speak of. If he disappears from this world, who would ever miss him?"

The scholar grows silent and allows his son's little

hand to grip his wiggling pinky. All the while, Dee evaluates Shakespar's potential, not only for learning—but, for fitting in as a Catholic among the Catholics of Illyria.

Moreover, the lad's theatricality may be an asset to gain the attention of the island's extravagant Count Orsino. Everyone loves a wit. And surely Will can play a role. There is a sticking point; the young playwright is only interested in Dee's library. Yet, this would-be poet is ambitious.

"Much like myself at his age," off-handedly to Jane, Dee mutters. *That's this actor's Achilles' heel.* Dee must think more on William Shakespar, but, first, a little tummy needs scratching.

8

A stinging Atlantic rain pelts the old wooden structures at Mortlake with full-throated clatter.

Doctor Dee glances at the meandering streams on his windows, taking his mind off the impending meeting with the young Warwickshire playwright. Shakespar will be arriving shortly—his third visit. Here in the *externa bibliotheca* where Dee receives guests, he intends to convince the young lad to give up London and follow him to Illyria. The library is what the boy is after, but the library—and certainly the precious volumes of the *interna bibliotheca*—shall not be traveling abroad. So the strategy will be to convince master Shakespar that access to the librarian is more valuable—a tenuous thesis.

Dee has formulated stratagems. His own life has taught him that no desire resonated so much in the mind of man as the envious desire to feel superior to competitors. Human society has an instinctive tendency to admire any man who has distinguished himself, jealously craving to better that singular person. Only slightly acquainted with the competitive life of London's theatre world, Dee knew of the petty feuds playwrights waged with pamphlets and parodies, published to shame each other. Greene objected to Nashe, Nashe reviled Kyd, Kyd reviled Chapman, and everyone was envious of Kit Marlowe. Dee hoped Will would accept his offer to tutor him in all the arts and sciences, and, in return, Shakespar would clerk for him. It was, after all, the rare opportunity of private instruction with a renowned scholar. Princess Elizabeth had had Cheke. Now, Will would have universally esteemed scholar, Doctor John Dee. What patrons and inner circles might not a young man penetrate if he had the same mentor as the Duke of Northumberland, the Earl of Leicester, or Sir Phillip Sydney? *Moreover, all London knows that I have the Queen's ear even if I do not have Her purse.*

As the nearby church bell rings out three, high-heeled boots approach along the wooden stairway that leads to his well-appointed study. *The lad is punctual,* Dee thinks, and, *there is undeniable excitement in his hurried march toward the door.* In a moment, the author of *Prince Amleth* has come knocking.

"Enter."

The boy is uncomfortably wet, cold, and expectant. Careful not to drip on anything, a shivering Shakespar crosses the threshold.

"Good morrow to you, Doctor. As you can see, despite the elements, I have returned."

"You are as wet as a hen. Stand by the hearth."

Will flings a curtain of rain from his sleeve toward the fireplace. "It was an evil ferrying from Southwark. I had much ado to keep the chill from my bones." He gives a quick glance out the one window. "It rains cats and dogs." Gingerly, he begins to unbutton.

The old scholar clears manuscripts off a stool for Will's benefit. Pouring a glass of canary wine, he watches as the traveler hangs a dripping wide-brimmed copotain on a metal hook by the hearth. Mindful of keeping what parts of him dry that still are, the traveler carefully eases out of his threadbare Dutch cloak with its long sleeves, placing it near the fire. Rivulets, like the crooked lines of rain beading down the window, trickle off the sopping woolen garment. The last things to be removed are a pair of expensive gloves very much out of keeping with the other dowdy articles of clothing. Will places them carefully on the mantel to dry, far enough from the blaze to keep them from shrinking.

Their anomalous nature breaks Dee's silence. "A handsome pair of gloves, master Shakespar."

Standing as close to the small fire as he can, John Shakespar's boy acknowledges the compliment as he drinks his wine like juice, color rushing to his cheeks, "Aye, they are a present from my father."

"Rich gifts from one you told me is now in penury?"

"Poor though he be, he is a proud tanner and would not stomach a son of his to wander London without a token of his craft proclaiming his love and advertising his profession."

Remembering his own draper father, Dee chuckles, "The English merchant never shirks an opportunity to acquire a potential sale." Generosity demanding, Dee pours another serving of canary. "A touch of that will heat the blood, and mitigate the chill."

"Gramercy." Shakespar downs much of it. Formality having long been dropped in prior meetings, William falls to the floor extending his sinewy legs toward the fire. Gossamer clouds of steam waft from the thin soles of his old boots; Will's head swivels as he takes note of the manuscripts that fill up the shelves around him. Young men, as a rule, are single-minded and lack patience; William Shakespar is no exception, and thus, he begins, "Reverend Sir, I am honored that you have allowed me entrance to your home and your good will." Dee acknowledges the compliment. "You promised to introduce me to your books." Dee nods. Will, who has rarely seen printed and bound volumes, looks longingly about at the bookshelves. "Is this the majority of your collection?"

"No boy, this is but books for decoration." That books should be decoration is a new concept to the young man. "My *interna bibliotheca* is more precious, and more private."

"Might I ever visit it?"

"I give leave to very few."

Will dares not be presumptuous. "Well then, Will I be allowed to continue to read what is kept here in your *outer* library when you are gone?"

Dee smiles slyly. "Here? There is nothing here of *worth*." This startles Will. Weren't all bound books of worth? Certainly, they were dear. "Young man, you are not the first student to ask such permission to partake of my *interna bibliotheca*. But, in those cases, when I was absent from home, I had the security of the boy's background and family to ensure against the theft or manhandling of my possessions."

"Doctor Dee, I swear I would not—"

"Aye, you will swear now on all that is holy that I should trust you."

"I grant you I am a player, and I grant our shame is such that we are much maligned. But indeed upon *all that is holy*, though I am unprovided, I am no false thief."

"I do not say you are. But, my books are delicate treasures suffering as we do the cruelties of time and use. Clumsy hands..." looking at Will's dripping clothes, "Wet hands do as much damage as rats, fire, carelessness. My treasures must continually be protected. I will not abandon them to the vagaries of fortune or the carelessness of the uninitiated. For this and much more, you understand they cannot be visited by just anyone. As you say, you are unprovided. You have neither capital nor family for me to use as collateral." He reaches out to the nearest book as if it is his dearest joy. "I have amassed my dear, dear collection for these many years. It is my passion and my life's work. Though you have been a familiar these past two weeks, you are, as yet, still a stranger to me. What trust can I have in you, an impoverished player?"

"Surely, your servants or your good wife can keep a watchful eye. I will but select a book and promise but to read. Outside, in the yard, if you like. No trouble to anyone." He further dries his hands on his breeches, insisting, "I shall be as loving to your books as a turtle to his mate."

Dee smiles at the simile but shakes his head *no*—a *no* that obviates any debate. Shakespar's hope of freedom from anonymity flickers and dies. Yet he cannot resign himself to return to the hard life that sped him to Mortlake. Opportunity is once more frustrated by humble beginnings. Sagging in adolescent disappointment, Will tells himself that he did not come through the downpour for *this*.

Dee drones on, "My volumes contain knowledge of which every gentlemanly man of Letters should be ware. But even should I give you license, a brief unguided sojourn with these pages will not sufficiently instruct you in the *divers* ideas, forms, knowledge, and philosophy that will make your writing esteemed, nay remembered. For that, one must needs be familiar with the wisdom of mythology, the courts, the law, rhetoric, poesy, Petrarchan love sonnets, the sea, weather, women, herbal remedies, dreams, mathematics, medicine, foreign affairs, the New World, the Spanish, the Italians, and the occult."

Waspish, disdainful, wanting to give offense, Will upbraids, "Preserve me from cheesy cant. This is but a schoolmaster's torrent of words. You would require of me years, and I have not the time nor inclination to dawdle giving myself to academia as you have." From his point of view, all this was pedantic claptrap and a waste of time. All the aspirant wants is permission to read a few books and improve on his conceits. *Another old man keeping me from my ambitions.* Uncaring about the wet that he flings, he jumps to his feet, "As you remind me, I am a poor *nothing*, wretched in every way, who must of necessity, make a living."

Dee motions him to sit, but the boy will not. Shrugging, understanding the boy's resentment, the antiquary continues, "Aye that you must. But though I tell you I cannot trust you with my books, I like you boy. Your ambitions do you justice. You remind me of myself—a man on a mission."

Shakespar shuffles, unsure of this new drift in the conversation. "Then trust me with your books! I will respect them as you do, Sir."

Not sensing any attempt at irony, Dee remains cordial. "It is not unknown to you that within a fortnight, I am for Europe. It is a wearisome journey, and, once arriving, I will need secretarial assistance. Might you see your way to companion me in my travels? I would pay you well and, more to your ambitions be tutor to you of all the literary forms and rhetorical niceties that your search implies."

The actor's eyes glance up. *What's this? Some chicanery?* "Why should I? I am after knowledge, not employment. Or, at least, not yours. What could I possibly find of interest abroad that I will not find in London?"

Ungratefull, spleenfull, rough, waspish non-entity are but a few invectives that cross Dee's mind, yet he remains calm.

"Will, I take you for an honest lad who would aspire to much," extols Dee feigning adulation, "Thus, I offer experience and travel, which were ever excellent teachers for erudition and invention."

A high price to pay for a little book reading. "But what will we study? What scriptural authorities may I consult? Unless you mean to trunk up your library and bring it with you."

Dee smiles. "Books are but reservoirs of wisdom and not wisdom itself. And each man drinks only a dram of their knowledge at the first meeting."

"But, I have told you I can remember all that I read."

"Yes, so you swear. But even so, all you will remember are the words not the underlying truths hidden in the text that sharpens the mind. *That*, my boy, comes through discourse and debate."

"Another indenture? Already, I have given a year to Burbage." Shakespar would leave at once; disinclined to suffer the rain again, he remains drinking the man's canary.

Dee presses on. "It is not unknown to you that for *divers* decades, I have pursued scholarship with its myriad avenues. I tell thee that the countless hours of striving after dull facts are as deadly and unprofitable a thing as the reckoning of grains of sand. What need you profit nothing from memorization when I can tutor you in all the mysteries of the consequential literary styles, forms, conceits whose value all the best patrons of the arts demand. Nay, pay good money for. The true poet must be as familiar with all *rationes seminales* as is the gardener who recognizes the first appearance of a hybrid rosebush and cultivates its sprigs for future gardens of unequaled beauty. Wit and reason are what you seek. And I can give you that. Under my tutelage, you shall have access to Promethean fire that will enflame your verses and send Marlowe packing back to school. You shall be not just a theatrical poet, but also a profound philosophical one."

Unafraid to speak truth to this graybeard, he bristles,

"You are nothing if not proud, Master Dee."

"Proud am I?" Here Dee rises to his full height with a dignity that commands respect. "Come with me, boy, and I shall give you ocular proof of my claims."

The scholar hastens out, stiff and tall, and determined. With determination, he advances quickly down a long hallway, leading to floors that suddenly creak badly, even louder than their thudding boots. They are in a section of Dee's home where the wainscoting is old and warped, where few ornaments hang on the wall, where the framework around the doors is plainer, older. It is evident to Shakespar that two buildings have been cobbled together and that his teacher leads him deep into the older wing. Outside a heavy oaken door they stop. Dee, self-absorbed, reaches into his gown and withdraws a heavy key. Ferocious in his intensity, he dramatically unlocks and throws open the portal to his private library, the *interna bibliothecha*.

"Proud am I? See for yourself."

Dee strikes a match, and Shakespar is dazzled by the first sight of hundreds upon hundreds of variegated books lined up on countless shelves and tables.

"Near four thousand." Dee finds a lantern and lights it. The ceiling is frescoed with white constellations and red planets. The walls are painted with interlocking circles with many-legged stars inscribed in their centers. The intellectual beauty is as majestic as any of the ancient wonders of the world. Stepping into this other world, Will is awed. If Will had thought their former room had shown an extensive collection of books, here is a chamber room thrice the latter's size and stuffed from floor to ceiling with manuscripts.

The lair, redolent with faded leather and lambskin and burned-out candles, is a paean to scholarly study. Also, there are oddities. A blue ladder is propped up against the window. A handsome square frame hangs empty on a wall. On the floor is a painted rectangle subdivided into nine smaller rectangular stenciled blocks, each with a different number painted on it. Shakespar's mind reels and his hunger to learn quickens.

"I am not proud, sirrah. I possess that which the greatest minds of all time have set down for our edification. Knowledge."

Will hesitates. He feels swallowed. Here is a reality that is alien to his limited background. Incapable of grasping its enormity, he stammers, "It would take me *divers* lifetimes to read even a small portion of these."

"Aye, and without the Latin nor the Greek—"

"I have the Latin," Shakespar defends his Stratfordian upbringing.

"But not the French nor Italian nor the Greek," Dee does not stop. "Nor the mathematics nor engineering. Without their comprehension, you would stand like a traveler at a border-crossing with no chance of passport into rarefied realms." With lantern in hand, Dee pushes Shakespar further into the room. "That is why you are in need of my help. I have read them all and digested them all. Their glories abide in the *pia mater* of my mind." Holding the lantern aloft, Dee points to his collection. "There is everything here that can inspire the imagination." He turns back to Shakespar with a baleful warning. "But beware, there also books with falsehoods that may seduce, betray, and debauch. Because not all truths are for all ears, not all falsehoods are easily recognizable." Shakespar stiffens at that. Lowering the lantern, the elder scholar takes a conciliatory tone, "Fear not. I shall be your Chiron and tutor you. Through my instruction, as Heracles freed Prometheus, I shall unshackle you from your ignorance."

Finding it still too much to process, t he glover's boy is impelled to say, "What care have I for mathematics or engineering? I have never been good at reckoning. It is a talent that more becomes a tapster than an artist." A disappointed, fearful youth continues, "They say your investigations into numbers, and geometric shapes have led you to dabble in the black arts and consort with devils."

Having heard it before, Dee looks Shakespar directly in his eye and remonstrates with sincerity, "By my very soul, I swear to you I have naught to do with devils nor evil spirits." Will nods in hearing if not acceptance. "Sure, there are men of small minds and evil intents who seek to blaspheme my work by calling it witchcraft, but my studies have ever been philosophical in nature, not magical." Dee sees Will's initial misgivings lessen, replaced by an aspiration to have his ambitions satisfied and delve into the exotic curiosities spread out before him. Using the lure of forbidden knowledge, the magus tickles the trout. "I will tell true, Will. I have on occasion communed with angelic entities. Should you vouchsafe to join me in my journey, I will require you to record what transpires between me and the angels I conjure."

The thought of that wholly heretical, impossible possibility forces the Midlands boy to sit in wonder. The faintest prospect of being in the company of angels bewitches Will's thoughts. It terrifies him, too, which makes him even more desirous of the opportunity—a chance at knowledge of the unknowable that few men could ever hope to possess.

In his black scholar's gown and tight skullcap, John Dee now stands before him like an elder of the Church hinting at secret canonical mysteries. Dee feels the boy's interest growing. He reaches for a nearby book.

"Here is something your Warwickshire schoolmaster never taught you." *Nay, never knew himself,* thinks Dee. "This is Marsilio Ficino's third book of his writings on life, *de vita coelitus comparanda,* that wondrously reveals how words have mathematical equivalents and those numbers are empowered with divine resonance." Shakespar cocks his head at this, as he has always believed the right combination of words in plays might weave magical spells. *Certainly, Marlowe's words have the power to weaken one's knees and conjure images that ignite the imagination and leave one's senses in disarray,* recalls Will. He knew there was magic in words, but when voiced, might they, in fact, really be incantations? Perhaps, Kit had learned these secrets of persuasion from Ficino or from his patron, the Ninth Earl, the *Wizard Duke,* of Northumberland.

"To what higher object or what greater wisdom can any mortal aspire than to look at the universal world around us, a puzzle that heaven has set before us, and seek to solve its enigma? Is that not the duty of the artist? Your duty, William Shakespar?"

Dee shows him Ovid's *Metamorphoses* and, the feel of the oily film of the old vellum is as sensual to the lad as any lover's kiss. Within are more wonders. Unaccustomed to actually holding an antique manuscript, Shakespar is slack-jawed at the calligraphied columns illuminated with faded demi-gods and heroes, and the lines of verse running perfectly parallel across the unlined yellowing page of that first book. Dee lets him browse on his own, and Will is Adam on the first day—all wonder. He lights on a handsomely-printed version of Chaucer's *Troilus and Creseyde* and, having little problem with the Middle English, he revisits the story with relish. Like a guest at the groaning table of a sumptuous feast, even as he reads, he lusts after what other foreign delights he might sample. Restless, Shakespar scans the racks of books and chance brings his hand to several that are in Latin and Greek. Two are written in utterly alien languages of which Shakespar can make neither heads nor tails. He guesses Arabic or perhaps Hebrew and realizes he is seeing the language of God. And had not his host just said he had read all the books here? It is not lost on him that it is a language—Christ's language—that Dee can teach him. A revelation dawns. Might Dee's angels talk to *him* in Hebrew in one of the master's séances? A harrowing more wonderful thought. *More.* To read the unalloyed words of the people of the Bible in their own tongue is a savory more mouth-watering than any appetizing sweetmeat. The cosmos had been inspired by *The Word* and that *Word* had been in Hebrew.

Curiosity ravishes the boy. Sitting perched on a small pile of books, a newer volume, *da harmonia mundi,* catches his attention. He fingers it gingerly, exploring its midsection, probing its dark secrets. The simple pressure of the large volume tingles his lap like the prologue to a sexual liaison. Consumed in lyrical prose, he discovers how herbs and flowers have symbolic significance. Each in its own way is endowed with celestial properties engendered by spirits of one of the seven planets that nurtures it. In his world, they were naught but plants; here, they have mystical powers. As he reads, his mind is on fire at each new artful revelation to be learned. Many pages are too complex to follow. Dee is right; he will need his tutelage. He moves on to other volumes.

Shakespar has no recollection of how long he has been reading. It might have been the better part of an hour when he notices John Dee lighting additional candles. With overblown niceties, Shakespar clumsily thanks his new benefactor for the visit and unabashedly agrees to serve as his assistant. He presses Dee on some of the things he has just read in a torrent of *wherefores* and *I-prithee-whys* that barely give Dee time to catch his breath to answer. Will's earlier role of London coxcomb has utterly faded away, and, in its place an eager student. Will is surprised that his new employer is unerringly patient and supportive; all the while, Dee marvels silently at Will Shakespar's ability to cite verbatim the passages he reads. Despite the lad's present ignorance, he will indeed prove very useful on this mission. This gladdens the old fellow's heart. The boy's indenture may well portend success.

{ 9 }

Like young gallants off to make their mark on the world, John Dee and Will Shakespar set out on a January dawn. At last, neither inclement weather nor inauspicious horoscopes postpone their departure again. By England's Julian calendar, it is the tenth day of Christmas, two days before the celebration of Twelfth Night, a time of traditional hospitality and remarkable cold. In an unusual seasonal act of neighborliness, Walsingham lends a driver and coach to Dee's departure—in Sir Francis' mind—too long overdue. Laden with trunks of clothes and seven large crates of books and pamphlets, heavy ropes secure the load despite the bumpy road. It worries Will that he has seen no weapons, except the coachman's personal musket hidden under a blanket. It seems they are to go naked abroad, trusting to the goodwill of strangers.

An inexperienced traveler, Shakespar, has an especial worry, *It is utter folly to go about unprotected. I sorely wish that I had borrowed one of Henslowe's broadswords from the theatre.* Dozens lay backstage— a professional necessary for depicting the casual cruelty London's playgoers salivated over. *Well, if wishes were horses, beggars would ride.*

With its unbalanced luggage, the coach staggers grotesquely down the road, due East to Gravesend avoiding the city of London and passing as the crow flies through Bexleyheath and Dartford. Though Deptford, London's main port, is closer, Dee avoids it as disembarking from Gravesend ensures fewer observers. Rumor cannot be muzzled once unleashed, and, with a public departure, all of England would have known Dee had stolen away to Europe. Admittedly, his absence from England will not stay secret for long, nor is his departure meant to be completely secret, merely obscured. With today's weather uninviting and many hung over from the holiday, most of the telltales will stay off the roads and sit by their fires.

"Master Shakespar," says Dee, his muffler covering his mouth to rein in warmth, "a full day's journey lies before us. Should we not beguile the hours with instruction? There is no fitter time than the present to commence your education. Take time when the time comes lest she steal away."

I am here to learn. Yet, in the early morn when his thoughts are muddy and numb with cold, Will is sullen and shakes his head *no*, indicating that it would be a great pain and to no purpose. Never having been East of London, Shakespar prefers to watch the rime-covered countryside pass by. Dee insists, and, not wanting to give offense, his new ward acquiesces. With an icicle smile, arms crossed, and wrapping one leg around another, Will looks like a man shielding his body from a beating or a sufferer of a wasting disease.

Not blind to this unspoken lack of enthusiasm, the

master starts the lesson with as simple a topic and as ingratiating a tone as he can muster.

"Education is the highest of Arts for it imposes forms—ideas and ideals—not upon the action as do other arts, *videlicet* painting or sculpture, but rather upon the mind. You, my boy, must collate all facts learned—whether that of literature or of mathematics or of human character—into a unified cosmology. A single house of ideas, as it were, but each room a separate compartment, easily connecting to another. Use your imagination as a hallway to visit each room for inspiration. Improve your wit by linking all together. But have a care. Style is not enhanced by merely memorizing random concepts but by acquiring observational skills to portray humanity in all its many behaviors."

Ignorant to all of this and resentful, Shakespar instead watches how Dee's breath puffs the muffler forward ever so slightly as he talks. Nice touch for a future pompous character. *Is that an observable behavior?* Will bites his tongue.

"Moreover..."

Is it going to be like this for the next four months? Though his throat is tight with the cold, Will cannot not stop himself from interrupting, "Aye, but, Sir, I desire only to learn the rhetorical figures of Wilson and mythological allusions of Ovid that the better dramatists have told me of. These are what shall make my writing learned, more descriptive. Can we not commence with these?"

"Child, all things may come soon enough if we can have the patience to stay for them. Remember the authors of my library."

The color in Shakespar's cheeks rises, but that could be from the cold, "'Child' again? You must cease calling me that. Sir."

"What should I call you then?" For warmth, the older man sticks his gloved hands deeper into the thick folds of his cloak that hangs between his knees.

"I don't know. Master Shakespar or Will."

"Then, you have forsaken the name of *Hall*?"

"Yes."

"And why?"

"It doth not please me anymore."

Unable to crack the dam of sullen youth, Dee accedes, "As you wish."

Breaking through a layer of frozen mud and ice covering a large rut in the road, the coach dips and sends them sprawling over their seats. Recovering his place and setting his feet firmly on the floor, Will suddenly, "Back home, they called me *Swan*."

"A strange appellation."

"They said I never left paddling at the riverbank. My mother calls me *The Bard* but only after hearing of my wish to be a poet, and gave me that name in derision. And you, reverend sir, do you have a pet name."

The elderly man chuckles mirthlessly, "My detractors call me the *Great Conjurer*."

"Not just your detractors, sir, but the Queen Herself."

"How came you by that?"

"Master Augustine Phillips, he of the Queen's Men, told me the night we met."

"Did he now?" *The villain. Effrontery from a rascally knave.* Dee wonders if this Phillips spat when he said his name. Her Highness might call him what she liked, but if the players were calling him such, it would not be long before he would be pilloried on the stage, *a basso il Doctore* hunching over a caldron speaking drivel in iambic pentameter.

"Well, then *Swan*, a poet who for want of art, only imitates ancient ornament never can hope to touch the heart of his listeners. You must find the essence of your characters and thereby reach the soul of your audience—through newfound conceits, as I say, will *illuminate.*" Dee smiles convivially. "...as well as entertain." Unable to stop teaching or patronizing, the inveterate lecturer pontificates, "That is what will make you great, and not simply an ink spotter of pages. The regurgitation of facts and figures is mere information and not worthy of being called Poetry since it does naught but burden the mind—dulling it instead of developing, enlightening, and *illuminating* it."

"*Dulling it*, I see," says Will, barely listening.

When leaving Stratford for London, "a higher purpose" was the ambition Will had set for himself: To leave behind the drudgery of middle-class life that trapped one's existence in one's birthplace and deadened the imagination in the repetitive labor of a tradesman. Such a man stales his friends and ultimately the drudge aspires to nothing more than a full belly and a tickle in the hay. Upon leaving, he swore to surpass his father's ambition for him as a glove-maker and escape the curse of eternally skinning horsehides and threading needles. His father's own lofty aspiration of rising in society to become town burgess had merely endowed him with the grand responsibility of nudging stinking drunkards home or the management of whitewashing walls. *Fie upon it. Fie.*

At school, *Swan* had chanced on Sidney and Cicero. Their words had ignited his imagination. The artistry of these men inspired a truly higher purpose that had made him envy their wit, their wisdom, and their language. As Will sits barely listening to his mentor, he realizes that he himself errs—or as the commandments sayeth, *sins*— in his assessment that it is their university studies that had made them so exciting, so close to perfection, so successful. This old pedant with his hands buried in his lap is right; the thrill that had swept Will up hearing Marlowe or Lyly was the acquired skill in which they plumbed mankind's many natures and portrayed inner depths. Will has a wolf's appetite for acquiring that ability.

The boy unclasps his arms and leans forward. With clenched fists under his chin, he smiles prettily, "With your help, I hunger for all you can guide me in, Dr. Dee."

The cold bright morning fades into a sunless afternoon. It is five and growing dark as they ride toward the seaport. Their first sight of Gravesend is the towering spire of the Mariner's Church standing watchman over the community. Tall and dignified overseeing the sloping countryside, it has been there since the Norman Conquest. Seeing the choppy dark water of the angry Thames, Will experiences a frightful apprehension. Tomorrow at this time, he will be in the middle of the broad Channel with unknown sailors—with his life in their hands. Storms can arise instantaneously and threaten for days, driving ships far off their course. Or, at least, that's what happens on stage. Shakespar has never actually seen the ocean. Many images of dread come to him in his dreams where he hangs helplessly to the back of a dolphin heading afar out to sea, or clinging for life to slippery timbers buffeted by infinite green waves?

He glances at his employer who falls into reverie, engendered no doubt he thinks by the lapping sound of the troubled river. Will is intrigued but does not speak. In fact, since stopping for a meal the two travelers converse very little. Shakespar is beginning to think of Dr. Dee as Sir Sullen or Sir Solemn, sitting as proper as an old church matron or as perpendicular as the church tower in the distance. As the carriage lurches along, Will sees Sir Solemn, trying to maintain his respectability. Keeping his knees pressed together and expressing a proper sense of decorum, his eyes fixed in front of him, the old man's mind seems equally fixated. Not Will. Each jolt pushes him toward a more uncomfortable imagining. Has he been foolish to leave the safety and relative familiarity of London? *Is not accustomed poverty less unsettling than the possibility of a threatening future? Why risk everything on the hazard of one throw?* Having put his trust in Dr. Dee and his own good fortune, he now has doubts about both.

As for the Sir Solemn next to him, he too slips into a dark *humour* realizing that each subsequent voyage abroad seems longer and more hazardous than the last.

This recognition links itself to his journey through time. When he was younger, his body did not hurt so much from the abuses of traveling. The liver spots that proliferate over his hands are as numerous as the lice in an ill-kept inn. How did they get there? When did they grow to such a number? He looks over at the boy; in the twinkling of an eye, these blemishes would be his too. *Our existence is but Time's fool*, he reminds himself. He is old. Forty-seven. When young, he had thought that at this age he would know so much more. *Nearness to one's death*, Dee observes, *brings no more wisdom than any other point in life's journey.*

Gravesend grows larger in view. The roadway to the outermost edge of London was never smooth. Winter's wet weather has worsened it, pitting the dirt surface transforming it into sucking sludge. The wagoner flicks his whip urging his team to avoid the road's muddier ruts, gouged into being by the city's traffic. Although more even ground reveals itself, with each quarter-mile, the wooden wheels rattle over rocks and tree branches brought down by the wind.

Sore and exhausted, both travelers are thankful as the coach finally passes through the city gate—Shakespar most especially. Though born in a rural town, London has given Will a preference for cities and their bustle and history. The carriage lumbers past the ancient chapel that was ransacked and torched when Henry VIII had forsaken the old religion, past the Tudor fort with its brass cannons, past men of all stripes and languages, some in the most outrageous costumes. Shakespar wonders what dramas have been enacted here by generations of Kentish families?

After stopping to ask Dr. Dee about lodging, the driver comes to a halt at a shabby inn. Above the massive stone-front entry, a sign reads, *"Crossroads–public house"*—its letters painted in black on two lengths of yellowing pine hanging from the roof by two long rusted iron chains creaking painfully in the swooping wind. Eponymously, the boards of the sign intersect and make the mathematical symbol for multiplication. Two flickering red lanterns light an unwelcoming entrance throwing a hellish glow upon the inn's flaking walls.

Will's misgivings rise again. *Surely there are better lodgings further up the road, closer to the water, and better suited to Dee's station in life. Why here? Crossroads is not auspicious for the start of our journey.* He sighs. The choice is not his to make. *My readiness is all that is required.*

Shakespar, with the coachman, immediately takes charge of unlading some of the baggage. The crates of books and most of the luggage will stay aboard until they find passage on a ship. Dee goes inside to arrange for rooms and finds a pot-bellied innkeeper whose scowl is embossed on his brow. Dee finds his thick Kentian accent nearly undecipherable when the small man offers a room.

"What direction face the windows?" Dee demands to know.

"Towards the East."

"Good. What is the room number?"

"The room number? Why the devil ask you that? I've never heard the like. What difference does it matter about the number?" spits the put-out host. "The rooms are all *blis'soning* alike!"

"Difference!? Why, man, all the difference in the world. Numbers manifest divine Providence. Through the investigation of the implication of a number's mathematical conclusion, we can come to understand everything that can be known. Starting under the influence of the right number betokens starting out in the right manner. It is as simple as that."

"Is it now?" The annoyed little man is named Bull. Needing the custom, he sighs, "What would you, sir? Odds or evens?"

A propitious room number is agreed upon and Bull, having secured a paying customer, is now eager to know more about whom he rents to. Escorting his guests along a narrow hallway to the room numbered *Nine*, Bull inquires of their backgrounds, their journey, and where they are headed.

This man is too nosey by half, thinks Dee and straight-faced lies, "Krakow."

"Krakow? Strange name. Be that in Scotland? What place is that?"

An attempt is given to inform the innkeeper as to where Krakow is in Europe. Though truly knowing nothing of Poland, Bull still nods in understanding. The innkeeper then shares what disagreeable knowledge he *knows* of Polish sailors over the years.

Patting the Doctor's shoulder with pretended consolation for his future, Bull warns, "Them Poles be scurvy bastards."

After hastening to light a candle and opening the

door of number *Nine* for Dee's inspection, Bull grunts something that sounds like, "Happy?"

The Doctor nods approval.

The innkeeper is now quick to help Will with the placement of bags in the modest room. "Heavy. What's *blis'soning* in'em?"

John Dee, seemingly unfamiliar with the term, matter-of-factly gives the innkeeper eight pence for the night's lodging. No determination has been agreed upon their length of stay.

"That will be all, g'day."

Begrudgingly, the little pot tips his hat, offering, "Ask if you be in want of aught." Both men know there will be no further communication between them.

As the door closes, Dee mumbles, "Insufferable fool."

But, Dee is wrong. Bull is no fool. University men often sailed from Gravesend to travel to the Continent, but rarely did they first travel the old road from London, being jarringly uncomfortable and having a reputation for highwaymen. A faithful Protestant, the innkeeper of the *Crossroads* is alert for strangers bound for Europe, especially those journeying to the coast of France to Rheims or Louvain to study at the Catholic Colleges. Some year or two later, with a haunted look, they return ashen-faced and eager to convert good people for the whore of Babylon, the Catholic Church. The governmental watchers of the harbor offer sizeable purses for news of such men, calling them recusants, men treasonous to the Queen and the nation's religion.

A disboweling is too good for them. But this one dressed in his black robes, Bull construes, *he who barely keeps a civil tongue in his head, has let drop he studied at St. John's College Cambridge and everyone knows that is a heathen school. But,* he thinks, *the coachman downstairs. I've seen him. Been here before. One of Secretary Walsingham's men.* Relaxing his scowl, the vigilant Bull concludes that the old man and his punk must not be papists. Almost smiling, he thinks, *Alright then, I've got his number.*

As Will unpacks, his employer busies himself consulting calendars, almanacs, and astral significances for their impending voyage; in this, he is as methodical as a bricklayer with his calculations.

"We must embark on the morrow."

"Sunday? The last day of the Christmas holiday? How may we ever find passage? Few if any crews will willingly forsake their holiday festivities... or their Sabbath debaucheries."

"There is little choice." Dee explains, "Hermetic resonances suggest tomorrow is the sole day for propitious travel this week." Will gives him an unbelieving, exasperated smirk. "Tomorrow, Sunday, the seventh day is named after the celestial body called *Sol*, the sun, symbolizing all that is majestical. Charity and Love stream out from the sun, and we must be ruled by these radiant virtues when they are at their mightiest?"

After two hours' discrete inquiry along the waterfront, Dee locates Moroccan-born Captain Samuel Pallache, now commanding a merchantman ship commissioned by the Dutch States-General. The vessel is *The Rachel*, crewed by Marrano Jews: Hebrews forced into Catholicism by the prejudices of the Roman Church. There being no Jewish citizens in England—at least not officially given that England sees no reason to show any kindness to Jews—Captain Pallache is eager to be on his way home to the Netherlands.

That evening, the captain, the doctor, and the player sup at table in a small nook wedged under the *Crossroads* tavern's stairwell. A dim oil lamp casts wan shadows. The singularity of meeting his first *exotic* so early in the trip piques Will's imagination. Neither Shakespar nor any of his Warwickshire family has ever met one before—not of any breed or creed. To Shakespar, Jews are romantic figures like the Chinamen of Cathy or inhabitants of the moon. This sojourn might be full of such strange encounters. He is indeed at a crossroads.

Still concerned about anonymity, John Dee wears a steeple-crowned hat to obscure his face. They share a flagon of rum as the quiet Moroccan, in a distinctly yellow hat, tells of his recent trip to Constantinople and provides *curriculum vitae*. Will feasts on the alluring details of Pallache's wandering existence, and, in the dark shadows of the cranny, wonder takes hold of him.

"I was born on the Barbary Coast, the son of a merchant family." Captain Pallache leans in. "I learned nautical skills from seafaring Venetians and the subtleties of commerce from nomadic sheiks. After I impressed the Moroccan Sultan, I became one of his advisors and was soon entrusted with the duty of establishing trade relationships with the Spanish Court. I was in Madrid many years at the Spanish Court where there is a great feast of languages. To thrive, you are compelled to bargain in another's tongue. I was lucky, on board serving with foreign mariners, I learned to speak my mind with most. I am fluent in not only Spanish, but, Arabic, Hebrew, and Dutch, as well as your English. My faith was a stumbling block to advancement in Spain, so I converted to Christianity, but my ambassadorial cache meant *nada* to the Inquisition." There the loquacious seaman spits between two fingers raised in a V. "I fled the country for the Jewish community in Amsterdam where I bargained with the Governor-General, William, Prince of Orange, for a ship and started a new maritime career under his protection. I have here delivered a shipment of—"

"—Why, Amsterdam?" Will interrupts.

"Because of the *Union of Utrecht*, is it not?" Dr. Dee suggests. The captain nods in agreement.

"I am ignorance itself in this," is Will's bewildered reply.

"You Englishers know naught of the world beyond the narrow borders of your little island," chortles the Jew, then in a more informative manner, "Nigh five year ago, the northern provinces of the Netherlands knitted their allegiances together in a compact called the *Union of Utrecht*. It forbade persecution for religious reasons. They are as forgiving about how you choose to pray as the Venetians."

"In defiance of Rome, freedom of conscience was

established as sacrosanct within the anti-papal states of the Low Countries," the ex-priest adds, unhappy with his former masters.

"Under the *Union*, my family is free to be openly Jewish and worship as our ancestors had meant us to. No outward signs of our beliefs are required, like wearing this *maldito*..." He indicates his yellow hat required for Jews in England. "...this, how you say, 'poxy' hat," he sneers, "my badge as a Hebrew. A stigma of shame enforced by the laws of your nation." He shakes his head in consternation and proceeds, "In Amsterdam, our property and goods are safe from the Church or the government's taking."

"So long as you say your prayers and practice your rites in private."

"Yes, under that proviso. But there, we no longer fear the fires of the Spanish Inquisition simply because we are born Jews."

"We live presently in a corrupted world, my friends, but the time will soon come when none need fear the rigors of religious persecution."

"How say you?" scoffs the Hebrew.

"You have my word," assures Dee, "Soon."

Dee wonders how well Pallache has studied his *Kabala. Is he aware of the coming end of days when the world will be restored to perfection? As a mariner, surely he must study the stars and thus know of the forthcoming grand conjunction.* As if in answer and with troubled eyes, Pallache nods in the Jewish hope of a better future, "*Aw-manin.*"

The conversation returns to the Moroccan's business

in Britain. Samuel Pallache explains that he has delivered a shipment of ornate Turkish rugs that day. He does not explain that that is only what he reported to the customs men and the watchers at Gravesend. Even erudite John Dee is not aware that privateers such as Captain Pallache often smuggle contraband and illegal aliens amidst their legitimate cargo. Nor does Samuel describe to Dee his experience of the Gravesend officials' justifiable suspicions of his manifest—a suspicion Pallache could live with. Englishers knew better than to provoke a ship flying under the *Prinsenvlag* of Prince William of Orange. Traders sailing under orange, white, and blue protection were treated with respect when they arrived in Britain, primarily when they trafficked valuable goods. Always eager for more tapestries, the English aristocracy sought Persian rugs to drape baronial tables, walls, and windowsills of the best manor houses. Even old King Harry had made a point of seizing Cardinal Wolsey's extensive collection of Middle Eastern arras as soon as Wolsey was forced out of his Cardinal's palace.

Pallache goes on to regale about his past in Spain, Africa, and the Orient. Shakespar is not convinced all Pallache's embroidered tales are true—souks and sheiks, and bazaars! Will listens intently. Wide-eyed, the boy feels awkward yet privileged to be in the company of this cosmopolitan traveler of ancient lands—a veritable Sinbad. *Dee is right about travel,* Shakespar abjures his rudeness this morning.

To Will's consternation, the scholar slips smoothly into Spanish to keep certain particulars from the youth.

Hearing the loathed speech spoken, nearby patrons grumble at being forced to hear the language of their maritime enemies. As the guttered oil lamp is refilled by a waiter, more and more of the conversation hides itself in Spanish. Finally, Dee excuses Will, but not before reminding him gravely, "Our particulars, Will, are to remain locked within your teeth and lips."

Shakespar inclines his head in reluctant acknowledgement. "You have reminded me many a time, Master. I shall not forget," Turning his back on his elders, Shakespar, in his imagination, has the last word. *Though it is beyond me why I must keep secret the little I know of our stopover at an irrelevant spit in the English Channel en route to Poland.* Oblivious, he shrugs. *Perhaps, it's because of the Jews? No, that cannot be.* His masters warnings of discretion were emphatic back in Mortlake. Dismissed, untrusted, and unregarded, Will skulks off tavern-haunting and chances upon a pair of tars eager to make his acquaintance. They remind him Twelfth Night is nigh and offer him youthful camaraderie, laughter, beer, and horseplay, pleasing antidotes to an arduous day of travel.

After a brief dalliance, Will gazes back to the cranny beneath the stair. The elegant scholar and the ruddy sea captain are a mismatched pair—their hat brims touch; a whispered conversation lapses abruptly as a drawer approaches and asks after more drinks. Though another round of rum is ordered, the two stare fixedly into their pewter tankards as if examining mysterious riddles at their bottoms.

What purpose their sotto voce exchanges, Will wonders, *They speak a foreign tongue. How many water-rats here can fathom their Spanish?* His youthful desire to share in his elders' secrets makes it impossible for him to ignore them completely. He sees the Jew dipping his forefinger into the wine and drawing an unfamiliar figure on the table. *I must remember that action and give it to one of my characters.* With some disagreement or misunderstanding from Dee, Samuel Pallache repeats the drawing carefully. This time, Dee exclaims—in neither English nor Spanish—as strange a sound as Will can imagine—heathenish in the extreme. The sea captain understands, nods. Dee grabs Samuel's arm, intent on some meaningful explanation spoken again in the unknown tongue. Heaven-knows-what strange sacrament the Jew has drawn in wine on the table.

At his own table, a strong strapping sailor grabs the playwright's chin and regales the boy of seas and tempests and strange lands. Tales of Barbados and pirates attacking off the coast of Tunisia intoxicate and frighten the teenager. The adventures seduce young Will's imagination as much as the young sailor's full lips and brawny arms. The *not-so-innocent* from Stratford draws closer to the English mariner both with the desire to learn more and to inhale the salty essence of the man's raven-black hair.

Having overheard bits of the Spanish conversation, Cuthbert, Will's sailor, inquires, "Those two... at your other table... are they Hispanicists?"

"Spaniards? No! Complete strangers. A necromancer

and a Jew!"

"A necromancer?" The sailor scoffs. "Has he shown you how to conjure lead into gold?"

"Alchemy, no!" Deftly, Will redirects the conversation away from essential details, "*You*, however, Cuthbert, have shown me how to turn something soft to stone."

Communing, laughing, their hands meet under the table. When he thinks about it, Will notes that his Cuthbert asks nothing of the Jew, and the fledging student realizes Samuel is not a rarity to one who has seen so much of the world. Looking back at Dee, he puzzles again about the secrecy of the two men's discussions. A part of Will would eagerly return to their table to find out more, but then another part aches to be mauled by the Adonis beside him. *Where does my true nature lie? A slave to my blood or as a seeker of higher understanding?*

Will's focus does not go unnoticed by Cuthbert. "I detest Spaniards. The pox take them. Olive sucking bastard sons of Moorish harlots! They trespass exceedingly in our waters, and our betters do naught to say them nay." Never lowering his voice, "They have purloined the frigates of Portugal and with their galleons have raised a mighty armada. Know ye that? Captain told us so. Told us too, war's a'coming on." He takes a swallow of beer then turns elegiac about the nobility of his fate at sea. "What honors shall be mine when we do finally take arms for Queen and country. And should that day come when they have scuttled us and sent us to our watery graves, by God's grace, there will be no finer glory."

"Will thee not take me in your arms, my *quean*?" Will twists Cuthbert's left nipple.

But, his companion has grown tetchy. He shakes his head at the thought of Will's day tomorrow. "Setting sail with Hebrews on an ill-named ship christened *Rachel*?" Then, so all can hear, "On a Sunday and during Christmas no less! A pox upon it! I like it not! " His back to Will. "What do heathens know about the tides or the Thames' sandy shoals? Jews are all Jonahs. They'll drown ye sure and ye poor ma will lament like that Rachel in the Bible that ye heeded neither the Sabbath nor my warning. I'd sooner saddle a shark than venture my life aboard a Jew's cursed timbers."

In case Pallache is Spanish, after all, the tar's animosity further extrapolates in his drunkenness. "*A figo* to Phillip the turd and all the scurvy wogs that speak that traitorous tongue. Let *them* all drown." Another serving of rum and Shakespar's sweet ministrations, bring Cuthbert back to laughter. A coy smile plays on the sailor's lips as he passes his roaming hand along Shakespar's downy soft arm to his little finger.

As wine spills, they both guffaw at Cuthbert's salacious tale of an evening well spent in a Brittany jail. Suddenly, Shakespar hears his name.

"Will, take heed, mind you." The old scholar stands beside him. "We set sail with the next tide."

"Aye, and when should that be, Master?"

"Three, this morning," interjects Cuthbert.

Shakespar pouts. "Must we away so early?"

"It is as it is set down. We must obey the waves,

winds, and stars, which govern our condition. I am weary and am away to my room," Dee scrutinizes Shakespar's drinking companion. "I suggest, young man, that you make your *adieus* and call it a night." With his forefinger and thumb, he wipes dribbles of liquor from his aide's beardless chin. "But you are your own man. You shall find the door unbolted."

With that, Dee turns on his heel and heads for number *Nine*.

Tracing Will's lips with a forefinger, Will's newfound friend simpers, "Stay. Shove not off with Mr. Pointy-beard so soon. The night is but new, and I will tell you a thing or two of lovemaking in heathen lands. They say..." he grabs a spoon and shifts its position to imitate his meaning, "Asian wenches have bird nests that are horizontal rather than vertical." The rake licks the bowl of the spoon with the tip of his tongue.

Blind with arousal, Shakespar seizes Cuthbert's mischievous hand, and licks its palm and yanks it into his lap. It is after all only two days before Twelfth Night, a bacchanalian night of revelry. Moreover, it is ten days past Christmas day: the celebration of the *coming of the Savior*.

Seeking the sleep of the dead that comes of total exhaustion, at two in the morning Will Shakespar tries the doorknob to *Room Nine*—blessedly unlocked, as promised. To avoid a waking lecture, he tiptoes in. Only to find it eerily lit by one flickering candle and Dr. John Dee wide awake. With a penknife, the scholar is hard at work inscribing figures into a circular piece of wax. No lecture is given, only a terse, "You must be packed and ready within this half-hour."

"Even so," says Will. "Just let me wash my face and mouth."

He pours cold water into his hands. Bathing his chafed face, and even exhausted as he is, the methodical scrapings intrigue Will as his master models the soft wax.

"May I know what employs you?"

"Aye," is Dee's curt reply.

"What ist?"

"A talisman for securing the gifts of Mercury."

Still facing the ewer and basin, "Ah, that explains it," sniffs Will ironically. Unsteady, Shakespar jerkily turns his head over his right shoulder, questioning, "Gifts of Mercury?"

"Are you ignorant of the planets' properties, child? Do they teach you naught in Warwickshire?"

Tired of the old man's attacks on his rural beginnings and with a surrender born of exhaustion, the boy turns back to his ablutions, answering resignedly, "Aye, naught... I am woefully ignorant."

"Then take a seat, here," says Dee, points at the bed, "We will mend your ignorance."

"Must we?" he groans "Oh, Lord, no. Can I not sleep for even a minute. There remain but twenty-five."

"Then best to it quickly."

Fighting off fatigue, the eye-rubbing reveler falls to

the corner of the soft bed. Dee takes Will's hand, giving him the waxen talisman. It feels strange and looks stranger.

"What do you see?"

"A figure of a young girl nursing a child," he says perfunctorily. "Beside her is a helmeted figure that, in this dim light, seems like he has wings attached to his heels. Mercury?"

"Aught else?"

"In his right hand, he holds what looks like a rooster. Eyes bleary, Shakespar strains to study the carving. "In semi-circles around these etched figures are strange— I'd venture—Greek symbols that float above and beneath?"

Will's employer agrees, grudging approval.

"Is it not Mercury? Though never as I have seen him depicted," Will whines sleepily. He hasn't the strength to hold up the graven image; instead, he lets it drop from his hand to the bed.

"Ignorant in Astrology," grunts the older man none too happily. "Can you not guess what these other figures are?"

Sleepily, Will replies, "That I cannot."

"Then harken. The girl is the image of Virgo, one of the twelve signs of the zodiac." The astrologer begins a lecture on the celestial calendar.

Being a country boy and well versed in the night's constellations and in no mood for anything but bed, the half-awake carouser complains, "Do not think me an ignorant in that."

Eyeing him, put off by the interruption, and caring

not a whit for the boy's fatigue or the unmentionable behavior that caused it, the magus continues, "...the qualities and virtues of each of the planets and how each planet was created is the 'seminal principle' and a result of the Divine will. Mercury is not just a literary symbol for wisdom but in fact, *is* some echo, taste, and substance of God's creation of intelligence. Yea, each particular planet *is* the actual warehouse and nurse of different virtues. These be entitled the planets' *spiritus.* Twixt the *spiritus* of a planet and each man's soul runs an effluvium, the *spiritus mundi,* a fluid of fine and sightless substance." Dee demonstrates setting Will's pliable hand over the candle to feel its flame. Will winces from the heat, and the magus waxes on, "The *spiritus mundi* is very like the sightless stream of vapors of this flame that conducts the *spiritus* of the candle's heat to your sense of it. Moreover, harmonizing with a planet's *spiritus mundi* a soul may take possession of its innate *spiritus* and become elevated by its incandescence."

Barely awake, Will nods feigning to understand.

"The ancients divined that all the particulars of the *Book of Nature* (stones, plants, liquids) had in the days of Creation bathed in the *spiritus mundi* and separately learned their separate seminal particular principles. Therefore, to entice the *spiritus* of a planet to flow into something, a Natural philosopher has but to learn which things in Nature are infused with which planetary affinity."

Though in a fog, Shakespar dully grasps that this is his first lesson in Alchemy. *A study best fit for dead of night*, he opines.

"One has but to study the writings of the initiated adepts to learn which animals, plants, scents, metals, or colors can be used to draw the correct *spiritus* from the *spiritus mundi* and incorporate it into one's own being." Dee crosses to the basin and flicks water in his student's face. "To that end, one needs a receptacle to catch the *spiritus* and give it time to flow into one's soul, just as this room will capture and hold the warmth of a fire. This waxen image, by virtue of its figures and incantations, is especially receptive to the gifts of Mercury. As a spiritual medium, Virgo and its attendant symbols call forth Mercury's *spiritus* and send it on."

Sleep deprivation competes with Will's desire to know more and is winning. In this school of night, when fancies are set free, Will imagines he can actually see the talisman's *spiritus* radiating around it. "But the Lord God is—?" he asks dreamily.

"The Lord God is the supreme ruler of Heaven and Nature," the Doctor intones, "And I acknowledge no law nor lord but the holiest of holies. He is the wellspring of all, and I am but an earnest pilgrim who struggles to seek and master what is secret to most men." Attaching a small chain to the waxen image, the magus hangs it about Will's neck. Too tired to resist, Will objects weakly, holding it out from himself with mild apprehension. "It is yours," Dee says. "It will bring you the solitariness you need to concentrate on your studies, and the seminal influences will improve your memory and wit."

In Will's anesthetized state, dream and reality mix. He cannot be sure, but feels tingling at his chest as he lets the wax fall against himself. Regarding the scholar all in black, Will feels loving-kindness for the wizened old man. An exquisite peace tugs at Will's heart. In that warm room where his body and mind are overtaxed, Shakespar nestles toward his benefactor and finds him a support even as he falls fast asleep on his shoulder.

{ 10 }

In its last quarter, the stark half moon wanes in the nocturnal sky, willing the insubstantial clouds to conceal her and her starry retinue. As the travelers approach *The Rachel's* mooring, they confront an ant's hill of activity. At this early hour, provisions are loaded for the voyage. Sailors roll six barrels of freshwater aboard while others count casks of imported salt beef and mutton as they are wheel-barrowed up the bowing planks and onto the main deck. Supplies of biscuits and salt fish follow. At dizzying heights among the shrouds, bearded men are stirring in the standing rigging, testing the seams strength of sails and weaving the lines to the forestay. These are Luna's minions, preparing for any eventuality, toiling under the moon's influence while others sleep.

From the docks, local carters and dock workers heave the chests packed at Mortlake up to waiting hands on deck. As Will and Dee start up the gangway, Will overhears unguarded grumblings and feels wrenching dread. It is obvious the ship's crew is none-too-happy about the extra labors and the strangers on their ship. Less than ten feet from England's shore and Shakespar is affrighted.

The faint moonglow reveals little, yet with trepidation Will watches hefty hempen ropes slithering around him at his feet. Looping in countless puddles about the deck, their moving coils threaten to snatch him. Players' backstage have their backs broken when—*halyard ho!*—they are yanked suddenly upward by being in the wrong place at the wrong time. Under his feet, the deck lurches suddenly, propelled by the wake of ships careening nearby. Startled, the sleep-deprived youth nearly drops the lantern, scolding himself for nearly setting the ship afire. Stabilizing himself against a bulkhead, Will scans the length of the small ship disappointed the ocean vessel is not more capacious, more capable of withstanding adverse weather. He never liked boats, not even the little skiffs that carelessly waft up and down the Avon. The *Swan* is fond of swimming in the river, but he cannot fathom how ships stay afloat. It is a troubling thought to drown, to gasp for air and find none. Belching up life in the icy waters of the English Channel or gnawed by leviathans of the deep is a thought too, too horrible.

Alert to the ominous, he sees his employer ahead of him loitering about unconcerned and sure-footed in the dark. Cannot his master perceive the dangers? *Should I warn him?*

"Master Dee, I would not have you think me cowardly or effeminate," ventures Shakespar, "...but what if a storm arises and we Christians are drowned for the sins of the Hebrews' sinning forefathers? I was warned of such last night."

In the wan moonlight, the sharp-eyed magus

assesses the boy's state.

"Lay by your fears, lad!" Dee reminds, "I have studied my astrological charts. That is why we leave today." The boy is still faint-hearted. "Confidence is needed. Make it your byword not only for your writing but for peace of mind as we travel abroad."

Another unsettling wake and the ship tilts again. Will clenches at what seems to him another warning omen. *A man in the wrong box never thrives.*

"Be not dismayed. Why look you, her poop and forecastle rise like twin ramparts—a floating castle," assures Dee. "Use your eyes and look up, there is no haze about the *demilune.*"

"Courage man, she is all of well-seasoned oak *and* near seventy tons!" brags Captain Pallache, clapping Will hard on the back as he passes toward the stern, "She has weathered many a tempest and is as yare and bravely rigged as when she first put out to sea."

More is needed. Trying to distract the breathless boy, Dee points to his left. "This boat there nigh us is of the Dutch herring trade. Their vessel is smaller than ours, and they oft make this journey in safety."

"Speak to me not of the Dutch," replies Will. "They live in London in better ease and more freedom than those of us native-born to England. They are lice, a foreign commonwealth feeding off our body, stealing our provender and employment in the City as well as pushing good Englishmen from their homes. Fie upon them."

If Hollanders disquiet Shakespar, the presence of swarthy Jews scuttling is much more forbidding. Every man's prejudices are shaped by general opinion and that has done its worst to Will. Every prophecy and malefaction whispered in his ear last night echoes in his thoughts, including that of the biblical Rachel losing all her children. Shakespar is further unmanned by the crews' curved daggers openly displayed at their sides. The thought of a single Israelite in a room full of Englishmen had intrigued the Midland boy's fancy. Now being outnumbered by a score of anti-Christs in the pitch dark is terrifying horror. What if they have more lethal knives for butchery concealed among the folds of their billowing robes? *What a fool you are,* he upbraids himself, *You should have swiped the porter of hellgate's sword from the theater.*

Low and confidential, Will is urgent. "Master, it is madness to entrust these infidels with our lives."

John Dee sees Will's face change and hears the boy's warnings, but remains as fixed in his resolution as the stars he studies.

"Hast not seen such men before?"

"No," the young Christian whimpers, "Nor never hope to again in all my time to come." He dares not speak more against the infidels, lest they overhear.

"They are as anxious of your presence as thee by theirs. Remember your Bible. *Deuteronomy:* 'You shall also love the strange.'" Adjusting the chain that holds the new talisman around the boy's neck, Dee advises, "Have faith. I have labored in the reckoning. Good angels look after us. The captain is lord over this vessel and an honorable man. Do not kneel to baseless fear." Shakespar wills himself to nod in agreement. "Good.

Now, I must attend to other duties. Be of good faith, boy, this day shall pass safely. You have my oath on it."

Without another word, the skull-capped man with his lantern disappears down the dark ladder to meet what fate has in store for him below decks. Will turns to face gibbering, mangy rogues and vows to give them look-for-look no matter how blood-thirsty their stares. Be steadfast, he thinks, constant... a line is yanked upwards... and stay observant. Feeling for Dee's protective medallion around his neck, Will steels himself. *Readiness is all.*

By half five that morning, the *Rachel's* boatswain gives a warning for all work to cease and the crew to come aboard.

Twenty minutes before sunrise, Pallache orders Dee and his servant—for so Pallache thinks of Shakespar—to the quarterdeck, pointing at the sky and demanding of the astrologer what intelligence he has regarding the cosmology of the heavens.

"Goodman Dee, I was well contented with our talk last night. But see, here above the rigging is the immense bowl of the firmament. I know you to be a great scholar of the arcane arts. Pleasure me with your points of science, as you call them." If Captain Pallache had seemed diffident on land, he is lordly on *The Rachel* where he is absolute master and free of the world's contempt for his people. Gone are the downcast eyes, the yellow hat, and the abject voice. "Doctor, I demand to be told what Fortune holds for the Dutch. I have studied *Kabala*, and know the properties of the seven planets and the twelve signs of the zodiac. But insights from you, the renowned astrologer Dr. Dee, have military significance. William the Silent, Prince of Orange, will pay handsomely for such in his war against the Spanish."

The request is understandable, thinks the Natural Philosopher. Favor from great ones, once achieved, must, like a garden plant, be nurtured and watered or it will wither. No fool, Samuel knows to take advantage of what Fortune gives him.

"Gramercy, good *senior*. How shall I begin?" He looks around and points to the ship's wheel, saying, "The night sky is like to that wheel. Round and spoked. There are twelve spokes to the wheel of the night sky, and that wheel we do call the zodiac—"

"Goodman Dee, mind you, I am no child. I have told you, I am well-schooled in the stars of the zodiac. What I seek are the influences their wanderings foretell."

Being in this man's care for twenty-four hours, it is best to accommodate.

Gathering his woolen cloak around him against the nipping frost, Dee apologizes, "I crave your pardon, Captain, forgive my nature for I am ever the pedant. It is a weakness in me, and oft our faults are to ourselves unjust." Dee beckons Pallache to follow him to the wheel. Will shadows them. "Are you familiar with the zodiac's polarity?"

"Aye, that I am, Doctor." With weariness, he recites, much to Shakespar's interest, "Polarity being the signs in opposition on the astral map."

"Good!" says Doctor Dee brightly, but is quickly scowled at by the captain for his preciousness. "Beg pardon," he looks to Heaven to avoid the Semite's scorn.

"And, are you equally familiar with the zodiac's *quadruplicity*, Captain Pallache?" This time Dee is greeted with a blank look. Dee reiterates, this time in Spanish, then Dutch.

"S'death goodman Dee, I know the word, but not its meaning in this present context."

"Then, Captain, imagine a perfect square placed on this perfect circle, allowing for three *quad...*" Dee speaks the word slowly to emphasize the Latin syllables, "*ru... plicities.*" Using his hands and arms to form a box, he continues, "These four points influence *cardinal* qualities." Rearranging his *box* to lie differently on the wheel, he says, "These four *mutable.*" Again he rotates the *box*. "And these four *fixed.*"

Pallache nods in understanding. Eager to discover how to read the future, Shakespar inches forward onto the open deck, all ears, despite the damp and rheumy air.

"Now," continues Dee, "superimpose over the square a perfect equal-sided triangle. This arranges the zodiac signs into four groups." Again he demonstrates the relationships by imaginarily connecting three points on the circle. "Each of these groups of three is called a *trigon* and is influenced by the elements of earth, air, water, or fire." Dee stops to let his listeners ask questions. None come. His words hang as puffs of air as he plunges on, setting the stage for his most cherished discovery. "Fours and threes, gentles. Fours and threes are Heaven's divine integers. Every twenty years, Saturn and Jupiter line up with each other. And each time they do so, it is in a different astrological sign. And for two hundred years, they have continued to do so, and they will do so in the same trigon." Again drawing the imaginary triangle over the wheel, he excitedly shares, "These two-hundred years is an *epoch*. As the new *epoch* commences, this relationship of the two major planets—or copulation as we nominate it—takes place in a sign that is in a new *trigon*. This being the first week of January 1584 in the English Queen's calendar—or ten days prior in late December of 1583 on the Julian in your home in Antwerp—calculations show that by the end of April of the Julian calendar, the planetary copulation will manifest itself in the last phase of Pisces, the final sign of the *trigon* ruled by water."

Out of nowhere, a monstrous creature slithers like a snake down a hawser from aloft with the end of a rope held tightly in his teeth. He grins dreadfully—rope and all—at the faint-hearted young seafarer and then secures the end around a pin attached to the taffrail on the leeward side.

"Why say you Julian calendar?"

"Because good Captain Pallache, Englishmen have foolishly not adopted your European calendar of Pope Gregory XIII, which wisely lags ten days behind ours. For the English, it is beyond New Years, and..." Pointing east, he continues, "...but in truth, according to the stars, for your friends in the Low Countries, Poland, today's destination, it is Christmas."

Will is taken by surprise. "Christmas has come twice this year!"

Neither the child born in Nazareth nor its celebration holds sway over Pallache. "Good Doctor, please continue."

The ship oscillates.

"...As that date fades into the past, so fades that watery *trigon's* influence and all the world shall then be subject to the choleric upheavals of fire."

"I tell thee again I am no schoolboy, *senior* Dee. I have no time for these quillets. Be blunt man. We stand upon the swell of a full tide! I know you can see into the nature of things. Come to what is important for Prince William of Orange. How will go the war with Spain?"

Two sailors follow each other up a rope ladder to man the masthead and disappear into the rigging.

Dee lays his hand to his breast again, begging forgiveness. Crinkling his nose and with his palm rubbing the back of his neck, as tired as he is and despite the cold, he endeavors to share what he has gleaned. "The end of any *trigon* has always brought momentous times, but a *trigon* of fire connotes a wondrous chaotic upheaval. New nations shall arise, and they shall be sustained in violence."

As if on cue, the ship yaws precariously starboard. Dee catches hold of the nearby wooden tabernacle surrounding the main mast to steady himself. Now with an intensity that seems to warm the air around him, he concludes, "In five years' time, the world will see an end of days, and the new *epoch* will be an *epoch* of peace with all nations and religions living in brotherhood." His listeners are transfixed by the extraordinary revelation. "A glorious period arising like the Phoenix that will flourish for two hundred years and more." With great pride streaming from his sleepless eyes, he swears

Elizabeth will become the "Sovereign of Europe," resolving all religious intolerance in the Christian and non-Christian world. Viewing himself a genuine prophet, he beams at Pallache. "And from this wondrous event, as I foretold you, the Hebrews will no longer be persecuted."

A wheelbarrow is noticed by one of the ox-like crew. He hoists it to his shoulder, marches port side, and heaves the contraption onto the wharf below. It thumps against the hull as it falls.

Pallache paying *no-nevermind* to the clatter, asks, "What of Orange? What holds it for him?"

"As Elizabeth, *Gloriana*, is already allied to William, the Prince of Orange, it follows that He will surely share in the *Pax Britannica*."

The Captain grimaces or perhaps after years at sea and squinting at the sun the muscles around his eyes have formed a perpetual scowl on his face. Like *all shamans*, thinks Captain Pallache, suspicious of any prediction, *full of riddles of vague prophecies and shallow abstractions*. Still, Pallache will share this hopeful prognostication with the Prince in Amsterdam, being a good omen for the fledgling Dutch State's General and signifying survival over the forces of the encroaching Spaniards. He gives the star-reader a feeble smile. It is Dr. Dee's only reward for services rendered.

William of Stratford is less enthusiastic, concerned that his peaceful youth will now be at an end, his life's ambitions mocked by a cataclysm. Worse, might not *The Rachel* indeed cry for her lost children soon? A fiery *trigon* only conjures associations with a fiery dragon.

And, despite his birthday, he knows he is no Saint George and swordless to boot.

The sky lightens with the dawn. Sailors cast cables to the wharf below. Two sinewy men fetch ratchets to turn the capstan and weigh anchor. A third, the cabin boy, a lad of the Levant who has been sent for orders about casting off, dares interrupt.

The captain spits, "Dog, have you not eyes? Hold your tongue when I am in conference? Be off with you!"

"Captain Pallache, I—" With that, Pallache throws a stave at the menial even as he turns back to his passenger in a gentler tone, "I am right glad of your words for the Jews and the Gentiles, Doctor. But I would know more. What particulars do your astrological charts say will specifically benefit the new Dutch Republic?"

"That precise information would require an astronomical map of meticulous exactness. We call it a questionary horoscope. They are outlawed here in England, perhaps even in Amsterdam."

"Might you do it Doctor when we are upon seas where there are no man's laws?"

Disheartened his prophesy has not caused more excitement yet unwilling to show obvious disappointment, the natural philosopher wraps himself in the folds of his cloak. "Upon my word, you are a clever, Captain Pallache. No wonder Orange trusts you." Grandly, Pallache accepts the compliment. "I find you a worthy man and an honorable. I will endeavor to share such intelligence ere we set foot in Illyria."

Illyria? So, thinks Will, *that is the name of the spit of land we journey to*. Dee had not even told him that.

It doesn't sound English. He is about to ask after details when a portside hatch slams open. Will leaps away like a frightened sheep. A sunken-eyed bearded walrus of a man glances at him with contempt then scans the quarterdeck.

"Reverend sir, tell me what articles are needed. You shall be granted aught that is required," promises Pallache.

"Heavenly music," murmurs the graybeard, as he grips the main mast. "Can you hear it?"

Not amused, the Captain swivels his head, "*Doctore,* I hear naught and naught but the lark would sing at this hour. Again, I ask what necessaries are needed for your questionary?"

Hearing only the sweet clamor in his ears, Dee continues, "It is the most heavenly sound. A rich and lulling harmony. It bids me listen..." His eyes flutter and his arms begin to undulate up and down beating the air like a heron flying off from a lake. "...and I fain would ...." Even as he stands upright, Dee's head and arms drop. Rigid against the mast's tabernacle, he drops into a trance. Shakespar's eyes widen in wonder as his master's voice modulates queerly, "Good Samuel... hold acquaintance with the waves... and deliver the unstrung viol that is lost and shipwrecked from itself. One face, one voice, one habit, yet divided. Rescue the deceitful maid and perish the man. How this may be and yet in two, as you will speed, preserve it you."

In the rosy light of that winter morn, John Dee breathes peacefully, his chest barely rising and falling as some celestial wonder breathes intelligence through him. His face softens with the lilting cadence of his words; his usual sternness dissipates.

"*One face, one voice, one habit, yet divided?*" puzzles the Moroccan.

Will stammers, "This is a strange transformation. Have you ever seen or heard the like?" He fears that Dee is bewitched. *Cuthbert was right—Jews, astrology, men speaking devilish gibberish. This infernal ship is damned and fated to drown us all.* He catches sight of the sullen-eyed mariner pointedly glaring at him. Fearing the ogre will lay hands on him, Will cranes his head, seeking a way to wiggle out of this demonianism.

A hint of morning light betrays panic in the boy's eyes. Samuel Pallache stays him in a vise-clutch before he can flee. Fearing one Semite and now held captive by another, Will is forced to become as docile as gelatin. Turning back to the possessed, *The Rachel's* master gently prods that which speaks through Dee. "What significance is this to me?"

"Your noble help will serve a noble spirit." After a pause, the voice softly intones further, "Though your name be lost, your action will n'er be forgotten."

Ire rises in the captain's voice, "What say you? Serve a spirit? What means thee?" Pallache is genuinely puzzled.

Will touches his master's arm; it is cold as death. "Good sir, are you in pain?"

"He who abideth with you," the other-worldly voice advises the captain.

The old tar barks out a skeptical roar of laughter.

"Do not vex him, Captain sir, my master is

entranced... or the like," Will cautions, now believes the heretofore unbelievable.

Pallache guffaws, delighted with the strange play before him. Had he not already pocketed their convoy payment, he would have taken them both for rogues.

"There is no noble spirit that dwells with me. My lads are good and able, but there is naught that is noble about them."

Mustering courage, Will tells himself, *Never mind childish fears.* He asks his benefactor, "And what for me, good master? Shall I prosper?" As the day's light quickens banishing the night, Will is aware that much of the activity aboard has ceased as those above decks stare at them as confounded as he is.

"By how much the heavens excel the earth," the alien voice tapers to a whisper from the necromancer's lips, "...so much doth what is given thee from above excel all earthly treasure. The best of you is diligence. Work, rework, work, rework, work, rework..."

"*Heyday*, another riddle?" Non-believer, Samuel Pallache, shakes his head in derision while appraising the old man's face.

Samuel's raucous laughter penetrates Dee's awareness, and, through his nose, he breathes in a lungful of frosty air as if he had breached the surface of the ocean after nearly drowning. Dazed, the necromancer's knees buckle and he sinks to the deck.

"You should distrust your informer, whether angel or devil," Captain Pallache jests at the inexplicable, "He is woefully ignorant of my affairs."

Shivering, weak, in recovery, the aged philosopher

informs, "You would not be such a scoffer if you knew that I have it from the Holy Spirit." Barely able to lift his arm, John Dee indicates the sky brightening with the dawn. "The Word of God is living and powerful." His arm and his voice drops. "I am a sometime messenger of Heaven and but pass on that which I am bidden."

Another laugh, this time not so disdainful. "Bidden? Like Moses or Elijah?" The haughty sailor snorts, his eyebrows furrow. Pallache knows not whether to give the prophecy some credence. He has seen mountebanks who professed communication with spirits. As well, he has witnessed the like from holy rabbis who, after giving their lives to studying the doctrinal books of the Torah, were reputed to commune with the patriarchs. He thinks back on what was foretold: *a sea rescue*. Plausible. Better to keep an open mind with the infamous, and learned Dr. John Dee. If nothing else, it will be a beguiling anecdote to amuse the Prince of Orange.

"You are fortunate," Gathering strength, Dee continues, "the Word is not given to me often. Heaven must desire you to be forewarned. Surely a future or past charity of yours is pleasing unto Heaven."

"*The Word*?" whispers Will Shakespar, who, tutored by a rational world, knows not what to make of such an irrational morning? *How can this be?*

"Strange your herald angel did not speak to me in either Hebrew or Arabic? My mother tongues," hoots the captain. The perplexed crew is reassured by their Captain's good *humour*. The old doctor seems to be doing better. Reminded of their departure by the rising sun, they return to their respective nautical duties.

The morning's chill revives the scholar and he reaches for Will's arm and stands erect before answering Pallache, "Aye, that is most strange. Yet, when the music comes, music heard so deeply that it is not heard at all; I see their thoughts—not see *per se*—my imagination senses a presence, and, loosing all my vigor, they speak through me to others, betimes in a foreign language. You are in the right, it is most strange to have been delivered to you in English." Looking at Will, he poses, "Perhaps, celestial powers meant for Will to partake of the Word as well and therefore in his tongue." Both of Dee's listeners have the same thought, *the man must be mad.*

"Hebrew?" The player questions doubtfully, "Can you speak Hebrew?"

"Hush, no one bid you speak," says the permanent scowl.

Despite the reprimand, Will pushes to know more, "Where did you study it, Doctor Dee?"

"In Antwerp... with a rabbi. But, Will, that must remain our secret." Pointing at a flickering lantern, Dee fixes an unwavering eye on his Doubting Thomas of a captain. "As all things on Earth have an affinity with their correlatives in the heavens, so might this little flame share knowledge with the Divine fires above us in the skies. I tell you plain, the everlasting flame within us that is our soul does share with God, who, you know, is all fire."

There is a silence as both listeners contemplate this inexplicable man. Pallache had heard of European Christians studying the holiest of holies, but never with a Jewish rabbi. He thinks of what monumental daring that was against social norms, and the commitment needed. Such a man, daring a thousand devils, might indeed be conversant with angels. Who was this old man with the triangular gray beard and deep searching brown eyes? What matter of men were these English? Perhaps, they are not the obese mindless eaters of mutton that he had always believed them to be.

Mystified, Will's scarf slips absently to the deck. "But, the Church teaches that the divine language of angels was lost to the world when Adam fell. How is it that you can understand what they say?"

Noting the utter confusion in the young boy's face, Dee stoops shakily to fetch the dropped scarf and gently winds it about the boy's naked neck. "They speak to me as they did to our father, Adam, in visions rather than speech."

"Do they not speak in the chosen tongue of Hebrew?" demands Pallache.

"You mistake me. Not in the vulgar Hebrew of your nation, but the celestial speech of paradise. If our heavenly father created this majestic existence with the Word or what we natural philosophers nominate as celestial speech, it is the beginning of all things. Then, must a god-fearing and thorough scholar endeavor to understand the Word, to enrich his enlightenment and guide others to theirs."

"Understand the Word?" Will struggles, lost in doubts. Though he is not religious, this is near heretical. "Why waste time pursuing what cannot be known? You cannot know God's mind."

"Because our souls cry out for it," interjects Pallache

sourly at Dee's servant and then shoves him toward the taffrail in irritation. His perpetual scowl deepens.

"But, it is forbidden," comes Will's weak response.

Pallache isn't so sure the impertinent young rascal is wrong. Still, he is very certain the boy needs another lesson—respect for his elders. He seizes and twists the boy's scarf.

"Leave off. Let the boy be." John stays his hand.

Bewildered, Pallache loosens his grip on the upstart.

The graybeard wraps a protective arm around the boy's hunched shoulders. "I swear to you by the living God and by my hopes for eternal salvation that I have ever practiced *magia naturalis,* natural magic which is not forbidden. I revile the diabolical, and reverently confine myself only with *spiritus mundi* and the wisdom of the ancients who discovered the sympathy between the divine and earthly worlds through the right use of prayer. In the hands of sanctified adepts, it is the pathway to universal learning."

"If you say so, master." He pulls his wool cap down around his ears.

Sensing his charge's doubt, Dee lifts his hand from Will's shoulder and kindly cups his mistrusting face, "I am drawn to the unknowable as I am drawn to food and drink. Unlike the beasts of the field, the Lord gave us rational minds and free will to piece out *this,* His creation."

"Do you really believe in what you say, sir?" The question seems a simple one to Shakespar. It is given with such heart-wringing dismay, the philosopher drops his hand, startled.

"Aye..." John looks out at the rising sun. "I am as certain of that as I am of the coming of this new day. The Bible speaks of angels. And I tell thee, they have made themselves known to me."

Pallache nods to the men at the windlass, as the anchor is winched up.

"Then, must I believe," says the boy with a servile tone and turns his face away.

At the helm with many men about him, Captain Pallache informs the pilot of the change of course to Illyria, which he hopes to make by late afternoon.

As the island is situated off the coast of Catholic France, it resides in dangerous waters for a vessel sailing under the Protestant Dutch flag. Hence, lookouts are trebled to scout for enemy ensigns. Sailors grumble. The Captain promises his men to be back in Antwerp's safe haven by the following night. To further mitigate the nuisance, he promises a tankard of rum and a guilder to each of his men after they have safely left Illyria behind. Though this raises a massive cheer, Will spies several men standing mute, critically apprizing their English cargo. As the *The Rachel* leaves port toward Illyria, Shakespar wonders, *With what riotous madness have I entangled myself?*

{ 11 }

December 25, 1583 of Illyria's Gregorian calendar
January 6, 1584 Queen Elizabeth's calendar

Westerly winds delay *The Rachel*. It is late sunset when Captain Pallache first sights Illyria from the quarterdeck. Even at this distance, the island twinkles in and out of reality in the crepuscular light. The shoreline, the color of faded ink, is as thin as a reed. Still, its nascent presence assures Will that his nautical ordeal is nearly over. Yet knowing little more than that Dee has come for intelligence on the island—and having lived in London long enough to know what horrors are reserved for those found to be intelligencers—bile churns in Shakespar's stomach. *What shall I do in Illyria?* He broods, nauseous once again. *So, this spit of green mirage is to be my home for a month or two before we set sail for Krakow? It will have to do.*

Pallache has given orders to *not* light lanterns lest their approach be conspicuous. A ship of Jews is not an everyday occurrence, especially flying under the Dutch flag. Dutch pirates who style themselves as the Sea Beggars and are Netherland nationalists have grown in power and audacity, and *The Rachel* must make every effort to *not* be mistaken for them.

Dee is eager for an opportunity to observe the thoroughness of the harbor officials. He needs to evaluate with his own eyes how easy it is for ships to dock, unload cargo, and head back to sea. Inconsequential Illyria, an English possession since the victorious wars of Henry V, is pivotal to English military strategy to keep a tenuous grasp on a Channel outpost. Despite English dominion, Illyria is culturally French. English may be spoken at Court, but French is the *lingua franca* in Illyrian homes. Parisian influence is evident in the architecture, as well as clothing, the calendar, and manners of the populace—mostly Catholic and Vatican-centric. Over the past fifty years, a growing number of Huguenots and Puritans, sons and grandsons of immigrants, mingle warily with the island's ancient families. Orsino's father and his people chafed at the Protestant changeover by Elizabeth from Mary's Catholicism, but as long as the government at Whitehall gives them freedom to celebrate Mass and observe their Saints days, Illyria remains begrudging loyal to London. Though the *Act of Uniformity* insists that all Englishmen must monthly take part in Protestant services, no one on the island expects this law to be as rigorously enforced as it is at London's St. Paul's. In Illyria as in many areas in England, there are those who think the Pope's excommunication of Henry's illegitimate, some say incestuous, daughter Elizabeth, has given them the moral obligation to wish her dead.

Below decks, Pallache's crewmen devour their

evening meal with gusto. The celebratory laughter of men ripples through the ship, excited at being only one day or two away from their families after months at sea—though some gripe about the present delay. Ever a sad brow, Pallache will have none of the ribaldries and goes above to converse with his distinguished passenger. Questions regarding this morning's manifestations still hang in the air, but hospitality must take precedence. He offers Dee a cup of Madeira. Nothing is brought for the young secretary who sulks a little way off, scarcely penetrating the Captain's notice.

The distant isle grows more substantial on the horizon. "*This*," Pallache intones theatrically, "...is Illyria." He hands Dee the pewter cup, and the pensive scholar is glad to have it. "You begin your new life here, no? You meet the noble vizier?"

Expressionless, Dee gazes at the blinking lights on shore. Savoring the Spanish wine, he says nothing.

Understanding the man's abstraction, Samuel continues confidentially, "Orsino, I have heard him named. No longer a bachelor, *eh*?"

"Nay, not anymore," Dee offers, "He has been husbanded these two years to a niece of the French *Duc*. She is a de Guise, a prominent family of Catholic zealots who like not—" About to say more, Dee catches himself and changes the subject. "Elizabeth, Our Royal Majesty and Her Royal Highness' Most Honourable Privy Council were sore vexed at Orsino's betrothal. But this island's proximity to Calais—ever within arm's length of Catholic Europe—compelled Our Queen to curtsey to the Count's infatuation, and, thus, She gave Her blessing." With the drink or the company loosening his tongue, Dee glances back over his shoulder to Samuel and adds, "Belike at the time, Our Bess, too taken up with Her favorite Leicester's betrayal of Her with his secret marriage to the Lady Essex, could give a tinker's-dam about Orsino."

"The Count's French bride is reputedly fair, and I'm told her husband dotes on her," Pallache notes.

Dee gestures toward the island. "We are to present the newlyweds with Christmas gifts from Her Royal Highness in a show of Her Highness' love." Dee fixes on his drink. Turning back, he salutes the island with his cup before drinking deep. "May their union be blessed in Heaven's eyes." Wiping whatever liquid has dripped onto his chin hairs, his eyes wander, then John Dee further confides, "We will make ourselves known to Orsino tomorrow..." adding obliquely, "If he will have us."

"But you do embassy for Your Queen. Must he not give you audience?"

"Orsino is reputed to have a dark *humour* and fits of choler disquiet him. My coming has been kept a secret from him. I am uncertain why," Dee lies reluctantly. "Out of displeasure, he may not welcome me tomorrow and could make me rather cool my heels for a fortnight... or longer. A longer stay will keep me from my appointments in Krakow. The time I would not lose while more important matters wait at home. As you know, I have a child on the way." There is a look of sadness chased by one of entreaty. "As my stay here is meant to be short and quick..." He steps closer to the

Captain. "...and for secret political reasons, I ask you to keep your oath to me and utter not a syllable of this to others, not even your Prince."

"Upon the *Pentateuch*, the Torah scrolls, you have my word."

Dee turns back with a smile. "*Toe-dah,* good Captain."

Pallache confirms the delicacy of their position with a nod.

"Your kindness shall hold sway in my memory. I am forever in your debt, Pallache."

"And I in yours. Both for giving me your respect and the gift of the questionary that I will render unto Orange." In thanks, the burly seafarer kisses Dee's palms, again repeating proudly, "The honor is mine to converse with such a renowned guest."

Much civility is expressed on both sides, some even heartfelt. But the Mediterranean will not be so discourteous as to allow this venerable guest to disembark empty-handed. Leaving the weather deck, he goes below to retrieve a gift from his cabin. Returning, Captain Pallache presents John Dee with a well-worn volume bound in Moroccan leather, a collection of lectures given by Moses ben Jacob Cordovero. Dr. Dee, ceremoniously and with great reverence, reads the yellowed title page of the book.

"*Pardes Rimonim.*"

"It is Hebrew. It means—"

"I know, Captain Pallache: *the orchard of pomegranates.*"

"Do you know of it?"

Dee nods. Not for the first time, Pallache acknowledges to himself the philosopher's extensive erudition.

Dee calls to Shakespar, knowing the boy will be unfamiliar with the revered text.

"This is the lofty compilation of all Kabalistic philosophy," the scholar explains.

"*Caba, caba* ...what?" The boy's ignorance is to be expected

"In Judaism, it is as prized as highly as our Christian *Book of Hours*."

Opening the old text, the Englishman again gives the Captain thanks in Hebrew, "*Toe-dah*." Even as his fingers trace lines of sacred aphorisms, Dee continues, "You have touched me deeply, to the depth of my thanks with this." Closing the book, he cavils, "It is a treasure I am loath to accept. It is too precious, too dear."

"You will not deny me," insists Samuel Pallache. "Knowing its worth, it pleases me that you should have it. Is it not your old English saw that 'to get is the gift of Fortune, to keep the gift of wisdom'? I'll brook no denay."

To decline would be an insult to both Pallache and his culture; Dee dares not refuse. Moreover, having spent a lifetime collecting such old rarities, the bibliophile would never allow hollow courtesy to keep him from so precious a collectible and, thus, he takes it with humility. "But where found you this?"

"My brother's offering, when we first set sail. Since our parting last June, it has lain by my pillow, watching over me these many months. So now, I bequeath it to your safekeeping in the surety that it will look after your journey."

Touched by the offering first given by a brother, a discernible tension plays in the corners of the philosopher's eyes. Leaning forward, Dee ceremoniously kisses the Moroccan on both cheeks in thanksgiving and respect.

"I will be your book bearer, then, and its abiding with me will be a continual reminder of the friendship of its giver. I praise God for you."

Within the hour, evening breezes blow *The Rachel* into St. Peter Port. Alerted of its arrival, Illyria's harbormaster—his Christmas dinner interrupted—descends grumpily to the wharf to document the boat's purpose and cargo. Fully prepared, Dee presents the Royal Passports given him by Walsingham, allowing him and the boy passage beyond the English mainland, mandatory documents for all English travelers for the past twelve years.

"No need!" The harbormaster waves away documents as if it had been froth on a head of beer tankard. "Illyria is within Britain's boundaries. Such niceties are not required here." This *blasé* attitude troubles Dee's sense of protocol; the bear of a man cares little for fine points. "Welcome, friends! Now, let us dispense with little nothings and finish up." He bellows at the mariners unloading Dee's baggage, "My joint of meat grows cold at the tavern." But there is no hurrying them. With each objectionable minute, the maritime official grows more irritated at the meticulous unloading of worthless cases of books for an old man and a boy.

Finally, he erupts, "I have not time for this. Jesu! It's Christmastide!"

Defying protocol, the beefeater poses no further inquiries as to cargo. Instead, the pier rattles as the big man stomps up the stair only to shout back at a scruffy carter who looks for trade, "Lock up after!" For all to hear, he yells, "And take our heathen visitors to the *Cubiculo*. Bad luck to them for ruining my holiday."

Arriving at the harbor's one inn, the *Cubiculo*, Dee proffers his Royal licenses for travel, the innkeeper reaffirms—albeit in a manner gentler than the harbormaster's—that papers are not required.

"After all, am I not the best judge of character on the island?"

Not giving away any of his vexation, Dee acknowledges his avowal and his courtesy, "*Merci, Monsieur.*" He wonders if a Spaniard with graft or a renegade Roman Catholic priest might not be equally judged and welcomed.

In the room he shares with Will, Dr. Dee encodes his first day's entry in his diary: "*St. Peter Port is as porous as a sieve. If a ship of Jews can come and go without provoking so much as a bored grunt, cannot a ship of recusants and traitors be harbored as easily?*" As he finishes encoding the names of those he's dealt with as well as his expenses, he ends with a postscript: "*The old fox might be right.*" This fool's errand may be more legitimate than he imagined. In no mood for Will's incessant questions, Dee blows out the candle. As he falls asleep, he pictures Jane in her sixth month and prays she is having an easy time of it. In unfamiliar beds—Dee in a straw one, Shakespar in a hard cot by the door—they sleep soundly throughout the night.

The bells of St. Peter Port peal at six o'clock in the morning, calling for the *Prime* canonical prayer. Heralded by the aroma of porridge, eggs, and frying fish, a new day dawns. In that shadowy transition from sleep, Shakespar imagines he is still in bed in familiar Eastcheap. Hearing his master's knees thumping softly to the pine-timbered floor, Shakespar is rudely reminded that this is not the case. By cocklight, he tells himself that he is now a changeling, ferried away to someone else's bed, to act in someone else's story.

Fingers steepled and undeterred by the floor's chill, John Dee prays in silence for guidance and success in the days ahead. Praising Heaven's glories, the wayfarer asks the Lord to watch over his family and all he has left behind. Noticing the change in Will's breath, the penitent invites the boy to join him. Not having prayed since he abandoned Stratford, Will obeys. On his knees in this way, he is surprised to find comfort in the doing. Nostalgic words from his childhood return readily. They say the Lord's Prayer in unison.

Intending to meet that day with Count Orsino, the travelers dress carefully. Good first impressions are critical. Dee forswears his brown doublet for a black cloth gown adorned with a fur collar that signifies his authority as a scholar.

"May this appeal to the student in Orsino," he murmurs.

Catering to Orsino's predisposition, Dr. Dee hopes the Count will, in turn, show preference to the new Royal Postmaster. Dee dons thick woolen leggings in the likelihood of an ill-heated castle. Next, he slips into his elegant smooth-finish leather boots reserved for special holidays. Adjusting his beaver hat, the scholar studies himself in a mirror then turns his attention to Will's gaudy yellow doublet.

William Shakespar is as garish as Dee is formal.

"Have you no other," frowns the academic.

"None, sir. Does it not glimmer like gold?"

Walsingham's man frowns. *Orsino has a reputation for flamboyance.* Perhaps Will's *habiliment* will be admired. The boy, after all, is of marginal importance to the mission and the lad has no other. Will's black ringlets, however, require correction. Out comes the brush. Superstition remains universal; when elves tangle hair by dead of night, adversity ensues by day. Grooming finished.

"Men's actions, Will, are the architects of their fortunes," advises Dee, attending his own long beard.

"If you deem it fitting, doctor..." Ever helpful, Shakespar reveals many blood red satin bits. "...might I tie off my hair with crimson ribbon? Gifted by a friend. French courtiers of the best rank and station wear these to much appreciation."

"Say you so?" Baffled, Dr. John Dee, master of mathematics, is wholly ignorant of Continental *couture.* Guided by the proverb that Fortune favors the bold, he gives his leave. "Then you shall dress yourself in them. But I shall bear an eye if any of the Count's retinue disdain your gorgeous attire. We come not today to be mocked but to be adjudicated as proper representatives of Her Royal Highness." Once again, he stares hard at Will's canary yellow doublet. "Have you no other but the yellow?"

"None. Have I not said?"

"Then it must serve. And those pretty gloves your father bequeathed you. They are sure to make a favorable impression."

Greasy smells of breakfast draw them downstairs. There, the porridge proves as watery as poor man's gruel, and the fried John Dory has a grey appearance. *Old oil.* The two travelers seize upon warm wedges of bread slathered with savory herb butter and cheese. Once sated, Dee is all advice as to how to behave when presented before the Court of Count Orsino. Patiently, Will harkens, recognizing Dee has no idea that Shakespar's fellow actors, members of Leicester's Men, have taught him more about courtly manners than the Natural Philosopher will ever know.

Sharp Channel wind buffets them just outside the large doors of the inn causing them to clutch at their hats and huddle in their cloaks. They press forth passed by wind-aided ducks gusting along, their palmate feet barely touching upon the hard earthen path that wends uphill to town. A commotion from four pigs penned nearby, catches Will's eye. Briefly he imagines huddling together with them, jibbering and snorting in protest against the weather's fierceness. Fruit trees fronting the houses along the road are as dull as the passing Illyrians. Unimpressed with the rural nature of this section of St. Peter Port, Will sniffs, "It's neither city nor town nor middling settlement. Here be only thatched barns and pelting shacks fit for the poorer sort."

"Nay, we are but in the suburbs, neither city nor town. Nor will the city be as populous, nor as ugly as London town. Have a care. We are guests here and must not appear arrogant toward this Commonwealth." Silently, Dee deplores the poverty. "Doubtless, the village will become goodlier as we approach the castle of Orsino. His residence is on highest ground, and there we shall discover what sort of governor he be—*Blast!*" Dee steps in manure.

"The ducks?" asks the young scamp referring to the gaggle ahead of them "What wager you, master?"

"Orsino is reputed..." Dee ignores the insouciant questions, attempting to rid his boot of shit. "...to be short of temper, and woe betides those unfortunates who do not acknowledge his prerogative. Justice in a small locality can be swift and cruel as an eagle's talon. Therefore, again I say, have a care about you, Will. We must be as deferential here as any courtier at Windsor who curries favor."

Giving up on his boot, Dee pulls his cloak about himself. They walk on.

"Fear not. I can force my soul to whatever stratagem occasion calls for, having played servile roles of deference afore now. We who tread the boards are always, of necessity, tactful."

"Then be so today," Dee commands. "Our future may

depend on it."

With that, the older man pulls his hat low on his head against the wind. He forces himself uphill along a roadway leading to St. Peter Port.

They reach the town that thrives below the castle. The high street of St. Peter Port, now bustles by full light. Purveyors of wares and food call out from their shoppes to solicit customers. Ironmongers' and ropers' merchandize is strung up or hangs on hooks from their carts and wagons. The stench of blood overpowers the salty air as fleshers butcher chickens and calves, while nearby, salters draw back the curtains on their spice racks and help sweeten the air.

A bleaker presence is a family, in mourning black, mounting the stair of the old city church. The father carries a small pine box fitted for a child and struggles to retain the traditional sprigs of bay that the strong gusts threaten to blow off the coffin. The mother weeps while her husband stops to retie the foliage and shifts the heavy burden to the other shoulder. The sight recalls to Will the distant memory of his mother's keening over the death of his infant sisters. Try as he might, he cannot remember their lost faces. Pausing in reverence, he sighs. John Dee, however, pushes on, heedless of human tragedy. In a world where so many babies die before their first birthday, a child's funeral is unremarkable to him. Already Dee is two decades older than the average Londoner.

Catching up dutifully, Shakespar, fears that a day started with a funeral cannot be the best of omens. *Surely, this superstitious carver of waxen talismans and straightener of my hair must know that.*

As they ascend the narrow cobblestone streets, the town clatter increases: worshipers off to church, seamen *en route* to the harbor, and tradesmen hocking them essential *mustneeds* before a long voyage to the Mediterranean or the Continent or Hispaniola. Cries of trade compete with thudding foot traffic. Will pauses to ask directions but cannot find a kind or friendly eye as the crowd streams uphill as if late to some festival or hanging. Moreover, the chatter in French dissuades him from making an inquiry. Self-conscious whenever an Illyrian stares at him, Shakespar is sure they know that he is a stranger and that his master is on a secret mission. Though truth be told, Dee has not informed Will of many details.

Often, with the wind full in their face, they double back to seek another route, thereby losing sight of their destination on the hill. Massive oak doors of large residences seem barricaded against them as if to say, "Foreigners must stay in the street—you have no friends here." Winding, undecipherable, foreign, foul-smelling, the unfamiliar streets weaken Shakespar's confidence. Back in London, the actor would swagger easily about, feeling at home. Here, in Illyria, *Swan* is lost, diminished to a child tagging along behind his dogged schoolmaster.

Still, the teenager can't help but be impressed by the old man's stamina and determination. The climb is not an easy one for the aged scholar. A horse and cart approaching from behind forces pedestrians to the walls. Yet to Dee, it is of no matter; one expects unplanned hindrances. "Neither carts nor cats ever thwarted a journey," declares the stalwart scholar.

"You *are* one for saws and aphorisms," murmurs the derogatory poet.

As Dee and Shakespar climb castle hill, the clogging traffic thickens. Just ahead, a Court musician of about twenty-two tries to shield his lute from the jostling crowd and the damp wind by nestling it inside his cloak. Despite the steep incline and the fact that the musician has already twice that week scaled this roadway seeking employment from Orsino's usher, he moves at a jaunty pace. Making his way, the lutenist babbles in English as if he were rehearsing his conversation with the heartless porter at the castle door. First, he must get past the porter to get to the usher. "Was it not just the celebration of the Immaculate Conception of the Blessed Virgin Mary? Why man that was eighteen long nights ago. Should not Our Lordship have a new song for his new wife *and* the birth of the Virgin's son?"

"Does not the change of dates strike you as wondrous strange, master?" asks Will.

"Strange it is that we English are so ignorant of celestial time. Here and in all Europe, as I have told you, it is eleven days earlier here than yesterday's departure from Gravesend. Yet, be assured the Europeans are in the right and we English—barren fools that we are—are not." How long and how emphatically Dee had argued the wisdom of the Gregorian calendar. "The stars have proved to me that the Pope is in the right, but the Puritans in Whitehall like naught from Catholic Rome. There are many asses in our nation who will not nor cannot trust in Science. Happily, Her Majesty yet weighs the change. We may live in hope."

"Changing the dates not to mention the celebration days would trouble my father. He and many like him would not countenance it, I can tell you that."

"The new papist calendar is a fact, a Mathematical and Astronomical fact." Dee mutters, "No matter what your father—or any other simpleton—may countenance."

Incoherently, the ambient din of townfolks' conversation swirls. "A thousand hopes you've given me that breed naught but the stool of a witch," and, "A hundred promises, and yet an infinite load of nothing but claptrap..." and, "...filthy worsted-stocking son of a bitch-wolf." The soliloquy of the adjacent lutenist is most discernible, "But that accursed fellow at the gate tells me Orsino is a solemn man and needs no ungodly playthings to waste his time. A pox on him. Why, all the world knows that the Count is as loving and as lovely a man as ever woman created, and a merry." A passerby hoots at that. In response, the lutenist thrusts his instrument toward the critic, and, plucking two strings, answers with a jarring discordant *plunk* in his direction. Undismayed, the musician continues his plea to the usher, "Indeed, just this past celebration of our Savior's birth, Count Orsino danced the night away—a fandango if memory serves—with his Parisian wife. I warrant the heat between her legs if put to good use would warm us all for a Norwegian winter." Here he elbows the striding Doctor John Dee who has made an assiduous effort to pass him. Winking at Dee, "And she is as pretty a piece of Eve's flesh as ever opened lips." Dee keeps his eyes averted, prompting the fool to turn his attention to the youth, who smiles at the bawdy humor as he walks along cheek by jowl. As he passes the monologist, Will can't help but drum a *rat-a-tat-tattoo* on the tabor drum, the Illyrian has slung around his neck and hangs at his back.

"Have a care boy, that is an heirloom."

"This..." He thumps the drum again. "...a pox on it. It is but a drum."

Playfully the drummer jests, "Go off. I discard you. Let me enjoy my private."

"Your private is too loud for the rest of us. Tell me, do you live by your tabor?"

"No sir," pointing down the hill, "I live by the harbor."

The lutenist cannot take his eyes off Will's expensive kid gloves. "A handsome pair of cheveril gauntlets my boy. Those must have cost your lover here a month's wages."

"Not from *him*," says Will, offhandedly gestures at Dee.

"Some other turtledove, per chance?" This conclusion is made with a smirk, then followed by a snigger.

Dee breaks his silence. "Come along, Will. And you, sirrah, we neither seek your company nor care to partake of your witless conversation. Save your reeking breath for toiling up this hill and spare our ears your naughty abuse." Dee lengthens his stride and, despite aching thighs, seeks to gallop away.

"*Pardonnez-moi.*" Mocks the musician shrugging.

He hugs his lute tighter, and gives others more space to grow the void between them. Will scurries to catch up with Dee while the musician's parting words carry to him on the wind: "This ancient scarecrow is as much contentious proud as that whoreson at the gate."

Soon, the wayfarers crest the hill and cross a broad bridge over a moat surrounding the castle. High stone walls separate the public area from the castle's inner grounds. The portcullis ahead defends the castle entrance. A crowd of men congregates on the moat's bridge in the shadow of the rusted barbican, prevailing upon the gatekeeper to allow them entrance to conduct business within. It is the last Monday of the month, the designated market day for the County's household to procure foodstuffs for the two-hundred-plus castle occupants and liveried servants. Some carry produce, others poultry, meats and eggs, and a few haul building materials. Others stand with sacks of barley or bushels of milled corn or wheat. Keen to market their goods within, the multitude of unruly farmers, poulterers, butchers, builders, and serving men shout their wares like roarers. Rarely does a single one of them catch the busy gateman's attention, and the trumpeting wind only adds to the pandemonium.

"Master Shakespar, your services are required." John Dee attempts to see over the crowd. "Please announce to yon gatekeeper that we are come from Her Majesty of England, seeking audience with his master, the Count Orsino, Her servant."

Bewildered how to do that, Will obeys with a begrudging and ironic, "But, of course, Doctor."

Aware of the sarcasm, the academic instructs, "You have talents, Shakespar. Use them." From his cloak, Dee produces folded parchment bearing the Royal Seal. "Make use of this."

From his employer's stern countenance, Will knows that further questions are pointless, and so, taking the document, he wades into the *mêlée*. But to no avail, being a head shorter than most of the crowd. The throng is not eager to let him pass. Merchants block him with backs and arms, thrusting him aside whenever the boy maneuvers too close. He persists, only to be pummeled by choice French words that would shame the rudest English street doxie. Luckily he understands little of the language. He takes consolation that a mob such as this in London would by now be brawling and hurling stones and gravel. Their swearing would be in choice Anglo-Saxon. Still, there is no lack of fist-shaking, shouting, calumny, and distemper amongst the Illyrian purveyors. Briefly, Will turns to see if Dee acknowledges the impossibility of this mission, but when the lad catches sight of him, Dee is obdurate—and worse, Will fears, disappointed in him.

The boy pushes one massive fellow a bit too hard and receives a ham-fisted thump to the top of his head that causes him to stagger, and then, nearly trampled, and without thinking, he finds himself announcing in an astonishing, theatrical voice:

By this my sword that conquered Persia,
Thy fall shall make me famous through the world.
I will not tell thee how I'll handle thee,

> *But every common soldier of my camp*
> *Shall smile to see thy miserable state.*

This piece from Marlowe's *Tamburlaine the Great* leaps out of Will as if some demi-god possessed him. *Why it?* Having no idea, Shakespar knows only that Burbage's son, Richard, bellowed it a dozen times in Will's presence. Those around him turn in amazement. Though in English, the words have rung with authority as if coming from a personage of rank and stature. Its very Englishness reminds the crowd of the aristocratic civility of the Court. Whatever the reason, the confused farmers and butchers step back from the strange creature with the yellow doublet, red hair ribbons, and fancy gloves. *Who is he? What is his business here?* Though amazed as they are, Will does not let the opportunity go unseconded, and he waves the parchment with its Royal ribbons and Privy Council seals as he proclaims further,

> *The god of war resigns his room to me,*
> *Meaning to make me general of the world.*
> *Wher'er I come the Fatal Sisters sweat,*
> *To do their ceaseless homage to my sword.*

He strikes an heroic pose, hands perched on hips; an argus of quizzical eyes fixes on him. Again, the young actor raises the parchment dramatically. It is a showy prop and further cows the crowd. The confused gatekeeper peeks his head out from the farmers and vendors. The beribboned document catches his eye; he beckons Shakespar to *come*. Instead, Shakespar, remains rooted where he stands as tall as he can make himself and solemn as his free arm extends to John Dee at the edge of the crowd.

"Come, sir," he calls, "take my arm. The bridge is yours."

Being offered the conquered castle, Dr. John Dee strides majestically forward. Those closest to the entrance are reluctant to give way to an old man and a youth who have neither coach nor horse—fancy scroll, or no. Still, they dare not deny access to their betters—for how else to explain the rich gaudiness of the boy's apparel or the older man's autocratic *hauteur* and fur hat and collar.

"Good Sirs, state your business with the Count of Illyria."

Opting to maintain the conceit that effected their advancement, the actor from London announces to the bumpkins around him, "Here be Doctor Johannes Dee, councilor from the Court of Her Royal Majesty, Elizabeth of England. He *shall* have admittance to Count Orsino, Elizabeth's good and faithful servant."

The mole-faced porter, almost as massive as the door he commands, draws up to his full height. "Nay, the steward of the household has given me no notice of your approach."

"This is not a formal official visit, but a courtesy to Your Lord to apprise him of my master's arrival to this far-flung island."

The porter appears confused. Should he abandon his responsibilities, lock the main entrance, and attend to this English dignitary? Should he show the English guests to the main hall, leaving them with the gentleman-usher as protocol demands? Or should he take them to Malvolio, the wickedly strict steward charged with household matters who might have him whipped for not alerting him immediately. Below stairs, Count Orsino's steward is more feared than the Count himself. And much more despised.

Malvolio, a former farmer with a keen eye for finances and a tight fist for savings, forsook his fields for a salaried position as Orsino's father's almoner and now lords it over the household as if he were born with a coat of arms. To facilitate manorial management, Orsino has ordered that anyone in the household may purchase goods or hire laborers, but this is an ordinance Malvolio despises. He is vigilant in employing his long nose to sniff out any abuse. Whatever the steward deems a waste of money is to be rebated by the man responsible, out of that man's own pocket—hence, the porter's reluctance to allow entry to uninvited purveyors. This very morning, Malvolio is to sit in judgment of a valet who bought too many candles for dinner, the poor man having only wanted to make the recent holiday celebration brighter.

Rattled, the porter surveys the quarrelsome crowd, now more surly than usual. For certain they will take their revenge on him in town for making them shiver an extra half hour in the icy winter wind. And then there's the ire of those within the walls expecting their suppliers. What is to be done? Jesu, but he hates these Mondays. Blast. How many times has he asked for help on these market mornings. Especially after last night's holiday festivities when castle larders are dwindled? He hasn't even yet gotten to the ale brewers yet. There will be hell to pay if the residents don't get their grog. *What is to be done?*

Nodding respectfully to his English visitors, the porter waves them to a smaller wooden doorway to separate them from the mob. "Would your graces have a mind to return later this afternoon that I may better inform His Lordship of your visit?"

With a defiant shake of the head *no* from his master, Shakespar indicates he will have none of that, "Nay, we are here now and look to be seen now."

The porter equivocates, "His Lordship has been sick of late and will need some time to properly present himself."

"Then tell His Lordship that Dr. John Dee is well versed in the arts of medicine and is willing even now to visit his sickbed and offer what remedy he may."

The porter is stymied, sensing in this English doctor something otherworldly. As if the old man's judgmental deep-set eyes can discern the lies one tells. "I will tell him when I may. But I am not of the opinion he has arisen."

"Yes, inquire. But, Dr. John Dee, Her Majesty's Royal Postmaster, will not wait out here in the cold. Take us inside where it is warm."

There seems no way of dissuading the herald from an immediate audience with Count Orsino. Further feeble excuses might infuriate the disagreeable old goshawk before him with the sharp beak.

Might as well make it Malvolio's problem. Let him

decide proper etiquette. "Honorable guests," deciding on a course of action, he says in his best English, aiming to strike the proper note of respect, "Honorable guests, I bring you to our gentleman-usher, Master Fabian, who will advise His Lordship of your arrival. *S'il vous plait, suivez moi.*"

"M*erci,*" is all he gets from the young grandee, which is pretty much the extent of Shakespar's French.

The crowd explodes when told that the gate is being temporarily closed. Clenched fists punch the air, and a vegetable or two is hurled at the porter's back as he locks up. He mollifies with promises to return before the tolling of the next hour. More vegtables.

Once inside, the travelers are led through a vast courtyard of gardens where herbs of the season shiver against the cold, and wives of court servants work weeding, noses and fingers purple from the cold.

"*Ici,* the kitchens, the bakeries, and the harness-maker's store," explains the porter. Along the way, a fatty cooking smell wafts out of the squat stone outer houses of the castle keep. The aroma reminds Will of a summer festival in Stratford. John Dee thinks of his last meal with wife and son.

Finally, in the corner of the bailey, they mount the stone steps of the chapel. Here the porter asks them to rest themselves while he fetches Fabian, the castle's usher. He barrels away to accomplish what he has chosen to do.

Left on their own, master and man loosen their cloaks and wait in silence.

"You did well, *Swan.*"

"Gramercy, *Arch Conjurer.*"

Cheeky, thinks the master, *but the lad got us through. I was right to bring him.*

The chapel's rancid scent of sacramental incense reminds Shakespar of having been cooped up too often and hushed into submission during Sunday services. He'd often wondered whether this smoky smell was the redolence of heaven or the fumes of hell.

The ex-chaplain, however, takes no notice of the fragrance, having been inured long ago to these occupational aromas. Looking about the small church and noting the fine marble sculpture of the Madonna presenting Christ to the world, Dee is struck by how such a likeness would now be impossible to exist on the mainland of England. Behind and above is a larger-than-life wooden graven image of Christ nailed to the cross. *Was this idolatry, as Archbishop Grindal and the other Anglican ministers maintain? Or beautiful art to inspire awe and worship?* Like many of his countrymen, privately he believes both. But he cannot feel the same about the silver plate and rich new vestments on view everywhere that have surely cost a pretty penny. The Puritans, he muses, are right to rail against them. *Either Illyria has prospered out here in the middle of the channel,* Dee concludes, *or Rome has financed its only foothold in Britain. Walsingham shall want to know about the Madonna,* the intelligencer thinks, *Oh yes, Walsingham shall indeed want to know about the Madonna.*

The visitors' reveries are interrupted when, out of nowhere, a clipped monotone drones from beyond a far bench, "Good morning to you, sir. I was not informed of your visit until just now and am most distressed at our want of decorum. Welcome to Illyria." The travelers turn to see an exceedingly tall, broomstick of a man with his equally thin white staff of office standing before them. This is Malvolio. He makes no attempt to bow. "You should not have been left uncared for here, where there is neither refreshment nor fire. I shall remedy that."

The effete official, all in black, regards them sternly. It is obvious he disapproves of Shakespar's yellow jerkin and crimson ribbons. Too irreverent, too ostentatious— it is an affront to Scripture. Right-thinking children of Heaven should be demure in thought and decorum. The dour man thinks the English doctor seems proper enough, yet what cheek for him to bring along this animal spirit, dressed in tawny foppery. Youth these days is perpetually cursed with sinful vanity.

Thrusting his baton of authority at his guests, he says, "The Count shall desire some explanations for this improper behavior." But whether this refers to the Count's own household or the visitors' unannounced arrival is unclear.

"I am here to inform His Grace of Her Majesty's business. England's will is that I am to set up the Royal postal system in Illyria so that communication may better flow between Her subjects here and on the mainland."

The Illyrian lowers his eyelids then peers at Dee as if he *mostly* believes what he is being told. The guest is a stranger and not to be trusted.

"Are you Master Fabian, the gentleman-usher to

Count Orsino?" queries Doctor Dee.

The broomstick Malvolio's eyes widen in surprise at the thought of *he* himself mistaken for one such as Fabian. The straight-backed steward pulls himself up further before he responds, "Nay, I thank Jove I am not." He intones, "I am Malvolio, steward to Count Orsino." He taps the wooden pommel of his little baton of office on his bony chest to make his position clear. In a thin voice he adds, "You are welcome to the *house* but as we had no word of your coming, I must ask you to remain here within until Count Orsino is prepared to offer you audience. Here you may partake of the warmth of the fireplace, which shall be replenished for you presently." He is quick to add, in a small squall of condescension he cannot resist, "You may profit by the time and place by repenting of your sins. I shall return as speedily as I can with Lord Orsino's wishes for you."

{ 12 }

Mulling their next move, the Queen's conjurer seems to look through his charge.

Will asks again, "What was that polished stick Malvolio held so firmly?"

Lost in evaluating the situation, the Doctor answers vacantly, "His mace. It symbolizes his authority. Our Lord Hatton, the Queen's Chamberlain, has a golden one. He is known to use it to discipline unruly courtiers, gently or rudely."

"I had a schoolmaster who had a rod like that," pipes Will. "Only he never used it gently."

As the chimney sweep stokes a comfortable fire in the chapel's hearth for Count Orsino's visitors, an odd assortment of animated persons passes through. The choirmaster and his eight boys arrive to rehearse antiphonal music. A valet, who, they are told, is not Fabian, brings refreshments of eggs and sardines, spending a minute or two to chatting up the new Royal Postmaster. But the valet speaks little English, and his island French is impenetrable for the doctor. Another member of the household, an ancient sacristan of the chapel, alerted to the Englishmen's presence, bustles in and suggests they admire the new stained glass windows crafted by the marvelous glaziers of Murano, a wedding gift from *Le Comte* to his new *Comtesse*.

"They cost *Le Comte beaucoup*," brags the sacristan, jabbing at the painted glass transferring light into colored majesty. "No matter the expense, says *Madame*, they remind her of *Notre Dame* at home." The priest, whose back is permanently bent, strains to look upward in quiet awe. Dee cannot tell if the reverence is for the splendor of the colors or the munificence of the Count. The sacristan's frailty hides a vigorous loquaciousness, and John Dee soon becomes weary of maintaining an expectant smile at each of the man's excited observations.

After a quarter-hour of docent enthusiasm in *Franglish*, the old priest takes a moment and painfully cranes his head and shoulders upward in spiritual reflection, followed by, "*Je vous demande pardon,* but I must *retourne* to my duties of *achetant, excusez moi...* buying wine and loaves of bread. *Mon fournisseurs...* my sellers... await in the sacristy, they are *tres en retard* this morning." Without another word, he leaves to negotiate with his vintner and baker.

As the priest vanishes, Dee's grin disappears as well; his attention is on young Will lying outstretched on a hard pew, sleeping away the time. He envies the teenager's lack of care. *The boy had a hard day yesterday. And today everything is unfamiliar. He did well today. He deserves his rest.* The Doctor smiles inwardly, despite the raucous laughter and occasional jarring notes from the prepubescent choir.

Resentful of the unexpected official visitation, Mr. Malvolio ascends the stairs to Orsino's closet to inquire if His Lordship has awakened. The night before had been a double celebration of Orsino's wife's childhood christening and the birth of the Christ child. Merriment and dalliance, augmented by great quantities of wine, inspired the Count to fall in love with his Countess all over again, calling her his beauty, his Guinevere, his Cynthia, swearing his love knows no bounds. She, in turn, had stroked his cheek and nestled in his arms—the night, the food, the music had made them giddy, and forgetful of the hours. But on hearing the church bell toll two, they reluctantly disengaged to their respective chambers, murmuring sweet words and eternal love.

A scant six hours later, at the door to Illyria's bedchamber, the Gentleman of the Privy Chamber, John Curio, informs Malvolio that His Lordship is sorely incapacitated, knowing full well that Orsino has risen and is at his toilet. Yet, insisting that he must not trouble *Le Comte* too much with matters of state, Curio allows the steward to enter. Granted audience, the censorious go-between informs His Lordship *Le Comte* of this morning's unexpected official visit and asks what answer is to be made.

Le Comte Orsino, in his early thirties and massaging the sore muscles of his neck and shoulders, has been recounting to Curio just how many dancing partners he hoisted the previous night while dancing the galliards.

"Right, left, right, left, *jump*... '*Cinq pas*' Dian called it, but some of the heftier sorts call it the *sinkapace*." He rolls his shoulders wearily to signify that the night's exertions have taken their toll.

Though the steward is practically invisible to *Le Comte*, Curio is eager to have Malvolio gone. "My Lord, Malvolio craves an immediate answer."

The tale is told of the Royal Postman's coming. "It displeases me that this unlooked-for visitor from London has come so thoroughly unannounced and unaccounted for," the Count says with a grimace. "First and foremost, you must impress upon—what the devil is his name?" This is followed by the gulping of a steaming beverage, and thence more rubbing on the back of his head.

Malvolio stiffens at the Count's infernal invocation, resisting the temptation to reprimand him not to invoke the Devil as the Bible preaches. Knowing his place and not wanting to arouse Orsino's mercurial black *humour*, especially after the rigors and intoxication of the previous night, he replies simply and obediently, "Doctor Johannes Dee, late of Mortlake."

The Count's cold fingers caress the warmth of heated wine in a porcelain cup. Staring at his puffy eyes in the paddle-shaped hand mirror that Curio holds for him, *Le Comte* is displeased to see his luxuriant mustache betraying some first signs of gray. Orsino's is the countenance of a rather handsome man, and one who knows his mind—a scholar in outlook who prefers forthrightness to policy, yet aware that government on occasion requires both. He had not, however, expected to make any decisions this early. Last night's surfeit of sweet wine is still well in effect. The nagging dull ache at the back of his aristocratic skull persists. Yet the world is in perfect order: Winter has not hit them too hard this year, and he is, yes, in love. Love's madness has ensnared his heart beyond understanding—love, in its fine frenzy, that gives the fresh vitality to things familiar, making souls thrill at being so alive. And with that joy, there is a second grace—charity to others.

Thus, despite this uncivil intrusion from England's barren Queen and a wretched headache—and on St. Stephen's day no less. Orsino opts to be amenable and excuse the visitor's lack of administrative decorum.

"We must foremost be gracious," says Curio, "despite this unlooked-for arrival. Say Count Orsino will give audience on the morrow. Today is a holy day."

Though the Puritan would argue that a Saint's day is no 'holy day' but a social distraction enforced by Rome, Malvolio has served long enough to know Curio can speak with Orsino's full authority. Unconcerned with the arrangements, *Le Comte* reaches for the whetting stone on the ledge of the window and begins to strop a bone-handled shaving knife. If there is to be more nuzzling, he must be kinder to his wife's sensitive cheek. He decides not to wait for the barber.

The steward prods further; his stiff ruff and stiffer neck make his head look pilloried. "Forgive me, Your Lordship, yon fellow swears he will speak with you today, pressing on me a *warrant of introduction* from Her Majesty of England. The porter and valet have both given me to know that the man and his boy are fortified against any denial."

Taken aback by his rebuffed offer, "What manner of man is this Ambassador?"

Orsino looks to John Curio for an answer but gets only, "Truth sir, no Ambassador. A Royal Postmaster." Curio, distracted, occupies himself with searching the room for the Count's misplaced shaving bowl. Malvolio informs, "Your Lordship, in my own estimation the guest is a wizened, gray, shrewd-looking fellow, falling into deterioration, and yet haughty of nature. And, according to the porter, a student of antiquities and books, foreign—and heretical. Weak in the hams and watery in the eyes." The description is made with derision and severity. Ill will never thinks well of scholarship. University studies and their *quadrivium* sciences are to Malvolio most assuredly not God-fearing pursuits, but rather soulless distractions of satanic numbers, distancing the faithless from the *Holy Writ* and as useless to a man's redemption as card-playing or blind man's buff. "This Johannes Dee is a doctor of philosophy," Malvolio adds distastefully.

Still in a haze by last night's merriment, Curio interjects, "Oh, *he*—I have heard of him. They say he foretold the Queen's long reign and instructs Her to strengthen Her navy in the channel. He has trained many in navigation. They say his angels—or perhaps devils—tell him of a secret passage to the Far East."

This godless behavior further irritates the steward but tickles *Le Comte*, whose charity this Saint Stephen's morning is as deep as the sea and swallows up even Malvolio's curdled reporting.

"If this be the Queen's astrologer," says *Le Comte*, "and he be adamant about audience today, then this day must of necessity be a day of good omens. Is there aught of importance that waits upon us today?" Not waiting for an answer from his servers, Orsino returns to his mirror and studies his grizzled, rugged face as if it were a celebrated painting. His looks please him for they please Dian. There is a redness about his cheek that is almost Titian red. He runs a hand through his mane of coal-black hair, which is oily and needs cleaning.

"No, My Good Lord, nothing is planned for today," replies Curio, who has found the shaving bowl and a towel for His Lordship. Noticing his master's hand is too shaky for tonsorial exactness, Curio withholds the bowl.

"Then..." says Orsino, his face brightening with generosity, "Then let him approach. We give him leave to make himself known. Today." He strides quickly to the door and calls to his groom of the bedchamber. "Tyne, fetch me some water. And perfumed soap!"

Curio tempers his objection, knowing Orsino will be pig-headed about this, "Your Lordship perhaps jests. Today? The day after Christmas? We are not prepared."

Orsino turns abruptly; his steely voice unnerves Curio, "Do not gainsay me, sirrah. I repeat, 'It is *Our* will that *We* affect this today'." Seeing no further objections, he orders, "We will entertain the doctor *this* afternoon. Tell your kitchen to prepare lavishly."

"My Lord, he is not asking for lavishness. He but desires a meeting of introduction."

"We will bestow courtesy where it is due." In the governor's mind, the introduction, now morphs into a state occasion. So soon on the heels of last night's dual celebrations, it will surely gladden his Dian and impress on the gentry the extent of his liberality. No thought is given for the burden this will place on his household. That is, after all, Malvolio's concern.

"Yes, Your Lordship," confirms Malvolio, deploring the waste of money, waste of time, and sin of pride this spectacle will engender. But propriety and obedience must eclipse scruples of conscience and husbandry. At least it is a market day and provisions will be at hand.

The groom of the wardrobe, Tyne de Val, brings water and soap. Orsino plunges his head into the cold, clear contents of the brass shaving-bowl. A breaching whale, he surfaces and reins in stray tresses and agitates the lot. Taking the soap from de Val he lathering up, and again submerges, at which time de Val scrubs his Duke's head. With an explosive snort, Orsino rises dripping from the water, right glad of his spit bath. Toweling his face and scalp, Orsino bids Tyne de Val fetch his brightest purple gown and the new ochre silk stockings that Dian presented to him the night before. He will flaunt his wealth with gorgeous attire and advertise to his household how pleased he is with his wife's gift. He sends word to his Countess to prepare herself in her winter best. And those of his Court, anywhere in the *demesne*, are to attend upon him at midday in the Great Hall.

"Our celebration must impress the old Queen," Orsino is adamant. "Show Her Puritan Court our especial generosity and graciousness in the season of our Saviour."

"The *Queen's Conjurer*," muses Curio regarding himself in the Count's mirror and cringing at the sight of dark circles under his eyes, "There's a man worth knowing. As learned and renowned a scholar as ever lived in England, yet poor as a beggar's louse."

"A strange choice for postman. He is two and a half score, if a day. His cheeks are hollow, and his hands are mottled. And a conjurer? A necromancer? Heaven preserve us," adds Malvolio, fearing he may have been infected by their earlier meeting.

"Mayhap he has come hither to die," quips the laconic Curio.

"It is a fairer place to do it in than plaguey London," hoots Orsino. "We will sift him and learn what news there is at Elizabeth's Court."

Pouring himself another goblet of wine to relieve the chill, the Count carries the drink to his unmade bed, and plops himself on downy pillows. There is no hurry to dress. De Val needs time to find and brush the gown, and the grooms must then warm the garments. Orsino gestures to Curio, beckoning him to the bed and, by his side, there they snuggle like co-conspirators. Malvolio, aware he is no longer required, shifts his eyes to the ground and meekly backs out of the room, deploring the sinfulness of the ostentatious, frivolous event to come. *Vanity. All is vanity*, he sniffs.

Alone, the two old friends enjoy the fire's warmth and the conviviality of friendship, discussing the best way to approach this new development.

"Why has he come now?"

Curio shrugs. "If England wars on Spain or France, a

sure line of naval communications will be essential to her fleet. We are at the last outpost of Britain and midway to Spain. A postal station is essential if ships are to be in readiness."

"You don't think it is because the old Queen's terrier, Walsingham, has smelled out that Madrid has sent us diplomatic letters this past fortnight?"

A shadow of concern tightens Curio's face. "Do you suggest an intelligencer is among us? Betraying our councils to Whitehall?"

"No, good friend. My people are all true as beagles to me. But this Dee may be sent here for just such a false endeavor." Orsino thinks better of that. "If so, he being so infirm of age will be easily manageable."

"Aye, but Your Lordship must be wary of what you say to him, nevertheless. And as to Spain? What of that? Spain and Britain are not presently at war. The Privy Councillors at Whitehall cannot fault us for our parleys or commerce with King Phillip, not when taxes on our trades with Hispaniola contribute so lavishly to the felicity of Elizabeth's treasury."

"Lord knows, Spain and England delight in bristling at each other," Hopping off the four-poster, Orsino strolls to the standing mirror. He feels the top of his head for dampness. "Speaking of bristles, Curio, fetch me a brush from the table there that I may properly comb my damp hair."

Some two decades and a half earlier—since late 1558 and the death of Queen Mary Tudor—Elizabeth, and King Phillip of Spain, Mary's ex-husband, like bantam cocks at the start of a match, have warily taken the measure of each other. Because of the open distrust that engulfs both countries, naval commanders are encouraged to fire upon one another's ships, respective Ambassadors are reviled and bullied, and shiploads of gold are captured and confiscated. Illyria, whose geographical position is of tactical military importance, tries assiduously to appear neutral and politically agreeable to both. Spain is especially strategic in keeping secret their warming relations with Illyria as the Spaniards are *not unhappy* that the English laws of supremacy and uniformity are flouted there. The Spanish opine that, in time, the island way-station will be brought into their Empire. After all, Illyria is Catholic and has a new de Guise aristocrat as its Countess.

The policy discussion that day is rather one-sided. Curio is a plain man, which is why Orsino trusts him. Instead of a brilliant schemer who is too clever by half, it is better to choose a friend of the more everyday sort who, when it is needed, ventures common-sense advice. He has Lord Griffin for brilliant scheming. Orsino believes that Curio is a man who does what is expected by his liege lord rather than follow his own bent. That is the success of their relationship. The two men grew up as companions. It is said that in their youth, the old Count's son and his comrade had both striven to outdo each other in the service of Venus. But Curio turned modest and subservient when Orsino became governor of Illyria. And when the old Count Orsino died, both young men had reformed their debauched lifestyles almost overnight and now think only to serve Illyria.

It was Curio who went to France to woo the young

French Princess to be his friend's wife. It was Curio who culled the best men in Illyria for Orsino's advisers. And as the household well knows, it is Curio, an expert at listening, who is best capable of forestalling his master's choleric outbursts. The household swears Curio can read Orsino's thoughts before God can.

As they wait for Tyne to bring Orsino's wardrobe, the Count intensely lectures his friend on the English vulnerability to the Spanish war machine, disdaining the doddering Elizabeth. Curio, his head cocked to one side in a servile, but forthright pose mastered long ago, gently reminds His Lordship that it is best not to underestimate the English Machiavels. They have outwitted the French diplomats' dozens of assassination attempts, Spanish and French statesmanship to draw England into foreign wars, and the Excommunication by the Pope—all while the English economy flourishes. "The Queen's age," Curio argues politely, "is a testament to Her political savvy and endurance. She is no Henry VII, nor Cromwell, yet her Burghley may be." His point made, Curio's posture returns to his natural, subservient slouch.

Orsino nods. "Long and faithful friend," he says, playfully throwing the brush at Curio, "You are the wiser."

Curio goes on to suggest that Lord Griffin be informed of Illyria's new visitor, with Orsino acknowledging the wisdom in that. The debonair Edmund Dotrice, Lord Griffin, though only thirty years old, is the Chamberlain of Illyria's Privy Council and well versed in policy and protocol. When de Val returns with the robes, Orsino sends word through him that Griffin is to be by his side in the great chamber and that he should wear his sword of state. All must dress in their best finery to bedazzle Elizabeth's old but new-come civil servant. *Le Comte* desires there to be reams of *communiqués* back to Whitehall praising Illyrian lavishness.

That morning, castle Illyria's Great Hall, site of the previous night's revels, is swept, and the oak-timbered floors are strewn with new rushes from nearby marshes to catch the dust motes and freshen the smoky air. The rectangular hall has a high, timbered roof. To insure winter's bitterness is kept at bay, the walls are covered with expensive Flemish tapestries that depict tableaus of hunting and feasting. At the back of the room, farthest from its massive oak doors, is a dais boasting a pair of sculpted high-back wooden chairs, taller than any other seats in the chamber. Behind the seats of power, from the rafters hangs a broad pennant with a field of purple and aqua-green. On it is emblazoned the ancient insignia of Illyria: a sea nymph seated in a fishing vessel, strumming a pearl-colored lyre while fish jump into the boat. The fisherfolk who populate the island retell their children the myths of their island as a playground of Thetis and Galatea. Beneath the flag, chamber men add logs to a fire that is dwindled to smolder. Fresh thin branches of kindling grow red in enflamed anticipation.

Shooing the dogs from the hearth, grooms of the chamber are setting several high tables with linen napery and silver plate. Carrying wicker baskets, the lower almoners prepare the trencher-boards, along with place settings of pewter cups and dishes. Most of the household staff are commandeered by the kitchen to collect herbs, slaughter three pigs, roll in vats of wine, fetch eggs, and any other chore of which the kitchen can conceive. Much of what is needed is fresh at hand from this morning's deliveries. Magically, last night's dinner meats are to be transformed into today's cold victuals.

At noon, the gentleman-usher escorts Dee and Shakespar into the Great Hall where they are astounded by the magnificence of the island's stateliest room. Will is awed by the dozens of liveried men, countless courtiers, lighted torches, and ornate settings set for dinner with Illyria's best and their master. *How magnificent a show of power and wealth*, observes the boy. Shakespar has n'er seen such extravagance. *Foreign aid and credit have surely abetted the Illyrian Court*, is John Dee's conjecture.

Presently, after four hours of waiting, the travelers finally get their first glimpse of the *Le Comte* of Illyria. Majestic and refined, Orsino strides purposefully into the Great Hall with a hardy and infectious laugh that comes of authority and prominence of birth. His long, handsome face is ruddy cheeked divided by a straight nose. Shakespar is taken with the Count's broad, lean muscular build and above average height. Dee notes a resemblance between Orsino and the newly appointed Royal Yeoman of the English Guard, Sir Christopher Hatton, who is accounted the most handsome man in England. Both have tresses that cascade down about their shoulders, dazzlingly dark and curled like walnut wood-shavings.

While familiarly clasping hands with many of his retainers in the room, the governor looks about in search of something. Dee at first thinks he, the guest of honor, is the one being sought. That notion is quashed when Malvolio points out Dee and, after a moment's inspection, the Count's search continues. The mystery is soon solved when Lady Dian enters. His agitation abating, Orsino, the king of courtesy, fixes on her across the space even while others engage him in conversation. He begins making his way to her. She is as ethereal as the goddess she is named after and like Daphnae happy to be chased. Like the chaste deity of the moon who is pale and white, the Countess Dian is fair with cinnabar red hair, and the unmistakable aquiline Valois nose, the mark of French aristocracy. No paragon of beauty ever became a room as majestically as this Lady, in her mid twenties and gowned in red velvet and tailored brocade. Her unusually red hair, in a fetching frowziness, is curled and double curled. Most of her female entourage are of her age and swarm around her like attending cherubs, fulfilling the co-equal functions of protection and adoration. In youthful exuberance, the Lady beams at all present, seemingly unaware of the effect of her radiance on every male in the room. Orsino quickly makes his way to her side and takes her in his arms. From where Dee stands, the Count's size and height nearly eclipse the Countess from sight. But like her irrepressible namesake, Dian appears again from his shadow to shine on those around her.

Posing like a fop on display at the theater, Orsino holds her at arm's length and demands her opinion of his yellow stockings. She plays at disapproval, only a moment later applauding enthusiastically at her last night's gift. The rest of the guests do likewise. Even as the hall reverberates, she snatches up her long skirt to lean over and whisper something in his ear.

"Later tonight," Dian purrs softly, "...when all have departed, I shall lure you to my chamber where I will peal those canary leggings from you with my teeth. Think on that for the nonce."

Orsino blushes a subtle crimson as Dian takes one step back and applauds him again. At this, the crowd, most of whom had been present at the previous night's festivities, clap and laugh indulgently. Truth be told, neither of the island's rulers hears any of this; they are too lost in their own intoxication and the sweet, silent communications of lovemaking. At last, His Lordship and Lady take their seats in their high-backed chairs and thank all for coming. The banquet room with three dozen more of Orsino's attendant noblemen and their attendants, all dutifully resplendent, heartily acknowledge their island's governor and their hereditary ruler. Toasts are called and wine is poured.

Shakespar marvels and asks, "Who be all these people, Master?"

"Courtiers and liege men," whispers Dee. Deciphering the iconography of the room as he had the stained glass windows that morning, Dee nods in the direction of the older men in residence. "Those by the dais are most likely men of import dwelling here in Illyria. Men of standing. Men of property. Men of commerce. The others farthest from the dais may be family of the elite or, like us, guests from abroad. Those closest to the entranceway are sons of these older men or important menials, men who may in time ask favors of Orsino. If so, Orsino, like any nobleman of England, will graft them to his household that the new relationship may form an unbreakable bond that safeguards him here at home."

"Safeguards from whom?"

"From whomever might wish his demise—other landowners or henchmen." Dee's sharp eye scans the hall. "It could be anyone," says Dee, noting that Orsino seems enchanted by a story an older, well-dressed guest is telling him, "Even that ancient fellow now tickling his ear." Dee smiles knowingly, adding, "Subtlety is better than force. By treating one's dependents well, a governor hopes to gain his people's trust and maintain his authority. From your own experience, being treated well would you wish a good master harm?"

Dee scans the chamber wondering, *Which of these men could be a suspect in the treason that I have been sent to smell out?* Seeing many proudly wearing Catholic crucifixes, he asks himself, *Where to start?* But in that moment, he smiles ingratiatingly at the cupbearer who offers him wine. *Anyone (including this servant) might be embroiled in the menace of sedition.* He smiles while taking his glass—*a Jesuit, possibly, on his way to an illegal Mass in Britain.* Dee sips the wine. The delicious luster of French grapes excites his taste. Better than any bottle in his wine cabinet. *If Orsino is most responsible, who else is involved? Walsingham has set me a daunting puzzle.*

There is a new toast from Orsino—and his yellow leggings—to the health of all. Countess Dian's eyes brighten at the sight of all the joy in the room. The young Shakespar fixates on the red ripeness of her full lips. Her speech has a sweet nasality to it that makes the throng feel that they are in the presence of another Helen. Orsino offers his hand to a personage standing closest to his throne on the steps of the dais, the debonair Edmund Dotrice, Lord Griffin. He is not handsome, and his short stature hints at neither strength nor virility. Yet, what nature has scanted him in physical power, in recompense she has given him a quick mind that towers over others in policy and government. A murmur of respectful acknowledgment ripples through the crowd as he climbs to the top of the platform and busses Dian's small proffered hand with a chaste kiss, as courtesy dictates. Indulgently playing her part, Dian gazes down at her assembled guests and gives them all a stern look, as if to demand Griffin's sweet obedience from all of them as well. All the room's guests love her all the more for the performance; many lower their eyes in deference as she gazes their way. Orsino is well pleased. Then, with practiced statesmanship, Dotrice turns to the Count's ear, whispering some counsel. The instruction completed, Lord Griffin retires to stand behind one of the tall chairs.

"Why, no show of humility, no bending of the knee?" inquires Will. "Is it not a disgrace to His Grace?"

"Bowing is the fashion in England," Dee whispers in reply, "not in France. Moreover, here it is not 'His Grace' but 'His Lordship'."

Will Shakespar would have asked the reason for that difference had not his reverie been broken by in imperious voice from the dais.

"Well met good friends," starts His Lordship. The room reverberates with a hearty applause. "Countrymen. We are honored today by the visit of a worthy from Her Royal Highness, Queen Elizabeth. In Her generosity, She sends us a Royal Postmaster, a man well known to scholars throughout Europe—a Postmaster who is erudite, well-grounded in philosophy and languages, both dead and quick. Honored guest, Doctor John Dee, come forth." Orsino gestures for Dee's approach.

Dignified and with measured step, John Dee walks toward Illyria. Dressed in his best scholar's black robe with its furred collar, Illyria's first Postmaster does not create much of a stir in the hall, causing many to wonder why Orsino has gone to such trouble for one so old and clearly of reduced means. Yet, all present marvel at *Le Comte's* openhandedness—two straight days of Christmas celebration—which they take as an honor meant as much for themselves as for the graybeard from London. Several even whisper about the strange menial attired in yellow doublet whom the Postman has in tow. Is this the finery in fashion at the Queen's Christmas Court?

Having taken notice, Dian's waiting lady, Maria, catches her mistress' eye, "Over there," pointing out Will, "observe the gauche yellow doublet, in the name of mockery."

"Shush, Marian," chides Dian. She looks anyway. "Yellow. *C'est bon,*" liking what she sees, "*il est tres brave.*"

Chastened, the saucy Maria dares not speak her mind. *Oh, yes, very brave. He obviously fears no colors.*

Paying no attention to the mystified murmurs, John Dee straightens his pointed beard and mounts the stair to the dais.

In the midst of the crowd, Will stands a little taller at his master's honor.

Meeting his guest for the first time, the Count walks towards Dee and clasps his hand.

"Duty to Her Highness has so besotted my reason that, childlike, I am powerless to greet you properly, more so in that you descend upon us like a meteor without forewarning from Her Royal Highness. But I am not so ill-bred or disobedient not to send everlasting thanks to Her Majesty who is my most gracious Prince, governor, and neighbor. Therefore, as your presence here betokens hers, be as ourselves in Illyria and welcome."

"Our Royal Prince greets you through me as her trusty and devoted counselor," Dee replies. "And forasmuch as by reason of the indisposition of your person and the freshness of your marriage, you could not conveniently partake of the late festivities of our Savior's birth at her Windsor Castle, nor could She earlier in the year here attend the solemnization of your joyous marriage union, She sends you by me tokens of Her happiness for your nuptials. On the morrow with your leave, I shall bring you rich gifts from Her Highness, who hopes that they shall ever be honored in your heart and that of your bride. She also sends by word of me that as Illyria's Royal Postmaster, I may bind the island more firmly to her breast."

There is tepid applause from the guests. Orsino has a disagreeable image of his face being roughly yanked against withered Royal dugs.

"For my own part, I stand in awe at the graciousness of your welcome and your liberality. I give you such thanks as duty and compliment may."

Orsino, without rancor, asks, "This honor from Our Queen is rather sudden. Was it effected on the whim of the moment?"

Dee chooses not to answer, allowing an awkward silence. The Count stares quizzically at his new Postmaster with a calculating, impudent stare waiting for an answer. None comes. Having made his point, Orsino turns his attention elsewhere, taking up another matter that has caught his attention. Dee, unsure of what to do or where to go, takes a doubtful step to descend from the dais, prompting the short man behind the Count to cough politely.

"Master Dee, may I present myself to you? I am Edmund Dotrice, Lord Griffin, counselor to the Count." His voice is as manicured as his nails. Indicating the number of guests, the lavishness, the gaiety, "More than you expected?"

"You mean this welcoming of me?" Stroking his beard, Dee acknowledges the bizarreness of it with a half-smile. "Yes."

"He is in love," confines Dotrice, "And because he is in love, he desires happiness for all. You and, of course, Her Majesty included."

"I will tell the Queen."

Indicating Orsino, "*Le Comte* will like that."

The point now made of Dee's reporting back to his masters, the new Post Master smiles politely, "Your servant, sir."

"And yours." The guest of honor turns to descend the dais steps when Dotrice gently touches his shoulder. "Truth be told, master Dee, we have met ere this, or rather I have had the good fortune to have been in your presence."

Turning back. "My apologies. I am at a loss, *monsieur*. Your riddle?"

"It was at university in Paris, *Docteur*. I was a student at your marvelous lectures on Euclidean geometry."

The men nod in recognition of a shared past, though Dee wonders, first Thomas Phelippes and now Lord Griffin, how many others at those lectures shall come forth.

"I was much saddened to hear that you left that position shortly after."

"My studies in philosophy, especially that genre which seeks to find communication with celestial beings, made my superiors uneasy. They gave me fair warning of dismissal if I chose to continue my course of study, and though I suffered for my actions, I have never regretted my decision."

"Your studies have made you famous."

Orsino extends an arm to Dian to join them.

"Infamous, rather," commences Dee, "Having shook hands goodbye with my university career, my unconventional pursuits made me invisible. I fear that my ascendant star of renown is now in its decline. I am the epitome of the poor pedant, whom Her Majesty now has taken pity on and granted me employment in a convivial location among friends."

"I have heard of your inquiries in hope of finding the Northwest Passage," says Dotrice eagerly, "Have you made much progress?"

Happy to have found someone who knows his work and its worth, "Just as all Europe seeks for a path to Cathay and its riches through the *terra incognita* of northern America, so I seek the same lost route through the study of ancient texts of navigation. But, though I advise Frobisher, Gilbert, and the Muscovy Company on routes, we are still disappointed by the results. As all men do, I live in hope of making my fortune. Angels have presented me a volume of *cronica wallia* that maps a course to the Far East discovered by the Welshman Madoc. Thus in the Far East, I hope to see the sun rise again on my good name."

"Lesser minds fear the dark unknown, and your fellow scholars criticize your explorations, both celestial and maritime," Dotrice reproves, then adds, "But in time, Heaven will weigh us all and judge us for our actions. I have no fear that your erudition in natural philosophy will be acknowledged throughout Christendom."

Is this man friend or foe? Illyria's Postmaster is not sure. *But when in time the new age arrives, all will be right glad of this prophecy.*

"Edmund," says Orsino, returning his attention on his guest and eager to parade his scholarliness. "Read you Cornelius Agrippa, a German theologian, who like our new Postmaster, taught us that the study of natural philosophy is both mathematical and deeply religious. The art of magic is the art of studying God."

"I thank Your Lordship and commend Your Lordship's conclusion." Dee nearly lays a hand on the young Count's sleeve in approval, remembering etiquette just in time to resist. "Yes, indeed. Agrippa's *de occulta philosophia* tells us the study of Nature, unlocking its secrets, and advice from Heaven can never be objectionable. On peril of my soul, I take that belief seriously and make it my life's work." Seeing no disagreement, he continues. "Guarding my soul and my investigations with heartfelt prayer, I humbly petition knowledge from angels above," but then quickly adds, "How more righteous our lives would be if we might know *God's* will." What a cordial to Dee's faith that he may say "*God*" in this Catholic company and not be constrained by Puritanical dictates to "not take His Divine name in vain."

"Amen, good doctor," concludes *Le Comte*.

Taking the Countess' hand, Lord Griffin introduces his former lecturer, "M'Lady, our new Postmaster, Doctor Johannes Dee. As erudite and grounded a man in philosophy and languages, both quick and dead, as can be found in all the world."

"Have you just said, 'petitioning knowledge from angels'?"

"Yes, Countess."

"And do they answer you?"

Observing her frown, Dee knows its origin:

revulsion. He is caught off-guard but determined not to ruin the afternoon's festivities. It is with utmost care he replies, "Yes, M'Lady, when Heaven deems it appropriate."

Lady Dian searches his face. "Do you speak in metaphor?" She is quite sure that is the answer, yet adds with a playful *moue*, "Or do cherubim and seraphim pay you visits?"

Cordial, half-smiling, Dee's stealth ensues. "When God sees fit to command them to educate me. For I have utter faith, Our Father wants us to know Him in all His glory."

Daggers replace her dancing eyes. "You equivocate, Doctor. That is not what I asked. But I have my answer and know it as sacrilege."

The philosopher chastises himself—lulled into imprudence by Lord Griffin's praise. Acutely aware of most of the world's suspicion of his studies, he knows better than to refer to his angelic conversations in public—the unsophisticated will always think natural philosophy diabolic. He gnaws at the inner flesh of his cheek. To his disgrace, his tongue has been too eager to share with strangers what his heart rejoices in. With resigned self-reproach, every muscle in his face assumes the mask of humility. "Most gracious Madam—" Dee begins.

"Doubtful, *perhaps*..." Blithly, Lord Griffin cuts him off so as to deal with the Lady Dian's dismay with his usual tactical compassion and keep it cordial, "...but sacrilegious, *no*. I should think not. Verily, Moses spoke with the Almighty on Sinai, Abraham did so at Isaac's sacrifice, a host of Israelites had conversation with angels, and our Lord Jesus Christ spoke with thousands. None were sacrilegious. Rather, it would be piety itself and wondrous well to do so again. The Church teaches us that the time of miracles is not over. The time is ripe for good religion to ripen, not wither. Our present world would certainly be a better place if we knew what Divinity's counsel was. *Isaiah 55:6, 'Seek the Lord while he may be found, call upon him while he is near.'*"

Far from placated, the Countess remains defiant, "You've not finished the quote, Sir Edmund: *'For my thoughts are not your thoughts, nor are your ways my ways, saith the Lord. For as the Heavens are higher than the Earth, so are my ways higher than your thoughts. Let the wicked forsake his way, and the unrighteous man his thoughts: and let him return unto the Lord, and he will have mercy upon him; and to our God, for he will abundantly pardon.'* We can only return unto our Lord through proper faith, only through the Holy Mother Church that teaches us that we can know Heaven's will *only* through a priest or prayers to the Madonna and the blessed saints. Not through sacrilegious incantations."

Dee's mask has not moved a muscle. "May I welcome the Count and Countess of Illyria to any of my scrying sessions to assuage Her Ladyship's doubts? Thereby, may she be reassured of my profound faithfulness."

"To commune and have sway over devils. I think not."

Sanctimonious reproof radiates from the courtiers who scorn Dr. John Dee in the Countess' presence. Dee chuckles to himself. He has known worse.

Illyria intercedes. "Sweet chuck, if God or any of his host desires communication with our new Postmaster, they will most assuredly locate him. If not, what harm? It would be pleasant sport to see him enchant with bell, book, and candle. Shall we not say *yes* to his invitation?" Dian is not to be mollified; miracles and prophecies ended with the Apostles. Too late, her husband realizes her antipathy and quickly seeks to humor her. "I'd venture that Professor Dee's now dwelling with us in blessed Illyria will make him the more desirous by Heaven to be found."

There is a courtly cheer of approbation.

Not amused but too well-mannered to give full-throated offense, Her Ladyship replies, "Perhaps our gracious Royal Postmaster is here in Illyria because Her Majesty knows he can find no angels in England." Eavesdroppers go silent, unsure if her *rapprochement* is an olive branch or a declaration of war.

"Well, most certainly, it is angels that have brought him here," quips Lord Griffin, to smooth tensions. "If money or angels will go before, all doors in Illyria will certainly open. If commerce can be made better with one or both, then either prospers our island."

The pun on seraphim and the English coin, *angel*, is approved of with nervous laughter and brings a halt to the uncomfortable conversation, which Lord Griffin directs quickly to the sea's conditions and other less controversial subjects.

When asked, John Dee is happy to pass on all the news of the English Court that he is aware of. And when questioned about the latest fashions, he points to Will, "My aide, Master Shakespar, is more knowledgeable."

"A tawny doublet to match my stockings!" declares the surprised Orsino, regarding Will's yellow *couture* with a tradesman's eye. Then he remarks wryly, "Richly suited, young man. Dian, what think you? In one of low birth perhaps unsuitable, no?" Dian commends her husband on the *bon mot* though with a sly glance reprimands, "*Tous les deux sont tres brave.*"

"We both are, are we?" Playfully Orsino pulls a face, tweaking her with a whisper, "You little harlot." Orsino drinks in his radiant Dian, content to look at her forever. But even the mighty imp, Cupid, cannot dissuade lunch from being served, and so the clatter of trenchers and the aroma of roast pig drown their coltish teases and blushing whispers.

The Lady Dian, though independent, knows the absurdity of resistance. Her Valois aunt tutored her well in her instruction that this is a man's world, yet educating her in the powerful strengths of manipulation. When she first arrived at the Illyrian Court she had expected an ugly, overbearing lout. To her delight, she found Orsino to be neither. His handsomeness is an exquisite joy to her, even as she begins to see where some laxity around the jaw will eventually lead to fleshy chins, and that his ears, usually hidden by his hair, are too large for his narrow head.

More delightful to her than his beauty is his gracious care of her. He loves her truly, with genuine warmth and decency that belies her aunt's one warning that men care only for themselves and will think of you solely when directed by their lower parts or as a means of propagating an heir. They will call you their flower—and prove it by assuming you to be witless and ornamental. The Valois aunt had further advised that marriages are but political chess moves, to strengthen military power, create patronage, or add to one's treasury—with the wife a pawn and her husband the king. A willful pawn may become a queen, yet normally in marriage a woman is checkmated.

So far, Orsino has proved her old aunt wrong—however, Dian is still young; there remains time, anon, for disappointment. Perhaps merely to bask in her radiance, Count Orsino never crushes her opinions, and instead makes a genuine effort to obtain her counsel. Nearly from the start, she had been invited into his privy discussions, despite the reproving grimaces of certain male Councillors. Orsino is tactful enough at the sessions not to question her; instead, when they are again alone, he requires her perceptions. He has listened for hours at her nothings, never missing the smallest nothing. Once or twice a tear has unabashedly slid down his cheek as he told her of his prayers for her.

But she is not so young as to fool herself into believing him some Galahad from old romances. Rather, his shortcomings make him a Lancelot, a Gallic knight, arrogant and proud and willful, capable of his own headstrong destruction. Ardor and willfulness are his two most powerful divinities. On that day when she was certain Orsino had won her heart—that same day when he had clung to her and engulfed her in his arms for what seemed like an eternity and had sworn by all Gods that he would cherish her forever—she had made a solemn vow to keep those same demigods from devouring him. She would do all she could to fulfill her wifely obedience. But her aunt's last words still echo: "Never forget you are de Guiche. Family is everything."

The harbormaster, having neither title nor property, Sir Toby Belch—or so Tobias Gassette is called—is not a *Sir* by anyone's definition of a gentleman. On the hierarchical ladder, Tobias Belch is too high to be called *sirrah* but too low to be addressed as *Sir*. His only attachment to nobility (albeit tenuous) is that Edmund Dotrice, now Lord Griffin, is Belch's cousin. They share a notable grandfather who received title and lands in Illyria from Henry V when the English King sallied forth for recovery of his rights in France. Fate and primogeniture having scanted Tobias, he is merely the second-born son of a second son making his way on a remote island far from the bustle of either England or France. Mercifully, Nature gifted him with good looks and a jovial personality. All else—his grandfather Griffin's wealth of moveables, title, patronage, and money—had all passed to his firstborn male heir, Gassette's uncle, Etienne. Regrettably, Etienne was a man with no love for Toby's father. The older brother stinted on charity to support his unfortunate or rather fortune-less younger brother, mirroring the time-honored sibling rivalries of English aristocracy.

Luckily, Illyria's old Count, Orsino's father, had a

fondness for Gassette and had taken him in, appointing him to several positions of importance, eventually making Toby's father the steward of the Orsino household. Old Gassette repaid his employer's generosity with unflinching fidelity, fulfilling his duties with enthusiasm and dogged loyalty. His prosperity, allowed him to buy a parcel of land. There, Toby's father kept his family well-housed and well-fed. His eldest son, Toby's brother, wanted no part of his father's ledger-book existence. Leaving the island, he joined the forces of Lord Hunsdon, the Lord Warden of the Marches, in the turbulent northern borderlands where he battled against the invading Scots. With little or no soldierly training, he served with early distinction: combating the rebels, whoring, drinking, and taking deep revenge for the most minor of offenses. Dogged as his father, young Gassette rose through the ranks and accompanied Sussex through Teviotdale, wreaking brutal vengeance on any Scot who had protected English rebels. His highland incursions were much applauded by his overlords for his zeal at burning castles, homes, and slaying whole villages. In time, he fell in love with one of Sir John Carey's daughters and was given leave to marry her. But, being barely able to write, he never got around to sending letters home about his nuptials, nor was he inclined to do so.

Accustomed to not hearing from their swashbuckling scion brother, the Gassettes were not surprised when they heard that two years had passed since the eldest was dragged from his horse and torn to shreds by Scottish hordes. Forever after, old Gassette warned his youngest of the evils of such an adventurous life, "Begin by taunting your father, and you will end up embracing calumny." Just the same, Toby had been awed by his brother's exploits, so much so that Toby became jealous of his romantic dead brother's life, hoping to best him in outrageous acts.

As a youth, Toby was part of the Count's household. As such, he was permitted to study with the children of Illyria's notables. Having more of an aptitude for study than his brother, he quickly learned to read and write, mastering not only English, Latin, and Dutch, but, of course, French. He developed significant expertise in the fine arts, excelling in calligraphy, music, rhetoric, and dancing. Had Fate been kinder, he might have become a successful courtier or minor diplomat. However, his education, refining the rougher aspects of his intrinsic roguishness, never led him to better his station significantly. His father exacerbated this failure. The old steward deprived Toby of leisure time and studious contemplation by ordering him to scurry about St. Peter Port on thousands of menial errands. To the island folk of Illyria, he became as familiar a messenger as the lark. Fond of their Count's steward, the populace regaled his good-looking son with all sorts of amusing quips, maritime adventures, and salacious gossip. Every now and then, they might even accompany a particularly long tale with a goblet of wine. Many a shoppekeeper's wife took pains to offer Tobias a little extra cake or a peek at her ankle just to have the good-looking boy malinger longer in her company. He grew up waggishly cheerful, self-assured, and adept at entertaining people.

His uncle, Etienne, Lord Griffin, had three children: Reginald, Edmund, and Olivia. Reginald, the eldest, died at fourteen in a boating accident. Then twelve, Edmund was suddenly burdened with the responsibility of being heir. Acknowledging the solemnity of his title, the new heir made life grimly serious for himself. Five years younger than Edmund, Olivia worshiped Reginald and mourned her eldest brother for years. Edmund's paternal instinct was strong, and he made it his duty to watch over his younger sister. She, in turn, treated him like a father. Children in a confining household often turn against each other. These two did not. As Lady Olivia matured, her obedience to her brother blossomed into loving devotion. All suitors were measured against his perfection. At holiday time, Count Orsino gave many lavish parties, whereby the estranged young cousins suffered strained hours together. Edmund and Toby grew up barely tolerating the other's company. Softer in her affections, Olivia, nevertheless remained dutiful to the opinions of her father-brother. And like Edmund, she regarded her surviving cousin as a familial burden. Never forgiving Toby for his mother's rural Basque background, Olivia opined Tobias as servant class— since she too sent him on errands—and therefore, not quite a blood cousin.

Despite the meanness of his birth, Tobias' panache blossomed. He absolutely believed destiny favored him, and that he would overtop the feats of his brother as well as many other notable breakers of the Queen's peace. His envy equally boundless, Toby was caught stealing from the old Count's pantry on more than one occasion.

Belch's *bonhomie* however made it impossible to remain angry with him, and sooner or later, he would be forgiven. The flirtatious, honey-tongued lout took pains to further his natural talents with poetry, beguiling the ladies and entertaining the men with song and sensational potboilers on high seas. In recompense, he was showered with coin from the foppish gallants and even sweeter gifts from *mademoiselles*. With good wit and drink as good compensation, Tobias Belch grew ever more confidant. Without scruples as a flirt, even as a young teenager, he was a fox in the henhouse. He cuckolded countless inattentive island husbands. The taste for drink acquired when on his errands grew among his addictions. When alone, drink silenced the discontent in his head, making him forget his family's deficiencies and drowned the hollow emptiness of his self-worth. When provoked, he barked and bellowed and roared to escape that awful inner voice. He knew that if he was loud enough, his boistering would beguile him into believing that he was happy.

Nature gave Toby wit, yet flouted him as the butt of a grand cosmic joke. As he grew older, his body grew intolerant to rich foods and was dangerously incapacitated by more than three tankards of ale. Too much and Gassette's stomach rebelled against the noose choking his sensitive mid-section. This leads to him stumbling, vomiting, or belching his way home after a night's carousing. Perhaps that is the origin of his nickname—perhaps not. No one, not even his family, is sure from where the title *Belch* originates. But, everyone calls him *Belch*, and he appears rather proud of it, amazingly never putting on weight, and magically staying at a handsome fourteen and one-quarter stone.

In the summer of his sixteenth year, he made the imprudent mistake of seducing his master's mistress and getting her with child. The old Count was furious, and his steward, Toby's father, even more so. Tobias was banished from the island. At the public expulsion of Belch on Good Friday, his father's words were harsh and unforgiving, "My rascal son is no better than the meanest beggar caught stealing at the castle alms door. He is a coistrel, sick of self-love, a heathen, nay a very *renegado*." Enumerating the great kindnesses the good Count had lavished on his son in the past, old Gassette slammed Toby further, "He is a reprobate and an unmannerly ape with no respect of place, persons nor time, I can hardly forbear hurling things at him." Well aware that his son's crime threatened his lifelong climb of stability and respectability, Gassette concluded with, "May he be cursed to the everlasting bonfires of Hell and suffer eternally for his degenerate sins. Ungracious wretch, out of my sight!"

Taking what few belongings he possessed, Toby slinked away like a beaten whelp. Forced to face exile in a world without security, familiarity, or sustenance, he cursed his fate and bred a fear of poverty that now rankles within him in middle age.

Where shall I go? he asked himself. Having grown up on an island, he felt most comfortable by the sea with its sound of lapping waves and the briny smell of weather-worn timber. Two choices prevailed, given Illyria's proximity to two mighty centers of power. A boat trip to Portsmouth was longer and more costly than one to Le Havre, so the outcast traveled East. Plus, the food was tastier in France, as were the women.

For the next nine years, he spent an uncertain life among the thieving wharves of Burgundy, making use of the talents some mischievous god had given him. He would latch on to a young gentleman and make himself his boon companion partying until dawn and always taking advantage of his benefactor's largess. Loans were taken while picking purses; clothes were borrowed and never returned. It was a life of abject penury and, when alone in his cups, he mourned his lost pampered life.

His notion to ship aboard a three-master to the West Indies was replete with happy imaginings of a life in the unsettled new world; there he would carve out a name for himself and bask in the love of a family of his own making as his older brother had done. Moreover, in the New World, he could live without constraints or the oppression of hierarchy. As he wassailed his youth away, carousing and drinking, his ambitions went unfulfilled. At thirty-three, the age by which Alexander the Great had already conquered half the world, Belch ferried himself back to Illyria upon receipt of certain obituaries. The old Orsino had passed on to his heavenly rewards, and his faithful Spaniel, Toby's father, had followed soon after. After some days of reacclimatizing in the downtrodden wharf area, Belch sent word to his wealthy cousin, Edmund Dotrice, telling grand tales of his reformation, and playing upon any shred of familial obligation.

Edmund, for kinship sake and prompted by tears

from Olivia, found him a position working in the harbor. In time, he became the new Count Orsino's harbormaster, keeping tabs on the comings and goings of the mercantile ships sailing through St. Peter Port. Contraband was to be reported to the Vice-Admiral and fees were to be levied on certain manifests. It turned out to be a post very much to Toby's liking. Not more than two or three vessels moored a day, and poring over manifests could be very rewarding. Having no qualms about turning a blind eye to contraband in exchange for a Captain's open hand, or, by appropriating ample samples of certain forbidden cargoes of food or wine, he could easily be bribed to countenance flouting the law. In his mind, the law was designed to keep the rich wealthy and the poor in their miserable shanties. No one would miss what little he culled for himself. With a spit between his fingers, "The law! A *figo* for it and those who keep it!" was his catchphrase.

With this kind of officiating came many an invitation to join a captain or first mates in the *Nous Trois* tavern, making the harbor alehouse a second home for Toby. There, the widow, Maria Roitelet, held sway. A capable woman well versed in cursing in four languages and, if not understood in those, supremely talented at wielding a bat. At his favorite table by the chimney, Belch reveled in the stories of the sea and of foreign lands. Like the sweetness of Palestinian dates, he savored the words of wandering tars, revisiting the exotic locations in his imagination, and then augmenting their glories with a drunkard's gusto to others whom he retold of the opulent watery palaces of the Venetians, the towering forests outside of Muscovy, the infernal monsters of the New World. So much of life he and his Illyrian audience had not tasted because of ill-luck and want of wealth. If Providence or unlucky stars had shut them out, they would not hold them out forever. Toby swore that he— and his companions—would o'er-master their Fates.

Black Bile, it is said, is the source of all bitterness and melancholy in mankind. Galen, and before him Hippocrates, had maintained that personality was the result of the mixture of the four *humours*: phlegm, blood, yellow bile, and black bile. Black bile, associated with the Earth and autumn, was the worst of the *humours* and prone to ferment. The amount and regularity of his eating was haphazard, dependent on when and from whom he could cadge a meal. It was often cold and swallowed hurriedly. The pathology created in Toby an alternation of anger and abject depression. When his maritime duties were tedious, any excuse to slip away to Maria's sufficed. He slumped himself into his booth waiting for travelers who might be eager for company and reciprocate by buying him a drink. Though the frivolity and charm of his youth that oft beguiled with bawdy tales and raunchy songs reigned in him, Toby Belch could, in a nonce, transform himself into a bitter old seaman. And, like Proteus, he was suddenly a raging Leviathan, murderous for blood and vengeance. On those evenings when he was unusually quiet, the tavern regulars watched him warily as he sat alone at his table. If he sucked at his lip or left his cup untouched, they knew to leave him be, and, if approached, to call him "Sir Toby" and then give him wide berth.

❧   ❧

In the spring of 1580, four years prior to Dr. John Dee's presentation at Orsino's court, Antonio Peretti met John Clinton. The latter was a sailor on one of Elizabeth's Royal ships. The former's father had been an artisan at the Vatican where England's Archbishop Woolsey had discovered him fashioning decorative glass. It was artistry the Archbishop thought could amaze and bedazzle young King Henry's Court. And it did for several years. Regretably, the Peretti family fortunes fell with those of Cardinal Woolsey in 1530. Neither the new courtiers of Edward's VI's Court nor the stiff-necked followers of England's next monarch, Mary, wanted to do business with anyone associated with the despised prelate, Woolsey. An impoverished Italian child in the fetid London streets with swarthy skin, tight black curly feminine hair, and a pronounced accent that tended toward a lisp rendered Peretti prey to ridicule. Often set upon, he was quick with his fists, and nothing provoked him more than the name-calling his racial difference prompted. Much to his mortification, he only grew into a sinewy short man. Though his domineering father had tried to bend his attentions toward the glass and ceramics trade, his son's striving mind wanted more than a life of blasting ovens and gooey glass. More, he sneered at the craft's enforced apprenticeship and pseudo-respectability. Antonio took to the sea, reasoning that he could jump ship when nearing his family home in Venice. But the frigates Antonio sailed never seemed to venture anywhere near his origins. It was infuriating. On every voyage Antonio made, Peretti inflicted his frustrations on those around him, leaving more than one sailor bloodied or maimed. Some had stood in his way; others had simply not succumbed to his sexual overtures. Yet, his nimble mind was quick to spot opportunities when they knocked. Diligently working his way up from seaman, an occupation too small for his ambitious spirit, he advanced to purser. But try as he might, he became trapped in that position, convinced that his naval superiors looked down on his Roman heritage and kept him from advancement.

John Clinton, apprentice to a butcher in Norwich, had abandoned his trade for the preternatural calling of the sea and the spray. Learning at an early age how to use an astrolabe and compass, he hired onto merchant ships helping pilots chart their voyages. He was able to navigate to the farthest harbors of the known world and bring them home again. His successes, along with the praise that accompanied them, eventually engendered in him haughty self-esteem that balked at the necessary chain of command essential to decorum at sea. Once saved from mishaps and set on the right course, no Captain seemed happy to have him aboard, unless his expertise was needed to discover a way out of unfamiliar waters again. Though his dead reckoning at sea was legendary, only the subservient seamen openly recognized his talents, as the ship's officers thought it utter insubordination to suggest that any captain could miscalculate.

One day quite by happenstance, both Clinton and

Peretti meet in a maritime tavern in Gravesend. They huddle over tankards of small beer, dissecting what is most assuredly rotten with the world and its authority. How fed up they are with "Aye, sir" and "No, sir" and of the certain destiny of drowning by their masters' incompetence. Whenever chancing upon each other over several months, they grouse in the dim light of anonymity. Others join them and their individual complaints against the mutiny of servitude grow into a chorus of discontent. Yet, no actions are taken.

Seasons pass, then unexpectedly on one winter's day, Chance and Fortune arrange that the two men's ships dock in Illyria. A devilish wind and rough seas keep their cautious captains from leaving the calmer waters of Orsino's marina. Crews allowed ashore make straight for the gossip and grog at the *Nous Trois*. Reunited, Antonio and John soon find themselves falling into old habits grousing once again about their pestiferous betters.

"S'Death, our pilot swore we were just off the coast of the mainland at Weymouth when the lookout sighted this island. Storm or no storm that's reckoning off by eighty or more leagues." Clinton spits in distaste upon the wooden floor. "If there had been shoals or rocks, we'd all been sodden timbers in a watery grave."

"Your *Capitaine, bas-tard*," Antonio says the word accenting the second syllable rhyming it with mustard "is not *fit-a* to sail a toy boat *in-a* pond."

"Aye, but his father is Lord what-a-ye-call-it in Devon and would have his son to sea." Mocking, Clinton impudently poses militarily, woolen cap askew, as he had once seen on a Portsmouth stage. Performing a pantomime of his Captain from Devon, he licks his finger to see which way the wind blows, then sticks it in the direction of his ass and lets go a fart. "Regarding our experience and our especial mastery of navigation, what malicious star cursed us to be no better than servants? When our minds are as fit and our spirits as brave as any blue-blooded milksop born of a lisping doxy," snorts Clinton. His ship-mates agree with shouts and curses that buzz about the table like horseflies. The tavern door suddenly opens and a sliver of sunlight cleaves the tavern gloom, but the new arrival is only an island man, and the sailors return to their grievances and cataloguing the injustices of the world.

"Aye," echoes the thin Italian, whose every word ends with an upward inflection, "I *hava* both the *judga-ment* and ability to *commanda*. But-a, the *gooda* Lord keeps me *bound-a* to benefit and *in-richa* others, a pox on them. I *have-a* served as *a-prentice* at sea *long-a* enough. *Basta*, I *have-a* learned my craft. It is *enough-a*!"

"That we have. It is time to be freemen of the oceans and prosper for ourselves." Clinton slams his pewter mug down on the table to emphasize his slightly drunken conviction. Either that noise or mere coincidence draws Tobias Gassette to them. Toby Belch slides a small stool over to their table. The Italian and the Norwich man are none too pleased with the arrival of an intruder who reeks of *stranger*, having neither sunburn nor rope-scarred hands.

"*Avast-a*, you donkey islander. No one *has-a* invited *you-a* here," snarls the younger man. He makes no secret of reaching for the hilt of an ugly fish-gutting blade scabbarded in his belt. Look-for-look with the Italian, Toby grandly breaks the silence by calling out, "More beer!" His barfly generosity an excuse to join their company, Belch consummately shares details of his own ill-fated existence, and welcomes them to swap tales of consternation and woe. Having introduced himself as the harbormaster, he further insinuates himself with the two malcontents by describing the witless inanities of their captains. Further elevating the mood, he recounts two vignettes. The first concerns a mustachioed pomp-and-swagger Turkish captain whom Belch has sharked out of cash and commodity. By imposing imaginary harbor fees on the Muslim, Belch has enriched his own pocket having insisted upon fictional English *usage* fees. Finding the Turk illiterate in English, Toby had then shoved an old parchment in front of the heathen, swearing, "This document spells out more charges." Toby risked mutiny by insisting on payment before anyone was allowed off the ship. At last, Toby had magnanimously waived *half* the imaginary fee, and the grateful captain had filled his benefactor's palm with eight Crowns of gold.

With Toby's next tale, he convinces two blue-blooded ensigns, both in love with the same girl, to send threatening letters to each other. He incites a duel that neither of the cowards dared to fight. The detailing of their womanish waving of swords and their shrieking when the weapons happened to collide accidentally provides a half-hour of riotous laughter. More importantly, it thaws the last icy barrier of suspicion.

With increased drink and the late hour intimate secrets pour forth, certainly rather more than they might have done otherwise. Often, the sailors return to snarling about their discontent and the maddening shackles of a life in service. They swear a beery oath of blood that they will do anything to rid themselves of their accursed chains.

"Action is the word!" they agree. "But every path of escape..." they tell their new acquaintance, "...is improbable and impossible to enact."

"What means courage to you, my good looking Italian?" asks Belch.

"*Cour-rag begins-a* with a deliberate constancy and *continues-a without-a* change," sniffs the young purser, overcome with grog, and stammering more than before. Toby waves for another round. "*If-a* you are constant in the belief of *your-a* own strength and skill, *your-a cour-rag* will *never-a* fail you."

"Say you so. Belike there is much truth in that," a nodding Toby sagely agrees. "And you, my son of Norfolk, what means courage to you?"

"The courage of a man is seen in the resolution in which he embraces death. Fools fear the threats of this world. But they are as thunder is to children. Nothing can affright a heart of valor if it is resolute and confident in his purpose."

"True. It is a coward's folly to fear that which he cannot change or escape. And whoso feareth every storm and tempest is not fit to be called a sailor, nor a man."

Throughout the evening, over two dozen shipmates have brought their benches over to this table and taken part in the general moan. After closing is called and Maria harangues them to shove off to their ship bunks, each man is resolute on curing his own miserable situation. "Action is the word!" they drunkenly regurgitate, weaving their way back to their berths.

The next day's weather is more miserable than the previous. After a morning of intestinal pain and a gut-full of self-pity, Toby spends the day brooding on his lowliness and what fate and a loveless father have deprived him of. In a moment of inspiration, a daring plan born of indigestion or some malevolent star overtakes his miseries and plants a plan whereby unnatural allies might unite with a common interest. Again at the *Nous Trois,* Belch rejoins the malcontents certain the band of mutineers will reconvene at supper to rehash their travails. At his table in the back by the chimney, Gassette finds Clinton and Peretti already in their cups, enjoying the hearth's warmth and their mutinous camaraderie.

"Well met!" booms Toby.

Bland smiles are exchanged, inquiring about their courage and resolution to hold to their solemn oaths. Both sailors swearing by their mothers' honor, that they meant every word spoken the night before. Admittedly, a good deal of what was said is now lost in a dim haze of debauchery.

What follows next changes the lives of all three men.

"Under little guard in the harbor, *The Tiger...*" said so softly by Toby that Peretti and Clinton must lean in to hear his nefarious suggestion. "...one of Orsino's barks, a small two-master, is moored unprotected, and well victualed for a year's worth of travel." He points two stubby fingers toward their previous night's fraternity of companions drinking and cavorting about the tavern. "Verily, they are tall men of action," he posits then proposes that Antonio and John persuade these seamen to arm themselves with muskets on this very night and seize the defenseless *Tiger*.

"A pretty speech, my bucko, but will we not be confounded by the watch?"

"Surely, it is a-guarded?"

"No. But one man is assigned the watch," Tobias Belch assures them that *The Tiger's* guard will be an easy matter to overcome, "The solitary boatman camps out on the main deck. Simply weigh anchor, and, once in international waters, use your good talents to pillage hulking vessels commanded by captains who haven't a thimble-full of your seamanship or courage."

"But—"

"No *buts*." The harbormaster smiles affably and informs them, "The key to the escape and your success, is that I will not sound the alarm until late next morn." Further, Belch adds, "I will provide you this very hour with forged *Letters of Marque* from England. These will furnish you with Royal permission to do violence on all who sail under the flag of England's enemies."

"And what do ye ask in return?" John Clinton is skeptical.

Toby Belch *née* Gassette has thought about this for a very long time. Now that opportunity has smiled, the second son of a second son is prepared. These villainous salt-water rats are not to be trusted. He cannot expect a share of their privateering or a modicum of safety on their ship if he chooses to escape his current existence. They would turn on him as quickly and as sure as night follows day. So, Tobias Belch asks for what is worthless to mutineers. Belch lifts his black tankard to his companions and wishes them fair sailing. "But..." says he, lagging, "in your spoilings, should you discover letters of state or correspondence from those in government, give it me that I may make use of it as I may."

Smiling broadly, Antonio readily nods agreement as he ascertains no discernable loss of profit. What good are ambassadorial letters to a man who can neither read nor write?

The wiser of the two vermin, Clinton probes, "But, how shall we deliver your share to you?"

Belch's voice remains hushed, "Every third month, on the quarterly anniversary of your freedom, you shall dock on the far tip of Candy and ask for an Andrew Aguecheek. He's a scamp of fourteen who frequents the waterfront bars. He shall be our courier, and I will ever be grateful to you."

"What is he?"

"He's a gull and a lackbrain, the son of poor ill-treated gentleman." In truth, Tobias is the latter, the former being his bastard. Andrew's mother, the old Count's paramour had fled to the island of Candy to lick her wounds, after having been shamefully whipped and abandoned. There she brought up their son with no inkling of his own patrilineage. Toby wanted no part of her shame, yet when she insisted, often he found it in his heart to send money for his issue. Belch would, however, be damned first before admitting publicly that the fatherless, flaxen-haired child was his. Toby's scorn was further cemented by his observation that *the urchin's an effeminate.* "He is my Spaniel and trusts me dearly. He hasn't the wit for deceit nor the courage the Good Lord gave a flea."

Espionage is a profitable business these days. A man in cousin Edmund's position could always make use of it. Toby would have value to sell, access to a buyer, and little or no risk. Having supped at the table of revenge for years, he relishes the prospect of finding something with which to blackmail dear Edmund Dotrice should he take the bait. Belch turns his cool, sardonic gaze on his new partners who are eager to comply.

The recent Channel storm has blown Toby a providential wind. The three clink pewter cups—*to better fortunes!* Thus, their spirits lift, Antonio cries aloud, "Saint George and the *Qu-Qu-Qu een* of England."

Like quicksilver, a ripple of excitement passes through Belch as his stratagem takes root. Finally, here is an exploit even his brother could not have matched.

{ 14 }

A week of settling in comes and goes, and the
familiarity of routine sets itself into motion.
Walking St. Peter Port each day, the Doctor finds
Illyrian islanders to be content and comfortable with
their lives. As the ambitions of each citizens appear
limited, so too are their desires. *A society not involved
with the quickening of international conflict,* Dee
reasons, *looks complacently inward for its own
wellbeing.*

The philosopher bisects Will Shakespar's days into a
demanding session of lessons from nine to two and then
leisurely work in the afternoon. Though not as early as
Will's sunrise trudges to grammar school, the first shift
starts at an unbearable hour—unbearable for a man of
the theatre. Dee tutors his pupil in many authors,
including Aristotle, Quintilian, Peacham, Chaucer,
Priscian, Plutarch's *Histories*, Virgil, and most
especially, Cicero's orations. Will's knowledge of Latin is
only passable, and his translation of texts is not easily
completed. Moreover, to the Doctor's horror, the boy
has never been introduced to the mathematical beauties
of Euclid. He should not have expected otherwise; after
all, the boy is but a grammar-school student from the

middling town of Stratford-upon-Avon. More, Will's lack of equations is indicative of England's general ignorance. The whole country prefers the darkness of superstitious blindness to the radiant light of geometry and mathematics. True Will Shakespar can count the iambs in a line of pentameter or tetrameter verse. But beyond a rudimentary skill as a metronome, in higher formulas, the boy is an unlettered zero.

Shakespar's uncanny memory, however, still astonishes Dee. *"Once a passage is translated, the savant remembers every word or trope or figure,"* Dee writes in one of his cyphered updates to Walsingham.

"What are you doing, Will?" asks the scholar returning from his walk.

Squirming unhappily at his master's tone, Will replies, "I am copying out my translation." Dee has insisted that Will rewrite all his Latin reading into the vernacular.

With a withering look, Dee responds, "That seems plain. Of what author, if I may ask?"

"Some verses from Priscian," Will reports, "from his *partitiones duodecim versuum aeneides principalium.*"

"Ah, yes, his Latin parsing of Virgil's *Aeneid.* Let us hear a few stanzas." But before Shakespar can start, Dee snatches his writing paper from him.

"From memory, then?"

Looking at the boy's scribble so unlike his own meticulous penmanship, Dee answers, "So please you."

Will recites,

I sing of arms and the man who first from the shores

of Troy,
  Exiled by Fate, and Lavinia who came to Italy and its
  Shores—having been tossed much on sea and land
  By the violence of the Gods on account of the
remembering wrath
  Of savage Juno,
  Having also suffered much in war, until he would
build a city
  And bring his Gods to Latium; begetter of the Latin
race,
  The fathers of Alba, and the walls of lofty Rome.

Looking up from the translation, Dee corrects, "In the phrase '*and Lavinia who came to Italy and its shores*', you have mistook the nominative for the accusative case, as you often do in your other translations. Be mindful of your declensions. It was better yesterday. Although I see your Latin improves."

"I was ever *willful*," replies Shakespar with a mischievous grin. "I'll be damned if I am not *willing*."

The instructor smiles inadvertently at the wit-play on Shakespar's name and then, thinking better of it, frowns, "Aye, that you are, Will, too willful and moreover you have the most unsavory expletives." Unhappy with the boy's constant preference for juvenile puns on his name, Dee continues imperiously, "*My* will is that you study the harder, lest you make me look like a fool."

"Well, God give them wisdom who have it. And those who are fools, let them use their talents."

There is a *harrumph* of displeasure.

Intensely gratified and pleased with his own cleverness, the young buck ducks his head from any of his tutor's open-handed rebuffs. Avoiding further discussion, Dee returns to the boy's homework. Though Will's familiarity with his master is too large and with his Latin cases too small, Dee has not missed that today's oral recitation is a letter-perfect recitation of the boy's written translation. Surprisingly, this *legerdemain* only happens with passages in English; his Latin lessons are not as easily remembered. There seems to be some disconnect there. Dee ponders, *Is the boy's partiality a side effect of a vivid memory or simply disregard for his studies?* The more significant threat is that this inability to retain foreign words may prove inconvenient—if not detrimental—should Will's mind be needed to capture correspondence from abroad during their investigations.

If Shakespar is to succeed at writing, he must master the subtlety and artificiality of language that the better playgoers demand of their poets. Besides a Latin education, Dee's exercises help Will with the niceties of classical rhetoric. Will knows little of the rhetorical figures or the means of invention.

Later that day, they are reviewing Ovid's *Metamorphoses.*

"This will not do! You were born a tradesman's son, and now you have transformed the greatest of poets into naught but dull commerce. Nothing here in your translation is commendable. All is a shambles. What is this..." Dee thrusts the paper in his student's face. "...but a great want of beauty in your writing? Neither antithesis nor zeugma nor paradigma! Scarcely any conjunction or transition. In short, no eloquence. Knowledge of which should have been rudimentary lessons in your grammar school studies. Really, what *was* taught you in that Warwickshire village? Did they not teach you any grace at all?"

It's near two in the afternoon, and the player-schoolboy is too exhausted to confront his teacher's reproving wagging beard. Listless, he parries, "I have not the wit nor years that you have, Master, but I do desire to learn. And I little deserve your bitterness. Master Jenkins was as good and as kind—"

"No doubt, your shoddy Midland schoolmaster was only concerned with how well you strung words together for fashioning a prologue before you butchered a calf. It is this—" The scholar stops himself from blurting out, *It is this want of style and memorable language that made your Amleth so utterly unbearable.*

Defeated, Will pouts; his hang-dog expression softens his master's exasperation. At least the boy seems repentant; his middle-class desire to succeed may serve him to achieve better. But, presently, he could be more diligent if not dutiful. *His mind wanders. He spends too much time gazing out the window.* What daydreams outside could possibly be more exciting than the fanciful adventures in the *Metamorphoses?*

Writing in his private journal later that day, Dr. John Dee inscribes, "*Gulielmus Shakespar has neither the virtues of subtlety, modesty, the grace of deportment, nor even the slightest grasp of the principles of reasoning. He is an inheritor of our nation's slighting of the virtues of education and, I fear, symptomatic of a future unlettered Commonwealth... but he is a good boy.*"

With the tolling of two and the day's lessons finally at an end, Shakespar runs outside, escaping up a pathway to the vistas of St. Martin's point that look down on the Channel. Exceedingly weary in body and mind, he welcomes the sharp winter gusts that blow the stagnation of Ovidian dactylic hexameter from his frazzled mind. This morning's stultifying Latin verses spread, cadaverous, in his memory. For the nonce, the tortures of the early morning's geometry with its angles and parabolas are shoved aside, together with the lessons in artificial arguments whereby he must create for his taskmaster's satisfaction entertaining rhetorical figures and conceits based on the classics he is asked to read.

"Fut!" mutters Shakespar, "What did Horace say? *'The mountain groaned in great labor, then bore a tiny mouse.'.*" Thankfully, he has learned the trick of marooning the tedium to a distant memorial shelf. He doesn't see how Aristotle can improve his *Amleth. If this is what Greene and Chapman studied at University, no wonder their plays are so pedantic.*

Shakespar's eyes travel upward; a pair of redwings flit effortlessly through gray vaulted skies. As if performing a soliloquy to this audience in the sky, Will declares, "I did not travel all this way to be a translator. I signed on to be a poet. The poet contrives living characters out of his own fancy. The translator merely copies."

In Will's imagination, he soars with the swooping birds, breasting the wind—free from terrestrial drudgery, looking down on earth-bound humans. He questions—not for the first time—the need to appreciate the wonders of nature by reading musty authors. *The proper study of nature's glories, he tells himself, is through meticulous observation of the world around him, and, using those insights to limn the workings of the human heart.* Like all apprentices overridden by masters, Will looks forward to spitting the bit the moment his study's bridle is slipped off, and he is free to practice his craft. "That day cannot come soon enough!" he shouts over the rattling wind to the redwings that cannot be bothered. Pulling his present pains about him and relishing the extreme weather, Will daydreams of grabbing hold of success as tightly as he clutches his cloak. For him, poverty cannot be an option. Having been given a chance to inherit either John Shakespar's tanning trade or farm his grandfather Arden's land, the poet had foresworn both. His family had nearly thrashed him for such a reckless refusal. Never caring for his father's tannery with its greasy skins—a loathsome business that stank more of mediocrity than its noisome chemicals—Shakespar could not allow his family's predictions of failure to come true. Trusting the stirrings of greatness within him, Will had a thousand things to say, and, in his heart he felt, men of taste and position would pay handsomely for a pretty phrase well penned. *Success is a golden angel to be followed no matter what back streets one trawls to capture it.*

A mocking inner voice intrudes and reminds him

Prince Amleth was disastrous—*a tragedy in so many ways.* Will tries to shake doubts from himself. *What if I have no talent?* a belittling voice whispers, *What if Burbage refuses to buy a second play?* Reminded of Dr. Dee's criticisms of his work, Shakespar fears that these scenarios are the more probable. *My writing, Dee has told me, has been but a toy. A comfortable and artless scribble.* Furious at his qualms of failure, he argues the contrary. *To succeed, a poet must shoulder the irksome weight of scholarship and make it a constant discipline. Success means that I, like Dee, must become an alchemist and continuously study how to transubstantiate language into precious dramatic catharsis. The strides of a man's work are measured by his commitment to the diligent pursuit of the journey.*

Most assuredly, Will Shakespar *shall* not continue squeaking out girls' roles forever. Granted, his first play landed far wide off the mark. *On the next, I must score.* If he can get it produced. *No qualms no doubts.* He must take full advantage of what Fortune is giving him. *Failure is unacceptable.* To the redwings and the skies above he swears aloud, "By all that is Holy, my future shall be better than my past!" To himself he declares, *No more, my former days of whoredom, where, following my theatrical ambition, I had sunk to canoodling in the backrooms of Eastcheap. 'Shakeshaft', that moneyed theatre-owner, Burbage, had called me and then ordered me to my knees to perform.* Burbage had not been his only *benefactor*—or rather *malefactor.* There had been too many others. *Thankfully, this Dee is not so inclined. But, what matter past depravities? No, no more of that.* The memory of things done could be burned away if one's celebrity blazes bright enough. *My past is but a means to an honorable end. William Shakespar will be a name to conjure with. Doubtless, the final couplet of my life will be written in gold leaf.*

Wheeling drunkenly beneath the cold sky, Will's wild ambitions career alongside his hopes, much like the crazed arcs of the redwings that have left him behind.

A small beagle, sniffing the hard ground for food, appears out of nowhere. Each looks at each other in head-tilting scrutiny. Instinctively open to qualifying and analogizing everyday experiences, Shakespar asks himself, *Is this creature, now before me, a noble hound or a beggarly mutt that has strayed from the stables and come here to piss? Has it the highborn mien of majesty or the bastard breeding of a base cur?*

Had not Will's instructor told him to recognize God's hierarchical order? Conversely, Will thinks, *What am I to him?* "Contraries," Dee impresses incessantly upon his student, "Seek contradictories in your thinking, and you will create conflict." *Am I a higher being to him or an irrelevant nothing?* There's to be no answer. A fierce gust suddenly shutters them both, and Shakespar's companion yips, wandering off for warmer shelter. Will's attention wanders as well. Leaning back and letting the weak sunshine bathe his face, the lad nestles in his cloak as he gazes at the open sky. There is comfort in knowing when the right metaphor is discovered, all prior straining is forgotten, and only the sweet taste of a perfect line remains.

Whistling louder through the pines, the Channel

wind ruffles his hair and stings his face. The ground is now too cold to sit on. The new rawness is like the afterglow of rough sex, and he sees it as a sure sign that Apollo is pleased with him. Shivering and loping from the open hilltop to a spot by the garden, he finds shelter from the weather.

I must not catch the ague, the boy warns himself. Already he's lost too many friends that way.

"I'll fer him, and firk him and ferret him, *pesante, par moi foi,*" comes a shout from far away. It is unmistakably the chaplain in an un-Christian fit of anger.

What's this? What's this? Will wonders bemused, *Is this the prologue to some comedy? How delicious is the contrast of the chaplain's reverend office and his expressions of irreverence. What a dramatic antithesis to exploit in a play. Wait,* Will thinks, *how did the priest say the word?*

"*Pe–san te,*" murmurs Shakespar. The word is peasant, but the man's unmistakable third syllable trips it into a tri-syllabic word. He rolls the pronunciation around in his mouth; savoring the accent, he mimics the way English is forever Frenchified here in Illyria. *If words can paint a feeling, a rustic accent can capture a character.* Not content to just imitate the voice, he begins to explore what physicality can add to the impersonation. He flounces along the grassy plateau ever spying to see if someone one is watching. A broad characterization emerges as he struts and scowls in imitation of his memory of other prelates. *It needs work.* Suddenly, another clerical curse is shouted below.

Perhaps these epithets are but prologue to a more uproarious performance. Needing to hear more, he runs down the hill toward the chapel, praying that the sacristan will continue in his scathing idiosyncratic performance.

While Will daydreams of worldly ambition, *entrées* to tapestried mansions, and a new character for his acting repertoire, the *magister,* John Dee, methodically puts away his teaching paraphernalia. The scholar discovers in his bag a forgotten volume by Pico della Mirandola. The exacting persona of the scolding teacher now melts into a eager student as he reviews the philosophical treatise into celestial influences on earthly talismans. Dee's boney forefinger travels methodically over the leathery vellum page, stopping here and there to ponder the subtleties of Pico's surprising suppositions. Reading and rereading the passages, Dr. Dee searches for any illuminating insights buried in the arcana. At the ready to preserve any such quasi-revelation is the doctor's companion diary. Pico and Pythagoras proved that certain geometric figures have natural magic that echo the perfect mathematics of creation. There is an intrinsic duality in numbers as they simultaneously affect both terrestrial and cosmic realities. He reaches for his diary; he has found something.

The chapel bell tolls the mid-afternoon canonical hour of *None*. Having always made a practice of praying when he hears church bells, the ex-chaplain lifts his eyes from his note-taking. "Blessed is our Lord Jesus Christ. Have mercy on me, my wife, our young son, and our child to be." As a cleric he had learned that it is a habit that not only cleanses his soul but clears his thoughts. With bowed head, he again asks heaven, to show mercy to his family, for enlightenment, and a speedy end to his travails here that he may go home to his sorely missed life.

Dee's prayers done, his thoughts drift back to Jane and Arthur; his desertion of them remains an open wound. He imagines little Arthur smiling up at him, his little fingers grasping at Dee's long beard, his lolling head nestled in the crook of his arm, a smile of unimaginable love beaming from his face. Remembrance of some wifely scolding of Jane's, some gentle reprimand for a chore undone gladdens him as well. What of her present condition? She must be near her time. He worries. Childbirth is dangerous. Before Arthur was born, Jane had taken precautions and written a will. The unknown and the absence of his family weigh heavy. *No,* he upbraids himself *wallowing in grief, only leads to the mortal sin of despair.*

"Down, down," Dee lectures his loneliness, *"...think rather on what's to be done. The sooner that is accomplished, the sooner the journey home."*

Focusing, he returns to his mission to uncover recusant activities in Illyria and the smuggling of Catholic materials on ships bound for England. Despite his visits to the harbor, and, seeing the unsupervised unloading of crates and barrels, he has yet to find an excuse to inspect their contents. Might there be religious or political materials, or even Jesuits hidden in those oak barrels? He needs a way of finding out. His duties as Royal Postmaster give him license to inquire after messages *from* England, but Dee is more interested in vessels and their cargo bound *for* England.

There is a scratching at the door. At first, he thinks it is Will. Then he hears the whining. He shooes the dog away. The solitary man finds that he is in need of human companionship. Wrapping himself in his cloak to face the weather's bitterness, the antiquarian departs to visit the *Nous Trois*. Perhaps Providence will provide an unwitting gossip and a line of investigation.

As John Dee canvasses the streets of Illyria, his long black robe swaying back and forth the briny sea air permeates his lungs and burns his eyes. His sharp nose leaks and his heels itch from chilblain. The ocean blasts of Illyria are more bitter than those of the Thames. Cramming his beaver hat well down on his head, thinking about how much is yet to be done, his thoughts sting as well.

Jane...

Between the squat St. Peter Port buildings runs a well-trampled pathway that connects Illyria's heights to its depths. As Dee follows it, his shoes and the hems of his cloak and robe are muddied. The winter wind whips leaves and dust into whirling eddies of debris. At times,

Dee is forced to stop and shield his face from swinging branches and driven dirt. From the steep descent, a dull throb has started aching in his knees and hips; he winces with each step. Thoughts of Jane flood his entire being. He cannot remember when he has felt so lonely.

Dee steps judiciously over bare broken tree limbs, the victims of the strong wind. Some old wives' tales warn about disturbing these. Better be safe than sorry. The imponderable problem of Orsino can be solved. The adage comes to him: *He who hath no patience hath nothing.*

One lone figure hurries into view. Like Dee, his head is tucked into his shoulders to protect him from the elements. Beneath the shapeless canvas hat jammed down on a large head, is the Harbormaster Belch, hurrying toward the long low frame house of *Nous Trois.* The swaying hand-painted sign above the door seems to wave them both indoors.

Within the windowless establishment, a low-burning seacoal fire burns. The owner has not seen fit to light any torches. As his eyes adjust to semi-darkness, blood returns to his extremities. The lonely old man perceives faces looking up, pointedly annoyed by the sudden presence of a stranger's visit. A quarrel comes to a sudden halt between a slack-jawed pimp and his middle-aged whore. Illyrian distrust is apparent.

Dee knows the locals consider him as unpopular here as the French are regarded in London, yet he loosens his cloak as if he were arriving home to Mortlake. His need for answers—and companionship—harden him against the islanders' sharp looks. Apparel proclaims the man.

Dee's embroidered gloves and beaver hat and collar signal prosperity. And, in an ignominious haunt like this, it is best not to appear too well off. To his benefit, the mud and the drizzle have gone a long way to further sully a bedraggled traveler. Quite deliberately, he allows the denizens of the docks time to get a good view of him. Impervious to their distrust, he judiciously stows his gloves and nonchalantly rubs his numb hands together.

In the gloom, he makes out about forty male phantoms, only two women, stained ochre walls that have been papered over with yellowing broadsheets either for decoration or to help keep the cold out. Cheek-by-jowl tables offer no privacy between conversations and gossip. All along a simple plank shelf an array of pewter mugs ranging in size and craftsmanship serves as crown molding around the circumference of the room. Cooling in a large basin of water on the bar a half dozen bottles of rum and wine await shouts of "Another round!" In three bowls at the far end of the bar, used mugs are bathed by the servitor, a pimple-faced half-witted character, whose face droops permanently from boredom.

Off to Dee's side, Tobias Gassette strips off his own outer garments, silently considering the newcomer's presence, *Intruder or possible gull?* In a seeming act of neighborliness, Belch breaks the silence. "Master Dee, are you lost?" The magus shakes his head, still taking things in. "If you've come for dispatches from England, Royal Postmaster, there be none here." Belch laughs. "The boat from London is not expected until the morrow." The fellow's chiding is none too welcoming yet passes for the appearance of cordiality as he adds, "If this blow continues, you'll have to wait even longer."

"Nay, harbormaster, I've come for a walk and..." The Doctor speaks louder, "...to meet what townfolk I can."

"The wind bites bitterly," says some carping sharp-nosed dice-player in the corner, "a bad day for an outing. You'll want your London comforts here and have a hard scramble back up the hill." Other choice words in rural French float in the haze; the xenophobia in the room is as pervasive as the chimney smoke.

Exchanging glance for glance with his detractors, the Doctor announces to the crowd in his best French, "It was ever my wont to taste my legs along the Thames—no matter the season. The sight of your Illyrian harbor called out to me, and the swaying boats reminded me of home. I thought I might learn what new news of the town." It is a practiced performance of bravado delivered in as loud a voice as any town crier.

"You eat with Jews at your home!" hoots one of his critics in the back of the room, while shuffling an old deck of cards. Unsure from where in the gloom the attack emanates, Dee is genuinely taken aback but dares not show his confidence wavering. His eyes shift about. The reference is apparent enough. In a small fishing town, everyone knows your business.

A whimsical Tobias Belch orders a cup of malmsey wine and watches the stranger's demeanor with curiosity. Usually, the condescending lords and gentry never leave their high ground in the city. *But today, the blasts of winter seem to have blown a wayward old ram to my door*, he thinks, *This lost muttonhead might prove to have some gold about him.* A most sophisticated shearer of sheep, Belch is no clumsy cutpurse or pickpocket. Fellowship and conversation are better at cony-catching than any rogue's nip and foist.

"There's naught that happens on this quay that I don't have the knowing of," Belch confides to the Royal Postmaster for all to hear, "The coming of a ship of Jews with a postman from England is a singular occurrence in our backwater of Illyria. We'd all like to know how that came to be." He looks about the room noting the doubting regulars who nod agreement. "Should you be in the talking mood?" asks Belch, pointing to a stool close to the fire and beckoning the tapster to ready a glass for their new guest. "What's your pleasure, Doctor?"

Scanning the tavern, John Dee purses his lips and considers the offer. The harbormaster's welcome to this hostile environment is a better *entré* than the aging spy expected.

He looks at Toby's inflamed cheeks and remembers the stinging of his own.

"Aye, marry, harbormaster, I will. Something for the chill." Turning to the bartender, he posits, "Canary wine?" Dee walks to the fireside seat Belch offers at a beer-stained table. The necromancer considers it unwise to sit with one's back to thieving rogues. Accordingly, ignoring the proffered chair's back and the stares of the pub's gimlet-eyed shanty-boatmen, Dee skirts the table to its far side. There he squeezes his thin frame into the gap between the rectangular table and the single planked bench near the wall. Standing erect, he takes his chances and launches into a pretty tale meant to put his critics at ease. "I was eager to set sail from Her Majesty's shores to serve the people of Illyria, and the Jewish *Rachel* was the first vessel headed this way, who else would sail on Christmas?"

There are a few ugly laughs. Most locals return attention to their own activities. They are disappointed that the old man has no silk lining within his Londoner's cloak, nor any items of finery about him but the hat.

Belch, however, sticks like a burr. "A scurvy lot to trust your passage to—not to mention your life." Dee shrugs at Belch's remark and sits on a backless bench along the wall so he can face the room. "The Jew craves Christian blood, you know, for their heathen ceremonies," adds Belch, beckoning to the barkeep to add another cup of canary to Dee's order. "I'd not have been so eager to venture the Channel all alone without protection. Especially as it was the Sabbath on which you chose to sail."

Any stalwart still eavesdropping prick up all ears, eager to hear what falsehoods this Englishman will spout. Was the foreigner an atheist? By God, once they'd picked his pockets, they'd take his clothes as well and leave him to suffer the cruelties of the Illyrian wind and chill.

Preoccupied with tracing his thumb along a crack in the table, Dee looks up suddenly and catches their intentions. Taking pains to move his purse to a safer position, he repositions it from where it hangs at his belt to deep in his lap and then folds his hands over it like a fleshy tent. He has a second thought and, with a forefinger carefully clinching the drawstrings of his purse, re-steeples his hands over his money. His gestures are less acts of security than a declaration to all that he is no gull.

That done, he sets about announcing his *bone fides*, "Dost thou know that in England I am well known for my metaphysics? Some call me the *Queen's Conjurer*."

"Say you so? That is not unknown to me." Belch grins mischievously. "Come, what is your reason for coming here today? Do you mean to bewitch us?"

"By Jesu, not for the world. Verily, the ignorant, not liking of my studies, have spread a plentifulness of false witness about my character. I know not what you have heard of me, but..." And he here Dee smiles wickedly before adding, "...*most* of it is rumor." He is rather happy with the effect of his subterfuge.

Superstitious patrons cross themselves against the warlock and imagine delivering the heretic to a raging pyre all while fixating still upon the stranger's purse.

"Well, ere setting foot on board the accursed *Rachel*, I investigated the stars for any warnings of danger. My sun sign had been in the ascendant..." At that moment, as if by magic, the tepid fire flames up. A cat-ate-the-canary grin widens on Dee's face. He beckons all round to listen intently. "Yet, knowing what peril I was placing myself in, I dared not leave aught to chance. Therefore, I took precautions that the Jews could not but be wary of." Dee is slightly distracted by what might have been a fly fluttering near his left ear. But it is winter; there are no flies. Mindful of chicanery Dee is aware of an angler twitching the graybeard's ear, watchful for an inattentive hand to wave off the insect and thereby loosen the necromancer's grip on his purse. A second attempt and the foist fails, so Belch subtly shoos off the catchpole.

Endeavoring to enthrall all eyes and ears in the room, Dee confides in a hypnotic voice, "Ere boarding, I hewed off a long thick branch from a gnarled oak. One that had stood on the bank of the Thames long afore my ancestor, Arthur was King. To its thicker end, I attached one of my scrying crystals. I then used it as a staff and paraded it around for all to see. Those heathens could not miss it. The crystal transformed the half-moonlight into diverse colors and shapes." Eyes squint either from the smoke or in bafflement. "The Captain inquired as to the rod's importance, and I informed him that this was the very staff that his prophet, Moses, had wielded in Pharaoh's land. It had hermetic powers and could divide the Channel, were I to see fit."

The crowd knows not whether to laugh at the gulling of the Jews or fear that this is a most nefarious magician. Belch chooses not to credit what is not as yet proven. Cunning men and women—charlatans—are amusing to Belch; he has seen many come and go.

"Were the *yellow hats* such asses as to believe you?" ventures Belch.

The storyteller looks about—acknowledges to himself that the room is silent save for the sizzling of charred mutton abandoned by the riveted cook.

"Verily, and after I was brought safely to your waters, I allowed them to buy the stick off me for ten talons of silver." And with a flourish, Dee delivers the punchline,

"Thereby I recouped all of my ferrying costs plus I had an excellent jest."

The room explodes in raucous laughter. Even the more skeptical gawkers have to admit that it is an exceedingly fine tale.

"Well told!" Belch smiles.

"And a just comeuppance for Christ-killers!" comes a shout from a cutpurse.

Nearly a century after forced expulsion, Jews continue to flee their homes in anti-Semitic France, Antwerp, and The Hague. Dutch Protestants did not mind breaking bread with Jews. The Catholics of Illyria, rarely having had any converse with Jews, were not so amenable. Their initial suspicion now fully shed, the tavern audience begs for scraps of gossip.

"And *your* Queen, how old is She now?" asks Toby Belch in a high quizzical voice.

Like the vice character in an old play, Dee screws up his face in mock confusion, scratches his head, and makes a show of counting the Royal years on his fingers. His performance gets its hoped-for laughter, instigating a second round of cackling at the Queen's expense. Stoking the crowd's disdain, the Doctor pulls at his ear and postulates, "Seems she's ruled *for-ever.*" He stretches "ever" ridiculously.

The older of the two doxies present—a rather obese transvestite—adds to the Queen's mockery by lifting her sagging fat pectoralis tits for a moment back to their youthful carriage, and then with a theatrical frown, lets them plunge to her girdle.

"*Alors,*" says Belch pointing at the he-hag, "Illyria's

very own fairy *quean*."

Ignoring the insults to His Sovereign, Dee chooses rather to ingratiate.

"I know not Good Bess' age, but rumor has it that She is in such need of new wigs. At Her command, the Royal Wigmaker has un-haired all the redheads of London. The man is paid by the strand and is fat as his shorn hairs are skinny. He is thought to be one of the wealthiest men in the city. At his sight, ginger-heads are quickly dragged inside by their mums. Of late, even the brunettes cover their heads in fear. In London, all Eve's daughters fear 'a dyeing'."

As is the way with wayfarers to distant ports of call, if you can thaw the native resentment with jocularity, all are happy to hear of things new. What tidings from the Court? *Who's in? Who's out? What's the cost of wheat, corn, and wool? Who's the Royal successor? Will there be war with Spain?* John Dee does his best to answer, always offering the caveat that he is but a rural schoolteacher who rarely frequents the Court. Despite the growing conviviality, never does Dee allow himself to forget the danger he is in. His hands remain pressed upon the contents of his lap.

Not all the questions put to him are political. Many patrons are genuinely eager to learn of Dr. John Dee's magical abilities. Wretches ask after spells and incantations to cure the toothache or a soporific to protect their young grandchildren from *incubi* and *succubi* during slumber. One goes so far as to ask for a spell at winning dice. Dee sloughs these off not a one, for there may be some within who shall provide information later. He prescribes the appropriate *paternosters, Aves*, and potions for each malady and protection. Dee even satisfies the dicer, cautioning, "Only play with your own dice."

By degrees, Belch becomes the Royal Postmaster's guardian, waving off known rascals, malcontents, and dips. At times, Dee asks casually after foreign influences on Illyria, especially Spain; at that, people either shrug or change the subject. It is revealed that English ships patrol the Channel for Spanish galleons, hoping to monitor and sometimes pester the economic lifeline to the Duke of Alva and his Spanish forces in Holland. Spain may be a constant threat to Elizabeth and Her territories' peace; Phillip II, however, is the defender of the Catholic faith and hence the defender of *their* faith. Here in the English hinterlands of Catholic Illyria, Her Majesty's power is attenuated. Orsino and his people live by their own rules, Dee is advised.

Until early evening, John Dee stays at the *Nous Trois* making friends, entertaining, and listening to fisherfolks' stories as hoary as the grizzled beards that tell them. Dee gives advice, commiserates, and pours from an endless pitcher of replenished ale. All the while, he studies faces. *Who might be a bribable informer?* The young dockworker already soured by a life of heavy lifting? The local fisherman who is proud of his mastery of the sea and the quickness of his boat? The barkeep who works the counter every day and never leaves the harbor? The rail-thin carter who is seemingly uncaring about worshipping saint days? Or the jolly harbormaster, across from him, who is courting him and has access to cargo manifests? Which of them needs money badly enough to compromise principles? Or forego their faith? Which of them hates Elizabeth the least?

Dee aches to ask whether any of them knows of Edmund Campion's influential legacy—if and when he was ever been here in Illyria? Or, could they point to any who might have aided him while he was alive? Just three years and a half years earlier, Edmund Campion, the University of Douai's most illustrious recusant, had penetrated the homeland's security by stowing aboard a ship inbound from one of the Channel Islands or so Sir Francis has told him.

What the world knew was that Edmund Campion, the foremost recusant to enter England with a ministry there of only sixteen months, had become a blessed martyr and a rallying figure for Roman Catholics. Braving death, the Jesuit had in secrecy preached to thousands of English papists about the heresy of Tudor Anglicanism and the sanctity of the Roman Church. Fervently and eloquently, he had begged his countrymen to foreswear the state's religion and return to the true faith. Papist Europe revered him universally not only for his religious zeal but also for his advocacy for freedom of speech. *A policy*, thinks Dee, *to which the English government gives lip service yet never truly honors.*

Walsingham had sworn to him that the seditious priest had been welcomed in Illyria. Dee was there to prove him right. The equally sinister, Father Robert Persons, a fellow Jesuit who had earlier come like a spy into Jericho to prepare the way, probably had docked here too. Together, they stoked the rebellious fires of Roman Catholic attacks against the Queen. How many of these grinning Illyrian faces might have abetted Campion and Persons to complete their journey to Northumberland and Leicestershire to preach their apostasy? How many of those here had heard the English ballad-maker's refrain?

His reasons were ready, his grounds were most sure,
The enemy cannot his force long endure,
Campion, in camping on spiritual field,
In God's cause his life ready to yield.

The unfortunate Campion had been hanged—then, while still alive—cut down, then emasculated, disemboweled, and finally the maimed corpse was drawn and quartered. John Dee and most of the English North, a citadel of Catholic belief, had been appalled at this cruel treatment. Campion, with no antipathy toward the Queen and her ministers, only professed the wisdom practiced by many of Europe's countries—Christian religious tolerance.

Sanguine that familiarity makes many a friend and excellent wit renders even more, Dee says nothing about Campion. In due course, he will inquire, after learning the inward nature of some of these poor souls and ascertains whom to trust. They had seen the purse in his lap. The advertisement was there. Undoubtedly, the promise of gold would tempt someone.

{15}

Mischievously, Will Shakespar enters the chapel door at the edge of the outer bailey. Will is happy to find that the comedy he overheard playing outside has moved inside.

"*Par ma foi!*" The stocky chaplain explodes inches from Malvolio, staring daggers at the steward's large nose and veiled eyes. "*Encore*, you will not lecture me on the liturgical anthems we are to perform." The chaplain's Burgundian temper sears the air. "I care not a fig for your self-righteous criticisms, and you, *Monsieur le Stewart*, can go to *hell*."

Giggles erupt from the boys of the choir whose rehearsal Malvolio has interrupted. Decorum long evaporated, the sweet soaring voices that engaged in Thomas Tallis' anthem, *If ye love me, keep my commandments*, are now discordant and chaotic. Seating himself quietly in the shadows, Will savors the abusive exchange.

Malvolio and his ilk, forgetting their principles of mercy and temperance, strike at others for not seeing the world as they do or for not following their scriptures' ordinances for the faithful. Yet, even Count Orsino, who can bristle at this chamberlain at times, admires

Malvolio's devotion, his incorruptible loyalty, and his meticulousness at rooting out active and potential problems.

"You swear, sir, and in the presence of children!" Malvolio, with his little wooden staff crooked in his elbow, adjusts one of the links in his chain of office. "Sinfully you take our heavenly Father's name in vain." His manner appears tranquil not because he knows his strength, but, on the contrary, because he fears he is weak and infirm. Scanning his surroundings, he adds, "This is language neither seemly for one of your profession nor fit for such a sanctified place..." Unable to stop himself, Malvolio's voice vibrates, "...for all its idolatry and superstition."

"Idolatry?" *Le Père* seethes, "The devil a Puritan that *vous est.*" The chaplain raises his fists combatively, "*Allez, allez*, vent thy folly elsewhere. I *can hardly* forebear hurling *zings* at you."

Sequestered in shadow, Will reflects, '*Vent thy folly,*' *I must remember that. And the accent! 'Zings' for 'things'!*

Though a foot taller than the chaplain, Malvolio retreats nervously, his face more ashen than the clouds on this grizzled day. His wand now tightly clenched in his fist, the steward whines, "I shall report your behavior to the Count. He shall know of it by this hand."

"Aye, you do so, and while you are at it, tell him that you criticized the singing of a motet *zat* Her Ladyship asked *me* expressly to perform for St. Valentine's. Will you tell him *zat*?"

Feeble, impotent Malvolio struggles to say, "You may

call it singing, but it is naught but caterwauling. This music is filled with heresy. Perhaps, Her Ladyship was not ware of its content."

The chaplain can scarcely believe his ears. "Not know *la pièce* she has chosen? *Quelle idiotie!*"

Like all the practitioners of his sect, the only music and words Malvolio begrudgingly approves of are the *Psalms* sung solemnly.

"Idiocy, but to you, sir." There is venom as the cleric says, "You, who follow not the true Roman creed."

While England constrained many aspects of Catholic practice, still, in the outlands of the English realm, Northumberland, Ireland, and Illyria, the old faith continues much the same as it always has.

"Our choice is as beautiful a composition as ever written. But being that you are a time-pleaser, an affected ass who cons state without book, a blasphemer, a monster, a..." here the chaplain sniffs with utter contempt and makes one more advance on his victim, heedless of the reed-like stick in the other man's hand, "...a...*Puri-TAN*" *The last syllable*, thinks Shakespar, *is contemptuously elongated*. The curate thrusts with a poking forefinger, his voice cracking as it climbs, "You have not the sensitivity of a blind maggot to appreciate the beauty of *z'exquise* motet."

With that, the cleric turns abruptly from the beleaguered Malvolio and walks away, secure in the knowledge that though the steward has sway over the household, he has no authority—*no, not a whit*—over matters of the Church. Slamming the sacristy door behind him, the priest leaves Malvolio alone with the sniggling boys.

Suddenly, Malvolio's wooden wand is animated. He holds it erect, its tapered end points to Heaven as he faces the youths. "Entertainment and disrespect are sins. We must all mend until the pangs of death shake you." Now the authoritarian's stick shifts and points to the floor—or is it to hell? "Pray on your knees, fasting for your errors!"

Obediently, the choirboys drop to their knees in prayer. Malvolio turns on a heel and leaves, brushing past Will. Shakespar does his best to appear, beyond all reasonableness, that he has not been loving everything he has witnessed. Behind a pillar, two workmen abandon their hiding place and return to brooming the floor rushes. No more than a minute passes before the still smoldering chaplain storms dutifully from his sanctuary to rehearse the choir. First, however, he requires answers of his boys.

"*Garçons*, did any of ye see where *le steward* went?"

There is a shaking of heads and universal response of, "*Non, mon Père*, we were in prayer."

"Did *Monsieur le steward* speak anything—after I left—of going forthwith to *Le Comte*?"

Again the same, "*Non, mon Père*."

Turning now to the men who are at work on the floors, "*Et vous*? Did ye see or hear aught?"

"*Non, mon Père*."

Hoping not yet to ring down the curtain on the comedy, Will steps forward to stir the pot, "I rather think he went off to pray or maybe to polish his chain of office. How you did shake his ears. I doubt not but the ass is braying to someone even now."

But the sullen Gaul is not in the mood to listen to a nattering stranger, especially as he has work to do for his *Comtesse*. He marches back to his virginal and takes up his seat.

"*Silence! Defénse de parler!*" he shouts and gets it by banging on the keys.

Quiet immediately reigns. A pitch is played, and the boys sing.

"And so ends our play. Alas," sighs Shakespar. Resigned, he opts now to sit in the back pews where he listens to heavenly sopranos infused with sensual contraltos. In time he is struck by the contraries of human behavior. This cleric, who was as choleric as any rough soldier, is now at one with the music. Like a doting father, the choirmaster has forgiven them their minor mistakes and is paternally proud of their elegant counterpoints and polyphonic unities. *Once noisy children are now obedient angels. How can this blissful shepherd of children be one and the same as the ungodly priest who had come before?* The young poet cannot but wonder at how changeable men's *humours* are. What then is the intrinsic quality of a man, and what the outer pretense? *Perhaps, a man's personality is neither black nor white,* Will tells himself, *neither good nor bad but a continuum seeking balance between extremes. What Dee calls temperance.* Suddenly, Shakespar is struck by his own introspection. Real characters, Will realizes, examine life as they encounter it in the moment as he is doing now. *That,* thinks Shakespar, *is how I shall breathe life into my works.*

Characters cannot be mere speechifying puppets. They must be self-aware. Damn, I must write this down. Where is there paper?

Behind Shakespar, the heavy wooden door opens again. *Malvolio returns?* Will glances back and is surprised to see *La Comtesse*, Dian, more surprisingly *sans entourage.* The narthex is engulfed in sunlight and the presence of the French beauty who stands resplendent in the open doorway. Chaplain and choir fall silent to give her their full attention. To Will's mind, it seems so disrespectful that not one among them bows to her. Never having been honored with the custom, Dian is ignorant of its absence.

"Forgive me, reverend Father, but I had thought to see how you and your charges progress. Please continue with your *musique*," gesturing to the keyboard, "*S'il vous plait.*"

The shadowed church interior illuminates with her smile. Men and boys alike bask in it while Lady Dian takes a seat in front of the intricately carved altar. The chaplain strikes a chord, and the choir, inspired by Her Ladyship, strives for perfection. Listening as contentedly as a nesting dove, soon Dian forgets herself and her bejeweled hand commences to animate from its perch in her lap. Bewitched, Shakespar shifts his seat inconspicuously to the Epistle side of the church to watch Dian's sympathetic fingers hold correspondence with the music and strum the air with the musical undulations. Though most women would not have been so shamelessly demonstrative, Dian is entranced by the performance. In turn, Will is entranced by her. Not quite sure at first, then, *yes, her green eyes are most definitely tearing.* He savors a gasp of passion that catches in her throat as her breath quickens with the *accelerando.* She is all fire and air.

By the time the anthem concludes, Will has decided that he must compose a sonnet to this paragon of women who now beams through her tears. He rifles through the possible classical allusions: *Venus? Too pedestrian. Helen? Beautiful enough, but unfaithful. Hecuba, a model of devotion? Too old. And the Countess' namesake, Diana? Too cold and too chaste.*

As the boys sing a new canticle; Dian claps appreciation urging them on. In her presence, Will feels the heady air of paradise surrounding him. Was there ever such beauty in a woman's eye? Such comeliness. Such Grace. Radiant. Exquisite. Unmatchable beauty. If his master spoke with angels in Mortlake, here, just ahead of him, was one newly alighted and enthroned in all her glory. The perfection of the ardent teenager's blissful moment is ruined when the church door opens.

Orsino's Chief of Staff, Lord Griffin enters. *Has he come in response to Malvolio?* wonders Shakespar. *Please don't let him lecture the chaplain and ruin my bliss.*

Instead, after pausing momentarily to appreciate the performers, Orsino's Chamberlain moves swiftly down the aisle and sits by Her Ladyship. Neither is surprised by this chance meeting; neither takes notice of Shakespar. Lord Griffin whispers in hushed tones.

"*Silence,*" she shushes him, "*Angels sing.*"

"But, I have come—"

"*Encore, silence.*" Dian is peremptory. "*Pas maintenant.*"

Reproved, Edmund joins Dian in rapt enjoyment as angelic tones waft over them. When rehearsal finishes, they lavish warm-hearted praise on the ensemble. Congratulating the chaplain on work well done and avuncularly tousling some of the boys' hair, Lord Griffin excuses himself. Having work to do, he leaves Dian with the children. Lovingly the Illyrian Countess greets each boy individually. Honoring and humoring one by one, she occasionally drops all formality by making faces at the boys and flirting innocently with the chaplain.

Shakespar beholds kindness in her every word, grace in every gesture, and boldness gets the best of him. He approaches the front of the pews without caution.

"My Lady, I am—"

"*You!*" Dian pauses to regard Will. "The Postmaster's boy, are you not? *Le philosophe's* boy?"

"If it please Your Ladyship to call me so." She has the noble bearing of Lady Montague, whom Will deems the most beloved woman in Southwark.

"Well, Postmaster's boy, did *la musique* not stir you?"

Yes, the music in her voice: her throaty, guarded Gallic-accented purring of the word *music*.

With her *this close* looking at him, her perfumed presence melts his swagger. "Aye, M'Lady, it was thrilling. And might a player from Warwickshire be so forward as to ask a favor?" Inexplicably, he looks down at the newly swept floor, berating himself even as he does it for taking liberties. Might he not look up again and behold transforming grace?

Dian smiles again. Wordless, Will is all too aware of her graciousness and her sexuality.

Out of his silence, she prompts, "If it *favours* you crave, then you must beg your *favours* of my husband. He alone has the power to *faire grâce*." The visitation being over, she gathers her skirts and turns to go.

Not yet. Don't leave me just yet. Bravely looking up, Shakespar speaks in a timid, self-effacing manner that he cannot believe is his own, "By your leave, Your Grace, but I ask nothing for myself. I seek a boon *for* you."

"*For* me?" This piques Dian's attention. She turns back. "What boon might I do for myself?" Prettily she cocks her head to one side as perhaps a lover might do, awaiting a charming reply.

"M'Lady, I ask only that you allow me to dedicate a sonnet to your beauty."

Her eyes widen at the flattery. "You are too bold young man. Too rude and too bold. Tell your employer I am not used to such tricks."

"Madam, forgive my audacity. My master is entirely ignorant of my request. This is a gift of my own. I have hopes to aspire with my art to describe what all of Illyria already worships."

"Worships?" she questions, doubtful but flattered. "Do they?"

"If you will but read of my lines, you may judge for yourself."

"Is it already written?"

"Upon my heart. Not on paper."

"Now, my young poet, you overdo." She lets go of the

sides of her skirt and places Will's beardless chin between her delicate thumb and forefinger as she had done with one or two of the choirboys. All Will's senses focus on that single spot and on that hand that frames it. Her touch is warm and smells of lavender water. "I forgive you. You have my permission to praise me in your verse. But, first, you must present our poem to My Lord Husband that he may approve. I warn you, neither scurrility nor impropriety may be contained therein, for assuredly, he will box your ears."

In the wake of her coquettish manner, Will nearly forgets himself. "That shall not be a problem, M'Lady." Will wants to say more, but Her Ladyship has heard enough.

Amused by his youthful blushing, she withdraws her hand from his face and quietly insists, "I must go now." Even remembering that it is not the custom, reflexively he bows deeply as he takes a step backward.

Startled by the unaccustomed compliment, the Countess adds, "One thing more, post boy, it would pleasure us greatly to have your verse come the feast of Valentine's." He nods in understanding. As she gathers up the pleats of her overskirt, Will deliciously catches sight of an alabaster ankle.

Dian starts up the aisle.

"Dee's boy," she calls without turning back, "what is your name?"

"Shakespar, Will." She is moving quickly away from him. He says his name again loud enough that she will never forget it, "WILLIAM SHAKESPAR." Rather proudly, Shakespar hears the sound of his name echoing back to him in the vastness of the large church. It is an effect no theater could ever expect to replicate.

The reverberating name that is a sexual innuendo tickles her Gallic sense of humor, raising the corners of her mouth into the hint of a wicked smile. Briefly, Dian turns back.

"*Shake spear,*" she murmurs. Then, with a smile broader still and in her exotic French accent, she savors each word and their meaning, "*Will shake spear.*" She laughs more like a maiden seeking a husband than a married woman, and then gives Shakespar a flirtatious look, reproving him for so suggestive a name.

Will beams, sharing in her delight of it. He even thinks he may change it to her way of saying it, accenting it the way she does. She exits, radiant again in the doorway, leaving him to his thoughts and a new commitment.

16

Saint Valentine is a fortnight off on the isle of Illyria. And Will has sworn by all that is sacred to him that he shall compose fourteen lines of perfect iambic pentameter for the unparalleled *Comtesse* Dian. *How does one write one-hundred-and-forty iambs of perfection?* Thus, the boy-poet spends in conflict countless hours that turn to days. As the scarcity of paper makes it impossible to write, he triangulates fierce sentiments and passions in his mind. Rejected similes and worthless metaphors litter his thoughts—foul papers of his imagination. Despite his extraordinary memory, worried that he might forget his better conceits, William Shakespar takes to penning the best of them on his arms and legs. The scratch of the sharp quill pricks his skin. A proper penance he thinks for his forwardness. He prays it doesn't rain.

Will spends days in the chapel, in the place of their first assignation, conceiving and reworking. As he searches for the right word, he sometimes voices the verse, hoping steadily to match each word's sound to its meaning. Those who take notice of him imagine that he is moving his lips in devout prayer. And when questioned, Shakespar replies, "And so I am." They are pleased, while he thinks to himself, *but not to the deity you think.*

Fashioning each of the sonnet's quatrains proves immeasurably difficult, but there is no success, none, at puzzling out the clinching couplet that must sum up her worth. His efforts are laughable. *I am inadequate. Shallow schoolboy sentimentality cannot plumb her godhead. To paint a word picture of a goddess—the minutest detail matters*, laments Shakespar.

When the eve of St. Valentine's Day arrives, Shakespar is still at a complete loss for the all-important final couplet. At his most despondent, he hates what he has written. His lines cannot stand. They will not do. They are unmusical, ungainly, and sophomoric. He can hear the mocking laughter and the twitting jests that *Le Comte* and the divine *Comtesse* will make when they hear his foolishness. The lash of shame will surely follow. The next day in class, when Dee complains of Will's lack of attention, Shakespar petulantly storms out having no stomach for Thucydides. Back in his room, he opens his jerkin and removes the two pieces of parchment that he filched, smoothing them out lovingly on a hard surface. One of these sheets must be presented to Orsino this very day. With fingers arched against his right temple and ear, the thoughtful poet stares at the parchment pen in hand, once more running through the lines in his head. He is feeling a little better about what he has composed, yet to what avail? *I have failed. I have proved what the Wits of the theatre have known all along: I am an untutored bumpkin... a mechanic at words... a tradesman's son.* Facing his inadequacy, he resolves to give up writing and go back to London and resign himself to acting female roles. His eyes swell. He thinks, *Yea, here are the womanish tears for it.*

But he cannot gainsay the reality of the deadline. That grudging fact necessitates him committing to paper in his best Roman calligraphy the first twelve lines of the sonnet. At least the penmanship may be praised. He dips his quill and writes. Then wretched at his failure for a perfect conclusion, he completes his work with two lines that are the best of the worst. The time has come. The Lady must have her sonnet and, come what may, William *Shake-with-fear* must live with his failure.

After blowing on the wet ink, he folds the paper into an oblong shape. Lighting a small candle in his cramped room, Will drips wax upon the folded ends to seal it. With a fearful heart all that is left is to present himself to Orsino and await the consequences. It is a feast day, and he knows the Count will be in the Great Hall. There this writing will either be the source of the Count's and his Lady's ridicule or (best scenario) forgotten that it was ever delivered. Will must leave it to Fortune.

"Fortune," he says as he blows out his candle, "All is Fortune."

Music swells in Illyria this morning. Merry as wedding bells, the sounds of joy resonate as islanders celebrate the feast of Saint Valentine. In the marketplace square, the Waits, Illyria's official musicians, fiddle furious jigs for the gamboling townspeople. Inside the banquet hall at Count Orsino's castle, couples dance pavanes, voltas, and brawls. The spirit of Love buzzes about from glance to amorous glance, gladdening hearts and reviving a community tired of winter. Orsino has commanded day-long festivities throughout the town in honor of the holiday. Heaven has blessed *Le Comte* with as fair a February day as one could hope for.

That morning, the boys' choir outdo themselves and delight the attendees with their anthems and oratorios. Malvolio, grumbling about frivolity, stations himself in the basement kitchen where he can supervise the preparations of foods and not have to partake in the madness. Upstairs, Lord Griffin has orchestrated everything to gladden the eye and enliven the festivities, hanging the walls with cloths of gold and tissue of iridescent silk, embroidering the trestle tables with broad velvet drapes, setting tables with polished brass plates that reflect the warmth of flickering torchlight. He has employed jugglers for the morning's entertainment and lavish fireworks at night. In the main hall, where corontoes and galliards are being played, dancing reigns. At the suggestion of the lead viol player, *a la Volta* is announced. Young gallants, divesting themselves of their rapiers and dancing in their best attire, leap and cavort and lift their ladies high into the air, kissing them as their feet touch the ground.

Edmund Dotrice, Lord Griffin, has donated two dozen casks of wine, three stags for roasting, and a team of pastry cooks to concoct countless trays of confections. Before the serving of the delicacies, the more informed guests in the Great Hall drool in anticipation. Later, when all are assembled, Orsino seizes his Chief Councilor and presents him to the crowd.

"Here is a sweet gallant." Then bussing Edmund on both cheeks, Orsino coos, "My heart swells with your enchantments." The entire hall roars in approbation.

For a short time, Griffin allows himself to be congratulated then discreetly retires to a niche near the archway far from the crowd where his sister, the Lady Olivia, demurely sits, still mourning a father who passed a year ago. The Lady is round and short, wearing a formless black dress that is purposefully unsuited to the holiday's festivities. However, Count Orsino has said politely of her gown that it beautifully sets off her enchanting pearl grey eyes. Her blond hair, tyred in a net configured like a swan, primly rests atop a simple linen-colored ruff. But, despite her filial obligation, there is redness in her milky-white cheek acknowledging the evident excitement in the Great Hall and the not so apparent liveliness that is bottled within. Bending forward in the chair her brother has provided for her, her gaze hungrily follows the gaily-dressed gentlemen preening about the room. She is not so obvious as to crane her neck at the celebrants, but her eyes do leave her brother's face often as he speaks, casting them around the room to anatomize the men's shapely legs and capable arms. Twice or thrice, she has to enquire as to what her brother has just said. Edmund is not in the least concerned, for he secretly hopes that Cupid will clap her on the shoulder and coax her out of her overlong mourning.

"Beg pardon, Your Graces, but might I have a word with Your Lordship." Shakespar stands sheepishly before them.

"What is your will, young man?"

Gay applause erupts in the great hall as a gavotte comes to an end.

"I was bid by the Countess to deliver a poem of my own making to Count Orsino for his approval, and perhaps Your Lordship might speak a word to him for me?"

As her brother is in conference, Olivia watches while new partners are chosen for a galliard. The music begins and her right foot moves secretly in tempo under her stiff underskirt. She has learned the steps yet does not grant herself permission to enjoy them.

"How came you by this commission?" Griffin is ever circumspect.

Explaining the history, Will is careful to over emphasize that it is a gift composed in the Countess' honor, done at her bidding, written as chastely as if he had been a maid, given to one who is celestial—not he, but she—and wanting no recompense. Babbling further, Will assures the Lord that nothing in the poem is amiss. Illyria's Chief Secretary acknowledges the request, giving every indication that the Count will have it ere noon. The sonnet, penned on small parchment, easily slips through the slit in the doublet sleeve of Lord Griffin for safekeeping. Sputtering a dozen thanks, Shakespar collides with the stone archway behind him as he curtsies and backpedals.

A musician strumming a lute wanders by

acknowledging them with a smile of courtesy and some plaintive notes from a love-song. Seeing the lady's mourning weeds, he concludes he is not wanted and then continues on his way following Will into the Great Hall. All the while, Olivia masks an amused smile with the back of a gloved hand.

"Tell me how he takes it," she says.

"Who?" says her brother.

"Orsino."

"In truth, I had thought to leave it unseconded on his desk," confides the sniggering Edmund. "It is a trifling matter."

"No! Thou must do more!" Her father-brother is startled by her un-Olivia-like vehemence. Even she does not recognize herself when she implores, "It is a matter of the heart, Edmund. The lad is obviously besotted with our French mistress. For shame, is this not St. Valentine's?" Intent, she pushes playfully, "Brother, you have given your word. Hie thee in all haste and present it to the Count within this half-hour. Surely, a *poésie* of Love must have the swiftest messenger possible on this Love's own day. Love's courtiers are winged, and so you must fly. I will not have you indifferent slow. Go, get thee gone!" Not allowed any excuse, Griffin, in all affection toward his sister, wades into the dancing to find Orsino. Breathless revelers catch up with one another barely noticing Lord Griffin pushing through them. A pavanne is signaled and the older guests elegantly rise from their chairs to dance to a more respectable tempo. Left alone, Olivia, scans the room, catching sight of Shakespar tracking her brother's progress.

A pretty youth, she thinks of Will.

In another room in the castle, Orsino is presiding over a wrestling match between his smithy and his groom. Locked in a tight embrace, the men clasp each other's back with one arm over the other's shoulder and one under. The strain of being squeezed in this bear hug is evident on both their twisted faces. They compete for a sovereign of gold that the Count holds over his own head, awaiting a victorious throw. Wagers have been made, and on-lookers noisily shout out moves and handholds to their favorites. The approaching Lord Griffin is loath to interrupt the match as it is evident Orsino is very much enjoying himself, shouting encouragements as loud as any muleteer.

At last, the groom is thrown to the floor with a resounding thud and Count Orsino, after presenting the smithy with his prize money, with great *noblesse oblige* helps the loser from the floor. Almost immediately, the Smith puts the Groom's head in a half-nelson and lovingly hugs his neck. They are the best of friends.

"*Alors*, who's next? *Qui est le prochaine?*"

"M'Lord," Edmund Dotrice discretely waves the sealed sonnet at him.

"No matters of state, today, Edmund." Orsino looks around for new contenders.

"'Tis no matter of state, but of the heart, M'Lord."

"*Yours?*" is accompanied by a look of mock surprise. Then with high expectation, "Or *mine?*"

"Neither, Your Grace. From one of lesser worth." A look of confusion from the Count. "Doctor Dee's 'prentice has penned a sonnet for Her Ladyship. He has given me to understand this was done with her permission, but must first be overlooked by you for its fitness. The best of these..." Edmund hands the Count the sonnet. "...artistically want matter or felicity. Fourteen lines dedicated to My Lady's eyebrow, I gather."

Orsino breaks the seal and reads. A furrowed brow is soon replaced by a look of surprise and antagonism. "This is the boy's, you say?"

"Aye, M'Lord, how bad is it? Has he offended? Is there aught amiss?"

"Bring him to me this moment," demands Orsino, his tone rattling the much put-out Chamberlain. Word is also given that the Postmaster, John Dee, must be fetched. In the interim, Orsino bids Lady Dian be brought, as well. She is the first to arrive, and they whisper together. The lady's smile turns to horror.

At the foot of the dais, Dee asks nervously, "What have you done, boy?" Taking a step up to address Orsino, Doctor Dee intercedes for his charge. "Your Grace, if this lad has in any way offended, hold me responsible."

"Very well, I make thee responsible for the penning of this." A choleric Illyria storms, waving the paper before the Doctor, "As the responsible party, are you aware of its matter?"

The Postmaster is at a complete loss. "I plead

ignorance, Your Grace, I know nothing of the matter."

Orsino waves Dee off in frustration.

Furious, the intelligencer turns to Will. "Without my consent!?" Betrayed, Dee's anger escalates. Shakespar's actions terminate access to the chief suspect of the spy's investigation. Having witnessed Queen Elizabeth cut people out of her life, he fears the worst. *Look what she did to Leicester, her favorite*, Dee recalls.

A hush crushes the room as all ears take in this controversy. Lord Griffin makes a move to grab Will by the neck, but Orsino stays his hand. The Count's undivided attention is now focused on his advisor.

Glaring, he demands, "Was it not *you* who brought these words to me?"

"Aye, My Lord, but I knew not the content."

"No one seems to know the content," he rages and growls, "Then, by heaven, you shall know it now." Addressing the chamber, he roars, "So shall ye all!" Glowering, Orsino thrusts the paper into Will's hand; the boy is stricken. "Read, that all may know what you have written..." adding with poisonous irony, "...on *La Comtesse's* behalf."

All the guests are well aware of their Count's ill temper, and doubtless, the boy will suffer the worst of it. Who else will bear the brunt? The *Comtesse*? Griffin? Surely, the Postmaster. An excellent day is ending badly. Speculations whisper around the room. At a menacing glance from the Count, all talk is forbidden. The room turns silent, except for the shuffling of stiff robes and starched ruffs around necks craning to see what is to become of the teenager.

Before daring to read, Will pleads silently for help from his mentor, who waves the look away, unable to do anything for him. Fearful of the coming infamy and shame, the accused stands like one on the day of his execution. Nameless terror takes hold. His heart pounds faster. Loud enough to hear it thump against Dee's wax luck charm that hangs about Will's neck. Atop the raised platform, with an entire chamber of dagger eyes judging him, the *auteur* succumbing to his *fate* gives voice to his words. The first line is barely audible. With the second and third and as the argument builds, the youth gains strength and theatricality. When Shakespar finishes, none speak. Orsino surveys the room and inexplicably his stormy visage clears. *Le Comte* beams with a patron's pride. As that moment, Dian regnant moves to the sonneteer and sweetly kisses him upon his cheek.

"Is it not well done?" commands *Le Comte*. "Has he not caught the very flame of my love?" In adoration, Orsino seizes Dian's palm in his and, with tenderness, buries his face in it. After many kisses there, he holds his wife's hand hostage and with both eyes fixed on his co-conspirator, his radiant bride, he intones,

"So while thy beauty draws the heart to love,
As fast that virtue bends that love to good.
But ah, Desire still cries: 'Give me some food!'"

Orsino entreats the room. "Is it not the perfect sentiment?"

Affirmation explodes. Perhaps its intensity is as much for the catastrophe averted as it is for the *poésie* or perhaps an appreciation of His Lordship's harrowing performance.

Joining the applause, Dian, truly touched, responds with tears of happiness. These she gives to patron and poet alike, adding, "Never was truer word writ."

The newlyweds embrace and kiss undeterred, perfectly comfortable with their public display.

"*Give me some food*," Orsino quotes the sonnet for Dian's ear alone. Playfully, she chomps her teeth at him and he is not slow to recall her meaning, nor last night's devouring.

Turning back to Will, Count Orsino claps the boy's shoulder. "We are well pleased. Come to me tomorrow, and I will set you to work on another. That is if your master will give you leave."

Dee acknowledges the demand with a dutiful nod of the head. Before returning to the party, Dian kisses Will's once more, more lingering than the last. Few kisses in Shakespar's life are so cherished.

Moving to the dais of honor, the noble couple lift goblets of wine, directing all to sit and join them in celebration. Eagerly, one and all do as they are ordered, lauding Orsino's wit and generosity—but all the compliments are soon lost in their desire to eat. The first course, a local delicacy, *ormers* or sea ears, is served along with Illyrian tea bread and *gâche*. Immediately, the metallic sounds of knives and spoons scooping out mollusk from shell mingle and quite overtake the pipers, strings, and brass.

No food for Will, rather he stands against a wall waiting for chastisement, having caught John Dee's eye before he sat down to eat. There is no question but that his employer is furious with him, having gotten such looks before when he started skipping Sunday services. Though it is a partial sin, he feels for the waxen talisman that perhaps had rescued him.

At table, Dee simmers through the first course even as he makes pleasantries with his neighbors. Plates being removed, he rises abruptly and beckons his lackey to follow him. In silence, they walk to a distant window seat out of earshot of the others.

"Sit," is all the fuming magus can say. After an inquisition of accusatory glares, Dee with much heat demands, "What permission had you to write a poem to the Countess of Illyria? Moreover, you kept this writing from me. You do that again, and you will rue the day. I will send you packing back to the pitiful nothing you call your life. This is inexcusable. You risked all we are sent here to do."

Nervous, making excuses, doing all he can to diminish that unsettling stare by focusing on the wall above Dee's head, Will narrates the facts of his conversation with the Countess Dian in the chapel, scrupulously leaving out any hint of his infatuation. With the explanation done, Shakespar rises to leave.

"Sit you down," orders Dee, "I gave you no leave to go." The tone is so peremptory that, even had he the will, pale Shakespar could not do otherwise. Like a predatory bird, the Queen's wizard peers down fixating on his mouse. "The last two lines..." is all he says.

So, thinks the poor wretch, *perhaps Dee knows.* Shakespar tries to brazen it out, replying seemingly unflustered, "Aye, what of it?"

"They are Sidney's. It is from his *Astrophel and Stella*."

Will's mouth opens, but nothing comes out. He has been caught stealing. It is not the first time in his life—nor will it be the last. But, each time he is found out, punishment follows. Still, he'll be damned if he is going to cower. Not today. Not after Illyria has praised him and the French goddess has kissed him—*twice*. Proud of his new celebrity and crossing his arms over his chest, he shrugs blithely.

"It was to His Lordship's liking."

"But not to mine." He grabs and wrenches Will's ear. "Mayhap, His Lordship is not as familiar with my old student's poetry as I am." Yanking the ear sideways, "That fiendish unnatural memory of yours has stolen verbatim from *Sir* Phillip Sidney." The "sir" is stressed to reaffirm the writer's aristocracy and honor. "Have a care," warns the cold voice of authority. "Blatant plagiarism will land you in a court or—worse in a duel to the death. Many a poet has murdered a rival for just such a thieving of his words. It is as dangerous a practice as filching a purse, one that will put you in an early grave. A tool mishandled can wound. Know you not that?" If Will thinks there is a hint of compassion in that, he is rudely mistaken. "Moreover, the gift you have given the Countess Illyria is now tainted with plagiarism and tarnished with pitch." He releases his hold on the boy's pained ear. "Do you understand me?

Rubbing the side of his head, Will murmurs, "I understand."

"Do you? Then have a care next time. For next time, you may not—nay you will not be so fortunate." Now that Dee has spoken his piece, the man's severity relents. Still, he has no stomach to be in Will's presence. The fearsome magus turns around to return to the table and glasses of wine. Begrudgingly over his shoulder, he adds, "But for the theft of the final couplet, the body of the sonnet is well-fashioned and true to nature. Pleasing to the ear. Your versification is precise and strong." There is a pause. "If it is indeed all yours."

Will lets that last remark go by unanswered. While receiving his master's chastisement, he did think of one thing only. "Though he asked me to come, will the County truly ask for more?" But Dee is already leaving. Risking more displeasure yet not wanting to put off asking, the chastised writer catches up. "Thinkst that I may get a commission? Sir?"

Pushing Will aside, Dee snarls, "Think not on it." But then the spymaster stops and turns back giving his aide full attention. He has had an epiphany. "Such preferment could provide us a continued access to Orsino." His eyes dart with future scenarios as he puts his index finger to his lips. "Best not say aught even in this concealed cranny." Dee remembers the pitchers who had ears—his students—at Mortlake. Glancing back at the feast, the doctor offers politic direction. "Count Orsino has for now culled you out for favor. Go, reap the applause that they will gild you withal. But, have a care for he is known to be inconstant in those whom he advances. And have a mind, he is a voracious reader, you may not get round him so easily next time." More *sotto voce,* "Play the little weasel and learn what you can." Louder. "Go. Off with you."

Left alone, John Dee ponders how they might proceed. Despite the boy's audacity and theft, the poem may well prove helpful. Maybe—dare he think it?—he will be home sooner than expected. On this day of Love, reuniting with Jane suddenly seems not as far away as just moments before.

{ 17 }

Good as his word, Illyria's Count Orsino commissions William Shakespar to pen fourteen sonnets as a present for his wife. The birthday of both the young poet and the Lady nearly coincide; both being born under the sign of the bull, Taurus. *Perhaps,* supposes Will, *that is why we both feel the need to be surrounded by love and beauty.* Orsino, infatuated with his own infatuation, and alone with Curio, beams, "Is it not an excellent day? And was it not a perfect celebration?"

"It is, and it was," Curio dutifully responds to his old friend, knowing that there is more on *Le Comte's* mind. Sitting in their respective chairs, facing each other, Curio, as is his wont, cocks his head to one side waiting to hear what Orsino has to add.

Leaning forward and laying a hand on his friend's knee, Orsino shares a profound truth, "The original cause of all good affections is Love. It is only proper that such a commendable virtue be chronicled, both here..." He touches his heart. "...and for all time. In honest recreation, poets distill the whole course of men's lives and are the trumpeters of accomplishment and commendation. Is it not so, good friend, Curio, that the best of Britain and on the Continent keep such poetasters in their household for their better enrichment and for their artistry?"

"The boy is but a youth. Scarce sixteen," cautions Curio.

Emphatic, the Count overrides, "I like him and what matter his age. He has obvious talents."

Curio shrugs in assent. He is out of his depth. What does he know of poetry or, for that matter, love? Love is a madness, a wasting disease that turns man's reason to jelly. Matters of importance are his bailiwick: financial settlements, trade disputes, setting the yearly allowable sales price for of bread and beef, obligations to Whitehall, and the unsolved audacious piracy of the *Tiger* from the harbor. *S'blood! Sex is a necessity. Love a distraction.*

"I want the world to know that she is beyond compare." Suddenly inspired, Orsino stands. His leg has gone to sleep and he sits again. "We shall invite both man and boy to supper that our sonneteer may learn of Dian's rarer parts, her virtues, her spirit." Each memory of her chases the next into a sweeter and sweeter place of adoration.

Ever tactful, the nuncio Curio, meticulously cautions against any public invitation to dinner until a private solicitation can be made of John Dee. "We should sue for permission of the boy's time," proposes Curio but is ready for more skirmishes to come. Exasperated at Curio's blindness in the matter, Orsino moves away. But, Curio will not drop his natural pragmatism, "...of our new Postmaster, before pressing the lad into service as the Countess' Petrarch. God forfend, the postman's secretary should scant his duties—whatever they may be—if that permission is not first given." He cocks an eyebrow and twisting his high-backed chair to better look at his liege lord asks, "What point supper?"

Orsino's eyes lock on Curio's. "But his master acceded with a full heart when I offered."

"That was in public view, where the old man could not with good grace deny thee. We must beg it again when he is not so constrained."

Thwarted and shaking his head, Illyria counters, "Curio, this is too fainthearted a consideration, even for thee." Orsino paces, scowling. Circling the room twice, *Le Comte*, biting his lip, softens, acceding to his old friend. "Though this be too nice and precise and I like not the idea of begging, do as you list," sulks Illyria. He moves to the window and fixes on the countryside. Curio knows it is his habit whenever his will is prevented. "The people must resign themselves to my desires. Be they citizen or visitor."

"Yet, your desires must give place to that of the Queen's." Though this is self-evident, Curio regrets saying it and turns to sit straight in his chair.

White with displeasure, Orsino, turns on his heel, remonstrating a low warning in his man's ear, "None but thee, Curio, could think that my offer of employment is aught but a loving gift of gratitude to this Postmaster and his Queen." He straightens and nearly shouts, "It must be instantly accepted."

Curio flinches, and, while fingering his ecru linen shirtsleeves fashionably exposed through the slits in his doublet, says what must be said, "And I doubt not but that it will be accepted, but first we must inquire."

"Have I not said, 'Aye'?" His hands clasped behind him, with his chin he waves his counselor away. There is nothing more to say, except, "Fetch Malvolio."

Fabian has served the house of Illyria proudly for two score and more, first as server and then head usher. His years of climbing up and down stairs, serving meals, and answering doors have taken their toll. Now in his mid-fifties, he is weak in the lower back and knees. Forced by age to bend forward even when trying to stand most erect, his posture is an ossified half-bow, a continual quasi-obeisance. Many of the younger staff inveigh that the old retainer is too proud, too feeble. "He should be replaced," they whisper. Fabian is well aware of the grumblings and cannot avoid admitting to himself that navigating steep roads, fetching visitors from the lower courtyard, and descending stairs is as hard on his knees as climbing back up. In recent years, he curtails, delegates, or craftily avoids most strenuous responsibilities, including the excruciating trudges outside the castle. Still, as the head usher of the Orsino household, it is Fabian whom Malvolio requires as the right and proper courier to deliver the Count's letter to Doctor Dee.

"Fabian, a word with you," clucks Malvolio.

"A word is all I have time for, as I am needed above."

Like all the household, Fabian is not fond of his steward. The man is, after all, a blaspheming Puritan.

"Then let me be brief." Militarily tucking his white wand in his armpit, Malvolio postures condescendingly. "You must to the *Cubiculo* to deliver an invitation from our Good Lord to the Royal Postmaster."

"The *Cubiculo*?" Fabian, annoyed, "That is an intolerable march almost to the water's edge. Cannot Roy or Henri manage it?"

The steward raises a haughty eyebrow, thinks to reprimand him, and instead ignores the question altogether as he looks through Fabian. "Have a care of your position here, Fabian. You are Illyria's usher and the fittest personage for such a formal assignment. What would our English guest think... or our honored Lord think... were a lesser worthy than yourself to perform the Count's desires?"

"S'death, Master Malvolio," Fabian grumbles under his breath, bridling his impatience with this pettifogger.

Countless instances of such Fabian mutterings have rendered Malvolio deaf to his menial's complaints. "You will do it then."

An ill-sounding sound of agreement is given. "I will do it then."

"I have your word that you will not pawn this off to one of your people." Malvolio looks at him sideways.

Have I not already said? Irascibly, Fabian retorts, "By the Holy Rood, you have it."

Ignoring the resentment, Malvolio waits for the usher to clean his hands of any household grime before the steward lays the sealed document unto Fabian's care.

"His Lordship desires this to be done before sunset tonight, sirrah. As I am told the sky threatens, and the rain falls again soon, I counsel you to attend to it at once."

Grunting, the feeble old retainer sets his shoulders as far back as his physique allows, and wrests the letter from Malvolio.

"I shall go," declares Fabian, coloring each word with disdain, "when *first* I have completed that which is presently required of me, *then* every jot and tittle of this..." He shakes the wax-sealed message at Malvolio, causing its ribbons of yellow and red—the official colors of Illyria—to tickle the steward's nose. "...will be done as His Lordship requires. Satisfied?"

"I am," Malvolio patronizes. "Do so then, and before you do, look to your fingernails—filthy as a truffle-digging pig's hock!"

Then without a *by-your-leave* and fixated, no doubt, on accomplishing the countless tasks that are in need of his management, the stone-faced steward pivots and hurriedly climbs the stairs, his bitter black robe flapping around him. As the self-important turkey-cock ascends to higher duties, head usher Fabian hurls silent invectives at the back of his superior's gyrating robe. Born of years of servitude, he is jealous of the man's agile ability.

Daunted by the long walk before him, Fabian sighs plaintively, *Great pains and little gains make men soon weary*. Then he blazes, though not loud enough to echo up the stairwell after the martinet, "To hell with you."

Shaking his head at his bad luck, one other curse escapes his bewhiskered thin lips, "You could have provided me with as poor a conveyance as an oxcart, you squinty-eyed Lombard." Two chafed fingers point heavenward before his lips, and he spits contemptuously between them at the vacant stairwell.

That afternoon, it chances that a wagon, over-laden with timbers, lumbers up a precipitous twisting dirt lane—the very route down which the old courier, Fabian is hobbling. Jutting out from the stores on either side of the street are three to four foot wooden shelves with goods for sale. Many are jostled roughly and gouged by the large dray's load on its uphill trudge to the castle. But having come to where the lane is narrowest, the cart and its freight are now inextricably wedged between two buildings. Having shifted precariously, the logs jam into every split-timber crevice flanking the cart. Attempting to rearrange the load to no avail, the Rottweiler of a carter stands among the logs confounded. The delay sets Fabian into a corybantic fit. Wanting neither to retrace his steps up the steep hill nor risk squeezing into a filthy rat's nest between buildings Fabian waves his walking stick in fury.

"*Bouge! Allez! Allez!*" shrieks the vituperative Fabian.

Laboring doggedly, the carter could care less what the old man shouts or wants. A delivery must be made and it is already late to the construction going on within castle grounds. Harsh words are exchanged in the winter cold as to right-of-way—ancient Court pedestrian versus honest workman—both on a needful mission for the Illyrian Count.

Thwarted from passage, the old usher is forced to retreat into the small alley rank with vermin droppings. None too happy, Fabian gathers his cloak about himself, careful to avoid contact with the plaster walls flecked with bird droppings or the foul-smelling trash in the tight space. Then the load shifts and, to Fabian's abject horror, his exit from the rattrap is altogether blocked.

"*Bâtard!* Whoreson dunghill!" rants the powerless usher from the rat hole, shifting his weight—yet never lifting a foot—from right to left like an ancient boxer spoiling for a fight. With his back bent in a crescent and his fist raised in fury, he sputters frustration.

The protracted tragicomedy ensues, minutes pass, until the Rottweiler muscles aside the obstructions and manages to launch his team through the bottleneck. Fabian's egress permits him to hurl himself from the caustic piss rank alley into the lane, shouting ever more egregious epithets at the driver.

Massively behind schedule, the delayed carter has neither time nor inclination for the luxury of a confrontation. Instead, he coaxes his team onward.

When the cartman is of a mind that he is safely past the curmudgeon, he uses his whip to flick his horses into a quicker pace uphill toward the castle. Not ready for the sting of the lash, the straining animals jerk. The freight shifts. Ropes and harnesses, meant to secure the large wooden limbs, slip, causing two massive tree trunks to roll off the wagon whereupon they roll directly toward Fabian.

Back turned, and only a yard or two below the cart, the old usher should be crushed and sent by Fortune to his rewards in the hereafter. But the aforementioned goddess places the quick-thinking Feste, the lutenist, contentedly in the plodding wake of the cart since it loaded its foreign-cut timbers at the docks. Just in time, the musician manages to yank the ancient out of harm's way. Feste's tug, sharp and forceful, inadvertently twists the old retainer's overburdened knees and misshapen back, sending him into excruciating pain.

"*Merde!*" is the Samaritan's reward followed by a string of ugly French epithets, so loud and so colorful that gossiping housewives, hanging out their laundry at upstairs windows, stop chattering to eavesdrop.

"Let me be! You fly-blown misbegotten son of a turd!" A glancing blow to Feste's head is given, and Fabian's savior surely would have been beaten brain dead had not the lute player's arm repeatedly parried the old usher's knobby stick. Not sufficiently mollified, Orsino's manservant spits more venom. "I shall have a charge of battery drawn against you, you rabbity whelp. You gross cogging hempen attacker of the good and true. You piece of base-born dust," spews Fabian.

"Good sir, have done," laughs the musician, good naturedly, despite the onslaught.

"Rash, wanton, ruffian," Fabian persists petulantly, "You nearly knocked me senseless. Have you not the sense God gave puking sheep? I shall have the Law against you, you rapscallion, you mangy *merde*-eater, you begetter of maggots—"

"Why, you doddering ancient toadstool, I have rescued you from certain death, that is sure. You'd have been crushed there..." Feste points at the two massive logs now resting where the old man had stood. "...like an apothecary's herb, you'd be naught but powder and pizzle. The gravemaker would have had no need but a ha'penny worth of pine to build one infinitesimally small coffin to house your withered, dried, enfeebled carcass had not I intervened. Charity, old Methuselah, or I shall cry the drayman back and have him unload on you another tonnage of timber to crush that evil tongue of yours. Charity, Father Bile."

Whether for lack of breath or finally realizing how close he'd been to Death's scythe, Fabian gasps and grabs at his chest. His choleric display has sapped his strength, and in frailty, he sags against his benefactor. They huddle together for a moment and then Feste slowly lowers him to the ground, careful not to increase the man's painful groans. The itinerant musician loosens the button on the older man's shirt and lays the wounding cane to one side. And there on the cold ground, the usher massages his pricking knees, grimaces, and feels the pain of every one of his many decades. Breathing easier and looking up to see concern on Feste's round face, Fabian's tone softens.

"Are you not the lutenist who played and sang for Count Orsino's guests, but last week at the open house in celebration of Saint Valentine's?"

"Aye, and are you not the Count's usher who kept us

waiting an hour past vespers until we were near frozen by the chill?"

"Neither your voice nor your purse were the worse for it." Curt, the usher squints. "For you gained a warm-hearted reception, and you reaped a hogshead of gold in gratuity once you were allowed in." Feste reaches out his hand in order to make Fabian more comfortable. "Jesu, your hand was always out for more. So much so, I took you for a modern Lazarus." Fabian recoils from the offered help. "Was *that* not worth your wait?"

"Then allow me to thank you, sir, for *your* benighted hospitality and *my* late resurrection."

Feeling better, Fabian reaches tentatively for Feste's hand in hopes of rising from the cold ground. Feste reaches for him and the two stand for a while holding on to each other, cognizant of how near to tragedy they came.

Though *sur ses pieds* Fabian is unsteady. Looking Feste in the eyes, he mutters, "No, sir, it is I who must thank you for the saving of my life."

In the interim, the lutenists is aware that his bruised head smarts and his contused arm throbs; he is also mindful of the usher's shaky legs. Fabian gestures for his cane but his rescuer waves him off, having genuine concern that the ancient courier is not fit to travel. Eschewing the walking stick, young Feste craftily poses him questions to waylay his elder into a longer resting period.

"What brings you out on this ill-fortuned and foul day, Sir?"

"I must deliver a message for the Count to one who

abides at the water's edge—an accursed English interloper." Fabian snorts, "What care you?"

"Can't be an easy outing with those knees and that back."

"Think you I am not fit for the task?" rebukes the old curmudgeon, letting go of his human crutch and making himself dizzier with the sudden movement. "Only fools and profligates shirk their duties."

"Your want of duty was never in my thoughts." This is said with a smile that shows that he is growing to like the foul-mouthed gent more and more. He stays Fabian and once again holds off retrieving the fallen staff. "And neither of us is a fool."

"I am not, certainly, and you had better not be." Taking his arm from the musician's grasp and venturing a step or two, "I told you I am fit!" Fabian flexes a knee to prove his point, only to twinge painfully.

"Mayhap, it would be the wiser to rest longer ere you proceed on your errand."

No, Fabian shakes his head, not open to persuasion. Forgetting what is already known, the dazed man vehemently repeats, "I am sent by His Lordship to deliver a message to the Englishman at the *Cubiculo*." But the movement of his head only makes him dizzy again. Waiting for it to subside, he informs, "There is much for me to do when I get back. I am needed from morning until night." He ventures another step.

"Can you make it?" the young man asks with obvious concern, having monitored with a peregrine's eye every twitch in the reverend usher's face.

Again, Fabian tests his knees and softens, "In truth,

un peu wobbly."

"Then, perhaps, you might allow me to take your burden from you by footing your delivery to its destination. The inn is but ten minutes further down the road. I can fly there in as one would count fifty and return presently to tell you how the Englishman takes it. We are in luck, look here is Pierre's. You may rest and recover in the warmth of his bakery."

"Nay, I gave my word to His Lordship's steward that I alone would perform the service."

Feste shrugs in understanding though he hears regret in the old usher's avowal. *I have offered what kindness I may*, he thinks, *Perhaps, one good Samaritan act a day is enough.*

Endeavoring to fulfill his mission, Fabian takes one more hobbled step; gauging the distance, he finds Feste's sleeve. "Wait, sirrah, I am now remembered," Fabian says with some degree of calculated chicanery, "I swore only to give not the responsibility to one of my people, and you, sirrah, are *not* one of those."

It is a very pretty equivocation, and both men know it.

"Alas, I am masterless," shrugs the minstrel, not too ashamed to say so, "I belong to no one. But in my heart I belong to Illyria, and as such, I am willing and able to serve His Lordship the Count by couriering his letter in your stead."

"I like not..." Fabian pauses to think it through. "...to be in any man's debt." With a sidelong glance from under his gray beetling brows, he opts to favor the musician. "But, do this small *embassage*, and, in exchange, I will forthwith endeavor to give you early entrance to the Count's presence whenever you come begging for employment. You shall never be made to loiter at my door again."

Without another word, the lutenist seizes the usher's hand and shakes on the bargain. They take baby steps to Pierre's.

"Gently, lad, gently. I fear I am still in want of my proper balance."

The written invitation with its Illyrian ribbons and seal is put in Feste's custody, but not before a lecture is given on the needed gravity of the musician's demeanor and the job's proper dignity. Either due to his age or the importance of the errand, Fabian explains this twice, as a mother would to an errant child.

In five minutes, the fleet-footed entertainer-*cum*-Mercury knocks at Doctor John Dee's door. Orsino's missive delivered, Dee instructs Feste to wait for a reply.

Laying out paper and ink, the Royal Postmaster pens an answer to the invitation. Feste, in imitation of a proper valet, waits, keeping one hand behind his back. He scans the room with approval.

Finally, Dee is content with what he has written:

"Count Orsino is most kind in asking our participation in this. He gives me a day to think on it. His noble character deserves a swifter answer. I and mine, with the greatest humility and thanks, will attend Your Lordship's supper on Wednesday, hoping to have many more profitable conversations with Your Lordship and the Comtesse in my sojourn to Illyria.

Sealing his *R.s.v.p.* with wax and signet ring, the Postmaster hands his response to the messenger.

Although he now has done all that he has promised, Feste makes no move to leave. He stands in the doorway like an obedient greyhound waiting for his master's whistle. Attempting to close the door, the doctor inquires testily, "Is there aught else?"

"No, not from the Count."

"Then, from whom, pray tell?"

Feste holds out his palm in the universal gesture of *tip*.

Being a born conversationalist and liar, Feste knavishly explains, "It is a long journey back up the hill, and then I must wait for Orsino to know your answer. Moreover, if he has further correspondence, your... Your Worship—" Feste would natter on, hammering on Dee's sympathies to wedge his wallet open, had not Shakespar bounded up the stairway at that moment. "Marry, young fellow, I know thee! Master *Fine Gloves*, is it not?!"

"Aye, we heard your rehearsal. You foolishly spoke aloud your hopes for employment."

"Foolery, sir," says Feste, acknowledging his past actions, "does walk about the orb like the sun—if you will believe the Polish star-gazer." Still waiting for a tip, Feste hints none too subtly to both men for the gratuity. None forthcoming, the performance goes on. "My labors are thrice onerous and thrice weighty. I serve the Count. I serve his fame. And I serve his business. Might not my labors inspire some remuneration?" His right hand opens and shuts several times like a feeding clam.

Aware of the overlooked protocol, Dee scavenges in his room and covers the messenger's naked palm with a coin. "There's for thy pains."

"A half-penny is as small a remuneration as one

could hope for," counsels the messenger. The good Samaritan looks up and re-engages the eyes of his miserly benefactor in a look that says, surely, the *Royal* postman can do better. "I would play Lord Pandarus of Phrygia, Sir, to bring a Troilus to this Cressida."

"'Tis well-begged," Dee acknowledges the wordplay, "Yet, I will not be so much a sinner as to be a double-dealer. My purse sleeps. You can fool no more money out of me."

Meaning it as a compliment and hoping to eke out more for a fellow performer, "This fellow is wise enough to play the fool, and having the good opinion of such wise men," offers a newly employed Shakespar, "and not their barbs and quips, is a right good investment." But, alas, nothing more is to be had.

"What you will," shrugs lutenist-*cum*-courier. Ever cheerful in misfortune, Feste concedes wit and persistence can get no more, and his open palm clamps shuts and disappears into his pocket. "I thank you, master Doctor, and I will conster to His Lordship that you will come. And lullaby to your bounty 'til our next meeting."

Briskly, Feste exits thinking of the warm tortes he shall buy Fabian and himself at the bakery. The sound of his footsteps trips down the creaking stair. Bright-eyed, Doctor Dee beckons Will into his room and retrieves Orsino's invitation, "My boy, I have great news to tell you. A feast is prepared for us. We are welcomed by Orsino and shall taste of their preferment."

"Oh Lord, sir, we have much to do to make ourselves ready."

{ 18 }

The church bell is pealing seven in the morning when Will's mind struggles awake from last night's sumptuous supper with nobility. Wine, heady company, late-night camaraderie! Shakespar is done in. If he has dreamed of kings or velvet gowns or medieval knights, he cannot remember; he is only aware of his fat tongue glued to his teeth and his body aches, stiff as though he had climbed a palisade of stairs. The smell of rancid sweat offends. He has drooled on the sheets. Not since *The Mermaid* tavern, **where he was lavishly entertained by a trio of pretty sailors who'd tramped in from The Pond, has Will guzzled this much.** This time, however, there is no need to explain away his escapades.

Dull swooshes inform Will that it is raining—not just raining, but pouring. A gurgling torrent outside curtails any hope of finding out sleep's sweet lassitude. Slowly, struggling to open one eye, he squints at the window for confirmation where rivulets of water madly stream and reshape on the pane. When wet air finds an exposed inch of his body, his muscles knot. Shivering, he reconfigures the thin blanket around his head to muffle the clatter outside. No remedy. Necessity reprimands him that he must not be late for class. More, he must submit to his loins' growing need to piss.

Dressing as fast as his cramped fingers will allow, he knocks on Dee's door. No answer. Strange, his master is rarely absent from his room at this hour. Inquiring of the innkeeper, Will learns Dr. Dee left word that studies are postponed. Upon further investigation, the innkeeper, covetous of his guest's privacy, reveals that the doctor has gone out less than an hour prior. Relieved at not offending his master by keeping him waiting, Will returns to his room angling to return to bed. Instead, he retrieves quill and ink and descends to the inn's main room. There procuring strong broth, he nestles into an empty chair repositioning it nearer the roaring hearth. The warmth relaxes his cramped muscles while the soup alleviates the intemperance. In repose, he focuses on his new assignment—penning love sonnets for Dian. Her sleek gestures come to mind, as do her small, firm breasts not yet suckled by babes' incessant hunger. But, whatever muse he calls upon is continually shoved aside by rain-soaked patrons sloshing through the public room, thundering about the bad weather. Despite the world's intrusion, he works assiduously, endeavoring to beatify the Lady Orsino with showers of praise.

Out of nowhere. "Are you not the postman's boy?" asks a servant dressed in Orsino's livery.

"Aye," answers the surprised Shakespar. "If you seek my master, he has departed I know not where."

"Nay, it is you I seek." Will raises an eyebrow in amazement. "You are asked for by My Lady Dian. She requests your company instantly."

Rain or no, Dr. John Dee too is struggling this day. Having overslept until six, immediately, Walsingham's man is alert to the need for an investigation of Orsino's library. His line of inquiry is to discover what books are important enough to be coveted and preserved by Illyria himself. A collection of books will speak plain what interests a man has and what is in his heart. Though the slate colored sky threatens rain at this early hour, the bibliophile is not deterred. Tying around his neck a rust-colored woolen scarf knitted by his beloved Jane's own hand, he finds that it still, magically, retains her familiar fragrance. As he scurries down the stair, he conjures her image in his mind.

"*Docteur* Jean Dee?"

"Yea." Dee is passing the innkeeper.

"*Ici est une lettre pour vous.* Came on last night's mail boat."

"*Merci bien.*"

"Has the Royal Postmaster need of my services prior to its departure from harbor later today?"

Eager to be on his way, Dee shakes his head *no*. His heart leaps at seeing the handwriting on the envelope—a letter from Jane. *But how?* Surely, she must think him in Poland with Laski. The answer is revealed as he turns the letter over and sees Walsingham's seal on the back.

Husband,
An eternity has elapsed since you journeyed from

me and the child. I do not know how long it shall be before I see thee again.

Ignorant of place to write you, as Count Laski wants for a permanent residence, I have leave from Arthur's god-father, Sir Francis, who is knowledgeable in all matters, to forward our present estate to thee abroad. His Lordship could not tell me where thou art, but his Honor hath assured me that thou art safe. Trusting in His Lordship and God's mercy and Grace, I pray for you. Sir Francis has done a great kindness in helping me, and I will remember him in my prayers. A good man and a true lamb of Christ. I and the child are well in health. This pregnancy is a milder one than before, God be praised.

But I am ill at heart. The frailty of life and health being what it is, I thought it good to inform thee of our adverse fortunes since last we embraced. A week after you departed, a Master Sledd, whom you know of late resided here and partook of our hospitality, came to me and bade me to understand that soon there would be a lawsuit in Guildhall Court brought against you by the old reprobate, John Prestall. More, Mr. Sledd had come for the £56 he lent of you, and I, having not so much, could not oblige him. He threatens to recoup his monies from my brother, Nicholas, as you left without payment. It is not unknown to you that my brother wants provisions to be of help. Nay, threatens to seize and sell off a portion of your library to recover his losses of you.

Further, a message has been brought me from his Eminence, Archbishop Cooper, that in June of this year, *you are to be deprived of your rectorship and ensuing rents from Long Leadenham, a loss of £1000 per annum. Archbishop Grindel, he says, likes not your past as papal priest nor your present as 'devil-worshipper'. Without Grindal's leave, Sir Francis has indicated to me that the loss of the cynosure will indeed come to pass.*

I would appeal to friends in your absence, but your friends at Court are of no help. They say your detractors have dissembling hearts and openly shoot at thee, with arrows of reproach.

Most grievously, my late mistress, the good Queen, has dismissed thy suit for a Royal pension, which only energizes the animas against thee at Court.

We are £300 in debt, and I have had to let go Walter Hooper, gardener, Mary Goldwyn, wetnurse, and two others, all but George Marley, who refuses to leave as he has sworn an oath to you to look after us. Our pantry diminishes daily, and without pension, patrons, students, nor friends at Court, I fear that we cannot thrive until the summer. Can thee not, dear husband, ask Count Laski to remunerate thee with what he owes you that you might ease our hardships here?

We miss thee dearly and know that with your succor and Providence's favor, our needful maintenance will be met. You are in my thoughts continually—especially now.

Thy loving wife,
Jane

He buckles, his stricken conscience rebuking him for

leaving Jane beset, alone, in need of funds, comfort, and a husband. *I have lost all. I have left her bereft and alone at her time of greatest need. What honorable man does such a thing? But then, I am not an honorable man, but an intelligencer, in the employ of Sir Francis Walsingham, who poses as a lamb to mask the appetite of a wolf. I should not be here scavenging, but home with those I love. Home with my experiments. Home preparing for the new era of progress written in the stars. Instead, I'm doing the wolf's business that is beyond my expertise and will scourge my years of good works. Why have I abandoned my family? Yet I gave my oath. What's to be done? How Jane will loathe me whenever I return and reveal the truth of my absence. Will she not revile me for my lies and the abandonment of her and our children?* A thousand reproaches stab with every turn of Dee's thoughts. *How can she understand that I have sworn to my Queen's government not to share any details of my mission— not even with my dearest, my wife? She will curse our marriage, heap scorn upon me, mayhap even abandon me. Might she take our child—our children—with her? Who would blame her? What happiness is there without them?*

Caught in despair and self-loathing, he envisions the poor state of his finances. The revenues from Long Leadenham had never been good, but they had, at times, been helpful. Now there would be nothing, less than nothing as there would be all the expenses for the Prestall case, the repayments to Sledd and Nicholas, his brother-in-law. Worse still was the unthinkable denial of a Royal pension. Her Gracious Majesty had promised, yet would she now be foresworn? She had always shown kindness to him. Had he been deceived in trusting... loving Her? Desperate imaginings take hold. How was he to secure loans to preserve his family and home when he was incommunicado in Illyria? *Would Nicholas be so base as to take advantage of my absence and sell portions of my library, my alchemic equipment, my property?* Public shame rises as the thought of having friends and neighbors know of his poverty and the loss of his touted princely patronage. Had Her Highness not told him that *"What is delayed does not mean denied"*? Had She royally misled him? Yet, all of this could be remedied were he not hundreds of miles from home. *Damn Walsingham! Damn him!* Could he not have offered Jane some money when she presented herself before him? *How did the tyrant expect me to do his business when my own is in such disarray?* No, Secretary Walsingham must help. He could do it in so many ways. *I will write to him this day and ask for remuneration for services rendered. He will not—he cannot deny me.*

But the Library? Impotent to help Jane and relying on his plan for assistance, John Dee shakes recriminations from his orderly mind, forcing himself to concentrate on today's mission; he considers the small events and what he has learned of Illyria. Yet still possessed, his insistent conscience whispers that none of this can compensate for deserting his family. He is on the rack—pulled asunder by the ties of responsibility and fidelity. The taste in his mouth is coppery foul. Out the window he sees storm clouds gathering. What is the nature of rain? *...to nurture or drown?*

He wills himself to think on the former. *Thou hast a puzzle to solve and doing so is your constant occupation. Look to it.* His venom toward Walsingham—and by association himself—abates, and, slipping Jane's letter into his cloak, he buttons up against the winter and the threatening weather. But the smell of her on the scarf conjures images of loving times: Their picnic on the day Will presented himself, her pleasure at gathering flower arrangements for their household, her abashed manner when he caught her unstitching some mindless needlepoint she had done, embarrassed at having been found being so lackadaisical. And he savored the memory of Jane's exposed, perfectly white and jutting breasts while she beckoned to him in their bed chamber—and their mutual shuddering that followed. How could he have abandoned her?

His mind is on fire, yet he starts the long trudge up to the castle and its collection of books where clues may be found. *Keep going*, he orders himself. On this miserable gray day bereft of sun and *her*, his memories and future cast a long shadow on his tomorrows.

Orsino's usher closes the door behind him, and John Dee finds himself alone in a comfortable room. It is home to all sorts of books, maps, manuscripts, pamphlets, and folios. Some of the texts—the older ones—are written upon vellum, though most are on paper. The chamber is divided into ten large bookcases, and each has six shelves. Above each cabinet on the coffered ceiling oval paintings depict biblical events, presenting a timeline chronicling the expulsion of Adam and Eve to the birth of Christ. In addition, various artifacts sit alongside the books: an Italian lute, instruments for measuring and numbering, artisan tools, and an assortment of stones and seashells.

Looking about and acclimating easily, the scholar thinks the architect, perhaps Orsino himself, is of a saturnine frame of mind like his own. Scholarship is revered here. Phelippes had been wrong, the Count's collection is a fraction of the size of Dee's at Mortlake, yet larger than he had expected, making his hopes of finding insights into Orsino's tastes and leanings measurably unlikely.

Still, he has come and he must start? The room's glazed windows face east, and so the western wall receives the morning sun. Only the threatened rain has come and left much of the room in shadow. Today's light, Dee observes, reaches only the sixth shelf. Above which, obscured, he counts another, perhaps, four tiers of tomes. Taking his cue from what sun there is in the room, he begins to read the titles of the works on the sixth shelf and below.

Scouting for forbidden materials, he mutters, "I've set myself a fool's errand. Yet..." *Surely, there must be something.* He glances over at the rain-streaked window. *It pours now,* he thinks, happy to have left the inn when he did. As he bends down to investigate the volumes on the bottommost shelf, his scholar's robe puddles on the floor. Suddenly, he is aware of Fabian at the door.

Unsure why the usher has returned, Dee remarks, "You have my leave to go, Fabian. I shall not require your further assistance." Fabian nods respectfully and turns to go as Dee asks, "Is this room oft visited?"

"My master the Count takes great delight in it, Doctor. Oft afternoons, he comes here to enjoy his dark pleasures. He will sit at yonder table pondering over some quibble... best left forgotten..." The usher points with his cane to a small table with two books on it and an oversize wooden chair nearest the window, "...for hours His Lordship loses himself in these big ones here. Likes the feats of valor performed, he does, or the ink stains of wisdom, or the wicked tales of demi-gods," says Fabian with barely hidden scorn, adding, "and their paramours." Sounding just as sarcastic as he intends, he asks, "Does the Postmaster like them? Such stories?" Not waiting for an answer, Fabian gives Dee a lascivious smile. "S'truth, all members of the household have leave to come in and read—though nobody ever does." Fabian crosses to a nearby bookcase. With a forefinger, he swipes the shelf and finds it not to his liking. With a full palm, Fabian dutifully brushes away a broad span of dust patina that forms a cloud of motes as it falls. "Waste of time in my opinion. Too much work to be done." He looks at the foreign academician. "Your Lordship may do as you please so long as you don't mark up the pages." And giving Dee the once over, adds, "or steal any."

Having given fair warning, Fabian leaves the old scholar alone to the yellowing parchments and the miniscule atomies adrift in the musky wet air.

{19}

Shakespar timidly enters Countess Illyria's private quarters finding Dian clad teasingly in a morning linen slip that hides neither her shapely breasts nor her sacred body. Though he turns away in modesty, his imagination races as his fancies get the better of him. In such a revealing garment, he imagines her in a masque, priggishly provocative like Cleopatra or proud and pre-eminent in a diaphanous sari like thrice-worthy Andromache. Donning a velvet robe, she allows Will to look while she does her toilet. Her fine Gaulish hooked nose is not off-putting as her nostrils are exquisitely narrow in the manner of all highborn French women. It is said such a nose denotes intelligence, status, and personality. Pitched lower than most English women, her voice has a throaty breathiness that Shakespar finds feline and exciting. She has an accent to catch a hero's ear and urge him to monumental deeds. In her red hair is a chaplet of gold braid that shines with as much brilliance as the golden crucifix at the base of a lengthy alabaster neck. The two accessories accent the dual aspects of her beauty: her radiance and her spirituality. She regards Shakespar in her mirror. His pulse races as the male at sixteen usually does in such circumstances.

"Your Ladyship sent for me?"

"I thought we should become better acquainted." She sips wine and laughs. "Look," she says to him, "my hand shakes." She shows him her hand, and he is unsure if she wants him to take it. But if Shakespar sees angelic perfection in her presence, he is aware there is *cerise* as well as sensuality, requiring that he batten down his coursing blood. He is also cognizant of the Gaulish determination of her will. He senses that it is a dreadful power kept in reserve as lethal—potentially—as the executioner's ax, remaining hidden until the last moment. As if within one face, one voice, one habit, live two people—a duality that is and is not. The warning prophecy from *The Rachel*.

They are not unaccompanied in her privy chamber. He had not expected it to be otherwise. It would have been unseemly for her to meet him alone, a sacrilege against purity. With head down but grinning playfully, Maria Burhou, with long looping gestures, is stitching a woodland motif on her wicker *petit-pointe* hoop. There is also a groom of the chamber who stands in silent attendance as befits his office and her virtue. Will nods to each—ignoring him, they are but human furnishings. Soon, he forgets about their presence as one ignores the paneling in a room. Dian owns his full attention.

"I would have tried to see you, *Madame*, even if you had not sent for me."

"Why is that? Have you something to tell me?"

"Just that..." Impulses fight with reason for control of what to say next. "...that I must know you better to write the best about you."

Charmed by his youthful confusion, she coos, "*Mon cher*, come here. Come sit next to me." He comes but does not sit.

"Why?" Will asks warily when he arrives by her side.

"Because," lifting her goblet, "I have wine to share."

He shakes his head *no*. He must keep his wits about him. She smiles at his lack of social ease. "Master, *Shake-spear*, the Countess continues to mispronounce his name, which he never wishes to correct, so taken is he with her broken pronunciation. "Your sentiments and your *poésie* have provided much delight for my husband. He hath known you but a brief time, and already you are no *etranger* to his happiness. You are like to be much advanced."

"*La Comtesse* flatters me, beggar that I am," Will is overawed. "I can but beggarly give thanks to both M'Lady and His Lordship." As Dian and Maria are seated, Will bends slightly at the knees, aware he is towering over them. It is an awkwardness that is hard even for a teenage performer to maintain.

"Will Your Ladyship still grant me permission to sit?" Gesturing clumsily toward a nearby three-footed stool.

"Her Ladyship *does*," replies the coquette with a gesture of great hospitality. Maria merely purrs knowingly, never looking up from her stitching.

Seated on the low stool, Will splays out his legs in front of him. *Legs of a stag*, he reminds himself confidently. His legs and thighs he believes to be his best feature.

"How old are you?" Dian is coy.

Born poor and intimidated by her nobility, Shakespar forgets his legs as his confidence withers, yet he puts on a good face deciding to add four years to his maturity to better impress Her Ladyship. "Come Saint George's day, I shall be twenty."

The human furnishings behind him stifle their condescending laughter. But, Dian remains discrete, allowing only the semi-circles of the corners of her pretty mouth to lift. Shakespar supposes, had she joined their ridicule, his heart might have been torn apart as entirely as love-struck Actaeon was by the goddess Dian after whom she is named.

With childish unease, his exposed legs curl up protectively beneath his stool like crumpled leaves in late autumn. "I *shall* be a score... soon," he insists.

"Aye, soon, enough, young master," laughs Maria as her needle again arches through the air and returns to its stitch point, "but certainly not this St. George's Day nor several more. For look you, you have not even the beginning of a beard."

On either side of him, the women are seated high enough, and the boy's stool sufficiently low, so that Dian can address Maria over his head. "Mock not the boy's reckoning," orders her superior. Then with glinting blue eyes and in her nasal accent, the Countess twits Will for his deception, "Master *Shake-spear* is no mathematician nor tapster, but a poet. His only cunning is the reckoning of numbers in his verses." Turning back to him with a glint of severity, the Countess demands softly, "Now, young sir, might you hazard another guess at your age?"

"Your Ladyship shows me great kindness..." He glances behind him. "...when others heap scorn upon me." In self-defense, he endeavors to trade Maria mock for mock. "'Tis not gentle, not friendly."

His barb has no sting; Dian's waiting-woman remains self-satisfied having tweaked the besotted boy for his puppy-dog adoration. Dian, being of tender conscience, admonishes Maria's self-satisfaction, wagging her finger at her companion to behave. Obediently, the Lady returns to her function as room ornament.

None in Stratford would have imagined such a scenario: a burgher's son—the glover's moony boy— incredibly, being defended by this magnificent daughter of the de Guise! Not even the poet's mother would have dreamed it. His father would have boxed his ears for even imagining it. John Shakespar's mind, if it ever experienced an ounce of self-awareness, was blind to any higher existence; limited financial security and local acclamation was the highest hope he had for himself. When, in servile drudgery, bloody hands tore and scraped away at sheep intestines or horses' cadavers, Will's father blinkered his thoughts to achieving nothing more grandiose than a modest portion of middle-class respectability.

Will had worked alongside him long enough to see his nose-to-the-grindstone father fined for illegal wool trading and usury, and stayed long enough to see his field mouse father betray his religion by following plebian orders to whitewash splendid Catholic murals of saints from Stratford's Guild Chapel, stayed long enough to see his work-a-day father shrink to a non-entity. The man—if you could call him that—feared ambition, the boldness of self-respect, and never dreamt of the satisfaction of besting his fellows—if not his betters.

Dull ox-like existence dowses the fires of enthusiasm and boldness as thoroughly as a smithy's trough does a hot iron. Conversely, to men of the world, bold action is a joyful sport to behold. Will's intention was to outrun his father's modest expectations and stagger the world with exceptionalism. A man's worth was only limited by the size of his imagination. He'd sneered at his father's yeoman aspirations and escaped the Midlands as soon as he could. The mercantile Thames was a river more fit to sail dreams on than the meandering Avon.

Having been caught in a lie by the Lady, Will has no other option but to tell true. Returning his attention to Dian, yet not daring to look her directly in the eye, and hoping to please with charm and maturity, Will does his best to sound *blasé*.

"I did indeed miscount, *Madame Comtesse*." Despite more guileful sounds of satisfaction from Maria, undeterred, Will's voice becomes more intent, "Upon my soul, come this St. George's day, I will be seventeen."

His confession seems to mean nothing to the young *Comtesse*; herself barely exceeding twenty-six, Dian wafts through the room with a languid assurance. Arriving at her screen to dress, she disappears behind it while Maria helps her disrobe.

Befuddled Will stares. "Shall I leave?"

"*Mais non*. Why should you? It rains, does it not?" comes the sensual voice from behind the screen.

Is this something they do in France? he wonders. *Or perhaps I am of no more importance to her than the rest of the room's furniture. If so then I shall be audacious.* He steals glances at her naked flesh through the gaps in the screen's panels as she lifts her arms to doff her *chemise* and receive the day's heavier winter wardrobe.

"Better to speak true and shame the devil," she says while Maria pins sleeves to Dian's bodice.

Thinking he's been caught, Will abashedly moves away toward the mullioned window. What is to be done to quash his proverbial spear? He peers intently out at the view of the frosty countryside, his evil angel chides:

Wilt thou be a hulking laughing stock, a country bumpkin?

Who calls me this?

Nay, it cannot be if you should play the dreamer thus.

"Courage", prompts his good angel.

The spirit within thee is noble, honorable, and unmatchable.

Do not act the wretch and, like a finch in a cage, peer pitifully at the world!

Turn and brazen out all bashfulness.

Be the man.

His bad angel merely chuckles at this presumption of his having a backbone.

Emerging dressed in a damask gown, *La Comtesse*

presents herself with a grand gesture.

"*Et voila!*" she rejoices awaiting Will's evaluation, his opinion, his praise.

But Will's middle class upbringing keeps his eyes averted. "Her Ladyship looks at me. Might I be given permission to look at Her?"

"It is the common way to converse, *no*?" There is flirtation in her husky morning voice as she allows Maria to pin up her red tresses into a silken caul. "You have come to know me better, *n'est-pas*?"

Playing suave and masculine, Will catches Dian's eye. Faltering, his tongue outruns his mind, "How old are *you*?"

"*L'enfant est tres mauvais. Il oublie les convenances,*" gasps Maria.

"*Tu devois lui excuse. C'est une jeune,*" corrects Maria's mistress. Switching back to English, *La Comtesse* playfully reprimands, "Master *Shake-spear*, it is impolite to *demander* a woman's age." This tiny correction is followed by a mischievous smile. "But I will tell you that though I have overlept twenty, I am nearer to it than *peut-être* you are."

Shakespar calculates, brightens. Dian returns to her seat plumping up a velveteen cushion before she sits. Positioning it behind her back, she leans back in it and twists at a lock of hair that has fallen from her headdress.

"Your Doctor has offered to cast my astrological chart. But, I would prefer that he not," she says with some concern, inadvertently touching the cross at her neck, "...as I was brought up to believe such calculations an abomination, workings of the damned." A delicate white hand pushes a strand of hair back behind her ear. "I mean no disrespect to your master, who is our guest."

"*Laisse- moi*," says Maria rising to restrain Dian's errant lock properly.

The Princess allows herself to be tended. "Forgive me, *ma chere*," says Dian, the vibrant aura about her is electric, "but I was given to believe that Your Queen— *ma fois, Our* Queen—and her prelates have outlawed the celebration of all saints' days."

"Aye, even so."

"Then how is it that you nominate your birthday as a holy day?" This quickens something in her. "Were you somehow brought up in the mother Church of Rome?" She leans forward, hoping to find a fellow Catholic. Her breast swells beneath the confines of her clothing in anticipation.

"My father and mother, like all the generation of England before me, were faithful celebrants of the Mass. I was brought up in Warwickshire—"

"What an ugly word. *Aussi laid!*" says Dian's sewing companion and wrinkles her nose in distaste even as she brushes her own hair. "Warwickshire? It sounds of badgers, briars, hovels, and bad teeth."

With light malice, *La Comtesse* reprimands her waiting-lady, "Peace, you bleating nanny goat."

Maria makes a gesture that begs pardon and continues grooming herself. Will frowns. This *woman has sucked mischief from the tit of a man-hating nurse.*

Rescued by his hostess, he continues, "Warwickshire... where there are many beautiful remnants and celebrants of the old faith." He remembers the sizeable religious mural again in Stratford's City Hall that his father had been ordered to whitewash. "But, as I serve the Crown by serving Doctor Dee who serves here as England's Postmaster, I have, as required, taken the *Oath of Supremacy and Uniformity*, sworn my fealty to My Queen and Her Anglican Church and must profess myself a Protestant." Equivocation rings in the way Shakespar says *profess* and *must*. It is as politic an answer as he can make to a divinity he finds hard to lie to.

Dian leans in, seeking something in his face, she discovers only regret that he will not or cannot say more. If he has played the lawyer with her, he does not appear to have played her falsely. Sighing profoundly, her hand returns to the cross strung at her throat. She is disappointed by the heresy of the times. It is a loathsome new world where the faithless, preaching false theology and sowing doubt, can make God's children abandon the true religion and their eternal salvation.

As a dutiful daughter of the Church, her duty was to bring others to salvation. "Only God knows what is in your heart. But, as you tender life ever-lasting beware of foul heresy and ignorant pride. Do not sell the best part of you for thirty pieces of silver. Wherein I believe many of your countrymen have transgressed. Lands are but mud, gold is but glittering dross, and positions of power endure but for the moment." She looks hard at him. "You may know your enemy by unsubstantial fair gifts and beauteous raiment. Do not you forsake the blessed sacraments of the Roman faith for such trumpery."

Seeing no wavering in him, the missionary zeal that had blazed in her eye momentarily recedes behind a look of resignation, tinged with sadness. But her adamantine belief strives one more time, and with an unflinching hand, she takes his prisoner.

"You are young, Will *Shake-speare*, prayer will absolve you of all faults. The power of repentance and confession can absolve us of all our trespasses. I have a care of your preservation. Return to the religion your ancestors knew so well."

{20}

Continuing his investigation in Count Orsino's library, the intelligencer, John Dee, spends more than an hour searching for something—anything. "Bootless," whispers Dee to himself. His preoccupation on hold, he discovers the downpour has ended and where there had been shadow, sunbeams pierce through the dark clouds like luminosity in a Caravaggio painting. In the growing light, the chamber seems larger, more impenetrable. Had he time and another mind set, he might happily enhance his learning by studying the notable works that he has stumbled upon. Time, alas, is passing and his present investigation may soon be disrupted.

Searching for clues, the necromancer chances upon a flat piece of polished crystal near the top of one of the bookshelves. *Perhaps, it is time to ask for help*, he concedes.

Usually, Edward Kelley did all his scrying while Dee recorded. It is a young man's occupation meant for a young man's eyes and a young man's stamina. Daunted again by the sheer number of books, Dee resignedly plucks the paper, quill, and ink that he has brought with him. *Help thyself and God will help thee*, he reminds himself.

Setting his writing *accoutrements* methodically upon the table, he surveys the room, and finds that Heaven is already helping by providing everything he needs, including a break in the weather and streaming sunshine.

In order to create a *sigillum dei*, his scrying chart, he starts by retrieving the mathematician's compass from its place in the bookcase and carefully inscribes a large circle on the paper. Then with the draftsman's ruler already on the table, he divides the circumference of the ring in sixths and thereupon inscribes a straight line between each designated point. He connects every second point with a straight line then constructs two rectangles from these connected lines touching the circle's circumference in several spots. Next, he bisects the rectangles running lines through their centers. These create geometric forms and six-pointed stars within the original circle. Within these sections, Dee, again using the compass, is able to draw in three smaller circle-like structures. In various sections, he labels the figures with Greek or Hebrew letters. When he finishes, he points the small circle which he has designated *Omega* in the direction of the sun and sets the smooth quartz in the center of the paper, hoping Orsino's stone is pure enough for the "action."

Placing his fingertips on his forehead and cheeks and concentrating inwardly, he intones the necessary prayers for humility and purity of mind. He takes the precaution to add a new invocation to his ritual, "let not anyone come in." After a quarter of an hour of kneeling on the floor, cleansing himself through prayer, concentrating on the light being reflected from the polished stone, he begins the ritualistic words to "the Lord God on High," asking that a good angelic creature manifest herself in the stone. To considerable satisfaction and relief, the angel *Anael* manifests.

"Your Excellency is good to come at my request?" Dee intones reverently. He *perceives* rather than *sees* her in a glittering gold raiment. And about her head, blazing stars beam and radiate in all directions. The experience is more daunting and so much more fearful than the unrequested blissful visitation of divinity experienced on *The Rachel* months before. His eyes sting, seared by the reflected light from the stone.

Why have you summoned me? appears in flaming red Hebrew letters upon the surface of the stone.

"I look only for kindness and help from thee. I fall upon my knees before thee." He grovels. "Will ye grant me instruction as to how I may discover treachery if there be such in this room?" whispers Dee.

Pointing with a finger of blue flame at the Hebrew letter *Dalid* on the paper below the stone, Anael writes in blazing light upon the polished stone, "*You shall find it there.*" But the light has become too intense to bear. And the scryer flinches away covering his eyes and regrettably breaking the communication. Blinking to continue, he despairs that the blinding vision has vanished. *Too soon, too soon. All my time spent in preparation and so little communication.*

Left temporarily unable to see aught but burning bright light, Dee blinks repeatedly in pain, then shutters his eyes tight, maimed by the intense radiance he has forced himself to endure. His knees throb from kneeling on the hard wooden floor; he finds it difficult to rise from his position. Needing to move—yet everything seems too bright, too vivid—he staggers over to Orsino's reading chair where he recovers from his exertions and waits for the sensitivity to subside. Knowing from Edward Kelley, that eyesight will be restored in time, he remains seated for ten minutes, using the time to consider the angelic implications, revisiting all that he has been shown. Yet, he is clueless as to the significance of the Hebrew letter *Dalid* that corresponds to the Latin *Delta* or the English *D*. Orsino's library texts are not in alphabetical order. Despite the agony, the necromancer squints one eye at the shelves. Those in the shadow are easier to look at as daylight still stabs. He closes his eyes tight. *Kabala* taught that *Dalid* was the fourth letter of the Hebrew alphabet and held the value of four. But there were many bookcases and six shelves per bookcase. *Could it be four books? The fourth bookcase? Fourth shelf up?*

Thinking he must return to first causes and original intentions, Dee reopens his eyes, and though the stinging glare of the light has minutely eased, it remains impossible to read any of the titles of the books on the table beside him. Further investigation of Orsino's taste in books is impossible. He fears that though *Anael* made sure no one entered during the scrying, someone might enter now that the angel has vanished. That dread impels him to rise as hastily as he is able, and return the crystal to its original place on the shelf lest someone might discover he has moved it. Yet, he tells himself, who would know the purpose that it was used for. But then, a wizard—as many supposed him—with a crystal might immediately invoke rumors of witchcraft. Lifting the stone, he stumbles his way back to return the stone to its shelf. On the shelf below it, just even with the height of the table, a series of four books of equal height catches his maimed eye. Desperately blinking repeatedly to clear his vision, he squints and catches blurry glimpses of the titles, none of which appears treasonous in any way. Unable to read the words, he haphazardly flips through the pages. In the midst of the third, a document slides out; its seal and ribbons have been compressed by the book's pages. He stoops to replace it when he discerns its broken wax seal is embossed with what he thinks is two keys crisscrossing—the mark of the Bishop of Rome. Foregoing the pain, he brings the image nearly to one open eye to be sure. Even though this clue of sedition may be what Dee is seeking, he hesitates to open it. If he is right about the seal, then this is a papal encyclical and will prove a Pandora's box for Orsino. If indeed, Orsino is the one who left it here. *But then, Fabian had said no one but Orsino ever comes here.*

Could it be? Squinting hard, Dee attempts to confirm whether this is the despised *Regnans in Excelsis* excommunicating Elizabeth and inciting English Catholics to murder their Queen. *Flat treason.* The necromancer is brought up short by a contrary thought. He had asked Anael for the source of treachery, and his angelic counselor had pointed at the *Dalid*, saying, *you shall find it there.* As *Dalid* is the cognate for the letter

D, the philosopher in him wonders whether Anael's message is of two meanings? Is not Dee himself being treacherous to Jane and Arthur? Is Heaven advising him of a more meaningful obligation? His heart clenches even as his mind ponders the possibility.

Suddenly, on the other side of the stacks, the rusted hinges of the library door creak. Sensible of being caught in a seeming impropriety, he rubs his eyes clear of the ebbing haze and moves toward the doorway to greet whoever has come in—only to realize he still has the offending papal document in his hands.

Will Shakespar regards the Royal beauty, hiding his disbelief. He has heard these little homilies many times spoken by others, including his own misguided mother and father, but never before by one with such noble bearing as the incomparable *Comtesse* of Illyria. He knows her words about returning to the old religion are meant to resonate with the pliant susceptibility of a childish trust in authority. Will is not an innocent. Faith in the words of zealots has scythed the streets of London. He reminds himself how friends mock the idea of Heaven, an airy nothingness of a pipe dream. Words of "trust in a merciful God" are continually drowned out by the screams heard on Tyburn's bloody scaffold, a theater of unspeakable and innumerable live eviscerations and decapitations. How often are vengeance and hatred preached in conjunction with '*Jesus is love*' in the heartless metropolis where a lonely boy's confirmation of his family's faith is repudiated?

The Countess cannot expect me to swallow the naïve falsehoods of her candied nothings, he thinks. *From her position of noble power, she can afford to indulge in such a luxury, but I cannot.* Her childlike insistence on a benevolent deity doggedly partial to a flawed Roman Church diminishes her in Will's eyes. Still she is the personification of femininity, despite this soiling of her divinity; her perfect French face, like Helen herself, renowned for launching countless imaginings on a sea of perfection, is now all too flawed, too human.

Hanging onto her faith and his hand with impassioned tenacity, Her Ladyship implores, "Tell me *Shake-speare*, will you embrace *our* way? Say, you will celebrate the Mass with me *privately* on the morrow."

"My worship is only for you, M'Lady." Flattery and pretense are his trade.

"Idolatry is heresy in any religion." She frowns at the impossible conceit.

"The boy has no shame," notes Maria.

Releasing her grip on him, Dian sighs, "I fear he has no chance at reformation." Her *égalité* treatment of him vanishes like the dream that it was. Will concedes that the castle gate to his spending time with her and having her admiration has been lowered; he has lost access. Still, consolation reveals itself. "It is a pretty compliment. My husband is right. You have an easy facility with words." She looks at him so that he cannot look away. "But of course, so does Satan, the father of lies." *There it is!*—the hidden steel, the executioner's blade. She withdraws within herself, having done what she should, she is now relieved of further obligations.

The hunt for nature's perfection is the wellspring of the lad's writing. Albeit schooled in taverns, he has been bred on disillusionment that fosters cynicism. And the two angels—perfection and cynicism—debate in his conscience, often suggesting what to believe and what to identify as cant. For a moment, Will wishes himself older that he might better cope with the rising surge of conflicting thoughts in his mind. Not least of which is whether or not to report back to his employer the Lady's attempts at his religious conversion. Since Campion's return to England two years before, everybody was advised of the new *Act* proclaiming that no one be permitted to even whisper the slightest reconciliation with Catholicism. It is a hanging offense. Even here in Illyria. Is this suggestion of hers "to privately worship Mass" an invitation to a treasonous act? The Doctor shall know of it, *must* know of it.

"Shall I leave? Have I offended?" Will offers weakly. Youth's impatient ache to embrace forthrightness lashes at him. Not for the first time, he is aware of his own double identity, his own duplicitousness that is and is not.

She gives him a tiny smile, less kittenish than those before. "*Mon petite,* I am, how you say? ...*écoeuré,*" he hears her say, "May time and Heaven translate you into a blissful soul. Yours is a dangerous obstinacy. I warn you, your simplicity risks damnation and hellfire, but I will say no more." Moving away to pick up her sewing, her hands tremble; she turns her back on him. Without her previous tenaciousness, she despairs, "I have faith you will come round to the error of your ways." Then perfunctorily, "I shall pray for you."

Gazing at her slender back, Shakespar is uncertain. He fears his last performance may mar his new court position. Dian turns around to grant him another practiced smile. He foresees her detesting him and the disfiguring grimace that will replace that smile when she learns the true nature of his being here. Shouldering his fate, Shakespar is too much the actor to let *this* show.

"I hope to be guided by Heaven," he replies with all the maturity he can muster.

The sudden entrance of Lord Griffin, Edmund Dotrice abruptly interrupts their exchange.

"Ah, so you are *here*!" The puffing Chamberlain is irascible and out of breath.

Quizzically, Dian turns to Edmund as do the others. The groom straightens as Maria rises. And Will, putting on a brave front, tries not to cower at being found in the Countess' closet.

"Where is your Master?" the Lord asks, animus in his high tenor voice.

"I know not," informs Will. *Why—this irritation in Griffin with the Doctor?* "I would venture he is about the castle, Your Lordship." Supplicatory, he adds, "He has spoken of the library."

"The library? What would he do there?"

"Read? Your Grace." Will shrugs clumsily. The comical answer does not entirely melt Dotrice.

"Yes, well thought on," replies the Chamberlain. "I have not looked there yet. But, of course, it is reasonable to believe our scholar has gone to commune with what he prizes. In all courtesy, we must send someone to attend to him at once."

Again, Will wonders, *Why this intensity?* Is there a diplomatic emergency that ignites this fire in the unflappable administrator? Or, with a sixteen-year-old's impending sense of dread, could it be the discovery of their mission that puts them both in danger? Will's recent evasions with Dian have sent him down a rabbit hole of second-guessing. He wants to be anywhere *else*, but not for the reason he gives.

"Thinkest thou, my master requires me?" posits Shakespar.

"I know not. He is *your* master, not mine," comes the aloof rebuff and with it a long stare that anatomizes the player, further testing Will's powers of performance. It causes *l'inconfort* in the room. "Tell me, boy, are not poet's false dissemblers?"

"Poets oft must dissemble in their words, but I am honest, Sir."

"Yet, you do not look me in the eyes when you address me. Have you some dark purpose that taints your honesty?" Will's fears are redoubled. Concerned that Edmund is being too hard on the boy, the Lady Dian moves to stand between them. To the Countess, Dotrice asks with denigrating concern, "*Comtesse*, what do we know of this London youth *or* his employer except they are sent by the English government. And who runs that government? Walsingham and Burghley—both Puritans—who have ever been known to disapprove of *your* marriage? Disapprove of *our* being faithful Roman

Catholics."

"M'Lord, my employer was sent by *Our* Queen, not Sir Fancis Walsingham!" Will lashes out.

Unaccustomed to being addressed rudely by a menial, Dotrice looks sharply at the teen. "One and the same," is his curt reply.

"You scare the boy, Edmund," whispers Dian. *The admonishing white finger again*, Will observes.

Grateful for the Princess' intercession, Will retreats a step or two, rueful of his earlier thoughts of her betrayal.

With the corners of his creased mouth lifting and his normal indulgent benevolence returning, the Chamberlain tenderly takes the hand in front of him, "I am sorry, Your Ladyship, I did not mean to offend. It is that I have just heard from the porter that Doctor Dee, our distinguished Postmaster from London, a man of international repute, is about the house, and *no one* waits upon him. It is a breach of etiquette and a grievous dishonor to our guest."

With that, his mustached lips gesture to kiss his superior's hand. While his brown whiskers brush her knuckles, his eyes communicate some unspoken message born of mutual understanding.

When Edmund Dotrice, Lord Griffin, turns once more to face the powerless player, the Lord's countenance is contrite.

"My apologies, young man." He then ruffles Will's hair, who acknowledges the act of *rapprochement* with a tight smile and gentle head shake. *I need to be elsewhere*, thinks Will. Anywhere else that is less confusing, less threatening.

"I seek your Master, do you care to come with me?"

"No, he cares to abide here with me," countermands Dian, again showing her steel. This surprises Shakespar; he believed she had finished with him.

But it is more of a surprise to Lord Griffin whose sandy colored eyebrows arch. Whatever ugly retort forms in his mouth is swallowed. *Irksome to be so publicly admonished, even in front of human furniture,* thinks Dotrice. Though a man—and widely respected—he is obliged to obey Her Ladyship; she is an extension of Count Orsino's rule, not to mention a de Guise. Yet, no matter his standing, he knows that Maria will eagerly retell his chastisement to other menials among the household.

"M'Lady, grant me now leave to depart from thee?"

A steely, "With all my heart" is the Countess' reply, and dutiful Edmund Dotrice, Lord Griffin of Illyria, flushes himself from the room.

That little interlude, thinks Shakespar, *cannot but turn him into a notable contempt. Will Dee and I be reproached for it? Surely, it is not my fault.*

Maria resumes her sewing. Her needle penetrates and comes up again to anchor a French knot. Eager to know more of Her Lady's thoughts, Dian's confidant must remain silent until Will has left the room.

As for the Countess, she politely informs the room, "Sir Edmund is too scrupulous about protocol."

The library door is ajar and no one there. The concerned Natural Philosopher quickly scans the hallway. No one. Yet, Dee is certain he heard the door open, certain he *saw* someone through the stacks.

Dee feels the dry flux rise in his throat. Bewildered and suspicious, he closes the door and returns to the writing table only to kick himself that he has left the *sigillum dei* in plain view. *Had someone seen it and then bolted from the room?* He thinks to leave, but realizes that he still holds the alleged death warrant *encyclical!* Looking at it, with eyes now clear of obstruction, his surmise is substantiated. It is the *Regnans in Excelsis*. He quickly returns the abomination to its nesting place in the tome. *No one the wiser*. Then he remembers the blue flame pointing to the *Dallid*. He must write Secretary Walsingham immediately. The sooner he can get a message to Sir Francis of this lead, the sooner he can please his handler that he is making progress. Fortune is smiling. After all, is not the mail boat to London, anchored in the marina, scheduled to depart that very day and not return for another week?

Returning to the *sigillum dei* and the reading table, the intelligencer quickly folds the scrying chart into a small square and hides it in his boot, intending to dispose of it later in a safer place. Dee finds himself holding his breath as he puts pen to ink and begins his report, frequently looking over his shoulder should the invisible interloper return. Though the message must be encoded, the cipher is an easy one that he has used many times, and, a short time later, the deed is done. Nearly all is reported: his finding the papist Bull, Orsino as a suspected enemy of the State, but not the prognostication from Aneal of the *Dallid*. Sir Francis would not look favorably on that, and it would only undermine his official report.

Yet, there is more to do: a second letter must be written to his employer, neighbor, supposed friend, but certainly godfather to his son Arthur. From his robe, Dee draws Jane's pleas for help and begins fulfilling the promise he made to himself; he asks Sir Francis for help. It cannot be denied that Walsingham must already know of her letter's contents as it bears his seal. Surely, it had been steamed and read prior to its being put on the mail ship. He asks himself, how does an esteemed scholar admit to the sin of poverty to Walsingham? Begging help of his tormentor who placed him here so far from home is the act of a desperate man, one whom God has forsaken. And yet Dee has always presented himself to the Court, to England, to the world, and to himself as one in control and one of God's chosen. Shame vies with need. Need wins; he writes to the old fox. First, he will remind the Foreign Secretary of their mutual enemy: John Prestall, his *and* Walsingham's stridently Catholic opponent, who is bringing a perversion of a lawsuit to rob the scholar not only of his reputation but of what little he possesses—and this, conveniently, while Dee is out of England. Can this be countenanced? Often, he blots, then writes again, scratching out more than he keeps. His attempts to write honestly are blocked and countermanded by each careful word he thinks he must use to gain favor.

The prefatory encomium is too fawning, too overwritten. Can he not just confess his needs and plainly ask for funds or even a loan? Does he need to inflate his employer's accomplishments and beg pardon for his own shortcomings? Yet, his own pride in his erudition and the Foreign Secretary's pride of office require the flowery language. It *is* overwritten, yet it will serve.

Then there is the lost pension. That must not go unmentioned. If Sir Francis has read the letter, the need is evident. *The scheming two-faced bastard must know I'm being rejected. Who knows? Maybe the rogue had a hand in that too. I wouldn't put it past him. What does the Queen call him? Her spider?* All this prompts the scholar to tear up his request and start afresh for the fourth time. But he cannot.

Glancing out the window, it is clear there remains little time; the mail ship will set sail today; he must be satisfied with what is written. He uses the last page of paper on Orsino's library desk to sign his name in his most impeccable hand. Blowing the wet ink dry then waving it in the air, he cannot fathom how his accounts and his creditors have bested him. *I have been misused by mine enemies. Yet, not so. I must not succumb to self-pity. I have done this and I am to blame.* Looking at the letter in hand he thinks, *Sir Francis will be merciful.* Scanning the room to be certain that he has left no incriminating evidence of his scrying activity, the anxious man speeds to the door that will lead him to the mail ship and a reprieve.

Just as he reaches for the latch, Lord Griffin plunges into the room. Startled, Dee steps back. With seeming composure, the Postmaster seems pleased with the encounter, giving Edmund Dotrice the most reassuring smile that he can muster.

"Good morrow. How does Your Lordship?"

"Dear Doctor how good it is to see you again. I hope you want for nothing," says the urbane Chamberlain. "I was not told of your arrival this morning. You must have slogged through a torrent of rain coming up from town. Yet you don't seem wet. You are a magician indeed."

"Not a magician, Lord Griffin, a Natural Philosopher. I was fortunate. I arrived just as the heavens opened."

"Very early for a visit." Suspicion lurks in his voice. He looks around to see if anything is amiss.

"I could not sleep." Indicating the room. "Knowing that the Count has a fine collection of works, I was ardent to see what I could find. Just last night, His Lordship had especially asked me to come at any time to study."

Subtracting the few steps between them, Edmund probes, "Yet," indicating the letter in his hand, "you seem more interested in writing than reading."

"A letter to my wife, good sir, she wrote me of her loneliness and I wrote to her of my love." He kisses it lovingly and quickly pockets it. "I really must get this to the mail ship that waits in the harbor."

Not really convinced of any of this, Dotrice merely says, "Indeed."

Again, the library door opens. There the dour figure of Orsino's Stewart, Malvolio, stands—posture erect—his chin firm and resolved. Not a link of his gold chain of office is out of place or unpolished. Drawing in a long breath, with great formality he informs, "My Good Lord, the Countess requests your immediate help with a matter. She has asked me to bring you at once." He points his wand of office in that direction.

"I must refuse Her Ladyship," Edmund Dotrice responds curtly, still grudging her humiliation of him in the presence of Maria and a footman, "Tell Her that I am involved with business of my own." *As most assuredly she knows. Why send the peg-a-ramsey to fetch me?*

Seeing none but the two men, Malvolio counters, "Perhaps, Lord Griffin, you might bring Doctor Dee with you and ask My Lady if he may join you?" Thus, making clear to the Chamberlain that Lord Griffin is subservient to the Countess and Dotrice's presence is being demanded. Wanting to post his messages, Dee would object to going but can think of no excuse.

Fixing a cold eye on His Lady's messenger, Griffin politely refuses, "Thank you, Malvolio for your suggestion, but we will continue here, *sirrah*." The last derogatory word strains Malvolio's civility and his pride of position. Aristocratic households are furtive, competitive, with feuding subtleties often lost on outsiders. However, Dee needs no angel to tell him that the lengthy distance between the two men in the room is too short for their individual comfort. Taking the opportunity to extricate himself in two steps toward the open door, Dee pretends to be unaware of the disdain between them.

"You may leave us now, *monsieur Le Stewart*. Your services are not required."

21

Just as Dee heads down the hill from Count Orsino's castle gate, the morning's respite of sunshine turns to a showery rain. *Weather is so mercurial on this floating patch of unanswered questions,* grudges Dee. Despite the wet, the Doctor is happy to have fled the castle and its intrigues—reminded how distasteful it and he have become. Since his early morning trudge uphill, the well-trodden roadway has become sucking mud. Going is made worse by the crazed winds howling through the narrow lanes of Illyria, making the day bitterer. Stinging brine etches Dee's face and discovers secret entries through his boots and coat. He tightens his coat around him and pulls down on his wide-brimmed hat. A moment later, a swirling blast snatches the battered beaver and launches it from his head like a Roman candle. He catches up to it just before it sinks into a rippling tide of waste guttering along the lane. The hat is wet and stinks, nevertheless his gloved hand smashes it down on his drenched head. Needing to concentrate on anything but the elements, he calculates how long to reach the warmth of the *Cubiculo* and a change of clothes. *I can only hope this blow will keep the ship delayed.* He prays for a storm. *Would that I could conjure one.* Concentrating on anything besides his untenable situation, he calculates the time to return to the inn. Thirty minutes. *Too long. Too long.*

There is a crack of thunder and with a great clatter his prayers are answered. A torrential rain pours down. With it comes an internal tempest, one of expectations and regret flooding his thoughts. In Orsino's library, Dee has managed to gather several clues, and he feels justified in having come to Illyria, despite the sacrifices. Peering through the driving rain, the intelligencer glances back at the castle, now almost imperceptible in the onslaught, thinking that for comfort's sake he might return to it. *No, no more encounters with Lord Griffin.*

Through the cascade of water, he notices that beyond an approaching oxen cart a sign hangs from a two-story stone building. The image of an open book flails in the wind; the wild wooden plank looks as if it might at any moment break its chains and tumble down. Despite the swinging and the sign's faded colors, distinctly legible, even through sheets of rain, is the unmistakable text: *Hilbred's Book Shoppe.*

Praise God, a shelter from the storm. In the grip of an inexplicable humour that comes over men in extreme circumstances, he laughs manically. Delighted, the bibliophile eggs himself on. *Who knows, I might discover some discarded relic whose worth is known only to men like me.* A touch more practical, he reasons. *My angels have given me rain. If Providence holds, there may even be a fire within.*

"*Go on, go in,*" good counsel whispers, from whither he knows not, "*Ill is the weather that bringeth no gain.*"

A bell over the door shudders brightly as he enters, and, then again as he muscles the heavy door shut against the elements. Gratefully, he detects that the emporium is roomier than he had imagined. Four or five lanterns hang about the open premises. *Regrettably no hearth fire*, thinks Dee. Still, he has escaped the wind and the rain.

On a high chair perched behind a higher desk, a boy of Will's age copies from one book to another. Atop his curly red hair, at an odd angle, a blue workman's hat sits. Clothed in an equally blue tattered shirt and cassock, the lad dips his stylus into a pot of ink. Dee notes the sleeves of the woolen jacket are too short, reaching only mid-forearm. Customer and clerk acknowledge each other with a respectful nod, Dee merely remarking, "Nasty weather," while brushing the rain from his hat and cloak onto the small rug by the door.

"Mind the water. The books." Dully, the boy warns the dripping man whilst clasping and unclasping stiffened fingers over a flickering taper. The nearsighted clerk sits in danger of singeing his bushy eyebrows as he dips his goose quill back into the inkwell, copying dutifully. Making no attempt to help or otherwise communicate, the young scrivener has long since grown used to browsers. Most never buy. This one surely must be a fool to be out in this weather.

"Where be thy master, sirrah?" asks Dee, noting no adult on the premises.

Without glancing up, the young scholar merely continues his copying impervious to conversation.

Unwatched and unaided, Dee is left on his own.

Invisible amidst the stacks of books, Dee scours the dozens of shelves and tables of bound and unbound volumes and broadsides, *feuilleton* and manuscripts. The thought occurs to him that he may have to replenish volumes if his brother-in-law has his way selling off parts of his Mortlake library. Had his back-biting brother-in-law, Nicholas Fromoundes, any idea how much he had sacrificed to gather and pay for his valued collection? Not just for himself, but for all of England's edification and enrichment?! A monument to learning! Dee shakes his head at his situation at home. *Temperance*, he advises himself, *temperance. What is gone is gone. What may be lost may be lost. Heaven and Providence will preserve the Dees.* He must have faith. *All is God's will.*

Unlike London where booksellers divide their merchandize into various areas of interest—histories, sciences, literature, Roman, Italian, or political—here, in Illyria's only book shoppe, no evidence exists of intelligent groupings whatsoever. *Here 'tis like a brothel*, thinks Dee, observing, *Poetry lies with Almanacs, History consorts with Astrology.* Dee forages. Most is inconsequential. *Authors who have nothing to say and no skill in saying what little they pretend to know.* Though the preponderance is in French, many are in Latin and some in English—none of any interest to the practiced antiquarian, claptrap, and dullness. As he hunts and thaws himself, he loses track of time—the sin of bibliomania being as deep-rooted in him as gluttony to an epicure. For a brief reprieve, Dee forgets the nightmarish problem of his financial affairs, the heartache of his family, and even his hurry to post his letters.

Thumbing through William Camden's historical work *Britannia*, Dee revisits some of the new tenets of the old era. He moves on to a tattered university copy of Pliny the Elder's *Natural History*. He thinks, *Young Will might like a personal copy of this.* Setting it aside, thinking he may return to it, he moves on searching for works of *poesie* to inspire Will with his Love sonnets. Unimpressed with the selections near the front of the store, the scholar moves to the back.

As Dee has lost all sense of time, there is no telling when the three men entered the shoppe. The tinkling bell must have chimed, but later in his journal, he writes that he had no clear memory of it, so immersed was he in his search for a rare book. As the rain beats mercilessly upon the roof timbers, surely the men must have shaken their drowned hats and stamped their sloshing boots, yet it is not until a hollow thump resounds within *Hilbred's* that Dee glances over to see a wooden chest the size of child's coffin, flanked by three sodden men. The coffer has a discernable naval quality to it. One of the men, too, smacks of the sea, being as thick as a cannon and having a permanent redness of face that only comes from years in the sun. He massages the muscles in his massive neck with a hand the size of a mallet.

"Master Hilbred, Sir, me thought thou was't above." The boy stands, summoned from his desk. Immediately he lugs an outsized ledger to the beckoner, to be examined. "Master, I have almost done the copying as you bid me."

The boy presents the papers for his approval.

"Not now boy. Fetch my purse that lies within my desk upstairs," instructs Hilbred, a short, thin man who is bald as a walnut and has a large wart on the side of his nose and the facial features of a wooden prow.

Dee glances up again from his reading among the stacks.

"But, Master—"

"But me no buts, boy," says the walnut, "be about it or I shall beat thee into a carbuncle. Quick feet now, about it!!"

Obediently, the lad rushes up a rickety stairway to the upper floor. The three men follow the boy; steps shiver and squeak under their combined weight. Behind them—none the wiser of Dee's presence—the carved sea chest is left behind. Enthralled reading Erasmus, the bibliophile makes no effort to make himself known.

Within the time to read a full page of the Latin text, the three men clomp back down the groaning stairwell. Each carries a stack of newly printed documents in his ink-smeared hands. Each stack is made up of about thirty unbound manuscripts whose pages are collated with small ringlets of thread. Master Hilbred opens the sea chest and the unbound books are stacked inside.

Concerned about the time and warm enough to continue walking, the greybeard sets down the Erasmus. Preparing to leave, he wraps his cloak about him.

"Boy," says the prow-faced owner, "fetch me the original. It lies within the attic by the press."

Press? Dee's full attention pivots. Neither within nor without the shoppe is advertisement to indicate that it acts as a printer's shoppe. *Most unusual.* Secret printing presses are a prime source of papist propaganda. *A secret press upstairs?* thinks Dee, studying the three men at the bottom of the stair. Illyria's Postmaster recognizes the silent third man. It is Tobias Belch, the harbormaster, who, at this instant, stands under the light of a lantern, palm uplifted, cheerfully receiving a fat purse from the store owner.

Even as he pays Belch, Hilbred wipes the moisture from his naked head and speaks painstakingly to the seaman, "Tell your Captain Brabantio, a man named Paget will call for these at Portsmouth."

At that moment, the shoppe boy appears at the top of the stair with the original manuscript. Before descending to his Master, he uses it to point out Dee in the shadows among the stacks. All the men turn and look at the random browser at the back. The face of each man turns ashen at being thus discovered.

Identified, the eavesdropper must swiftly exercise civilities, "Good morrow, gentlemen. Miserable weather, is it not?" Dee ejaculates merrily, hiding any interest in their activities.

"I thought we had been alone," mutters the store owner, straining to mask his emotions. "Boy?" demands Hilbred, elongating the monosyllable in utter consternation for not having been alerted at once to the stranger's presence.

Disconcerted, the eyes of Tobias Belch and the ox-like marine betray suspicion and menace respectively.

The naval giant takes one threatening step toward the stranger, "Belay there friend," says Belch but pausing him from attack. Identifying the intruder as, "Her Majesty's emissary from... Whitehall." Louder, Toby remarks as he points at their wet clothes, "Morning, Royal Postmaster. Miserable weather indeed, Doctor. It rains cats *and* dogs."

"Indeed," replies Dee jovially.

Continuing in the same unconcerned tone, Tobias shares, "We just now got the last of a shipment of broadsides to a ship waiting to embark for Portsmouth. The vessel stays but for this consignment and for the raging waters to quiet." Brazen Toby leans down and latches the trunk as if nothing is amiss. Another crack of lightning shears the silence. The other two men and the lad shuffle and look to the door as if they long to be out in the storm—and its relative safety—rather than here ensnared in red-handed treason. Confident of his skills at camaraderie and cordiality, Belch shares a Mephistophelian grin of oily camaraderie.

Whitehall? thinks John Dee, *Why mention that?* Convinced that he has stumbled on some illegal activity, the spymaster commences a non-stop monologue that Kemp, Armin, or any improvisational thespian would envy.

"Indeed, sir, you are in the right, Tobias. The rain raineth villainously, does it not?" But Dee does not wait for an answer. The garrulous Belch cannot get a word in edgewise. "Gentlemen, I can scarce believe my good fortune. I have found the most wondrous text in this quaint shoppe. Despite the stormy heavens, the gods have blessed me today. For look you, gentlemen, behold." And the Royal Postmaster General holds up a leather-bound edition. "Gentlemen, gold and silver, jewels and the most exquisite finery, homes and horses are but dross compared to *this*." He waves *Erasmus* at them and splits his focus between them and it. "Words of wisdom live forever here..." Raising *Erasmus* ever higher in the air, Dee rants, "...far surpassing worldly riches that momentarily please the eye, a show of wealth that only serves to recommend one's capital worth to a stranger's assessment... Jewels and mean trifles are but very little. A work like *this*, ahhh, sirs, with its virtues, its wisdom, its words of comfort, and wise counsel can transform our bodily rectangles of dust into the excellence of an angel. Here be excellent words. Understanding, gentlemen! Knowledge and Understanding! Does not the old reprobate Socrates teach us to 'know thyself'? And how can we expect to accomplish that task without help from the ancients whose lives were once touched by true enlightenment." Briskly, Dee walks up to face his startled audience—in fact angling strategically toward the front door and a safe exit. "Which of you be the master here that I may purchase this priceless text? I must have it!" He reaches inside his wet coat and finds his purse, shaking it vigorously in their sight. The sound of clinking coins only adds to the men's bewilderment. Getting no immediate answer and as spry as any greyhound, the wizard scholar suddenly races up to the top of the stair and to the gaping boy standing there. Dee insists, "Here lad, you shall have these four Sovereigns."

"Four Sovereigns," says the mystified apprentice. "It is not worth four, farthings."

"What matter the cost. I shall be the richer for it."
Turning back to the three man audience below, "...*and
your master shall have made wondrously happy an
aging scholar.*" The necromancer thrusts the money at
the apprentice. Seeing the boy's difficulty in handling
what he is being given, the magus grabs the forbidden
manuscript from the boy's hands, freeing them to
receive the four Sovereigns. "Never mind *this* modern
claptrap. Here, here, take your remuneration."

Flustered, the boy does as he is told. At the same
time, Dee rifles furiously through the pilfered pages with
mock disdain dripping with contempt. He sees Hilbred
aiming toward the stair. Careful to locate the title, Dee
then throws it down the stairs onto the floor where its
pages disband. The balding head stoops to gather the
pages.

Pretending to ignore all, Dee continues his diatribe
as he descends, "This pennyworth of nothing is but
dross, worthless dross, compared to the celestial wonder
I grip now in my hand. I am the most fortunate man
alive to have found it." When it is clear that the stranger
is not trying to climb further to the shoppekeeper's room
and see the press, the conspirators silently expel bated
breath.

As the doctor turns his back momentarily, Dee can
almost feel the others winking at each other. Surely
feeling safe for the nonce. *No danger here; the intruder
is a popinjay.* Though Dee has rifled the pages, it is
beyond reason to think he has read anything that could
be written there. Moreover, he knows he has given every
impression of not hearing a word of their private

conversation.

Striding to the door with his purchase, Dee makes one last speech, "Long have I hungered for this very text," he warbles, "And I cannot wait to return to my room and absorb the wonders here writ onto the blank pages of my mind. I cannot thank you enough for introducing me to it, Master Hilbred."

The shopkeeper rises from the floor with an enforced conviviality. "Glad to be of assistance." Turning, the little man addresses the brawny porter, "By the sound of it, the weather is passing." He then waves the sailor on his way into the abating drizzle.

Shouldering the chest, heavier now with its contents, the mariner lumbers to the door to which Dee leaps and opens for his convenience. The large man exits. The weather has indeed eased and Dee's only thought now is the mail boat. Convivial, book in hand, he leaves as well, but not before suggesting to the owner that they must share a glass together soon.

Outside in the piddling rain, Walsingham's agent hastens on as he weighs the encounter. The encyclical is small news compared to discovering a secret recusant printing press smuggling contraband into England. *So, Walsingham's suspicions have been well-founded. The title of the manuscripts... 'Letters to the Lords of the Council'... No wonder the trio looked fearful.* Though the author's name was nowhere to be seen, *Letters to the Lords of the Council* is infamous as any pamphlet throughout the length and breadth of the European world. All knew it as *Campion's Brag*—Edmund Campion's Roman Catholic justifications for his coming to England. Its reprinting, even its reading, are punishable offenses in the English realm.

Dee is no lover of censorship, but a devout believer in the maintenance of authority. The similarities between England's old religion and the new one far exceed their differences, Dee believes. Why should zealots overthrow everything that is so excellent in England for a few incomprehensible, irrational Catholic rituals? *Transubstantiation, the sacrament of the Eucharist, consecrated hosts? Did they really believe Christ's body could transmogrify magically into a wafer? Did the Almighty really care if his people prayed to him in Latin or in English?*

A decade of Elizabethan policy has done away with huge numbers of Catholic clergy. Since Campion's martyrdom in 1581, many ardent English Catholics are joining the Jesuit's mission of ministering to abandoned parishioners. However other recusants who are less godly men than Campion—preach a violent overthrow of the government and the placing of Mary Queen of Scots on the throne. It is Walsingham's worst fear and the reason Dee has been sent here to Illyria.

By Heaven, Elizabeth must be protected. It is not my place, the intelligencer reminds himself, *to judge the truth of Orsino's moral convictions only to find the facts of any treachery. I must get these letters posted before the boat leaves the marina. The storm is nearly exhausted.* He quickens his step. A novel idea dawns as he walks: *if Campion had been morally justified to keep in hiding and dissimulate for his religious beliefs, have not I equal validation to do the same for my Queen.*

❧   ☙

Emerging from his reverie, Dee realizes he has covered much ground and is closing in on his lodging. The wet weather has done its worst and the skies are clearing. Relieved, he can see in the hazy far distance that the mail boat is still berthed in the marina.

He asks himself, *is Hilbred working on his own? Is he merely a hired printer, or is he attached to other subversive activities on the island? Are there further activities? Is Hilbred a codename? Had Orsino a hand in this?* How can the intelligencer ascertain any of this? He must find out—happy that clues have finally presented themselves. Obviously, harbormaster Belch is involved, but to what extent?

Turning a corner, the open water spreads out before him. Though obscured by mist, he now sees six ships anchored in the marina below. *One of them will soon set sail with its cargo of printed contraband to Portsmouth. But which one?* There below, the sea-chest trudging to its unknown destination can provide the answer. Intelligence about the ship and its cargo will be of great interest to Sir Francis. With such valuable information and the name of the man in Portsmouth— one *Paget*—Walsingham can use it to alert the maritime watchers to future arrivals. But, with the weather abating, has he time to discover the particulars of the one ship before the other sails? He feels for the letters to Walsingham, feels their urgency. He prays that he can do both.

Having forgotten the *Cubiculo*, Dee reassures himself that he and the behemoth in the bookshoppe that he is following are almost to the harbor.

"Doctor Dee!" comes a voice over the wind.

"Will? What are you doing here?"

"I returned to the inn, and saw you in the distance from my window." Breathless, Will stops, assuming his master will do the same, but the old graybeard continues in his brisk pace. Surprised, Will scurries after, "Wait, wait, I have much to tell you. Dian... I mean, *La Comtesse*—"

"I've no time. Do you see yon fellow... the big one with the chest... I must not lose him."

Seeing the porter carrying a chest on his shoulder but not at all knowledgeable about why he is looking, Will responds, "Fine. I'll come with you." Then asks, "Why must you follow him?"

His master tartly answers, "Because I must. Have a care, fall back, do not let him see us."

"Intelligence gathering?"

Dee deigns not to answer then picks up his pace leaving Will muttering to himself, "Well, if we must, we must."

As Will catches up, Dee inquires, "What is it that you have to say to me that it brought you out into this weather?"

"I had a remarkable encounter this morning. The Lady Dian sent for me to join her..." He adds theatrically, "in her closet." Not a modicum of a rise out of Dee. "I wish you had been there with me. She was—"

"Why would she invite you to her privy closet so early? And why on such a rainy day as this?"

"I was commanded. I think she likes me. She..."

Dee, despite his desire to keep an eye on the moving chest, gives his ward an ugly look. "Does she now?"

"She offered me wine and stood near naked before me. It was something to behold. You've never seen the like."

"Indeed." Dee can picture it easily and what he imagines bodes no good. "For policy, do not sneak around behind my back. Do you hear me?" His voice more bitter than the recent storm. Dee has time for neither tawdriness nor disobedience. "You cannot deal with these people alone. You have not the capability." He punctuates this with as rigid a look as he had ever shown the intractable boy.

Though Will wants to offer that he has lived on the streets of London where he was capable enough, his obdurate employer leaves no room for argument. Having no other friend in the world right now, Will holds his peace and follows in apprentice obedience.

Under a leucophane winter sun, master and pupil approach the harbor. Chill has rendered Shakespar unusually silent throughout their march to the docks. It could not please Dee more. Their quarry boards a small boat flying a Venetian flag. Though the cold brine stings nose and lips, Walsingham's spy is warmed by the sight—another piece of intelligence for his master. The ship's name is faded on the hull.

"Go boy, determine what she is called. Be discrete."

At the bottom of the water-stained stair that leads to the end of the pier, the doctor now fixes his attention on the mail boat anchored far out in the marina. A sudden concern arises, and he fishes out his letters to Walsingham to make sure the damp has not spoiled them. They are unharmed. A radical consideration strikes him while he returns them to safety whispering why *send* letters? *Just board her, deliver the letters in person to Sir Francis, make your report, and then speed to Mortlake to family who are in need.* A consummation devoutly to be wished: The aching for Jane, feeling her embrace, remembering her teary anguish embedded in every line of her letter casts a spell that tugs at him more and more as he considers the option. "Go home," his heart cries, "go home before it is too late." Yet, the sworn agent of Sir Francis' subterfuge knows he cannot just turn tail and run.

Looking to the anchored ship bobbing in the marina, the philosopher's attention volleys back and forth between the ignominious letter in his pocket and the English mail boat. The foresail and the foretop sails of his passage home on the mail ship are being unfurled from the foremast, all in readiness to quit Illyria. Its departure may be as fateful to his future as those of the ferryman, Charon, passengers, who on the River Styx leave the land of the living for some unknowable existence. Would God that he could be sure of this day's business. Beyond the protected marina is the tide-tossed English Channel stretching to the horizon. It stands a forbidding slate-green fortress wall that bars him from home, from his happy life, and the completion of his studies.

Staying in Illyria, fulfilling his mission, and not returning to Mortlake surely will mean lifelong estrangement from wife and children, and the dishonorable stain of abandoning both. To return to Jane now, while it may save his marriage; in the eyes of Walsingham and of the Court, means forsaking reputation, future success, oath and honor. Elizabeth's spider would most assuredly make good his threats and unloose the Privy Council to prosecute him for witchcraft, shutting him out of all preferment. *Unbearable humiliation.* No matter the path taken, either choice leads to hopeless ruin, and neither wholly ensures the security of Jane and their babes.

Like a big galumphing puppy, Will returns excitedly with the name of the Venetian ship.

"*The Doge,*" gasps Shakespar. Noticing his master's face knotted in constraint, Will, concerned, asks, "Are you well, Master?" But Dee is facing a whirlwind of recrimination. Shakespar, feeling for the man, approaches the sad-faced penitent, touching his sleeve tenderly. "What has happened that has shaken your usual demeanor during my short absence?"

Glancing at a compassionate face, the anguished man discovers a maturity in William Shakespar that is new to him and dear. *He is growing up.* Dee briefly considers taking the orator, Cicero's, advice, of lightening an old man's heart by sharing with the young. But, his self-imposed restraint will not allow it. *No, no, I cannot.*

"It is only the wind," Dee replies gloomily and hunkers deeper into his cloak, "The chill makes my old bones ache."

Mildly rebuked for his act of kindness, Shakespar nods in some understanding. Betimes the old fellow could be as petulant as a girl in her monthlies. *Something is amiss, yet this 'nothing' he gives me is but a concealment of some unsettling something*, thinks Shakespar.

"Perhaps," suggests Will, returning his own gloved hand inside his cloak, "we should return to the *Cubiculo*? What need we stand here? We have followed the fellow and seen where he has gone?"

"No, I want to be certain he should not leave the ship and board another."

"Ah," replies Will, to Dee's dubious answer. Doing his best to make conversation, Will adds, "Then may we walk to the end of the wharf where there is more sun?"

"*Bonjour, mes amis*," halloos Toby Belch from behind them, descending the stairs from his home. In either feigned or delighted greeting, Belch shouts, "Good Doctor!" Surprised to encounter the Royal Postmaster so soon, Tobias offers grandly, "Are you in need of my assistance, Sir?"

"Harbormaster, I have an urgent message for the mail ship," cries Dee above the wind. "Can you row me and the boy in a skiff before she sails so that I may immediately talk with the Captain?"

"The mail ship? I thought we were watching for...?" Shakespar stifles that thought. They are not alone.

"Row?" Such exertion through ice-cold surf is anathema to Belch. "No need, Goodman Dee, you are in luck. The ship cannot quit our waters unless an officer signs the disembarking papers, and he has not come. Though I do expect him presently. He can ferry you to his Captain."

"And the Venetian? What cargo holds she?"

A wary look flickers in Belch's eye. *Why that one?* "Only spices. Spices and commodity from the Indies." That detail will go in Dee's report to Walsingham. Changing topics, the harbormaster offers, "No point standing in the cold. Much warmer in the custom-house. You can read your new book, there." *Erasmus* is still in Dee's hand. Toby points the way. "We shall have good drinking ere he arrives."

"Gramercy, but I shall wait here and watch for their tender."

"As you wish. I am for warmer climes." Toby turns and mounts the wooden stair toward his home. The wind perks up and helps to blow the big man away.

Will shivers but not as much as the old man whose thin legs are locked together against the elements. On the wind comes a softly spoken invective from behind the fluttering grey beard. "Damn me, I should have asked for a skiff and rowed myself."

Will cocks his head at the seldom-heard profanity. "You are in an ill-temper today, Master," ventures Will. No response. "I merely mark your displeasure, Sir."

The pier shudders as a large wave explodes against it, suddenly forcing Dee to clasp the piling to maintain his balance. *Had he been closer to the edge, he'd have fallen in.* The concussion of icy water against timbers has soaked his outer garments and the shock of cold breaches the Doctor's ingrained inhibitions.

"Would a scholarly man, a celebrated teacher of mathematics, allow himself, his family, his very home to become the victim of debts?" A bitter word to speak aloud, but the dam breaks and Cicero's advice is taken. "I tell thee Will, I am unquiet in my mind having not sufficient and needful provision for my family."

This is startling admission from a man who has never shared before. Yet, nothing this morning makes sense. Will asks, "How has this come about?"

"I've had word from my Jane. My goodwife Jane."

"Then, you must home on the instant."

"How can I? O, how can I. I have been given a mission—though I have told you little—to stay here and learn what I can of the business of Illyria. I am enforced into sequestration. Upon my loyalty to Crown and Country, I am compelled to fulfill this mission. I have written to Sir Francis for... help," Dee cannot make himself say 'monies'. "I have a petition here," patting his breast where the request to Walsingham rests, "that must sail with that ship out there. My family is in dire need. I am both a man in poverty and a prisoner to my honor and loyalty."

"You paint a dark picture, Doctor."

"Darker still," acknowledges Dee, "If the Secretary will not help, to whom can I turn for loan? My assets are my books and my reputation. If the latter be lost at a public proceeding, surely the former will be lost at Mortlake." Having spoken his anxiety, he turns silent.

The Channel wind blows them nearer each other as Will watches his mentor shivering and shrinking into a despairing old man. Anxiety for another is worse than any anxiety for one's self. The youth realizes it is finally his moment to teach.

"Do not doubt yourself, Master." Dee is surprised by Shakespar's familiarity. Taking another tack, Will points to Dee's beard wet with brine, "White hairs become fools and jesters. You are neither." He continues hoping to make a difference. "Loyalty, Sir. What is it? Show it me. It is but a word that masters use to bind their menials to them. Can it be divided into parts and defined? Can you smell it or can you smell its antithesis, *disloyalty*? No, it is but a word, a breath of air that is bred in us by Church or parents. And why do they breed it in us? To bind us the closer to them and their especial needs. Loyalty held to knaves doth make our faith mere folly. As long as you are loyal, true, and crimeless to yourself, you are free from the reproach of Heaven, my good Master."

Above the long grey beard, anxious eyes acknowledge a modicum of comfort. Will, emboldened, yet respectful, falls back a step then adds, "Heaven, you have told me, hath always smiled upon you."

Dee does not, *cannot* answer.

"If that is so," says the student-turned-teacher, "God could not have put into your soul a yearning contrary to His will."

Doctor John Dee nods and turns to look out to sea.

"Doctor Dee, what are you searching for?"

"The purser," the intelligencer responds, although that is not the truth.

To be continued in...

ILLYRIA
BOOK TWO

Find more exciting titles from

Jumpmaster Press™

www.jumpmasterpress.com

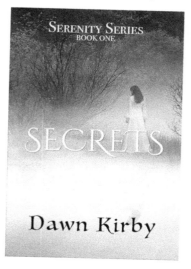

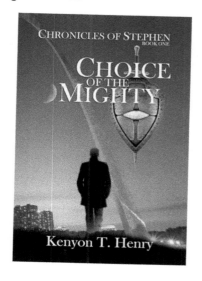

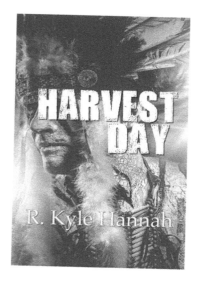

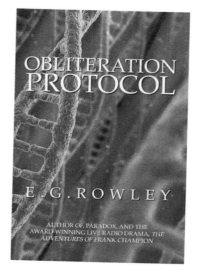

About the Author

Though known to the world for his acting work, Armin is a passionate bardologist. A graduate of UCLA, with a degree in English and a specialization in Shakespeare, Armin has performed a third of Shakespeare's canon at many major Regional Theatres (and Shakespeare Festivals) around the country.

He is an Adjunct Professor at USC and a sought after Shakespeare acting coach. His past novels, The Merchant Prince series, are also based on John Dee, Elizabeth I's controversial occultist and counselor.

"Betrayal of Angels ... is a way-back machine into the mysteries and intrigues of Elizabethan England, delivered in a poetical prose felicitous to both eye and ear."

Ira Steven Behr,
Showrunner, Star Trek: Deep Space Nine

"... Shimerman's vivid adventure ... lyrical ... voyage to worlds poised on the very edge of invention..."

David Rodes,
Professor Emeritus, UCLA

"... a mesmerizing period mystery ... enthralls readers with intrigue and captivating plot twists ... a riveting journey with the rich cast of intricately crafted characters...utterly gorgeous..."

Elizabeth Berman

"What a treat to discover that such a remarkable actor would be an equally remarkable writer. "Betrayal of Angels," ... One hell of a story (and storyteller). I impatiently wait for the last two installments."

Rick Berman,
Star Trek Executive Producer

"... delightful book ... Shimerman creates a charming ... wonderful tale ..."

Mike LoMonico
Institute Director, Folger Shakespeare Library

"Until Elon Musk invents a time travel machine ... Shimerman's fact-packed, historical adventure [is a] ... must read ... He had me at the first word ..."

Scott Carter
Emmy-nominated TV producer